# ROGUE UNBROKEN

# ROGUE UNBROKEN

## ANGIE DAY

RAHNE
PRESS

Rahne Press is a publisher in the United States. The city of publication is Cedar City, Utah.

www.angiedayauthor.com


Cataloging-in-Publication Data is available upon request.

ISBN: 978-1-7338144-6-1 (hardcover)
ISBN: 978-1-7338144-7-8 (paperback)

Edited by Suzanne Johnson
Cover Design by Sarah Hansen at www.okaycreations.com

First printed in the United States of America.
10 9 8 7 6 5 4 3 2 1

To my mom.
You always encourage me to dream big.
So I do.

# PREVIOUSLY IN

# SHADOW UNBOUND

Mara is a Legend, born with unmatched power. More than that, she is a Shadow: ruthless, feared, and lethal. But all of that changed when she became Kate and fell in love with a perfectly human life and the Legend that showed her how to live it: Kylan. After battling the Shadows and uncovering the memories they stole, she was free. Free to be with Kylan, his family, and the Rogue life they had chosen.

When a new human is brought into their lives, everything unravels. The family she has grown to love is thrown into chaos. Kate can't save any of them. But Mara can.

As Mara steps back into her previous life as a Shadow, it fits a little too well. The longer she walks with danger, the more she sees in common with the Shadows she left than the Rogue she was pretending to be.

When her two worlds collide, Mara should be faced with a choice. But a greater evil awaits her, one with the power to shatter both worlds.

# NOW IN

# ROGUE UNBROKEN

Kate had survived. She had lived through pain and torment and now she was on the other side, where all the happiness was supposed to be. But with Alec's vengeful punishment for escaping him, she can't touch anyone without hurting them.

Alec still wants to create a Level Five and he's dangerously close. That power under his control would mean unraveling the world as it stands. The world Kate has not yet started to enjoy. She won't be able to rest until her body, her mind is fixed, and Alec won't get his beloved power without her help.

The two warring sides of Rogues and Shadows will have to meet. Kate will have to confront Alec and his cruel ambition once again. But every moment with the Shadows is detrimental to those she loves, especially Kylan. So she must find a way to outsmart the person who taught her everything she knows, the most feared Shadow in the world.

Kate is strong. She survived once. But even the strongest people can break with the right pressure, and Alec is ready to tear her life apart.

# CHAPTER
## ONE

My hands were shaky as I rode up the elevator. Enclosed spaces reminded me of the small cage I had been held in.

The beige ceiling was plain and soft, nothing like the lab. No harsh fluorescent lights. No thick smell of salty sweat or dried blood assaulted my nose.

I was at my old office building. Safe. Warm. Free.

If I repeated those words often enough, maybe I'd believe them. It helped to have Kylan at my side, staring at the carpeted floor. Lisa was in front of us, clutching three letters to her chest.

"I still think this is a bad idea," Kylan whispered in my ear as his hand touched my lower back.

I smiled and shoved his shoulder, only touching his shirt. Kylan cracked a smile, barely enough for me to see.

I kept walking, carefully following Lisa down the main hallway from the elevator doors.

"Well, I think she deserves to say good-bye to her human life. And, it's a Saturday so no one's going to be here," I whispered back.

Kylan kept his wide eyes forward, watching Lisa's every move. She held a resignation letter for each of us. Well, really an explanation letter. We had all worked at this company together, back when Kylan and I were pretending to be human, but Lisa was the only one who cared to officially explain.

"I think us not showing up to work and not responding to Mr. Lyle's calls explained enough," Kylan said quietly.

"We did respond to some of them. Well, you did mostly," I answered, throwing him a look.

He didn't catch it and continued his protest. "To let him know we weren't dead and keep him from asking more questions."

"I can hear you," Lisa muttered, then she mumbled quietly to herself. "Huh, I actually heard that."

I glanced at Kylan and smiled. He rolled his eyes, but the corner of his lips pulled up anyway.

Her voice still sounded surprised at her own ability. She was a Legend now, like us. Recently changed by Alec as a form of torment and manipulation to get me to open my locket for him.

The necklace turned out to be as useless to him as I had claimed it would be. But he hadn't listened then. And now I had to help Lisa understand her new life and end her old one. Every step of it was a painful reminder.

I remembered the cell. The needles. The white coats. I remembered wanting nothing more than the pain to cease. Sometimes I felt like it never had.

Kylan noticed the shift in my steps, the slip in my mood. He slid his hand automatically to mine. I sucked in a breath, waiting for the touch of his skin.

The energy wouldn't stop if he touched me, even if I wanted it to. Not after what Alec had done. My entire mind lit up in red, blaring lights when the tip of his fingers finally grazed my skin.

A flush of power circled my hand despite me mentally screaming to stop it. Kylan winced and pulled his hand away again too quickly. He shook his hand out, flexing his muscles against the pain.

I didn't apologize. No amount of apologies would overcome the pain of Alec's *insurance* plan. The lack of physical contact was killing me. Kylan understood, even if he hated it too.

He put his arm over my shoulder and pressed a kiss to my hair, safe from my exposed skin.

"We get in, drop the letters off, and then we are out of here," Kylan announced louder.

I walked ahead and put my arm around Lisa. She clutched the letters in her hand and kept her focus on the door ahead of us.

"Don't listen to him. Take your time in there. Okay?" I pulled her closer to me.

She nodded and gulped nervously as we approached the door. Lisa slid her key into the door and I opened it for her. She stepped through carefully, as if the floor inside the office would shock her. To be honest, I felt the same worry.

I looked up at the familiar sight around me. I had spent nearly a year here, dabbling in a human profession and deciding what I wanted in life. I had found it.

Kylan walked far enough behind to give us some space. I smiled at him as all the happy memories surfaced of us flirting, discovering the other was a Legend, and starting to fall for each other.

All of it had started in this office.

It was so innocent and perfect, nothing like what my life was today. Now, I jumped at loud noises. I worried that anytime I looked over my shoulder Alec would be standing there, smiling. I held my breath when I walked into a room.

It had been three days since we got back from the lab. I had spent an entire day and night sleeping. I think Lisa did too.

It was harder when I woke up. I would name every item in the room around me to make sure they were real. Every morning, I was convinced I was still in that glowing cell. Every first breath of the day was a relief.

Lisa walked down the hallway to the head offices. I turned the other way and looked at the cubicles of desks, the receptionist area, and the windows that looked out into downtown Portland.

"Seems like a lifetime ago." Kylan came up behind me and slipped his hands around my waist, careful not to touch any skin.

I couldn't touch his hands. Not without hurting him.

"So much has changed since then," I muttered as I played with the corner of his coat sleeve.

"I still love you." Kylan turned me around. "That hasn't changed."

My eyes softened as I looked up at his beautiful, green gaze. As long as he looked at me like this, I knew I would be all right. My hands may shake slightly, and my nightmares may keep me from falling asleep, but I was going to be all right.

"Crazy to think this is where we met." Kylan smiled and glanced at the offices behind me.

"Maybe it's a good thing for us to be here. To say good-bye too." I shrugged.

"You're always one step ahead." Kylan looked down at me and grinned.

"Not always. But most of the time—" I started.

"Kate? Kylan?" Chase's voice called from behind Kylan.

I leaned my head to the side and saw him standing there in a t-shirt and jeans with a fist full of papers.

"What are you guys doing here? Where have you been?" Chase stepped forward, setting the papers down on the receptionist's desk.

"Not good," Kylan grumbled and sucked in a breath.

I glanced down the hallway for Lisa. She must have heard Chase's voice, which meant we were in for a big problem.

"Is she with you?" Chase asked me, following my gaze.

Footsteps headed our way. I wasn't sure if Chase could hear them yet, or if he only wondered. Either way, I needed to get him out of here. Lisa would lose control when she saw him.

And no one deserved to see their loved one hurting because of the energy you can't stop taking. Especially Lisa.

I started again, trying to keep my voice down. "Chase, listen to me, you need to leav—"

"Chase?" Lisa's voice came before I saw her walk around the corner.

"Definitely, not good," Kylan said, louder this time.

He bolted over to Chase to block him from taking another step toward Lisa. I rushed to her and held up my hands.

"Now is not the time. You haven't had energy since you got back from the lab. Your body is weak and you're going to hurt him," I rushed.

Lisa didn't even glance at me. She probably wasn't even following what I said. All of it would be foreign to her. She kept her eyes on Chase, her anxious fingers pushed me aside to get to him.

I tried to yank my hands back in time, but she grabbed them anyway and moved to step around me. The energy from her body immediately flooded into mine.

I should have wanted to stop it, but the warm, intoxicating

feeling was impossible to ignore. My breath stopped as the muscles in my hands and arms ignited.

"Lisa, let go!" Kylan shouted as he raced over to her and ripped her arms away from my grip.

The energy crashed to a halt and my body lurched forward, wanting more. I balled my hands into fists to keep me from reaching for her. I looked in her scared, drooping eyes and the warm brown color instantly reminded me that I didn't want to hurt her.

Lisa gasped for air in Kylan's arms. She stumbled against him, trying to understand the feeling of energy being torn from her body so quickly.

"Hey, hey, you're okay. Your body is just adjusting to less energy. You're so exhausted and it's gonna take a second. Just breathe," Kylan calmly coached her.

"Let me go," she snapped at Kylan and stepped toward me.

"Lisa, I'm sorry." I said and it hurt that even if she was scared of me, she was scared of Kylan more.

"What the...w-what are you?" Chase asked.

I looked at the human, who was still standing too close to a starving, newbie Legend and another Legend that couldn't control her ability to steal energy.

Lisa straightened at the sound of his voice. She leaned away from us to get a better view of Chase. My blood raced with new energy and anticipation for how Lisa was going to handle this.

I wished I had advice to give her. A way to break the news that she now wanted to feed on humans by siphoning their energy, and that included the boyfriend for whom she was head over heels. I didn't have anything to say that could make this easier.

"Lisa?" Chase asked, his light blue eyes on me as he walked toward her.

"She's a Legend. Kylan is too," Lisa answered before taking another step toward him.

Chase froze. He looked specifically at my hands that had just siphoned Lisa's energy from her body. He changed his stare to Kylan, his mouth tightening. Kylan stared back as he moved to stand by me.

"You're not serious." Chase shook his head. "That's impossible. Legends aren't real."

"Yes, they are." Lisa nodded and walked toward Chase.

"They've just been Legends this whole time? That doesn't make sense. We would've noticed if we had been working next to demons," Chase fumed and put his hands on her clothed shoulders, trying to force her to look at him.

Lisa flinched at the word *demon* but she kept her eyes glued to the floor. I glanced at Kylan. We both knew what was going to happen next.

"Maybe this is their idea of a prank. Have you been with them all this time? Are you all right?" Chase asked, lifting his hand from her shoulder to her face.

"It's not a prank," Lisa answered just as Chase touched his finger under her chin.

I tensed my muscles and sucked in a breath. Kylan wrapped his hand around my clothed arm to keep me from jumping forward.

The second Chase's hand touched her skin, a faint yellow light swirled from his skin to hers. Lisa stopped breathing as soon as she felt it.

"I'm one too," Lisa managed to whisper as her eyes met Chase's concerned gaze.

The light from the energy fused into her body. Her shoulders relaxed. She took in a deep breath, settling the worry on her forehead.

Chase yanked his hand away when he realized his energy

was leaving. Lisa's eyes popped open when the energy stopped. She looked at Chase like he was the source of relief to the ringing pain in her exhausted body.

For that one moment, I realized the person Lisa had turned into. No longer caring and selfless. She felt that raw desire all of us dealt with every day.

"What did you just do?" Chase pulled away from her.

He lifted his hands to defend himself. That seemed to snap Lisa back to reality, if only temporarily.

"I...I didn't...I didn't mean to do anything," Lisa stammered.

"You're a human. I know you're a human."

She winced. "I...I was."

"She was turned into a Legend just a few days ago," I interrupted.

Chase's eyes fell on me and glared. I stepped away from Kylan and moved toward Lisa. I touched her back with my hand and stiffened.

"You did this to her?"

His eyes burned with rage and fear. He wasn't the intimidated employee that needed a confidence boost to reach his potential. He was a man who just had his love ripped away from him and I was the reason for everything in his confused, blue eyes.

"No, she didn't," Lisa said.

"Yes. I'm the reason she was turned. She came to a lab in Louisiana to save me." I hung my head.

"How could you do this to her?" Chase screamed at me.

"You need to calm down, right now." Kylan stepped in between the two of us, holding up a warning hand.

"You're monsters, both of you." Chase clenched his jaw.

I moved to step forward, but stopped when a synchronized click sounded in the room. The computers behind us played a message. But the first words sent a spear of shock and anger through my chest.

"Please pay attention. The next few minutes could save your life," Alec's voice announced.

# CHAPTER
# TWO

I spun around as all the computers in the cubicles lit up. They should've been shut down for the weekend. We should've been alone in this office. I glanced at Chase and he seemed equally surprised.

A cold feeling came over me. I don't know if it was the flashing lights as the computers loaded a video, or the screeching sounds of all of them synchronizing, but my back seized up.

That would've been enough to make my heart race and require me to breathe and remember where I was to calm me down.

But the video message finally played and the star of the show was Alec Stone.

"Legends are real," Alec continued on the screen.

The video changed to footage just outside of the lab. It was a take of the fight just before Alec and I had made it inside to rescue Rachel. But the only person who was visible in the video, identifiable at least, was me.

My dark hair fell over my shoulders as I drained energy

from a Legend until his knees hit the ground. My head snapped up and my icy eyes locked on the next target. I stepped over the man's unconscious body.

"What is this?" Kylan asked, moving closer to the screen. The video changed to another shot of me.

"They survive on human energy. Without control, they are dangerous to every person on this planet." Alec's calm voice seemed out of place for what he was saying.

On the screen, I stood over Raven with crazed eyes and a syringe in my hand. My hair looked like it hadn't been brushed in weeks and my skin shone with old sweat. I shoved the needle in her neck, killing her within minutes as I watched her blood spill on my hands.

"Is that you?" Lisa asked from behind me. My eyes remained glued to the screen in front of me.

I couldn't answer her. I didn't want to. All I could do was watch my worst memories unfold in front of me.

"They will kill whoever they come in contact with. But they can be killed. They can die, just like humans can, even if they are harder to kill," Alec explained.

More footage of me flashed on the screens. I was stuck behind the glowing bars in the cell. My hand shot through the bars to grab the man standing in front of me. The video never showed his face but I remembered exactly who it was.

Alec. He was keeping his face hidden from the viewers. He only wanted me shown in the announcement.

"I want to drain all of the energy from your body," I said in the video. "I'm desperate."

The energy glowed even brighter than the light of the bars, illuminating my face further. My hand remained clamped on his neck. My expression changed the longer I held on. As the energy entered my body, I looked less like an innocent captive and more like the villain.

"This particular Legend is named Kate Martin. She has been seen residing in Portland, Oregon." Alec's face appeared back in the video again.

"It is her," Chase whispered behind me.

My eyes stayed focused on the screen. I couldn't feel Kylan standing next to me or hear Lisa's strained, nervous breaths. All I could see was Alec, ripping my life apart.

"She's a monster," Alec accused. "If you see her, kill her on sight."

The computer screen went black. I held my breath, waiting for someone to tell me this wasn't real.

At the word monster, something in me came alive. A slow, burning anger smoldered under my skin. The hatred that lurked inside of me surfaced. A tingle moved from my fingertips, to my arms, to the dagger mark on my right forearm.

This monster that had been trained for centuries by the Shadows to hate humans. This monster was only aggravated by the endless torture in the lab at Alec's hands.

A gun cocked behind me.

I turned. My eyes snapped up to a pistol pointed at my chest. Chase held it. He looked weak, easy to toss out of the way. His light eyes and gleaming blond hair made him look like a teenager at best.

All that Shadow training flooded down my arms. Chase needed a distraction and I could talk him into one.

"Where did you get a gun?" I stared at the weapon, already planning how to take it from him.

His hands shook as he tried to keep it pointed toward me.

"Shelley's a crazy conservative who always keeps a gun under the reception desk. I never thought it would come in handy until now." Chase rushed through the words.

He was nervous. It made his chances of actually hitting me with a bullet decrease, but even I didn't want to take that risk.

I raised my hands in the air, showing him he could calm down enough to lower the gun.

"Chase, what are you doing? This is Kate. She's our friend," Lisa begged next to him.

"She's not a friend. She's a Legend, a murderer," Chase spat at me.

"No, she's not. She's good." Lisa choked back a sob, looking at me for help.

Neither Kylan nor I dared to move. One stray bullet and we wouldn't have near enough energy to heal before the wound became fatal. Unless Chase was offering his energy up, which I obviously doubted.

"You just saw that video! She hurts people. Look what she's done to you." Chase didn't move his gaze away from me. "You were perfect. And now..."

The heartbreak crushed Chase's expression. His mouth turned down, like he was trying to hold back the emotion raging inside of him.

"I'm so sorry this happened, but please, please don't hurt her." Lisa reached a hand up to his sleeve.

"I'm going to fix this." Chase narrowed his eyes at me, his finger twitching next to the trigger.

"Chase, don't!" Lisa cried as her hands shot up to his, wrapping her fingers around his grip.

She shoved the gun toward the ceiling, and it went off. The shot shattered a light above us. Glass shards scattered across our shoulders. Lisa didn't let go of his hands.

"What are you doing?" Chase asked in a strained voice.

Lisa stood, still holding onto Chase's hands with bright energy swirling up her arms. Chase's knees buckled and he fell in front of her.

"I…I…" Lisa stuttered, her eyes focusing on the yellow light around her fingers.

Her grip tightened on Chase. Her eyes widened, wanting more of the energy flooding into her body. She was starving and nothing had prepared her for how her body would crave human energy.

I held still, watching the person she had become. She didn't see Chase anymore. She saw the energy that her body so badly needed.

"Stop." Chase's eyes drooped as the gun fell to the floor.

Lisa still held onto his hands, pulling the energy from his body. Her knuckles turned white.

"I can't," Lisa answered, trying to focus through the haze.

As soon as the gun hit the floor, Kylan rushed to Lisa. Chase's eyes closed and his body slumped forward, held up only by Lisa's grip. Kylan ripped her away from Chase.

"Listen to my voice," Kylan coached as Lisa fought to get back to Chase, a feral look in her eyes. "I know the energy feels good. Your body needs it, and we will teach you how to get it. But you have to stop! You care about him."

"This is his fault," I muttered. "This is him."

"What? Who are you talking about?" Kylan looked up at me, still fighting to hold Lisa back.

"Let me go!" Lisa struggled against Kylan.

"Alec," I answered. "How do you think he's doing all of this? He's here. He has to be."

I moved toward the door. Kylan's eyes shifted between me and Lisa.

"Kate, don't go out there," Kylan called. "Kate!"

His voice faded behind me. Lisa's screams bounced off the walls and then vanished the farther away I got.

I knew he was here. I had to find him. What I did after that was still to be decided. All I could hear was the blood pounding in my ears as the hatred burned through my veins.

# CHAPTER
# THREE

*Kylan*

"I want more," Lisa begged. "Why? Why do I want it?"

"It's energy. You're exhausted and it's what your body needs," I explained, trying to hold her arms tight enough to stop her but not enough to hurt her.

"Kylan, let me go!" Lisa shouted, digging her nails into my arms.

"Look at him!" I shouted back at her.

Lisa's crazed eyes finally landed on Chase's face. His body lay awkwardly on the floor, his chest barely rising and falling. Lisa slowed her fight against me, her motions becoming halfhearted.

"What…what did I do?" Lisa stopped moving.

"He's going to be okay. He's just unconscious. His body will wake him up once he's had a chance to rest," I slowly explained to her.

"He's not okay. He's on the ground. I did this to him." Lisa's eyes darted around the room, looking for anything to make this better. "I hurt him! I hurt him!"

She rushed forward as soon as my hands lifted off of her.

"Be careful not to touch his skin. It's easier to resist energy that way," I coached, following closely behind her.

She knelt on the entry floor next to him, holding her hands in front of her mouth to cover her quivering lip.

"What can we do?" Lisa looked up at me.

"Nothing for now. He'll wake on his own soon," I answered her, looking toward the door where Kate had left.

I pulled out my phone and clicked in Kate's contact. The ringing sounded in my ear, over and over until it ended with her voice message.

"Come on," I growled and shoved the phone back in my pocket.

"We have to do something. We can't just leave him here," Lisa begged.

"I can't help him," I sighed. "We have to go. Kate is not in her right mind and she might get herself into more danger. I need to follow her."

"Wait, just leave him here? No. I can be here when he wakes up. I'll explain everything." Lisa shook her head.

"We don't have time and I can't leave you here alone. Let's go find Kate and then we can come back here later." I tried to soothe her as I pulled her up.

She yanked her arm away from me and scooted closer to Chase, careful not to touch him. Chase stirred, shifting his head to face where Lisa's voice was coming from.

"He needs me to stay." Lisa stared at Chase with hope shining through her tears.

I pulled out my phone again and called someone who had always been ready to jump to my aid. The person I chose to take with me over the past century.

"Hello?" Derek's voice answered.

"I need you now," I said into the speaker.

"Where?"

One simple instruction was all he needed. He was my brother in every way I could imagine other than blood.

"At my work building. Kate just ran out. She's not thinking clearly. After everything that happened in the lab, she's...she's out on the streets. Get Cassie. Find Kate and take her down," I explained, looking at Lisa rocking next to the man she loved.

"How am I supposed to do that? You picked a Level Five girlfriend," Derek said, laughing.

I ignored his humor. "Do whatever you have to."

"You sure?"

I bit my cheek. "Yes."

"Done." Derek matched my serious tone.

I ended the call and put the phone back in my pocket before I turned back to the former human who was not understanding her new world.

"Lisa." I knelt down next to her. "When he wakes up, he won't want to see you. You're a Legend now and that changes the way people think about you."

"No, you're wrong." Lisa shook her head again. "He loves me. He'll be able to see past...anything else."

"Maybe eventually, but not right now, not when you literally just stole almost all of his energy." I put my hand on her shoulder.

"I...I don't understand. I didn't mean to take anything," she stammered.

"You don't have to. It's instinct built into your DNA now. When you changed to a Legend, your body started needing energy. I don't know if they allowed you to access any at the lab. So, you're probably starving," I explained calmly.

"I'm not hungry though." Lisa looked down at her stomach.

"It won't feel like human hunger. It's more like an

overwhelming exhaustion. You feel angry and anxious, almost to the point of physical pain. That's your body desperate to get relief. At that point, any time you touch a human, you'll take their energy whether you want to or not," I said slowly, watching her eyes follow my words as best she could.

"I felt that before. I mean, maybe I did. I think...When I was walking to Mr. Lyle's office with the letters. My head was ringing," Lisa rambled, touching her temple.

"But it's gone now, right?" I asked.

Lisa nodded her head, looking at her hands and then looking at Chase. None of this made sense to a human. They didn't spend their whole lives learning about the relationship between their body and energy.

"So, I can't control this?" She leaned away from Chase, not wanting to hurt him further.

"You can, eventually. Once you have enough energy, your body won't force you anymore. You can choose whether or not to take it when you touch someone." I noted Chase's uncomfortable position on the floor. "Like this."

I reached forward and moved Chase's head to lie flat on the ground. I grabbed his arm and pull it out from under him so his back could straighten out. My hands touched his skin, but nothing happened.

His limp muscles tensed when I touched him. Chase stirred again, this time turning his head and twitching his hands. His eyes fluttered open.

"Chase?" Lisa leaned closer to his face.

"Lisa?" he asked, still delirious.

"I'm right here. I'm so sorry. I don't know what I was doing, but you're going to be just fine. It's just gonna take some tim—" Lisa tried to cram all the words in one breath.

"Get away f-from me," Chase mumbled, looking at her before his eyes closed again.

A human may not have caught all the words. With our enhanced hearing, I knew she understood. Her face dropped as she sucked in a breath.

I waited for a moment, letting Lisa take in what he just said. Her human life was over. Even if Kate was on a mad search for Alec outside, I was more worried about what Lisa might do if she lashed out.

I had to hope that Kate had enough control to hang on until Derek found her.

"What..." Lisa stared ahead at Chase, her eyes wide.

"I'm so sorry." I touched my hand to her shoulder.

"What is this? I can see..." Lisa squinted her eyes, still staring at Chase.

She wasn't talking about what he said. Her eyes moved back and forth like she was seeing something in front of her. The new energy in her body could have been forcing her to do something she couldn't do before.

"Tell me what's happening." I watched her face carefully.

"He hates me. I can see it. But, that...that's not real. I can see myself like he is looking at me." Lisa's words choked in her throat. "I can feel it, like it's my emotion. It's not...it's my imagination?"

I knew the feeling she was describing. The sensation would be too unimaginable for a human, or for a new Legend who had never read someone's mind before. It was so much more than just seeing through their eyes.

"You're reading his thoughts. It's one of your new abilities as a Legend," I explained gently. "What you're feeling and seeing is what Chase is thinking."

"That can't be true. He loves me. I know he loves me," Lisa said as fresh tears spilled over her eyes.

"He did love you, but you're different now." I put my arm around her, careful not to touch her skin.

Lisa crumbled against me. She pulled her hands into her chest and the tears soaked into my shirt. She was one of us now, but I still had a hard time not looking at her as human and weak. I took steadying breaths as she leaned against me.

"I want out of here," she muttered into my shirt.

"We can come back," I lied. "We can talk him through all of this, but we need to—"

"Find Kate." She nodded.

"She needs us," I begged.

"I don't want to come back here." Lisa stared coldly at Chase, her eyes welling with old tears.

I didn't waste another second. I knew Lisa was nowhere near ready to say good-bye to Chase, but Kate needed me too.

Lisa followed closely behind me as I ran out of the doors and toward the stairs. My phone buzzed in my pocket. I lifted it out and saw a news notification. I clicked it and the same video played on the screen. Lisa reached for her phone as well, where the same message displayed.

It wasn't just in this room. Alec had posted the message publicly. Anyone with a connection to the internet could see it.

Kate had just walked into a trap with every human pitted against her and, unless she stopped to look at her phone, she had no idea.

# CHAPTER
# FOUR

The bitter Portland air stung my face as soon as I yanked the door open. My mind was too scattered to think about Kylan or Lisa.

My eyes darted around, trying to find anything that would prove Alec was close. Flashes of the video played in my mind. I wanted to blame him for painting me as a monster.

But all of those things I had done were of my own choice. The memories pounded in my mind.

*My hand clamped around Alec's vulnerable throat. His energy crashed through my body, the exact kind of ecstasy I had been denied for so long. His eyes fluttered shut and I should have been scared then, but the energy distracted me. The sweet, tantalizing energy bonded with every aching cell in my body.*

I shook my head and narrowed my eyes on anything that looked like my target. People swarmed up and down the streets, but none of them looked like Alec.

I turned and started down the street, scanning everyone's faces.

He had to be here. It wasn't like Alec to miss this big reveal moment. He wanted to isolate me, to remind me that I shouldn't look like the Kate he had grown to loathe. The woman that had replaced his precious Mara.

The next memory stung as it slithered into my head.

*The cold metal in my hand, the syringe changing to a dagger was pure power. Raven's warm blood running across my hands, coating my knuckles and sticking to my palms. Her life was spilling all around me. I was in control for one fantastic moment. The dominance tasted like possibility.*

The feelings lingered past the memory. My fingers jolted with the desire to kill. It was a perfect plan. It was always perfect. Not only did I want to find Alec, I wanted to hurt anyone that got in my way.

The people around me changed from looking up, or at the ground, to looking at their phone screens.

My skin crawled as the voice came from the devices surrounding me.

"Please pay attention. The next few minutes could save your life," Alec said.

I stopped and all the phones, tablets—any screen around me—joined in unison with the same message.

"Legends are real," Alec said.

I knew what came next, the video of me. I knew the humans had seen it when they looked up from their screens. All of them stared at me. They checked the phones until they were sure. I relaxed my shoulders.

"He's even better than I thought," I sighed.

Alec's plan wasn't to bring up my guilt. It was to expose me to the world. If I wanted to look like Kate, then all the humans around me would attack.

The video was meant to spark the hate in them and ignite the killer in me.

"It's her," one tall female human finally whispered.

"That is her," a stocky male human agreed.

My heart beat steadily in my chest. I waited for one of them to make a move.

The man rushed forward. I smiled. His body had more energy and he was the one I wanted first.

His hands reached out for me. I shot my arm out and caught his wrist. The energy immediately flowed from his skin into my body. The power ignited everything inside of me, awakening me for the attacks to come.

After a few moments, the man fell to the concrete, just in front of glass panels of another high-rise building. I dropped his arm, leaving his barely conscious body at my feet.

More phones came out, not watching the video this time. They were recording me. I cracked my knuckles, feeling the energy swirl around my bones, my muscles.

Maybe it was the overwhelming energy or the threat from Alec, the reminder of that dagger on my arm. But I rolled up my right sleeve and narrowed my eyes.

"Who's next?" I called.

Anyone that touched me would suffer the same fate. They knew it. Unfortunately, they didn't have to touch me to kill me. They just didn't know that yet.

*She's a monster.*

A woman rushed forward, ready to snap her handbag across my cheek. I ducked and caught her body as she fell forward with the unexpected momentum. My hand touched the small of her back, ripping the energy as fast as I could.

She stumbled a few more steps before falling. I released her and readied for the next.

"You're gonna have to do better than that." I almost felt a smile on my lips.

Two of them came at me now. Both men. One of them grabbed my left arm. I twisted around until I heard his wrist pop out of place. The other went for my legs. I tripped over him and hit the grimy concrete.

When I flipped on my back, I faced a short metal rod point directly at my chest. A man stood over me, holding it and ready to run it through my body.

"You filthy Legends. You think you're so powerful," the man sneered.

Energy blazed in my body, begging me to move, to use it. I watched his eyes, too weak to plunge the metal down.

*If you see her, kill her on sight.*

"But you'll die just like a human," the man said, an empty threat.

I smiled, automatic and taunting.

I concentrated on the metal of the weapon. It was simple, organized cells all bonded together to form the shape he now held. I closed my eyes and used my energy to break apart the cells, destroy the connection.

The strong rod turned to dissolving, black pieces. It scattered into the air, fluttering harmlessly onto my body.

"I'm more powerful than you can imagine." I stood as the other humans backed away.

They were scared of me.

*She's a monster.*

I raised my stare to their fidgety gazes and short breaths. They were right to be afraid.

"And yet, you still haven't figured out the art of subtlety," Derek called from behind me.

I turned to face him. His brown hair looked even darker in the overcast light. He stood easily a foot above me, with a build that would scare most people into doing whatever he asked.

But he was too polite to use it against anyone. Let alone me.

"Kylan called you."

"He said you weren't thinking clearly and that he needed some help to calm you down." Derek smiled a big grin that should have made me relax.

"I'm fine," I snarled.

"Clearly." Derek nodded. "Attacking humans in broad daylight. Yeah, that sounds like you."

"What do you want me to do? Alec just told everyone around me that I'm a Legend. Who knows how far that message has gone? I am *screwed*." I clenched my fists. "Any future I wanted with these people, this life, is gone."

I wanted him to leave me alone. I was scared, but I also didn't want him to watch when I turned into the Shadow I used to be.

"Any future as *Kate*." Derek took a step toward me. "We've all changed our names and you're supposed to be pretty good at changing your looks. I'm sure you'll be just fine."

"That's not the point." I shook my head, touching the side of my face.

I kept shaking my head, closing my eyes. Those vicious words played over and over in my mind.

*She's a monster. If you see her, kill her on sight.*

I didn't want them to be true. But I saw the way the humans looked at me, the way Derek looked at me now. I snapped my eyes open, clenching a fist.

"Then what is?" Derek stepped even closer to me and the tether inside me broke.

"Alec!" I screamed. "That's the point. He's never going

to leave me alone. Any face I choose, any place I live, none of it matters. He'll always find me."

"That sucks." Derek shrugged his shoulders too easily. "It does. But these people don't deserve your rage."

I paused, staring at him. He had his hands raised to restrain me or surrender, I wasn't sure yet. Either way, his eyes were kind. He didn't see a monster.

I relaxed my shoulders a little. Derek extended a hand toward me. I would have taken it.

But a gun fired in the crowd. The bullet pierced my left shoulder, sending an excruciating pain shooting under my collarbone.

"No!" Derek shouted.

I touched my hand to the hot blood pouring out of my body. I needed energy to heal the wound. The power in my body raced to close it, unable to finish the job. I was too weak. Always too weak. My eyes snapped up to the nearest human body.

"Kate, don't do it," Derek asked. "We can bandage that up. You don't need the energy. Just come with me."

The human woman standing in front of me cowered under my gaze. She was short, with frizzy black hair and long nails. The others backed away from her, eager to offer her up instead of themselves.

She wasn't the one that fired the gun. Her hands were empty aside from her phone and oversized purse. She was innocent. Just a bystander.

I sensed the flickers of energy roaming in her body, contained only by her skin. One touch and all of it would be mine. The throbbing pain in my shoulder would stop. The ache in my stomach would vanish.

Everything would melt away except the sweet, tantalizing sensation. I wanted it.

I glanced at Derek as my face hardened. He dashed in front of me, shaking his head. "Kate, no."

"Come stop me, little Two." I wiggled my fingers.

I was a Five, meaning I had the maximum number of abilities possible for a Legend. There were three Levels of power between Derek and me. If he wanted to attack me, he needed to be stronger than me or outsmart me. But he was kind and a Legend version of a teddy bear. I doubted his ability to do either.

I faced the human woman again, already reaching my hand for her. She backed up into the metal frame of the revolving door behind her. I heard Derek's footsteps move, not toward me though.

Even he knew not to fight me.

My hand latched onto her fragile throat. She was too scared to move, and now it was too late. Her energy jumped from her body into mine. The adrenaline flowing through her only intensified the feeling. My mouth watered as the energy melded with mine.

The blood stopped pouring from my shoulder. The pain lessened to a dull ache. Her energy warmed my hand, reminding me what it feels like to have something to hold. To touch skin.

"I'm sorry," I muttered.

The human's hands gripped mine, hoping to push me off. The extra skin contact only sped up the amount of energy leaving her body.

"I'm sorry he wasn't strong enough to stop me." The words choked in my throat.

My grip tightened on the human, just as a blunt object stabbed through the top of my left shoulder. Pain surged down my arm and filled my chest. My hand immediately released the frizzy-haired woman I held.

I whirled to look at who delivered the blow. I recognized the red hair almost immediately.

"Good thing he's not alone." Cassie smirked as she let go of the object that she left sticking out of my shoulder.

I grabbed it and yanked as the pain screamed through my body. What I held in my hand was a piece of a metal doorframe that had been ripped off. It had two jagged edges where the gold paint separated from the steel underneath.

Hot blood trickled down my arm again. I leveled my stare on Cassie.

I opened my mouth to tell her to run, that I didn't want to hurt her but I would. Before any words formed in my mouth, my eyes caught on to something behind her.

Kylan.

He rushed forward, looking at the situation in front of him. He saw the blood on my body and Cassie's weapon in my hand. That's not what worried him, though; it was the seething anger he saw burning in my eyes.

"Don't." Kylan shook his head at me, looking at his little sister.

My grip tightened on the metal as my muscles coiled, ready to strike.

"Look at me, focus on me," Kylan said as he walked forward.

I couldn't. I knew I would see something to calm me down, and I didn't want calm. I wanted the rage. I looked at Cassie instead.

Thoughts spun in my head too quickly. I wanted to be free, and that meant away from them. As much as I cared about him, as guilty as I felt for playing a role in Rachel's death, I had to run.

They weren't safe with me and this was the only way he would let me go. *She's a monster.*

I raised my hand, stopped only by the sound of fast footsteps behind me. I didn't have time to turn around before a hard object crushed against the back of my head.

Splinters crashed around me. My body fell forward. The consciousness in my mind shattered as I hit the ground.

# CHAPTER
# FIVE

*Kylan*

I shoved past the people clamoring to get somewhere. I couldn't tell if they wanted to move toward the commotion or away.

I finally got past the last line of people and saw Kate sprawled on the sidewalk, bleeding from three places and wooden splinters scattered in her hair.

Derek dropped the remnants of the wooden sign and Cassie stepped into view.

"What was that?" I shouted, falling to her side to check her pulse. Energy peeled out of my body.

She was alive.

"You said to do whatever it took. So that's what I did."

"You could've done that without hitting her over the head. Or stabbing her in the shoulder. You could—is that a bullet wound?" I pointed at the circular hole under her collarbone that had clotted.

"She was high! I watched her disintegrate a metal rod in seconds." Derek jumped over to Cassie, just out of my reach.

"We've got to get her out of here," I ordered.

Panic was seeping in as I looked at all the humans closing in on us and the cameras pointed at Kate's face.

I picked up Kate in my arms and started running, far away from the prying eyes surrounding us. I bolted down the busy street and ducked into the first promising alley.

"Wait," Cassie called.

She walked around the corner alone. Derek had thrown Lisa over his shoulder and she batted him with her fists.

"She's a Legend now and this really hurts!" Derek grumbled.

Lisa twisted off his shoulder and landed on her hands and knees. She jumped out of Derek's reach. I swallowed hard.

Every second we waited was more time for the humans to catch up. My eyes darted between Lisa nervously twisting her hands and watching another drop of blood trickle off the tips of Kate's fingers.

"Please, let's get back to my house. We can figure out what to do from there." I nodded to Lisa.

She stared at me, unmoving, firmly planting her feet on the dirty asphalt. The stench of grease and wet trash floated in the air, stinging my eyes. We couldn't stay here.

"Done. Come on, Li...Liza, is it?" Derek reached his hand out to her.

She pulled her arms away from him, staring at him like he was going to hurt her. Derek raised his hands in surrender and backed up, firing me a glance.

"Lisa," she shot back at him. "My name is Lisa."

"Okay, Lisa, in case you haven't noticed, all of those humans are particularly vested in killing Kate over there and we need to leave now." Derek walked toward her and grabbed her arm, this time latching on.

"Leave?" Lisa asked, trying to rip her arm away from Derek. "I'm not going anywhere with you."

"Kylan," Derek growled.

All he said was my name, but he wanted to know what to do. How to get her to follow us. Shouts and footsteps of the hoard of people we left behind echoed off the alley walls. They were coming.

"Derek, scaring her isn't going to fix anything," Cassie interrupted and pulled his arm away from her.

My sister turned her soft gaze on Lisa, putting her tiny hands gently on those cowering shoulders.

"You remember me from Kate's house, right? We made caramel popcorn together?" Cassie lowered her voice.

Lisa stared at her, crossing her arms in front of her chest to stop her hands from shaking. She nodded her head, slowly, still not releasing her vise-like grip on her own arms.

"Okay, I know you're scared, but you need to come with us." Cassie nodded back, moving her hands down Lisa's arms, slightly pulling forward.

"Listen to her, Lisa," I encouraged.

Her eyes shot over to me, angry and overwhelmed. She looked down at Kate again. The sound of humans got closer and closer. Instead of relaxing her arms, Lisa shook her head again.

"No," she said, taking a step back. "I don't trust any of you. How do I know you aren't lying, or planning to hurt me again?"

"Lisa, we wouldn't hurt you." I shook my head at her, taking a step toward her.

"Wouldn't hurt me? Look at what you did to my best friend!" Lisa backed away again. "She needs a hospital and you're taking her to your house?"

"I promise, she'll be fine." I started, acutely aware of Kate's blood soaking through my shirt. "I know it seems impossible, but you have to trust me."

"I have no reason to trust you!" Lisa shouted back at us, finally releasing her arms.

Cassie moved back to Derek, giving him a look that I didn't like. Derek nodded and looked over to me.

"Let me take her, bro." Derek reached for Kate.

His brown eyes stared at me, unflinching. He knew what he was doing. Lisa may not be able to trust any of us, but I knew I could trust Derek.

"Don't." Lisa shook her head. "You don't know what he's going to do to her."

"I'm going to save her life." Derek shot back at her as he lifted Kate from my arms and into his.

I pulled my hands out from under her, watching her body settle into Derek's arms. The blood coated the center of my shirt. I looked to Lisa, her eyes wild with worry.

Derek stepped away from the sound of the thundering crowd as it approached. He leaned in closer to me, lowering his head.

"Take it," he whispered.

My eyes widened, and I shot my gaze over to Derek. He was talking about her energy. I didn't have to ask to understand his tone.

"I can't," I whispered.

"Then find a way without dragging her kicking and screaming. You'll draw too much attention. If we wake Kate now, we don't know what she'll do. This the only option." Derek raised his eyebrows at me.

"You know what that will do to me," I begged.

Cassie stepped forward, touching her hand to my arm. "But waiting will kill us all."

"Meet us back at your house." Derek nodded.

He looked at Cassie to make sure she was behind him before he took off running. Cassie followed and they both rounded the corner in a matter of seconds.

I let out a breath as I turned back to Lisa.

"I heard...heard what he said," Lisa's voice shuddered, interrupted by short breaths. "W-what is he talking about?"

"You won't come with us, will you? Not even me?" I asked, hoping she would take the out.

"I d-don't know. I'm so scared." She pushed her tight curls away from her face. "I don't know what to do. I don't want you to hurt me, not like they hurt her."

"This isn't going to hurt." I raised my hands and walked toward her.

My heart pounded in my chest. I didn't want to do this to her. She was already scared and untrusting. This would only make it worse until Kate woke up to calm her down.

"Get away from me. You'll take my energy?" Lisa asked. "I thought you...we took human energy. I'm not a human anymore."

It was the perfect excuse. I wanted her energy. Her Legend energy soaring through her body. I could sense it from here.

Human energy was easier to avoid overindulging. But Legend energy was completely different. Better. And worse.

"Another power that Legends can have is the ability to extract energy from other Legends," I explained, walking closer to her. "I have four powers—I'm a Level Four—and that's one of the things I can do."

She shook her head, moving away from me. Tears welled in her eyes. Her breath couldn't keep up with how fast her lungs wanted to pull in the air. Adrenaline spiked in her body and she turned to the open street to run.

That only made me want her energy more.

"No," Lisa hissed, running as fast as she could.

I had more energy than her already, so I was faster. I flashed in front of her and blocked her path. I put my hands on her arms, feeling her energy just underneath her skin.

For one more second, I needed her to be a person, someone that I didn't want to hurt. Her curly hair crowded her face, her hands trembled at her sides, and she nervously shook her head.

"Let me go," Lisa sobbed. She turned her face toward the street. "Help! Please, someone help me."

"Lisa, stop." I gripped her arms even tighter. "They won't help you. They will kill you once they find out what you are."

"No. No, I'm not like you." She tossed her head from side to side, still trying to shove me away. "Help!"

Her eyes were bloodshot. She wasn't going to calm down. The only thing I could hear over her screaming was the sound of the humans getting uncomfortably close.

She was drawing them right to us.

"Yes, you are. Whether you like it or not, you're a Legend, just like me. I've seen humans attack like this and you will *not* survive if I let you run out there." I rushed through an explanation.

"You're lying."

She slammed her eyes shut, jerking away from my body.

"Listen to me. If you don't calm down and come with me right now, I won't have a choice," I begged her.

"You're gonna kill me."

Lisa froze, locked in my gaze. Her arms were warm under my hands.

*That energy.* I shook my head gently.

"No, I won't," I answered for both of us.

Her body twisted awkwardly. Hot tears poured down her cheeks. Her heart rate skyrocketed. The blood pumped through her veins, enough to turn her face red despite her brown skin.

The energy in her blazed. My mouth watered.

She was scared out of her mind. There was only one way for me to fix it.

I focused on that, on her fear, as I pulled the first energy from her body. The raw, unfettered power scorched through my arms. Every cell inside of me wanted a taste.

The energy flooded through my chest, down my legs, up to my head. Any part of me that worried about Kate or feared for Lisa's reaction when she woke up was silenced by the roar of new energy in my body.

"But I'll want to," I breathed.

Her chin dropped, her eyes fell shut. She didn't hear my answer. Didn't know how dangerous it was to have this Extractor pulling her energy.

She didn't notice it was leaving at first. It was easy for her, like falling asleep. She was scared and tired all at the same time.

I was just giving her the opportunity to rest. I was helping her let go of all that anger and fear that now raced through me. The energy tasted like tangible beauty, like crisp perfection.

Her knees buckled and her head slumped forward. She tumbled into my arms, just enough energy left in her body to keep her heart beating.

When she fell, the view behind her opened up to the street. Human after human raced around the corner. I tried to focus my vision through the swirling heat in my head.

"I found them!" a man shouted.

More humans followed. The energy slammed like a frenzy in my body. But she was so limp in my arms already, and they were so close. I gritted my teeth and stopped pulling her energy just in time to keep her breathing. My eyes snapped up to the people behind her.

"He's a Legend too," another man announced.

I swept Lisa's legs out from under her and pulled her into

my bloody chest. The humans were only a few bounds away from me.

Part of me was grateful for the distraction. The other part hated Alec for turning our lives inside out with one video.

I turned and ran in the opposite direction. The shouts of the humans faded behind me. I listened to Lisa's heartbeat to distract me from the buzzing energy in my body.

Now that I had this much, I only wanted more.

Kate would never forgive me if I killed her. I would never forgive myself either. It had been so long since I had killed a Legend. That last burst of energy was the best. My fingers trembled at knowledge that the feeling I craved was one touch away.

Her heart continued beating. I clung to that sound, hoping I could hold on long enough to get to the house.

Once I saw Kate, everything else could go away. The ringing temptation of Lisa's final energy would fade.

I had to hold on just a little longer.

# CHAPTER
# SIX

Warmth seeped into my cheek, moving down my neck.

The dark parts of my mind awakened, wanting to focus on the warm feeling. My hands felt the surface underneath me, soft and comfortable. A bed?

My eyes shot open. I sat up and searched the room for anything I recognized. My eyes landed on Cassie first. She sat at the end of the couch that I was on. I turned and saw Kylan kneeling on the floor next to where my head used to be.

"Hey, hey, you're okay," Kylan's voice whispered gently.

"What happened?" I asked, feeling a stinging pain in the back of my head.

I put my hand to my head. As I did, I looked down and noticed the blood that covered my left side. Both of my shoulders felt raw, uncomfortable to move.

"Do you remember leaving the office?" Kylan asked.

I thought back through my memories. The only thing I could remember was Alec's video. The message playing footage of me hurting people, his voice telling everyone that I was a murderer.

"Alec," I muttered.

"Yes, a video from Alec played everywhere, and you left because you wanted to go find him," Kylan continued.

"He called me a monster…I hurt people," I said slowly, remembering in pieces. "The humans, they came after me. I wanted to—"

"You didn't kill anyone," Kylan interrupted that thought.

"Then whose blood is this?" I asked, pulling at my shirt.

The sound it made when it unstuck from my skin turned my stomach. A pained look was on Kylan's face.

"It's yours," Cassie answered. "Derek tried to stop you from killing everyone. He almost convinced you to leave, and then someone shot you."

Flashes of pictures circulated through my mind. They didn't make sense, almost like they were out of order.

"Yeah, I remember that. I had someone in my hands, a human. I wanted to drain all of her energy to heal the wound. But…I didn't…" I stopped, glancing at the redhead. "Cassie, did you stab me?"

Derek laughed, walking in from the corner of the room. He sat on the arm behind Cassie, putting his hand on her shoulder. Cassie smiled.

"Yup, she jabbed a metal doorframe right above your shoulder," Derek answered for her, lifting his hand for Cassie to high-five.

She did. Kylan shut his eyes, embarrassed by them.

"I had to get your attention somehow," Cassie shrugged, laughing it off.

"And then you knocked me out, didn't you?" I asked Derek now.

"He wasn't supposed to do that," Kylan jumped in.

"You said, and I quote, 'Take her down. Whatever it takes.'" Derek snapped at Kylan.

"You said what?" I asked, turning to look at Kylan.

He lowered his head for a second, annoyed that Derek had spilled the instructions he gave. Cassie snickered even louder now.

"It's true, I heard the phone call," Cassie confirmed, intertwining her fingers with Derek's.

"I meant take her down, like to the ground. Not out completely." Kylan rolled his eyes.

"Well, that's comforting." I smiled down at Kylan.

"I'll do anything to keep you safe." Kylan caught my hand and brought it to his mouth in a kiss.

His energy trickled into my body through the connection. He was touching my skin, actually touching me. My heart filled with a mix of his energy and my own excitement. But his eyes looked different.

My eyebrows furrowed. It was odd that he touched my skin at all. He never had very much energy to give and he didn't seem to mind losing it. I pulled my hand back to myself.

I noticed another person lying on the couch opposite to me. Her unruly curls covered most of her face.

"Lisa," I breathed, immediately standing up from the couch.

I rushed over to her, feeling the blood move away from my head. A light, floaty feeling spun in my head, forcing the room to twist in weird ways. All of my wounds ached, almost to a throbbing level.

"Careful." Kylan followed me. I felt his hand rub down my back. "Just take it slow."

"What happened to her? What about Chase? Is she hurt? I don't see any blood." I tore through the questions. "Is she... Is he—"

"Chase is fine, I think," Kylan started.

"Well, I don't think they're gonna be together anymore, but physically he should be fine. That's what you meant, right?" Cassie quipped.

"What?" I didn't understand.

"He did not take her being a Legend very well. I'll explain the rest later." Kylan tilted his head to the side.

That motion from him settled my stomach. It meant that everything would be okay, even if he couldn't explain it all in the moment. I took a breath and let the air take some of the fear with it as I exhaled.

"Why is she unconscious then?" I asked in a slower voice.

"That's a longer story." Kylan hung his head.

"No it's not," Derek scoffed. "You were out cold, thanks to me, and the humans were chasing us. Lisa was freaking out hardcore and wouldn't come with us. So, Kylan, in all his Extractor glory, drained her energy and brought her here on the brink of death."

"Oh, stop. It was not the brink of death." Cassie smacked Derek on the arm. "It was the only way to calm her down enough to get her away from the humans."

I turned and looked at Kylan, his eyes glued to the light carpet of his living room. I glanced at Lisa, lying silently on the white couch. The dark blood on her clothes and her brown skin made it look like she was lying in her own casket.

They all knew what this looked like. Kylan twisted his hands together, squeezing them until his knuckles turned white.

I reached forward and put a hand on his shoulder. He looked up at me with big, green eyes laced with pain.

"Thank you for saving her." I smiled at him.

His shoulders dropped and the worry melted from his face. He pulled me forward and wrapped his arms around me. I tried to not touch any of his skin, but it was hard to focus when all I wanted to do was enjoy the moment of bliss.

My body warmed against his hard chest. Heat saturated all the way down to my fingertips. With each deep breath, his shoulders moved under my arms.

"I don't know how you handle it. The energy…it's…" Kylan pressed his mouth into my shirt, muffling his words.

"It gets easier with practice, I think," I whispered back.

I wanted to stroke his hair, or rub his neck, anything to tell him that I cared. Instead, I kept my hand perfectly still.

Lisa stirred on the couch next to me. I pulled away from Kylan and moved to be at her head. Her eyes fluttered open as her face twisted in discomfort.

"Lisa?" I asked, letting her hear my voice.

"Kate." Lisa's eyes flew open and scanned me, the room, and then back to me. "Are you okay? You're bleeding. Where am I?"

"Shhh." I put my hand on her shoulder to tell her to stay lying down. "You're here with me. I was bleeding, but it's all dried up now. I'm a little tired, but I'm fine. Just like you."

Lisa looked past me at Kylan, the person who knocked her out. Cassie and Derek stood behind him, warily watching her.

"Dried up? That doesn't make sense. None of this makes sense. Kylan, he…he took—" Lisa sat up, tears welling in her eyes.

"I know." I rubbed her shoulder as she sat up. "I asked him to keep you safe and that was the only way he could. I'm sorry I couldn't be there for you."

"I'm so sorry about that. I was never going to hurt you, I swear. I was just trying to help you," Kylan added.

Lisa looked between me and Kylan. Her eyebrows

furrowed while her lips pulled into a tight line. She shook her head softly, holding back her tears.

"I was so scared," Lisa mumbled, her fingers tapping against her legs.

"I know you were." I leaned forward and put my arms around her, careful not to take any more of her energy. "It's okay, though. I'm here now and I won't let anyone hurt you."

Lisa's weak arms wrapped around me, holding onto me with all the strength she had. Her sobs turned into short breaths until they eventually calmed down.

"Things are going to be different now." I pulled away from Lisa to look in her eyes. "You're a Legend. Humans tend to react in an extreme way if they know that, which you just saw. It's one of the reasons I never told you about me. I didn't want to lose you."

Lisa shook her head. "You wouldn't have lost me."

"That's sweet of you to say." I rubbed my hand on her knee. "But do you remember your life before? Imagine if I had told you that I was a Legend, with the ability to kill people, even you."

"I…" Lisa stopped, probably comparing her reaction to Chase. "I don't know what I would've done."

"You saw what everyone was like. I hope you know that we can't stay here. We have to leave," I explained.

"What? And go where? I've never been outside of Oregon or Washington." She looked outside the window.

"That's a good question, ya know," Derek said. "As you pointed out, we don't know how wide that video has gone. We can't just pick up and move again."

"We'll find a place, remote enough that no one has heard about all of this," Kylan answered confidently.

"And do what? Hide out while we watch you and Kate dance around the fact that you can't touch each other?" Cassie raised an eyebrow. "I'm all for a good bout of angst every now and then, but I've overheard a phone call or two between you and Derek. You two are gonna have to get that fixed."

"We can worry about that later." Kylan shook his head, reaching over to touch my clothed leg. "The overhearing phone calls, though, I think we should address now. You wanna tell me more about that, man?"

"Hey—" he started.

"Derek's right though," I interrupted. "We can't just pick a new place. Technology is everywhere. Humans are everywhere. We need a place that no human can go, but close enough that we can still get energy."

"Please don't say it." Kylan closed his eyes and sighed.

"The Shadows' mansion," I finished.

"Absolutely not." Cassie stood and moved to stand behind the couch, anything to put something between me and her.

"Cass, she has a point," Derek argued.

"She didn't make a point, she just disagreed," Kylan said.

"That's the point." Cassie shook her head, crossing her arms in front of her. "I am not stepping foot inside of that place. Kate can go by herself. They're only after her."

"I'm not leaving her." Kylan stood. "If she goes, I'm going too."

"Kylan, you can't." Cassie stepped forward again. "You know what the Shadows will do to Rogues like us."

"We know what they *used* to do to Rogues like us. Alec isn't in charge anymore and Kate's on our side," Kylan shot back.

"Why do we all have to go down with her?" Cassie groaned. "No offense, Kate, but our lives were so much easier before you got here."

"A little offense taken, but I understand..." I muttered.

"Kate is with me." Kylan stepped toward Cassie. "That makes her family. And we stand by our family."

"Besides, all those humans saw me and you fight her." Derek came up behind her and put a hand on her back. "There were cameras and witnesses. We're not safe out there on our own."

Cassie didn't say anything. Derek just stared at her back, hoping to see her change her mind. Kylan waited, not moving.

"Shadows are real too?" Lisa broke the silence, standing up from the couch.

We all turned and looked at her wide eyes. I already knew that everyone else would be glancing at me, waiting for me to explain. I sighed, stepping toward her.

"Do you remember the mark on my arm? The one that a lot of people in that lab had?" I asked gently.

Lisa nodded, looking down on my arm where she remembered the mark to be.

It was a reminder that I had been a Shadow. A twisted kind of Legend who enjoyed human pain if it meant more fun for me. Things were different now since I had joined Kylan's family and deemed myself a Rogue along with them. We were Legends that weren't affiliated with the Shadows. Good Legends.

But I was still marked otherwise and always would be. I looked down at the ground. The fear of ruining her trust crushed me inside.

"There's one more thing that you need to know," I started.

# CHAPTER
# SEVEN

I held Lisa's hand in mine, gloves covering my skin. She warily followed me into the town.

We had been driving all day. It took longer than running, but we didn't have the energy like Shadows to run that distance. Stopping anywhere was a risk. This way Lisa got to sleep most of the way in the car.

In the car, Kylan had held my hand over those gloves, and I tried to smile. I had settled for resting my head on his shoulder and letting my emotion show on my face when I stared out the window.

"I'll just be around the corner," Kylan whispered in my ear, bringing me back to where we were walking now.

I nodded and watched him walk off, leaving Lisa and I alone. I pulled her gently to a stop.

"We still have a day before we get to the mansion. Maybe half a day with how fast Cassie has been driving."

Lisa cracked a smile but returned her gaze to the crumbling road under her feet.

We had made it to a small, quiet town. All of us were

wearing hoods, hats, or sunglasses to obscure the way we looked. I had all of them on, every precaution necessary, down to my gloves.

"The energy in your body will probably last that long since you haven't read anyone recently," I explained.

"Read?" she asked.

"Sorry, reading minds," I explained. "When you use your abilities, it will drain your energy faster. Since you've only broken through that Level, I don't think we'll need to worry about others until you have more energy anyway."

She nodded, trying to be polite and quiet. I noted the way her hands were still trembling. They had started twitching in the car. Being outside, near the energy of humans, the shake was too visible.

I put my gloved hand on top of hers, hoping to shield the tremors from her. The hood covering her head made the bags under her eyes stand out less too.

"This is the important part, though. You need to learn how to take energy," I started.

Lisa shook her head.

"Not like how much you took from Chase. It will be different this time," I tried.

"I can't…I don't know how to—I can't stop. Kylan said when I'm tired that I can't—"

I tapped her hands, pulling her attention again. "He's right. It's harder to stop when you're hungry. But you can. Trust me, you can."

"Are you sure? I'm not sure. I don't…No, I can't," she stammered.

She needed more than just my explanation. She needed to know she could do it. I took a glance at the humans walking out of the grocery store nearby.

It was old, colorful, and far from a chain franchise. The

bricks outside had been painted with a mural of fruits and vegetables.

I watched the people leaving, hands full of grocery bags or pushing carts to their cars. I pulled my gloves off and tucked them in my pocket.

Lisa started biting her nails before I had even stepped away. I looked back at her and walked toward a woman who was carrying way too many plastic bags on her arm. She had missed a loop and some of her items were threatening to topple out.

I ducked down and caught the other handle of the bag.

"You missed a handle there," I said, raising my voice to a more innocent pitch.

"Oh, thank you darlin'," she said, blowing a piece of long hair out of her eyes.

I slipped the loop of plastic over her hand, letting my finger drag along her arm. Wisps of power warmed my hand. I glanced at Lisa just as I untucked my finger and pulled my hand back.

"It looks like you've got quite the day ahead of you," I remarked at all the bags.

"Just the weekly grocery trip," the woman nodded, smiling.

I reached out and tapped her hand again, pulling more energy. I laughed to distract her. "Make sure you get to your car in one piece."

"I will," she laughed with me and started walking. "Thank you!"

I waved at her and took a look at Lisa. Her face had drained of color. It looked like she was going to slump over or pass out.

I rushed to her at a perfectly human speed and caught her arm.

"How do you..." Lisa whispered, disgusted. "How is

it so normal? She didn't even know. Did…did you do that often?"

I guided her to a bench near the entrance, the new energy barely even felt like a change in my body. It was too little. But even that amount would do wonders for Lisa.

"I will tell you anything you want to know," I said, wrapping an arm around her shoulder. "But let's focus on you right now."

Lisa ignored that. "Did you ever do it to me? Did you take…"

I winced before speaking. I tried starting to explain the reasons for each time I could remember taking her energy. But she didn't need to hear any of that. Not yet.

So I simply nodded.

Her face dropped. Her bottom lip fell as she looked back to the entrance, back at me. "I didn't even notice."

"That's a good thing." I shrugged. "These people, they won't know anything is happening to them. I will make sure of it."

I expected her to shrink back down in her seat. I thought I'd spend the next few minutes talking her through it all. But I was wrong.

Lisa stood and immediately walked to a human about to enter the store. He was shorter than her, probably about ten human years older too. He wore a tank top with chest hair poking out of the neckline.

"Hi," Lisa interrupted his walk. "I'm Lisa."

The man smiled. "Hello, there."

I cringed at her technique, but I didn't know if I should try and stop her. Instead, I stood and moved a little closer, within a few bounds so I could step in if needed. I pretended to inspect the clearance products in a wooden bin outside.

"I'm a…I have a question, I hope this isn't too forward," Lisa said, dragging a hand through her hair.

*Was she trying to ask him out?* I wanted to gag, but kept my back turned to them.

"Let's hear it then," he said, in a deeper, more confident voice.

Now I definitely gagged. I put down the figurine I was holding and reached for a different one.

"I'm just…I'll just come right out and say it." Lisa took in a breath. "I'm really, really tired and I need a little energy. I'm a Legend. Maybe I should have started with that. But would it be okay if I took some of your energy?"

He laughed. "You want what?"

Lisa offered a hand out to him, like she was going to touch his arm. He lifted it up to her.

My jaw dropped. This wasn't normal. Even for a beautiful Legend asking a human who was way below her league. The fear was coming.

Energy flowed into her skin, too bright and fast to not be hurting the human.

"Not good," I muttered to myself and dropped what I was holding.

"What are you doing?" he shouted and yanked his arm away from her.

Lisa grabbed on harder, unable to tear her focus away. More energy spun around her fingers.

I knocked her arm off with too much force. She curled her hand back and shot a stare at me.

The human was already backing away from her, bumbling about meeting a Legend. He had his hands held up like he was going to fight her. Lisa was already backing away, her shoulders turned in and scared.

He pointed a finger at both of us. "Legends!"

I dug my nails into Lisa's coat and dragged her away. I had seen too many scenes like this. With the Shadows around me, I actually liked watching the humans devolve into insanity. We would play with them and kill them all.

It was easy and fun. A game we played when things got boring. But this was no game. I wasn't a Shadow with the protection of so many powerful Legends.

I was a Rogue, alone with a new Legend who didn't know anything about her new life. So I took her behind the store, out of sight, and we ran back to the van.

She stumbled and tried to keep up, broken up by sobs or shaky breaths. When we were a safe distance away, I stopped and released her arm.

Her hands immediately reached up to cover her face. She sank to the dusty rocks that people used as landscaping here. They were hideous and uncomfortable, but they were away from people.

"Lisa," I started. "Lisa, I should have explained more. I shouldn't have just let you walk out—"

"I can't do this," she said, and moved to hugging her knees to her chest.

"That's not true, you can. I promise it's easy once you get used to it." I patted her hands.

"How can I get used to this? I can't just take their energy. I can't...Not like Chase," she said through a shuddering sob.

"It's hard to see through everything right now. You're emotional because you're so exhausted. But you can do this. You can do this life," I whispered.

She wiped a sniffle away and looked up at me with red eyes. "You're right. I am so tired. I've never ever felt this tired," Lisa said. "I want to go back."

Alec had changed her just to hurt me. Seeing her struggle made the hurt worse than ever. Maybe I was right about the pain not stopping when I left the lab. Maybe Alec knew that even if I did escape, I wouldn't really be free.

Lisa didn't understand what it meant to be a Legend. I didn't understand what it meant to be human. It was like a bird trying to explain to a fish how to fly.

I lowered my chin and settled onto the rocks next to her. "We've talked about this. We can't go back to Portland."

"Not there. The car. I want to go back to sleep. Please, please just let me sleep," she said, drying her tears.

Her hands were still quivering slightly. Her breaths were too uneven. I tucked a curl behind her ear, careful not to touch her cheek. The energy she took had brightened her complexion slightly, but it would only last a few days if she was careful.

"We can go back, if that's what you really want. I won't force you to take energy yet," I promised.

Lisa nodded, letting her shoulders fall.

"But you should know that sleeping won't fix this. It will help take the edge off, but you need human energy. Your body won't survive without it," I said, quietly and carefully.

"You said I could wait," she interrupted. "That I could make it to the mansion? And I just took...I should be good now, right?"

I raised my eyebrows. "Honestly, I don't know how much energy is in your body. You're probably fine but—"

"Then I want to wait," she answered.

Before I could talk again Lisa shook her head. She was biting her lip now to keep it from quivering. So I didn't say anything. I couldn't fix the fear that was controlling her.

She had to give it up if she was going to make it through whatever came next.

"We could give it another try, go slower this time," I started.

"No." Lisa released her legs and looked me in the eye.

"I just need some more time to think about everything. I can't—I need to process this. I can make it to the mansion."

"It's not just making it there that I'm worried about," I confessed. "The Shadows' mansion…it's an easy place to lose your energy. Everyone there uses their powers and energy freely. It…it might be more overwhelming and taxing than you think."

"I know what Shadows are," Lisa grumbled.

"You know what you've heard Shadows to be. It's different experiencing it for yourself."

She looked at my covered arm, the one with the dagger I had shown her earlier. I had given her the briefest explanation possible, but even after she found out, she still trusted me the most out of Kylan's family.

I wanted to be happy about that, but she really didn't have much of a choice but to trust me. Her life depended on me taking care of her, at least until she knew how to be a Legend on her own.

I still wondered what she thought of me now. Legend. Shadow. If I had changed in her eyes.

"But you used to be a Shadow, and you're still kind and caring," Lisa said and I relaxed a little. "The others can't be much worse, right? They're your friends."

"Yes, they are." I lowered my gaze. "But they are a part of who I used to be. I was very different a few decades ago, even a few years ago."

"You befriended me when everyone else in the office was practically shunning me." Lisa reached for my arm instead of my bare hand. "You helped me stand out and matter. I can't think of the last time someone did that for me. I need you to be there for me now. I promise, *I promise* I will wrap my head around all of this and we can try later."

"Lisa..."

"Just," her voice broke. "Just don't make me do it now. Give me a little more time."

I scanned her eyes, red and weepy. I looked at her frail body, her cheeks almost shining and her lips had turned pink again.

Her body was better, but not far from falling apart. It was operating on too little power after what Kylan took. I wanted to protect her. I wanted to give her all the energy she would ever need.

But short of forcing her hand against human skin, I wasn't going to do that. She needed to take this step on her own.

"I can't lose you," I finally said out loud.

As much as I saved her in that office, she made me more humane. She made me care about a people I had loathed for centuries. She reminded me that being good could be a happy thing.

Lisa pulled me into her arms. I whispered into her mess of curls, "I want to fix this, fix all of this for you. I can't stand to see you in this kind of pain."

I knew what it felt like, the border between having barely enough energy and your heart stopping. I had been on that border too many times in the lab. Lisa would be there in days if she didn't get more.

"You won't lose me. But this isn't my world," Lisa said. "And I need some time. Just a couple more days, please."

I pulled back, not looking at her like a lowly human or even a newbie Legend that needed guidance. I looked at her like an equal, a friend.

She knew the risks, or at least I hoped she did. I had to let her make this choice. She deserved that much freedom.

"Okay," I answered. She sighed. "I don't want to take

anything else away from you. This decision should be yours."

Lisa nodded, finally cracking a smile. "Thank you."

I stood and hoisted her up along with me. I tossed my arm around her shoulder, friendly but mostly to support her.

"We'll figure this thing out, one way or another, right?" I joked.

Lisa smiled even wider. I might have even heard a laugh. "I never imagined I would be friends with a Legend, or be one myself."

"I can promise, it's not all bad," I said. "Being a Legend can have its perks too."

"It's really that different?" she asked. "I mean, you seem so normal."

I looked ahead, keeping an eye on the surroundings and any humans who might pass.

"You just wait," I whispered.

# CHAPTER
# EIGHT

The mansion grew closer and closer, somehow feeling taller than it ever had. The old stone looked the same as it always had. Familiar and intimidating all at once.

"Why would they let you in?" Lisa asked, quickening her steps to catch up to me. "If you aren't one of them anymore, I mean."

"The person in charge now, Thayer, he's a friend." I smiled at the memory of him.

Lisa linked her arm with mine and our steps fell into the same pace. I wanted to touch her hand, but clenched my fist at my side instead. I had just enough energy to function and my body would pull it out of her too fast.

"But, he's still a Shadow, they all are. Should we be trusting them?" Lisa whispered even quieter.

But that didn't stop Cassie from hearing. "See! That's what I've been saying this whole time."

"And yet you sped like an absolute maniac to get here," Kylan said. Cassie rolled her eyes and Derek winced. "We're out of options."

"Whether you like it or not, sweetheart, this is the safest place for you," Derek reasoned, and all I heard was Cassie huffing in defeat.

"We can trust Thayer." I smiled over at Lisa as we walked closer to the doors.

I pushed the blond hair from my face and tucked it behind my ear. I couldn't look like Kate when we traveled, not with that video. So, I went back to being Mara. Blond hair, sharp features, and the same blue eyes.

I took a breath and looked at my once-home and once-prison. Lisa's hand fell away from my arm as we stopped in front of the door.

"Maybe, just let me do the talking?" I glanced at the group, mostly at Kylan.

"We'll follow you." Kylan nodded, giving me a soft smile. "Even Cassie."

Cassie stomped her foot and Derek stifled a laugh as he put his arm around her. Lisa backed away from me, still trying to not stand too close to the other three.

I turned toward the door and closed my hands into fists at my sides. I wasn't sure how to proceed, despite how much I had mulled it over in my mind before arriving here. My fingers latched onto the large metal knocker and I slammed it two times.

The door opened and a rush of warm air swirled at my feet. Then a face I didn't recognize stared back at me.

"Can I help you, honey?" The man grinned at me as his eyes wandered up and down my body.

"Who are you?" I asked in a sharp tone.

"Better question. What are you doing here?" The man pursed his lips. "A group of Rogues, I assume? This is a place for Shadows, not you. I mean, unless you want to come inside and not come back out."

"I'm gonna ignore almost all of that." I furrowed my brows. "Let me talk to Thayer."

I stepped forward to brush past him. He stepped in front of me, forcing me to stop.

"No one comes in without clearance," the man snarled at me.

"You're gonna want to get out of my way." I narrowed my eyes at him.

I pulled the sleeve on my right arm up. I rolled it high enough to rest above my elbow, showing my dagger mark.

"You're a Shadow," the man gaped. "One of the old Shadows."

"Old?" I asked.

"Yeah, one with a mark. They don't…I mean we don't do that anymore." The man stepped away from me, staring at me with wide eyes and a slacked jaw.

"Tiran! Tiran!" a familiar voice shouted from down the hallway. "Shut up, you are not gonna believe—"

Fiona stumbled around the corner with a wide smile on her face. Her eyes snapped over to me as her words froze.

"Whoa," Fiona breathed, pulling her black curls behind her ear.

"Nice to see you again too." I smirked, reaching to pull my sleeve back down but deciding to leave it.

"What are you doing here?" Fiona asked.

"Thayer's new guard was being ever so rude and I was just waiting for common sense to smack him." I glared at the man.

He stepped farther back into the wall behind him. Fiona punched his arm and he yelped.

"Don't you know who this is?" she scolded.

"Yeah, yeah, she's an original Shadow." He rubbed a hand over his arm.

"No, this is Mara," Fiona explained. "As in Mara Hayes, the Level Five."

The man's eyes widened even more. He bowed his head to me and started a stream of apologies faster than I could understand.

"Hayes?" Lisa's voice asked behind me.

Kylan started explaining, too softly for me to hear. I focused back on Fiona and the unaware person next to her.

"Can I see Thayer now?" I asked, raising my eyebrows.

"Of course, come in." Fiona stepped to the side. "But your friends will have to wait out here. Thayer's orders."

"They're with me. They can come inside if I want them to," I scoffed.

She shook her head at me. "We don't let anyone else in without his permission."

"Fiona—"

She cut me off. "You can explain it to him yourself."

"Fine," I sighed. "Take me to Thayer then."

"Wait, what?" Cassie piped up. "You're gonna just leave us here with this idiot?"

I turned around to face all of them. Lisa stood a little closer to Kylan than before. Cassie crossed her arms in front of her, although they had been like that the entire trip.

"Yeah, let's insult the guard. That sounds like a solid idea," Derek muttered under his breath.

I shook my head at them and smiled before my eyes turned to Lisa.

"You'll be fine." I nodded to her and then looked to Kylan. "I'll be right back to get you."

I spun on my heel to face the entrance to the mansion. I looked at the guard, leaning against the wall casually, and Fiona had already started down the hallway. I walked through the threshold, feeling a weight push on my shoulders.

Being here made me different. Here, I wanted to be Mara more than anything else. It felt more right than walking in here like Kate.

Before I turned the corner, I moved behind the guard. I brushed a finger along his cheek, feeling his energy warm through my fingertips. He jerked his face away from my touch.

"Just a little advice," I whispered to the guard, looking at Kylan. "That one's an Extractor. Best to keep your hands to yourself."

Tiran stiffened at my words. Kylan's eyebrows raised. It felt odd acting like a Shadow right in front of them. But it was only for their safety. As Mara, I still held a lot of respect here, especially now that it was revealed I was a Five.

But all the swagger was a ruse. That's what I wanted to tell myself anyway.

The guard stood up from against the wall, keeping his eyes locked on Kylan. I smiled and watched Kylan shake his head while a smile spread on his face.

He didn't need to say anything else. I knew he would protect the people around him at any cost, and that was the only reason I stepped around the corner and left them behind.

I straightened my shoulders as I followed Fiona's bouncing, black curls down the grand hallways. The ornate trim on the ceiling and the stone floor wrapped around me.

"How has it been with Thayer in charge?" I asked. "I mean, I guess it makes sense he'd step up if Alec was out of the picture. But you and I both know he was never quite the leader type."

"All things considered, I think he's taking his new role pretty well." She shrugged and kept walking.

"What does that mean?" I asked, a little nervous to see Thayer as the leader instead of Alec.

Fiona stopped just before we neared the courtyard. She held a hand in front of her to direct me.

"See for yourself." She smiled and I braced myself for what I was about to see.

# CHAPTER
# NINE

The roar of laughter and excitement hit me like a wall when I stepped around the corner.

The ancient, stone courtyard sprawled out in front of me, lined with way more Shadows than I had ever seen. Most of the new faces were female, and I couldn't help but roll my eyes. Thayer was nothing if not predictable.

Another wave of cheers crashed in my ears as I walked closer to the center of the crowd. A flashing dagger swung, followed by the sound of cloth being sliced. A smile tugged at my mouth as I recognized this game.

I kept walking through the marble pillars, noting the Legends who saw me and stepped out of my way without my asking. The cheers died down as everyone turned to stare at me. The Shadow in the game sliced the second strike against his opponent's arm, creating an X. His victory was met with silence instead of the normal roar of applause.

I turned to see Thayer at the head of the courtyard. On the raised dais stood a gaudy, golden throne where an empty space once was.

I raised my eyebrows when I saw Thayer sitting on the floor instead of on the throne. Sage sat on his lap, with Thayer running his hand up and down her arm. He hadn't been paying attention to the game at all, just enjoying the thrill of the atmosphere.

It was nice to know leadership hadn't changed him too much.

"All fun and games," I called, and Thayer flicked his attention to me. "I guess I shouldn't be too surprised."

"Mara," Thayer sighed. His brilliant white teeth sparkled in the sun streaming through the open ceiling.

I walked through the empty center of the crowd and straight to Thayer. He stood, shifting Sage from his lap to a standing position in one swoop of his arm. He jumped off the stage and landed directly in front of me.

"It's good to see you." I smiled at him.

He stepped closer to me, but he paused when I leaned away, folding my gloved hands in front of me. Thayer nodded in recognition.

"I heard about what happened. I mean, what Alec did," Thayer said. "How are you doing?"

"I'm hanging in there," I lied, hoping he wouldn't catch it.

"Oof, Alec was right. Your lying skills are trash now." Thayer laughed easily.

"Yeah, that was pathetic," Sage agreed with a wrinkled nose as she leaned against the throne.

At that I smiled and shot my eyes back up at both of them. Sage let out a small laugh, easing the tension. Thayer smiled right back at me with the kindness that I needed. He stepped forward, getting dangerously close to me.

"I'll be okay eventually." I forced my smile to stay on my face.

"Which means you're not okay right now." Thayer lowered his voice.

I shrugged, hating how much he knew me. My face flushed and I lowered my head to avoid any emotions that I didn't want spilling out in front of the entire Shadows.

"That's why I'm here." I lifted my head when a blank expression solidified. "Kylan and his family are outside and—"

"No doubt being held up at the door?" Thayer sighed, nodding to Sage. "Of course Tiran picks today of all days to comprehend how to follow orders."

He twisted to look at Sage and asked, "Would you mind bringing Mara's guests inside?"

"Sure." She stepped off the stage lightly and started walking toward the entrance.

"Hey," Thayer called and Sage paused to look at him. "Hurry back, princess."

He winked, and Sage blushed. Against her nearly translucent white skin it was too obvious. She spun on her heel and disappeared into the sweeping hallway without a word.

"Princess, huh?" I asked. Thayer turned back to me, still smiling. "Does that make you the Prince of the Shadows?"

Thayer pursed his lips and looked back at the glaringly obvious gold behind him. He shrugged his shoulders. The Shadows around us fell silent, waiting for the response.

"I don't know, I mean with Alec gone"—Thayer turned back and locked his brown eyes on me—"I think that makes me the king."

A cry of support and joy erupted through the crowd. I peered at all the people that loved him. But that was what Thayer was best at, making people love him. I smiled.

Thayer stood a little taller and smiled with brighter eyes than before.

"I think the throne suits you." I nodded.

"Yeah." Thayer dropped his head. "That was a gift from Sage. But anyway, tell me what's going on. What brought you back here?"

"Have you seen the video?" I winced in anticipation.

"No…" Thayer narrowed his eyes at me. "What video?"

"You should see this." I pulled out my phone from my pocket and clicked on the saved video of Alec's message.

I listened to the words I had memorized from hearing them play in my mind every night. I watched Thayer's face drop when he saw me come on the screen, then his eyes hardened when Alec called me a monster. The video ended and Thayer clutched the phone in his hand, unmoving.

"Every time I think he can't go any further, that he can't possibly do anything else to you…" Thayer shook his head as he shoved the phone back to me.

"Believe me, I know," I grumbled and stuffed the phone back in my pocket again.

"So what do you need? Do you want to go to war against the lab or just hope that Alec will take silence as defeat and move on with his life?" Thayer asked. "I mean, we both know which option is more likely to happen."

"As much as I want to fight," I smiled, filling with contempt and remembering the thrill of winning a battle, "I have other things to consider now. I can't just go storming the castle like old times."

"Yeah, okay." Thayer bobbed his head.

I raised an eyebrow at how fast he backed off. "Uh, you're actually okay with that?"

"Oh, no." Thayer shook his head. "But I can wait until you come around."

He winked at me and I shoved him away. His smile broke through as he took the blow.

I glanced to the left and saw Sage sauntering back to Thayer's side. Behind her was the rest of the group, looking every bit as out of place as a Rogue in the mansion should.

"Until then," Thayer announced, turning to the group. "You and your friends are welcome to stay as long as you need. The Shadows are probably going to be as courteous as can be expected."

A series of laughs and snickers rippled across the crowd. All of them looked at the Rogues like new toys to play with. Thayer looked around at his people.

"But you will leave them unharmed. Anyone who decides to do otherwise will have to answer to me," Thayer purred.

It wasn't a threat like Alec would have dealt. Instead of cowering, the people around him smiled and cheered. He beamed and extended his arms out to accept the praise.

"Under one condition," Thayer added, looking directly at me.

"What?" I crossed my arms in front of my chest, taking a glance at Kylan's wary face.

I waited for his response. A hush fell on the people around us. Thayer smiled, his bright eyes staring directly into mine. The blood roared in my ears as I tried to pull in regular breaths.

He stepped forward and my heart pounded.

"Play me," he challenged.

I narrowed my eyes at him. Thayer waited.

"I can't." I dropped my arms and the crowd wailed. "I'm not a Shadow anymore and I don't have near the energy I'd need to face you."

"Mara, you know I always have energy to spare," Thayer said and opened his arms. "Get over here."

I looked at him standing with his arms extended. The short sleeves he had on would hardly protect him at all. My fingers tingled as anticipation burned through my body.

I held my stance for a second. Remembering where I was. Inside a massive courtyard with ornate carvings on the stone trim. The smell of dust and angst washed through the air. It felt like the home in my memory, not a home I would want now. But familiar at least.

With as much restraint as I could muster, I looked back at Thayer, open arms and grinning from ear to ear. I could play a game. It was easy. Even if my stomach twisted at the thought of the Rogues seeing this life, seeing me in this life.

But if they wanted to accept me, then they had to know part of me would always be a Shadow. After all, there were far worse things I could have shown them. My body took over after that. I shot forward, straight into him.

My arms wrapped around his neck, touching his hot skin. The energy released immediately. Thayer caught me and pulled me in tighter. My breath raced from my skin touching his.

Energy careened into me, too fast and hot. I tried to stop it, tried to slow it down. But the power crashed through my body, igniting every nerve.

After a few seconds, I stopped trying to stifle it.

This was the first time I had hugged another person without worrying that I was taking a small amount of energy in their body. Thayer moved his hand from my back to my neck and slid it underneath my hair. The new point of contact exploded with energy too.

My heart soared. All of my burdens fell off my shoulders.

"I missed you," I whispered into his shirt.

"Me too," Thayer answered easily.

He lifted his hand and smoothed the back of my hair. My entire body felt as though it was on fire. The energy swirled inside of my body, raging into a hurricane.

I opened my eyes and saw the world in crystal clarity. Every dust particle in the air stood out. I could sense everything. My muscles tensed like they were ready to run.

With all this power, I could fly.

I had forgotten about everything else around me. The rest of the world didn't matter. I hardly even remembered it was my best friend that was hugging me. My mouth watered at the thought of more energy. I sighed in absolute bliss.

"That's enough," Thayer breathed and pulled away. "Wouldn't want to give you an unfair advantage."

"Fair." I shrugged and pulled my hands back to myself.

My stomach dropped when Thayer fell forward.

He caught himself with his hands on his knees. He heaved a breath and blinked hard. Sage stepped forward and put a hand on his back.

"Wow, I forgot how much that hurt," Thayer choked on the words.

"Are you good?" Sage asked, her red eyes locked on him.

"I'm good." Thayer waved at her. "Just need a minute."

He shook his head and groaned. Another deep breath and he stood to his full height. His eyes still sparkled with energy, just not as much as he had before.

"Now that we're even"—Thayer shook off his shoulders—"ready to play?"

Sage stepped away, back to where Kylan and the others stood. I looked into his green eyes and hoped to see him encouraging me. Instead, his eyebrows pulled in confusion and his mouth tightened in disappointment.

He didn't understand why I was doing this. The best answer was to show him.

I nodded to him, hoping to convey that he should just trust me. His face smoothed slightly. I turned my attention back to the all-too-eager Thayer standing in front of me.

Energy roared through my body, barely contained by

my own skin. I lowered my head and narrowed my eyes on Thayer.

"Game on." I smiled.

# CHAPTER
# TEN

A pair of sleeves formed around Thayer's arms, and ended in gloves that covered his hands.

"Ladies first." Thayer pointed a finger at me.

I dropped my eyes to the worn stone floor, avoiding his gaze as I lunged for him. One stare would allow him enough time to get in my mind.

My arm swiped at his legs just before he stepped to the side. I faked stumbling past him and his chuckle told me he bought it.

My knee slammed down while the other foot launched me toward Thayer again. My hand grazed the gritty floor, feeling it change to an impossibly smooth surface. I hurled myself at him, sliding on my knees toward Thayer's leg.

I held my hand out, a dagger already solidifying in place as I shot it forward and slashed a diagonal line across the back of Thayer's calf.

"Ah," Thayer groaned and his hand flew to his leg.

"One more and I win." I smiled, still keeping my eyes on his legs as I stood on the floor that turned to solid stone again.

It was like fighting with Medusa. One look and I would be at his mercy.

"Not if it heals before you can reach it again."

Thayer ran at me. He was done waiting.

I let him get within arm's reach and I jumped. The dagger flashed in the light as I spun in the air above Thayer's head. A strong hand reached up and yanked me down.

My back slammed into the floor, sending the blade clattering out of reach.

I tumbled toward the edge of the circle of Shadows. I finally stopped and felt the disorienting pain ringing between my ears. The energy in my body raced to heal any bruises that would have formed.

I snapped my head up, just high enough to see where Thayer was and instead I saw Kylan just on the edge of the circle.

He stepped toward me, hands already reaching out to help me. Sage put her hand up and cut him off.

"Ah, ah," she chided. "You step in that ring and you're fair game for Thayer to use. If you want her to win, I suggest staying right where you are."

I forced a smile through the dissipating pain and Kylan rested back on his heels again, worry still cringing in his eyes. He didn't understand this was a game. I could only imagine what this looked like to Lisa.

A strong hand clamped around my ankle.

"No," I muttered under my breath.

The hand yanked on my leg, launching me into the air above Thayer's head. I braced for the fall.

My hands shot out, catching the floor and I landed on my front. Pain sparked in my wrists and surged up my arms.

"Oh, sorry," Thayer teased. "Did that hurt?"

I glared at my hands. I was letting him use his physical

power. There was no way I could win this fight if I kept playing into his hand.

I let out a breath and felt all of the Rogue parts of me flutter away. A cold concentration spread through my muscles. I was all Shadow now.

I kicked one of my legs around and caught Thayer's ankle. His body hit next to me with a thud. I shot my hand forward and grabbed his clothed wrist.

My other hand reached back in anticipation.

The air around the dagger lying in the corner forced it forward, skittering across the stone. The cold metal pressed into my hand and the air dissolved again.

I gripped the handle, feeling the power in my fingertips as I pulled it forward to Thayer.

His wrist was pinned, like his other limbs shackled in metal cuffs that I had created. He yanked against them. Creating wasn't my best talent and he'd be able to rip through them if I waited too long.

I pierced the dagger through the cloth that covered his hand. The fabric peeled away, leaving his skin vulnerable. I touched a finger to his open palm and more of his energy poured into me.

He was exciting, fun, and far more emotional than most people and his potent energy felt exactly like his personality flying through me. It almost made me forget what I was doing.

"Like what you feel?" Thayer crooned, still struggling against the restraints.

"Not as much as I'm gonna like this," I answered him, not hearing my voice over the sound of the blood pounding in my ears.

My teeth clenched as the thrill of impending victory raced in my blood. Black tufts of smoke floated around the metal. He was trying to destroy it.

But we both knew it would take him too long.

"No, no," Thayer's voice begged. "Don't do it."

He sounded genuine and scared. I didn't hide my smile as blood spilled from his hand. I drew a line from the bottom of his thumb to his little finger.

"Please," Thayer muttered.

That word meant nothing coming from him. Glimmering red pooled in the split skin. I moved the dagger to scrape the next line. More black sputtered around his wrists.

"You're gonna have to do better than that." I kept my eyes on his hand.

The tip of the dagger stabbed through his skin, blood already forming a trail to the white stone floor. The Shadows around us were silent, waiting.

"Kate," he whispered.

Immediately, almost instinctively, I looked up. I had to know if it was Thayer who said it. If he had actually called me by my fake name. A strange shudder moved down my spine as I thought about Thayer referring to me by that name. It was wrong.

That was exactly what he wanted.

My gaze locked on his bright brown eyes staring up at me. One second passed, two seconds. I tried to turn away, but it was already too late.

*Calm.* Flooding through my veins, freezing everywhere it touched. My body resisted any movement at all, even breathing. I stared ahead, perfectly and totally at peace.

"I didn't think you'd fall for it." Thayer's smile peeled across his face.

I pulled in one breath as a response. I just stared ahead at him, waiting for the next emotion. He ripped free of the cuffs, sending pieces of black and broken metal scattering into the crowd.

They rippled around the movement, whispers flying. I held still, perfectly still.

"Drop the dagger," Thayer commanded, smiling sweetly as he pulled his hand away from me.

*Fascination.* Thayer seemed to transform in front of me. He was beautiful and caring and I wanted to do anything for him. Anything at all, including giving up the fight.

My muscles struggled against my mind, despite the command. I had to fight this, I had to try. I clutched the blade tighter.

"Now," Thayer added, narrowing his eyes on me as he sat up.

My fingers released with the next breath. The dagger clanked to the floor. I sat on my knees, making my eyes the same height as Thayer's. My distracted mind wanted to rest my hands on my thighs, but my fists remained clenched and unyielding.

A little defiance. I held on to it.

"Let me go." The words burst out of my mouth from behind gritted teeth.

My body shook in the brief second of freedom and I blinked, almost a wince. Every nerve in my body was at war. I wanted to fight, wanted to reach for his vulnerable throat. But I needed to obey him above all costs.

He was amazing and perfect and deserved all of my attention. He was Thayer. I focused on that. He was Thayer, I knew him. I knew his tricks. I forced myself to see through the fog.

This was just a Shadow standing in front of me. A boy trying to be king.

My eyes narrowed.

"Ooo," Thayer cooed. "You're fighting me."

He saw the true emotion in my eyes. So he changed and used that instead.

*Anger.* Slicing through every thought. I wanted to hurt

him. I wanted to rip his controlling eyes out of his head. The emotion crashed through my body, forcing every muscle to remain in place. My chests heaved as the madness coursed through me.

"Not a fair fight," I grumbled, the only words I can manage.

"Oh, I think it's a fair fight against a Five, don't you?" Thayer smiled at me as he rose to stand above me.

I remained on my knees, rage pinning me to the floor. I narrowed my eyes at him, unable to look away.

"In fact, I think it's about time you fell for my tricks instead of the other way around." Thayer picked up the dagger as he finished standing. "Is there anything you'd like to say before I end this?"

A brief moment of relief lifted the astounding anger inside. I only had time for one breath, one word.

"King," I spat. It wasn't what I wanted to say, at least not everything but it was all I had time for.

*Happiness.* It danced across my shoulders, flowing through the rest of my body. My fists unclenched, my breathing evened. The scowl on my face softened into a smile. I wanted him to win. He deserved it.

"That's right." Thayer smiled. "I'm the king now."

The dagger moved to the bare skin of my chest, just above the collar of my shirt. The blade sliced from my left shoulder, moving down, forming the first line of the X he needed.

Pain flickered across my face, the only true emotion I felt past the blinding joy. A sharp breath filled my chest, raising Thayer's target closer to the tip of the dagger.

"Stop," Lisa's voice cried, "Stop that! You're hurting her."

The hold dropped. Every influence of emotion scattered, leaving me totally aware and in control of my own body.

Fast footsteps approached and my heart froze, completely encased in icy fear. My real fear. Lisa had stepped inside.

Thayer smiled even wider as he turned to look at his new prey.

Fiona and Sage moved to stand in front of Kylan and the others. Their hands up, ready to stop anyone else that wanted to go through. It was too late for Lisa, though.

"Well, well, well," Thayer said.

He caught Lisa's arms, pinning them to her side as he spun around her to face me. Her back was pinned to his chest, his ear pressing into her hair.

"Looks like someone just couldn't stand idly by." Thayer smiled. "What's your name, gorgeous?"

"Thayer, don't." I shook my head, crouching in an effort to make myself look less threatening to him.

I had to do anything to get him to let her go. This was a game that Lisa wasn't ready for. A Shadow's game. Her wide eyes looked at me, exhausted and frightened. She already realized her mistake.

"Come on. You won't tell me?" Thayer whispered in her ear.

"Lisa," she answered, frozen in place.

"Lisa. I think I remember you," Thayer pulled his eyebrows together. "Didn't Alec say you had a human friend?"

The blood rushed in my ears as everything around me fell away. Thayer was not Alec, but he definitely had no sympathy for humans. He wouldn't hurt her, not really. But he might enjoy using her in a game.

Lisa's eyes stared back at me, her mouth trembling as she pulled in uneven breaths. Her hands shook at her sides, and I knew I had to stop Thayer from exploiting her for sport.

"Don't tell me you actually brought a human into the mansion," Thayer tsked. "You know even I can't resist that."

Lisa shook her head, her arms struggling to pull away from him. He let her go enough for her to turn around and face him. His hands clasped her wrists, easily holding her in place.

"Let me go," she begged. "I'm not human anymore!"

The smile dropped from his face. He looked at her hands, probably trying to pull her energy. Those curious eyes fell on me again.

"Alec turned her into a Legend," I confirmed.

Thayer turned and looked back at her. She stopped fighting as hard when she caught a glimpse of his softened gaze. He released her wrist, but she didn't run.

"You were the one they carried out of the lab?" Thayer asked.

Lisa nodded and gulped down the last bit of her remaining fear. Her hands rested peacefully at her sides.

"You said you wanted to play me. So come and play," I said, stepping toward her.

I reached my hand around and grabbed her clothed arm, pulling her away from Thayer and toward me. She stumbled back into my grasp, still watching him.

Thayer stared at her with a solemn look weighing on his brows.

"You've been through enough, sweetheart." Thayer bowed his head to her. "I'm not gonna add to that."

Lisa nodded back to him, still watching him carefully. I nudged her toward the rest of the group and she reluctantly turned away. Kylan held out his arm for her and she ran into him, throwing her arms around his waist.

At least she trusted him a little more now. I smiled.

Before Thayer looked back for me, I vanished into the crowd. He turned and his eyes immediately darted around, searching for me.

I was already weaving in and out through the people. As I walked behind someone new, I morphed my hair, skin, and face to look like theirs. I blended in easily as I kept my gaze on Thayer's feet.

He lunged for a few people whose eyes might have passed for mine. As he got closer to each one, he knew it wasn't me.

"Come on out, Mara. Let me see those pretty blue eyes," Thayer called across the room. "The game's no fun if I don't know where you are."

I stood next to a Shadow in the crowd. My hair turned black and pulled into tight, wiry curls around my face. My skin darkened as my face rounded out.

A copy of the girl standing next to me, only with blue eyes instead of her dark brown ones.

I stared straight ahead at Thayer.

"I beg to differ." I shrugged, and Thayer whipped around at the sound of my voice. "I'm having fun."

Thayer glanced between me and the girl who I now looked like. He settled his eyes back on me a little too late. I had already ducked behind the next person, moving away from where he was now running toward.

I crept around people as the Shadows twisted every way, frantically trying to find me. A moving crowd was the easiest to sneak through.

I walked up to Kylan and the rest of them, watching their eyes search the room. Kylan's eyes moved, landing on me. Or what used to look like me. I had flaming red hair, freckles covering nearly every part of my pale skin. But the eyes were mine.

I smiled at him and his mouth fell open. He glanced around to see Thayer, searching the opposite side of the room by forcing everyone to look at him in turn so he could study their eyes before throwing them out of the way and moving on.

When he looked back at me, I winked. He smiled wide, sending a shiver down my spine.

"Watch this," I said and faced the center of the room.

Thayer heard my voice and spun around. I created a dagger in each hand, feeling the energy fading. I didn't have much left, which meant this game needed to end soon.

I tossed the daggers right toward Thayer, one at a time. He dodged the first and caught the second in the air. That gave me enough time to race forward with a fresh dagger in my own hand. I slashed the first mark across his back, a long line spanning the distance between his shoulder blade and the top of his jeans.

Thayer grunted in pain and stumbled forward, dagger in hand. He spun around to cut me, but I wasn't standing there anymore. I had ducked around him and faced his back again.

I heaved the dagger the opposite way and cut the second mark on his back, tearing his shirt away from his skin.

The only thing that remained on his bare back was a bloody X spanning across his many muscles.

The game was over.

A roaring in response, everyone jumped and cheered as their king had finally met his match. Blood trickled down his olive skin as the energy swirled around to heal the cut. He turned to face me with a dark smile.

I still had a few moments of being a Shadow left. I walked toward him and grabbed a fistful of his shirt. I stood on my toes to reach his ear.

"The first part of being a king," I hissed, "is learning to bow down to the queen."

I stood and focused on the cheers that surrounded me.

Shadows clapped and stared at me in wonder. I glanced back at Thayer who donned a humble smile.

He bowed low at the waist, gracefully raising his arms to either side. Dramatic and a bit too much, that was Thayer. He stood again, smiling at himself.

"Welcome back, Mara." He nodded.

I couldn't contain my own smile when I looked around at all the Shadows, at Thayer. Everything about this perfectly fit.

Through all the happy and excited faces, there was only one that I wanted to see. I looked up at Kylan and saw his expression had changed.

He clapped his hands, smiling at me. I was happy being this way, playing this game. He understood that.

"Well done," Kylan mouthed.

My heart filled my entire chest and pushed a lump in my throat. I reached out to shake Thayer's hand, keeping my eyes on Kylan.

"I love you," I mouthed back.

He put a hand to his mouth and then laid it in front of his face to blow his kiss toward me. My heart pounded in my chest. This was a life I could get used to.

Part Shadow, part Rogue, and always, always a Legend.

# CHAPTER
# ELEVEN

We had left the courtyard and met in a room too grand for what we talked about. The decadent velvet drapes and golden candlesticks that were taller than I was crowded the room.

I didn't need all of the lavish trinkets anymore. I just needed the people that came in the room with me.

Cassie and Derek stood in the corner, keeping a wary distance of Thayer and Sage. I didn't blame them. Kylan was behind me with a hand pressed to his mouth, thinking. We had too many things to fix and all of them needed attention.

I couldn't touch Kylan, Lisa was scared to take energy, and Cassie was about to lose her mind if we forced her to stay in this mansion any longer than necessary.

Lisa was curled on an oversized chair, a plush blanket thrown over her legs by Thayer as soon as she sat down. She now clutched the fabric up to her chin as she watched us.

I had explained my idea, and no one had said anything for a full minute. I finally spun to face Thayer, knowing he was the most likely one to voice an opposing opinion.

"So, what I'm hearing is you've *actually* lost your mind," Thayer mused.

"I haven't lost my mind. I'm coming up with a way to fix everything." I narrowed my eyes at him.

Thayer pursed his lips and raised his eyebrows to show everyone else that he still thought I was insane. Kylan stifled a laugh.

"By walking back into the lab?" Derek scoffed. "You just got out."

"But it would be different. We'd be on the same level as Alec. He has something I want, and I have something he wants." I gestured with my hands, but judging by the crossed arms and skeptical looks, nobody was buying it.

"No offense," Cassie started, "but I don't think that's gonna work."

"The redheaded one is right," Thayer said.

"Cassie," Derek cut in.

Thayer ignored him. "We don't need Alec necessarily. We just need that stupid tablet he carries around with him. We could send one person in undercover to find it?"

"Yeah, good luck with that." Sage put her hands on her hips. "Alec never lets that out of his sight."

"What if he started to trust the person? Maybe that might be enough to get him to hand it off?" Thayer asked.

"Maybe." Sage sucked on her teeth. "There was one time that he left it with Nikki. For a few seconds. They'd have to get close to both of them in order to get it."

"There we go." Thayer raised his hands. "We have a new plan."

"Okay, I can watch the lab and make myself look like one of them. I think in a couple days, I might be able to—" I offered before Kylan put a hand in front of me.

"No," Kylan interrupted.

"No?" I challenged. "What do you mean, no?"

"I mean, I've been pretty understanding of your plans in the past, but I am not letting you walk back in there by yourself. Sorry, that's not an option." Kylan shook his head.

I narrowed my eyes at him, about to open my mouth and rant about how he always had let me make my own decisions, but Thayer stepped in front of me.

"Cool your jets, Mara." Thayer raised an eyebrow at me. "Your lovely boyfriend's got a point. Alec would recognize your eyes in a heartbeat. There's no way you'd pass for anyone else."

"You can't wear colored contacts?" Lisa asked, her voice almost too quiet to hear.

I pointed at her, raising my eyebrows. That was an idea we could use. Plus, I still wanted to insist that I was right, and even though I knew it wasn't a great option, it was an option.

"Wearing contacts for twenty-four hours a day for who knows how many days is not only uncomfortable, it's impractical for a Legend." Thayer shook his head and pointed to Sage. "Just ask the expert."

"Contacts are awful. Your eyes will be in pain the entire time and if the tears don't move them, your eyes will eventually blink them out," Sage explained and before I could open my mouth, she continued. "And unless you're planning on keeping enough energy in you to fool *everyone* in the room at all times—which would be a struggle for even me—your eyes are staying as is. And Alec would be able to pick out your charming voice too."

I took a step toward her. She just smiled and waited. Kylan touched my arm and reminded me that we weren't the only two people in the room. I rested on my heels again.

"Good point. Have I told you how smart you are?"

Thayer smiled down at her in a way that made everyone else in the room uncomfortable.

Sage rolled her eyes at him and focused back on me instead.

"Fine." I crossed my arms. "It can't be me then. But I'm not going to ask any of you to go in my place."

"That's sweet." Thayer teased. "I can't speak for everyone else, but I personally would love to have a front row seat to see Alec eat it."

Everyone nodded except Lisa. She looked at me with confused eyes and I reminded myself that I would need to explain more in-depth as to why I hated Alec. That conversation was going to take at least a few hours.

"So, it has to be someone that Alec hasn't seen that much, or talked to." Thayer looked around the room, his eyes settling on Derek and Cassie.

Cassie shook her head, her eyes already lighting up in a fiery rage. "There's no way I could stand in the same room with Alec."

Derek shook his head too. "I can't change. Also, I don't think a Two is the best option to go up against Alec, and I will not leave Cassie."

I pulled my eyebrows together and looked at Kylan. He had the same expression. Derek was so in love with Cassie that sometimes it bordered on codependence, but that wouldn't be enough of a reason for him to back down from a fight. Honestly, I expected him to volunteer.

"Plus," Derek added quickly, avoiding Kylan's eyes, "Labs kinda freak me out and the less time I can spend in one, the better."

I opened my mouth to ask another question, but stopped. I wouldn't force Derek to go if he didn't want to.

"Well, then, we are back to where we started." I shrugged.

"I'll go," Kylan said, and my heart dropped.

Thayer raised his eyebrows as he considered the option. Sage immediately nodded as she looked him up and down. The breath in my chest stopped as I thought of sending Kylan in. I immediately started shaking my head, unable to form words.

"Not bad," Thayer said.

"No. Bad," I corrected. "Very very bad idea."

"Oh hush. You're only upset because you know he's right." Thayer dismissed me with his hand. "They've talked a total of, what, about three times in centuries? Alec might think he's familiar, but probably won't be able to place him."

"True," Sage agreed. "Someone at that lab has to have green eyes too. If Kylan keeps his mouth shut and picks a wallflower-type person to imitate, that might work."

"How would we know he's safe?" Derek asked.

"Send someone with him to stay on the outside," Sage shrugged and continued, "I'll do it. I wouldn't mind a trip out anyway." Thayer winked at her.

"No." I shook my head again.

"Mara, this is the best idea that anyone's come up with. You got something better?" Thayer challenged.

"I...I..." I wanted to say anything. Any words that would let Kylan stay here, safe with everyone else.

Nothing came to mind. I knew they were right. My fists clenched so hard that my hands shook at my sides. I looked at Kylan, but all I could see was Alec. How much Alec would love to get his hands on him.

"Could you guys give us a minute?" Kylan asked.

"Ah, yes," Thayer sighed. "When it comes to persuasion, nothing works like good, old-fashioned *alone time*."

"He can't touch her, idiot," Derek smacked Thayer's shoulder. "Way to rub it in."

Thayer wrinkled his nose and turned back to Kylan. "Sorry. Good luck with that."

"Get outta here," Derek said.

He shoved Thayer toward the door. Thayer smiled as he staggered forward, dragging Sage with him. Cassie took Lisa by the arm and gently led her out the door.

A stinging pain filled the void in the room.

His soft touch reached forward and rested on my clothed shoulder. The body heat spread through the cloth and into my skin. I turned my head away, trying not to look at him.

"Hey," his quiet voice called. "Come on. Please look at me."

"I can't." I shook my head.

"I'm trying to fix this," he begged.

"I'm not asking you to fix it. I can do this. I just have to get in there for a moment. I heard a lab assistant say something about Antidote 17B. I was too far gone to really care at that point, but I think it may be the solution. I just have to find it." I spun and finally looked up at him. "I can fix this on my own."

"I know you can, but this is the best option that we have at the moment." Kylan peered down at me with those big green eyes.

"Let Sage go," I suggested. "She could create a better illusion and maybe even—"

"Alec would recognize her. She's been at his side for how long now, a year? That's not a real option," Kylan whispered.

"A different Shadow then, one of Thayer's new recruits," I sputtered, desperate for any other option.

"They won't have the skill or the loyalty to not be swayed. If they got caught, he'd only gain another person on his side. You and I both know Alec is too persuasive," he whispered again.

"What about—"

"Kate," he stopped me.

"Just give me more time." I was the one begging now.

"I want to. I wish I was fine with waiting forever, but I'm not." Kylan winced.

His hands reached up to my shoulders, tracing the line of clothing on the collar of my shirt. His body burned a trail of fire against my skin. My heart raced to keep up with the fast breaths I now needed.

"I want to touch you," Kylan whispered. "Without any barriers."

His hands moved to my hair, pulling it back and off of my shoulders. They moved back to my shoulders and down my arms. My entire body ignited. One waft of air and I might have blown away.

"I want all of you. And every second I spend knowing that I can't be with you is pure torture," Kylan groaned as his hands latched onto my waist.

He pulled me forward, as close as he could before my face touched his. Our bodies pressed together. I didn't want to blink, I didn't want to miss a moment of his hungry eyes or his tensed muscles.

"Seeing you today, in the game," Kylan whispered in a low voice. "You were so strong and completely in your element. It felt like I was meeting Mara for the first time. And she was incredible."

"Really?" I choked on the word.

Kylan had fallen for Kate, the persona I created to blend in and make people care about me. It worked, and he fell hard. But ever since he had seen the other part of my life, he hadn't left and I couldn't see why.

"Really." Kylan smiled, letting out a breath. "The more of you I see, the more I love."

I wanted to jump into his arms. Desire scorched through

my veins. A lump formed in my throat from all the bottled-up emotions.

"Is this killing you as much as it's killing me?" Kylan asked in a desperate, soft voice that crushed my heart in one breath.

I couldn't speak. I only nodded.

The motion made my forehead touch his for a moment. His hot skin flashed against mine and his energy flooded through the brief connection. The throbbing power bursting through me was like warm liquid against my bones. I shuddered, relishing in the pure joy.

Kylan groaned and my eyes snapped open. His eyes cringed in pain as his lips pulled back over his teeth.

"I'm sorry," I rushed, reaching my hands forward to make it better, but halting before touching him again.

"Don't." Kylan shook his head. "Don't do that. It's my fault for not keeping more energy in my body."

"I'm sorry anyway," I cringed, pulling away from him.

Kylan dropped his arms by his sides. He looked at me with all the desire welling up in his eyes, but a scowl remained on his brow. The space between us could have filled the depths of the oceans.

"Please don't feel like you have to do this, spy on Alec, for me," I whispered.

"I'm not," Kylan answered quickly. "As much as I love you, I'm not doing it for you. I'm doing it for me."

"Then keep your head down, remember 17B, and good luck," I said, hating the words as they tumbled out of my mouth. "And I'll see you soon."

"See you soon." Kylan gave a half smile.

# CHAPTER
# TWELVE

*Kylan*

The trip was long and exhausting. Sage ran faster through every terrain, slowing down only to accommodate me.

I caught myself watching her white skin too long when I got tired. Her energy must be incredible, different than anyone else's. One of the most talented creators I had met.

I shook my head, focusing on Kate. But that bled into thinking about her energy. Wild, fierce, and in love with me. It would feel like magic in my veins.

I stumbled, and Sage finally stopped with me.

I couldn't handle Kate's energy. Not without wanting more, wanting too much. I wasn't ready for that kind of temptation yet. Any Legend energy would be too much.

Sage dragged me into the nearest town and flung me away from her. I stalked through the town, slowly and deliberately. The streets were too narrow, the buildings were uncomfortably close together. I'd hate to live here, but it made it easier to walk next to people. Every flicker of energy helped take the edge off the pain.

But I had a huge task ahead of me. Changing my entire

appearance would be a struggle. I had only tweaked my looks when I needed to.

At the rate I was siphoning energy, I would hardly have enough to make the change yet.

"Ugh, hurry up," Sage whined. "We've been in town for two hours and you still don't have enough energy to make the change?"

"Sorry. Not all of us are okay with murder." I gritted my teeth.

Originally, I thought it would be a good idea for Sage to come along. But, wow, her personality had been nothing but shrill and annoying the entire trip. We didn't stop enough, we stopped too much. She wanted to leave bodies and I wanted to leave people still awake. Nothing pleased her.

"I'm not talking about murder." Sage raised her shoulders. "Just knock a few people out and move on."

I spun around, the anger teeming inside of me. I knew exactly how much more energy I would need. I knew how long it would take. She just thought this was only painful waiting for her.

"Listen." I raised a finger at her. "If I'm the one that has to go inside, then I'm going to do this my way. No one wants this to work more than me and I am trying. So shut up for two seconds and let me concentrate."

Sage closed her mouth, her red eyes widening at me. I let out the air in my chest and turned back to the street.

"Sorry." I shook my head to not think about her energy again. "I just need another minute."

I searched for the next group of people through the street covered in wooden awnings that almost touched each other from across the street. It was a tourist street. I could siphon energy from the people weaving through the tables put too close together and the store merchandise on display.

"You could just take my energy." She offered so quietly I almost missed it.

"What?" I asked, knowing what she meant but hoping she would deny what I had imagined.

That white skin, her flowing energy. I wonder if it would taste delicate, or red, or—no. I forced myself to keep moving. She stepped faster and walked beside me, looking at the freshly oiled asphalt.

The strong smell mixed with the wafting bakery scent and a shop that must have been selling perfume because too many humans passing me smelled similar.

"You won't have to feel guilty about hurting any humans, because I'm the one that did it." Sage shrugged and raised a hand out to me. "Just take mine and we can get you back to Mara or Kate or whatever you're calling her now."

I stared at her hand. My fingertips went numb, sending a tingling sensation up my arms. My mouth started watering at the thought. It wasn't human energy she was offering.

Human energy was warm, comforting, and filled the hunger inside. But Legend energy was intoxicating, exciting, and anytime I thought about it, I shivered with anticipation. When I looked at that pale hand, that same shuddering feeling overtook me.

"It's not that simple," I said.

I couldn't describe how this would change me. How easy it would be to take hers, to take more Legend energy in the lab. To become so used to it, so high by the time I got back to Kate, to my family.

I'd hurt them. I gulped, trying to remember the scents, the awnings, the people, anything to pull me away.

Her fingers wiggled, drawing my attention back to her again. All I could do was stare at her pale skin.

"What do you say?" Sage asked, moving her hand toward my arm.

I wanted it. I needed her energy in my body. It would be plenty of power to make a change. But that was the rationalization that covered up the real reason I stopped walking.

"I can't." I shook my head.

"Come on," Sage crooned. "I won't tell."

I glanced at a group of human girls taking pictures and laughing as they walked through the street. I hated siphoning groups, they set me on edge. But this time, they looked like my only source of salvation.

"No." I stepped around her, heading straight for them. "Just wait here and I'll be ready in a minute."

It took longer than a minute.

I walked by every person I could see. I touched shoulders, arms, hands. Thank goodness it was spring in the south and everyone wore far less clothing than in Portland. I found Sage trying on sunglasses and scaring little kids with her red eyes.

I walked up to her, hands shoved firmly in my pockets. The energy thrummed in my body. It wouldn't be much, especially after I used it at the lab, but it was enough. She flicked her red eyes up to me when I got closer.

"Finally," she sighed and slipped the pair of glasses back on the plastic rack.

"Thank you for being patient." I tried to hide the sound of irritation in my voice.

Apparently, that didn't work based on the look that Sage gave me. Both of us ignored the most recent kid running crying to his mom.

"I'm at your service," she mocked and bowed her head.

"Let's just get going." I rolled my eyes and didn't wait for her to follow me before I started walking.

"Lighten up, prick." Sage came up behind me and smacked my arm. "I'm just trying to have a little fun."

"This isn't fun," I snapped. "We are about to infiltrate a lab run by my brother, and all our hope hinges on him not being able to recognize me enough to catch on before I can get my hands on his information. No part of that is fun."

"All right, all right, I get it. No energy, no jokes, no more fun." She nodded her head firmly.

A few seconds burned away before she turned to look at me with a knowing smile. I should've let it go, but with all the energy racing in my body, I couldn't stop the words.

"What now?" I asked.

"I see it." Sage pursed her lips.

"See what?" I prodded.

Sage looked at me, her creepy eyes moved up and down my body. She turned back to face the road in front of her as her smile widened.

"Why Mara is so enamored with you." She shrugged. "You're good. Like ridiculously, virtuous and sympathetic and just…good."

"Thank you," I added awkwardly.

"I didn't say it was a compliment. But Mara appreciates it and that's all that matters," Sage sighed.

I smiled. Being good had been a part of me for so long, and nothing had challenged it until Kate walked into my life.

I thought about her on the way back to the lab. I wondered how my life would look without her in it. I didn't even want to picture it. I needed her. She was the fun spark that made my life not so righteous and bland.

We arrived back at the lab and sat in silence for the next few hours. The one blessed time that Sage didn't chatter on and on.

The person we needed had to be quiet, someone that blended in. He also needed to be about my height and same build, and hopefully similar eyes. That narrowed the list quite a bit.

"This one. Isaac," I whispered, barely audible at all.

Sage followed my finger to the man we had been watching. His name was Isaac. The other Shadows avoided him, and he only spoke to the lab assistants in grunts or short sentences.

From here, his eyes at least looked green. The shade might be off, but it didn't matter as much with him. He had thick glasses that were just for show and dark, straight hair that hung down enough to cover most of his eyes.

Sage shook her head. "Too flashy."

I turned around, so my voice pointed the other direction. "What are you talking about?"

She turned around and sat closer to me, lowering her voice even further.

"The glasses—no Legend actually needs glasses. He's one of those timid types that wants to be noticed," Sage explained.

"He's our best option." I raised an eyebrow at her.

"No, what about that one kid, Julian?" Sage offered.

"You're joking right? He has black skin and eyes way darker than mine. If I change into him, my green eyes will stand out. I'll be spotted immediately," I hissed at her.

"I'm telling you, we need to find someone else." Sage glared with her sparkling red eyes. "I know people. I spent centuries altering their minds to show them what they really wanted, anything that would draw them to me so I could kill them. This is not our guy."

"How old are you?" I asked, temporarily distracted.

She grinned. "Didn't anyone ever tell you not to ask a lady her age?"

I shrugged. "Let me know if you see one."

Her eyebrows shot up. She lunged forward and stopped her hand just before it reached my throat.

She may as well have been touching me because I felt my throat crushing. I couldn't pull in air. My hands shot up, trying to stop my neck from snapping in two.

"I'm quite a few centuries older than a brand new Extractor who has a hard time wanting to keep his hands to himself," she whispered.

She dropped whatever hold she had. The pain was gone too fast, but I touched my throat and it didn't hurt. None of that was real.

I looked up at her, finally impressed. She rolled her eyes and looked back down at the lab. "We need to wait."

"I don't want to wait any longer. Every second we spend here is another second we could get caught. And there is a girl waiting back at the mansion that I am *dying* to get my arms around," I explained. "I have to do this now."

"If you mess this up, Alec will catch you and do who knows what with you. There's nothing I can do to stop him from out here." Sage narrowed her eyes. "Let's wait."

"I appreciate your concern," I nodded. "But I'm going with Isaac."

Sage sighed, looking around for any other option she could rush to present. "It does me no good to waste more energy fighting you."

"No, it doesn't," I agreed.

"This is a mistake."

"Then it will be my mistake," I whispered.

Her shoulders fell as she looked down at Isaac lingering near the entrance. She flicked her eyes back up to me.

"Let's grab him," she mouthed, her voice almost too low for me to hear.

# CHAPTER
# THIRTEEN

The alcove just off the main courtyard had become Lisa's favorite place. She could watch everyone from the shade and stay out of sight.

But Thayer eventually found her and asked every prying question he could think of. I got the task of explaining how she would need to take energy from people and Thayer volunteered to help her break through to her Levels of power.

The two of them huddled on the stone floor, tucked behind the ornate columns that spun into a glistening carving of flowers above.

"Just concentrate," Thayer whispered. "Focus all your attention on the paper."

We had been at this for hours. Neither of us had been terribly successful at helping her adjust.

Her brown eyes narrowed at the paper sitting on top of her hands. She held her breath and stared. Nothing happened.

"I don't understand what's supposed to be happening here," Lisa sighed as she continued to stare.

"You're trying to destroy the cells of the page. Think of

them as individuals. You want to rip apart the very DNA, turn it black, disintegrate it," Thayer coached, not giving up.

Even I was holding my breath, hoping for something. She had been trying for four days and nothing had happened yet. The grocery store human's energy was wearing off too quickly. I was surprised she was still awake.

"That doesn't make any sense. I can't focus on *the cells of the page*. That's not possible." Lisa let the paper fall to the ground and her shoulders slumped.

I closed my eyes and let the breath of air out. We weren't going to be making any more progress today. A short while ago, she was a human and none of what we were asking her to do would've been possible.

"Hey, it's okay," Thayer comforted her.

"It's not okay. Stop saying this is okay," Lisa groaned.

Her eyes glanced over to me, and then down at my arm. I knew what she was thinking without having to read her mind. She would never say it out loud, but a part of her blamed me for all of this.

I didn't fault her for that. She was right.

Alec had only come for her because she was special to me. He needed one more thing to drive me into utter insanity. It had worked, until Kylan came.

Thayer put his hand on her shoulder as she rested her head in her hands. She was frustrated, exhausted. We hadn't taken her out to get any new energy yet. But at least she had stopped refusing to go, even if I stopped asking.

I thought maybe if she understood what energy felt like moving in her body, she could recognize it in someone else.

In truth, I had no idea how best to help her.

Thayer stood and Lisa sat on the floor, reaching out for the paper again. She focused her eyes, straining the veins in her neck from concentrating so hard. Thayer walked over to me, turning his back to her.

"Can I talk to you for a moment?" Thayer said and nodded his head toward a winding hallway that would eventually lead down to the dungeons.

I followed him out but took one more glance at Lisa sitting on the floor, pulling at her tight brown curls. My heart twisted in my chest.

I turned the final corner and stepped through a familiar doorway. This particular room had been soundproofed to human standards. It was the one place in the mansion where it would be difficult for anyone outside to hear what was going on behind the thick, iron door.

Needless to say, it was one of Thayer's favorite rooms in the mansion. Second only to his extravagant bedroom. When I stepped through, I pulled the iron door shut behind me.

"This isn't working," Thayer whispered to me.

"It's only been a few days," I said.

"What Legend have you known that hasn't found at least their talent in the first few hours of trying?" Thayer asked. "You said she already figured out reading, so the rest shouldn't be too far behind."

I wasn't even a decade old when I discovered my first power. No one had to coach me on what to do. I was able to change cells without even really thinking about it. The older I got, the more powerful I became.

"Maybe she's just a One." I winced. "Please, tell me she didn't go through all of this to just be a One."

Thayer shrugged. "That's not so bad, I mean, Sage is a One."

"And we all know how much you like Sage." I smiled and squinted at him.

"What's not to like? She's pretty and fascinating and kinda scares me a bit sometimes." Thayer's smiled widened.

"So you and her are together?" I asked, honestly hoping I could see Thayer happy and end up with someone.

"Eh." Thayer shrugged and leaned against the gold-framed painting behind him. "She and I are together as much as you and I used to be together."

"Are you sure?" I teased.

"Come on, Mara." Thayer let his head fall back. "You know I'm not the settle-down type. But for now, Sage is quite nice."

I shook my head at him. "I think you just need to meet someone to change your mind."

"I dare you to find someone who can." Thayer grinned.

"Hey guys," Lisa's voice interrupted.

The door flew open and iron crashed against the old stone walls, sending a crack to the floor.

"Oh, sorry." Lisa grimaced as she looked at her own hand. "Still getting used to the whole strength thing."

We both chuckled at her innocent discovery. Thayer turned to face her, shifting to lean closer to where she stood. He dropped his head and looked up at her in the most seductive way possible.

"What can I do for you?" Thayer asked in a voice that sent chills down my arms.

Lisa's face instantly flushed, staining her cheeks a red color. Her eyes darted from Thayer to me. I hid my smile as she blinked furiously to try and remember what she was talking about.

"Um, I think I did something. Come look." Lisa waved us through the doorway.

Thayer and I glanced at each other before following. He was skeptical that she had made any progress. I was hoping with everything in me that she had.

Lisa flew from the doorway, back down the hall she came from. Thayer started after her and I tapped his arm before he walked too far ahead of me.

"Tread carefully," I said to Thayer and pointed to Lisa.

"What? You don't think she actually did something?" Thayer asked, hiding his smile.

"You know what I'm talking about." I raised an eyebrow at him. "She is not Sage. That woman means the world to me, and your shameless flirting and meaningless relationships are only going to hurt her."

"Yes, ma'am." Thayer winked at me. "I will be on my *best* behavior."

My muscles tightened at the way he said the words. I shot my hand forward and grabbed his bare arm. I purposely pulled his energy as fast as I could.

His hand clenched and he dropped his shoulder to stop the pressure from my hand.

"Okay, okay," Thayer conceded.

"I mean it. If you break her heart I will take you down." I glared into his bright eyes.

"I give you my word, I will not intentionally hurt her," Thayer answered in the most serious tone I had heard from him in a while.

He followed me down the hallway to where Lisa paced back and forth. As soon as she saw us, she sat on the floor with the paper lying in front of her. She stared at it with a big smile.

"Just watch," she instructed.

I stared down at the paper. Nothing about it had changed. It was a regular, white piece of paper. I pulled my eyebrows together and looked at Lisa. She stared intently at the paper, holding out her hands as if that would help direct her mental energy at all.

It moved. The corner of the paper lifted slightly from the carpet and then rested back down again.

"There! Did you see that?" Lisa asked, sitting straight up and pointing. "I moved it!"

I raised my eyebrows in surprise. Maybe she found the creating Level. I looked over at Thayer, who still looked down skeptically. I knelt on the floor in front of Lisa, turning my attention back to her.

"That's awesome," I congratulated her.

As soon as I lowered myself, I felt it, the small waft of air coming from the hallway. I turned my head and realized the pack of readers behind us were playing a game and had sent enough of a breeze to lift it.

"That wasn't you that moved the paper," Thayer said in a soft, flat voice.

Lisa followed my gaze and must have felt the breeze. Her face twisted in disappointment and her shoulders fell.

"Well, how was I supposed to know? I have no idea what I'm doing." Lisa grabbed the paper and threw it.

The paper floated easily in the air, mocking her effort. She growled and crumpled the paper in her fist. The tips of her fingers went white as she dug them into her skin.

This was totally unlike Lisa. I recognized why. The drained look in her eyes.

"You're hungry," I admitted and sat back on my heels.

"Finally," Thayer huffed. "I've been waiting to go out."

"I don't know if she's ready for that yet," I edged, hoping Thayer would back me.

His brown eyes widened and my stomach turned over.

"You're going let her just starve? She needs energy. Plus, I could go for a teenager or two right now anyway. Maybe even a mom," he said and every word made Lisa tense up more and more.

Her eyes widened as she thought about what she was feeling, and the crude way Thayer had talked about the race she used to be a part of. She looked down at her body, at her hands.

She looked back up at me. Her eyes flipped back and forth between mine as she waited for the rest.

"She can make it a little longer." I knelt forward resting a hand on her knee.

"Why?" Lisa asked.

Her soft eyes used to be so innocent. Now they had an edge to them. She was curious and I didn't blame her. Her body knew what she needed even if she didn't.

"Are you ready? I mean, you know what happened last time," I said.

"Scare tactic. Smooth," Thayer sighed, clenching his jaw. "There's no need to sugarcoat it. The energy is incredible and it's so much fun. Once you get over the fact that people might di—"

"Thank you, Thayer," I interrupted.

"What if I hurt someone?" Lisa looked at the stone floor, the weight of her reality resting on her back. "Like I did to Chase."

"You're just new, that's all." I softened my voice. "We've never known a human to change to a Legend."

"Only one way to find out," Thayer edged.

I watched Lisa. She pulled at her the corner of her sleeve near her elbow. Her eyes darted around the room. She shifted in her position on the floor. She was distressed, hungry, and suffering right in front of me.

"What do you think?" I asked Lisa.

Her eyes snapped over to me. She glanced between me and Thayer. When her gaze landed on me again, pain pulled at the corners of her stressed brown eyes.

"I don't know." Lisa watched my face. I didn't move. "I know I don't want to feel like this."

She hung her head as if she had already done something wrong. I rubbed my thumb against her clothed knee. She needed to know someone cared about her, supported her. This would be the hardest decision of her new life.

"I want to try," she said.

"That's my kinda girl." Thayer smiled.

He squatted in front of Lisa, lowering his head to her level. She looked up at him with full, innocent eyes. He smiled at her with a genuine kindness that I had missed from Thayer.

I watched the two of them carefully.

"Trust me, this is gonna be fun," he said in a seductive voice.

I could've smacked him but I looked back to her, thinking I would see shock or fear. Instead, she just smiled back at him.

Not in a dazed, Thayer-fascination way, but with anticipation for what lay ahead.

# CHAPTER
# FOURTEEN

*Kylan*

The outside camera was easy to disable. I knocked it off with one fist-sized rock flying at the right angle.

The lab was designed to test and further research Legends. It was now under Alec's rule and followed his pursuit to find a way to create a Level Five. That means they could've had better outside security, but no one would be stupid enough to attack a lab full of Legends, especially ones led by Alec Stone.

The guard looked up at the sound, giving us the time we needed to rush him.

Sage was an excellent diversion. Her eyes instantly threw anyone off that looked at her. Isaac was no different.

She tapped him on the shoulder while I waited just out of sight.

"Hey there." She smiled as Isaac turned.

He froze when he saw her eyes. He took a staggering step away from her while Sage grinned at him with a malice I had experienced earlier.

"You....your eyes..." he stammered.

Sage stepped closer, keeping her arms crossed behind her back. I moved fast, taking advantage of his lack of attention. My hand shot out and grabbed the back of his neck.

I yanked him around and locked eyes with him long enough to get inside his mind. I sliced through his scared consciousness, tasting the fear for myself. I looked around for anything that would prove useful, any clues about his personality or past.

Disjointed memories flashed in and out of my view.

*He wanted to be a Shadow, but Alec didn't agree to give him the mark before Nikki lost her powers.*

Good, but not terribly important.

I searched on. Isaac remained frozen in my grip. He had wide eyes and a vacant expression. Sage kept her focus on him, creating the distraction that occupied his mind.

*Nikki's hair. Nikki's eyes. Nikki's tattoos on her bare shoulders. The way the tattoos extended under her clothes—*

I shook my head, trying to focus on anything besides Nikki. I glanced up at Sage, her red eyes trained on me.

"What's wrong?" she asked, already tightening her grip on Isaac's coat.

"Nothing," I lied.

An obsession with Nikki would be hard to fake. I couldn't see how far anything had gone, and right now it looked like a harmless crush.

"I was right, wasn't I?" Sage hissed. "This isn't our guy."

"Too late. We already picked him," I said, trying to focus back on the connection I had established.

"Kylan." Sage grabbed my arm with her tiny, deadly hand.

"You only get to choose this once. I can't save you once you walk in there."

I pulled my arm away from her. "I don't need saving."

I closed my eyes and felt for the connection again. When I found it, I dove into his mind and out of the reality around me. Sage was no longer standing next to me, it was just my consciousness viewing Isaac's mind.

*His room number was 028 and he always left it unlocked. The only things he was worried about people taking were the many, many pairs of glasses he kept in pristine order.*

*He wasn't actually a guard, just filling in for someone else on an energy run. He was a mediocre assistant but one that worked with Alec more than Nikki. Much to his dismay.*

Even more perfect. The closer I could be to Alec, the better. I dropped him from my grip and he landed on his shoulder.

He scooted back, right into Sage's legs. She looked down at him, upside down, and he started to choke.

His breath halted, his hands flew to his throat. His gaze darted from me to her with eyes that looked like they were ready to pop out of his head.

Sage glared down at him. She was creating this. I knew that feeling. I shuddered.

Everything he thought was happening wasn't real, but his body thought it was. Isaac writhed on the ground until his eyes closed and his hands finally dropped.

I studied his body, his face. I focused on my own cells, feeling them pull and morph with the Change. My hands lightened to match his skin tone. My hair grew, hanging in front of my eyes. I matched the features on his face as best I could.

I lifted my face to Sage. She studied it and nodded.

She reached down and pulled Isaac's glasses from his face. I put them on, hating the awkward way they sat on my nose.

"You good?" I asked, trying to change my voice to match Isaac's husky tone.

She nodded again, waving a hand toward Isaac. Air whooshed underneath him, sending his body floating in the air next to her.

His unconscious body lifted easily. Sage moved her fingers and he moved through the air toward the trees.

My stomach knotted when Sage looked at him like he was something to play with or eat. I nervously looked at her, already feeling sorry for the fate I had sealed for Isaac.

"What are you going to do with him?" I asked.

Her red eyes locked on mine. I thought she'd smile or laugh, the way I imagined most Shadows would. She just stared at me, blinking.

"None of your concern." Her low voice made me shiver.

I couldn't help the assistant now. Sage may leave him alive. But the dagger on her arm would suggest otherwise.

I turned to face the lab door. My new appearance reflected in the glass windows behind the iron bars and I no longer looked like myself.

I smiled.

# CHAPTER
# FIFTEEN

I pointed at Thayer walking in the middle of the crowd a short distance in front of us. Lisa and I sat on a half-wall that was set far enough away from prying ears, but allowed us to see everything.

The outdoor mall was filled with people. They carried bags and took pictures of each other. It was an easy place to find distracted humans.

I knew it set Lisa on edge, and I hoped the fake, decorative stream gurgling behind us would help.

"Okay, I'm sorry, what am I supposed to do again?" Lisa looked at her hands nervously.

The storefronts were all aged and designed to look like a European city. Halls and people stretched in either direction. Fake ivy even grew up some of the bricks. The greasy food court smells reminded us that we were far from any foreign country.

It was a Saturday and there must have been a big sale or event going on to attract this many people.

"Watch him." I focused on Thayer. "He's walking by like nothing's going on. Until…"

He stood out from the crowd with his darker olive skin and his gorgeous face. I waited for Thayer to make a move. His eye caught on a pretty human girl and his bright smile sparkled in the daylight. He walked past her and brushed his hand against her arm.

"Right there," I pointed. "Look at his hand touching her arm. See that yellow light?"

"I think so." Lisa nodded with furrowed eyebrows.

The girl turned around and Thayer smiled at her, keeping his hand on her arm and the energy flowing. She blushed and when she looked down her hair fell in her face.

Thayer caressed his hand up her arm, pulling her energy all the way. She didn't move.

"That's her energy entering his body. You touch their skin and you force the energy to leave them and come into you. It's like second nature, easy as breathing," I explained.

"How much is he taking?" Lisa asked. "I mean, how do you know how much to take? Because he just keeps going and…"

The Shadow lifted his hand from the girl's arm, stopping the energy flow temporarily. Then he brushed the fallen hair out of her face and tucked it behind her ear.

As soon as his skin touched hers, the energy cascaded from her blushing face to his fingertips.

"Thayer is more…brazen than us. We don't take as much energy as he would," I said.

It was the simplest explanation possible. I left out that part where I used to be just as bad, if not worse, than Thayer was now. I didn't mention how many humans I had killed because I wanted their energy when I was a Shadow.

I was the one person she trusted, and I didn't have the heart to shatter that illusion.

"But he's not hurting her, right? Back in the mansion,

you kept talking about how I could hurt people if I wasn't careful," Lisa asked.

I shifted on the wall and looked back at Thayer. His hands had moved from her face, to her arms, to her neck. He was touching her all over.

Wisps of yellow energy lit up in all the places he touched. They were still too faint to be caught by a human.

"For them, it doesn't actually hurt to have their energy taken, not unless you take enough to kill them. Even then it just feels like falling asleep. For Legends, it stings and your body kind of aches when it adjusts to having less energy, but again, that's only if you take a lot," I described.

"And he isn't taking enough to...to kill her, right?" She stared at Thayer and the human girl wrapped up in his hungry arms.

"Thayer is probably siphoning a little each time. He does it more for fun than anything. But it would take all day to explain Thayer's reasoning. Watch the human girl," I instructed and diverted her attention.

Lisa flinched at the word *human*. A word that she had always used to categorize herself. But she wasn't one of them anymore. She was one of us. I moved the conversation along.

"Notice how she isn't standing as straight. She keeps shifting her feet. She's getting tired," I explained.

"So, this is the point where he should stop, right?" Lisa asked, her wide eyes locked on the human girl.

I hopped down from the wall. I reached my gloved hand out to her to help her down. She kept her eyes on the girl instead.

"He's not stopping," Lisa whispered loudly, as if Thayer could hear us. "Okay, he stopped...wait...he's kissing her."

I rolled my eyes and turned to look at Thayer. I was

seriously second-guessing the benefit of bringing him along on Lisa's first hunt.

Where their skin touched was empty. He wasn't taking her energy anymore. I smiled and looked back at Lisa. Her mouth hung open as she stepped down from the wall.

"That's Thayer for you. He likes to use himself as a distraction for the energy he takes," I said. "Others tend to choose a more subtle route."

I wanted to add in the part where he didn't always hide the energy he took, because he planned on taking it all. A dead person can't tell anyone else about a Legend they saw.

Secrecy only matters when he planned on leaving that person alive.

"But she doesn't even know him. I mean, he is a complete stranger and I don't think he even said anything to her. He just started kissing her. How did he know she wasn't going to say no?" Lisa asked, still in awe at what she had seen.

"Thayer can be *persuasive*," I smiled. I lowered my voice as we walked closer to the people. "He is very good at creating emotions. Extremely good."

"He's forcing this on her?" she balked.

I made a face and tilted my head. "Maybe not. Thayer's also very attractive and there's not a lot of people that would even want to say no. I mean if he tried to kiss you...you know, don't answer that."

"Did he ever mess with your emotions?" Lisa asked.

I paused and looked at her, grateful for the change in subject.

She raised an eyebrow at me, and it was like the old Lisa was back. It felt like we were in the office and she was analyzing emotions between me and Kylan. She noticed things that I sometimes wished she hadn't.

"Yeah," I nodded and scanned for Thayer in the crowd. "But that was a long time ago."

There was so much about me that Lisa didn't know. It broke my heart to think of telling her, but I also knew I'd have to eventually.

I looked back at her and took in a slow, steady breath. The next few minutes consisted of the condensed version of my past and watching Thayer flirt with every possible person on the street.

"But you still trust him?" Lisa pushed further.

"It may seem strange, but yeah, I do." I looked back at her.

Those brown eyes were serious and inquisitive. Light purple shaded the underside. When she blinked, she closed them for a little too long each time. She was tired, and her body knew it.

"I trust you. So if you say he's good, then I believe you." Lisa nodded.

"I never said he was good," I added and Lisa's eyes squinted. "But that's a topic for another time. Right now, let's focus on you."

"How was that?" Thayer asked as he stepped up behind Lisa.

He stood a little too close and Lisa flinched away. I snickered and Thayer shot a glare at me.

"Great demonstration," I said and stepped toward him. "I just need you for one more thing."

I took off my glove and Thayer's eyes narrowed at me again.

"Not again. Go get your own." Thayer pulled his arm out of my reach.

"Come on, this is for Lisa," I offered, smiling at him.

I did want to show Lisa up close what taking energy could look like. Now that Thayer had extra energy in his body, I could take it and explain it to her.

Whether or not Thayer wanted me to didn't matter as much as his desire to impress a new potential fling. He didn't need her to like him, but no doubt, his ego did.

After a brief second of staring, he gave in. He moved closer to me, which also brought him closer to Lisa. He smiled down at her as he extended his muscled arm, completely flexed, out to me.

"Watch closely," I said to her.

She leaned her face in to where my hand was about to touch his arm. Thayer didn't move, not wanting to scare her off again.

"At first, before you even touch them, you can feel the warmth from their body. You'll feel yourself wanting it. When you make contact"—I explained and laid a finger on Thayer's skin—"that desire inside you grows even more. You *have* to have their energy, and your body takes over."

Bright, yellow energy flew around my finger and spread into my palm. A warm, buzzing sensation raced up my arm and into my shoulder, my chest, my entire body. Thayer hid his pain under a smile.

"Does it hurt?" Lisa asked Thayer.

Thayer pulled his arm away from me and the energy immediately stopped. My body ached for more, but I yanked my hand back instead. I shoved the glove back on my hand and focused on what was happening.

"Only if she holds on for too long." Thayer smirked at me.

Lisa moved her eyes to me instead of noticing Thayer's wicked grin. I refrained from rolling my eyes at him again.

"Why can you take it from him?" Lisa asked.

"Remember when Kylan took your energy?" I asked. Lisa nodded. "One of the abilities is being able to take energy from other Legends and I have that ability."

"So can you do it too?" Lisa pointed to Thayer.

"No." Thayer smiled at me. "Mara is special."

"Hmm, and why do you call her Mara?" Lisa asked.

Thayer's eyes squinted as he looked back over at Lisa. She didn't know the whole story, but I hadn't told Thayer that yet. He was about to open his mouth and my stomach dropped.

"Mara is my original name. Back when I knew Thayer," I rushed to explain before he did. "We don't age as quickly, so we have to move around. When we change places, sometimes we change our names too. When I came to Portland, I changed my name to Kate."

I looked at Thayer and recognized the new energy fueling his body. He didn't smile. His brown eyes stared at me carefully.

I nodded back to him before Lisa spoke up again.

"Wait, if this is a Level, then I could probably do that too? Then I wouldn't have to...you know," Lisa said and glanced nervously at the humans walking around us.

"It's possible, I guess. It's just not very likely," I answered.

Determination burned in her eyes. She was focused. If she was going to break through a Level, it was going to be soon. With the motivation of not wanting to hurt other humans, and provided she was an Extractor, then she could do it.

"Can I try?" Lisa asked quietly and held her hand out to me.

I looked down at her hand and pain rushed through my body. I stepped back from her, very aware of where her hand reached toward my arm.

"You can't touch me," I explained. "I won't be able to stop taking your energy, and you don't have very much to give."

Lisa lowered her hand and her eyes fell again.

"But maybe if you ask Thayer very nicely..." I turned to look at him. "He might be willing to let you try on him."

His only slightly bright eyes turned cold. "There's a limit on how many nice things I can do in one day."

I punched his arm, and he moved with the blow to make me feel better, even though I knew it didn't hurt him.

"May I?" Lisa's voice uttered, barely above a whisper.

Thayer instantly looked down at her. She pulled her arms close and looked smaller than normal. Her big brown eyes looked up at him.

He tried to keep his tough façade, but after a few seconds of staring, he melted.

His shoulders relaxed and he threw his head back in defeat.

"Ugh, I just give and I give," Thayer groaned as he turned away from us. "I'll be back in a minute."

My eyebrows shot up when I looked back at Lisa. She waited until she knew Thayer was out of sight before cracking a smile.

"Wow, I haven't seen Thayer crumble like that in a long time," I smiled back at her.

Lisa shrugged, uncomfortable. Her eyebrows pulled together and she looked at me with her mouth open, ready to talk. "Can I ask you something?"

"Of course," I answered and touched her shoulder.

Whether or not I would answer honestly would be a different question. I didn't want to lie to her anymore, but judging by the look on her face, I might have to.

"When you were a Shadow, did you ever....you know... kill anyone?" Lisa asked, keeping her eyes firmly glued to the ground as she cringed.

"Things were different back then. I didn't think of

humans in the same way I do now. I hadn't met you yet," I smiled and answered as evasively as possible.

"I changed that?" She raised her head and looked at me.

"Yeah you did," I said. "I didn't know that humans could be so caring, that they could be worth anything more than the energy they held. I know that's harsh, but they just didn't matter to me. Until you."

Lisa opened her mouth wider and took in a breath just as Thayer jogged up to us.

"All right, I've got fresh energy. Ready for it to be taken away *again*," he said with a pointed look at me.

Without hesitation, he stepped as close to Lisa as he could get before she leaned away.

Lisa looked at me, waiting for what to do next. Thayer raised his arm to her, closing his hand in a fist so he could inconspicuously flex his muscles.

"Put your hand on his arm." I nodded toward Thayer. She lifted her hand slowly.

"Don't worry, I won't bite…unless you want me to," Thayer whispered in a low voice.

A strange feeling crawled on my skin as I witnessed Thayer try to flirt with someone who wasn't responding. I had seen many women and men—human or Legend, it didn't matter—fall all over him, but I hadn't seen him actually try in so long.

The best part was, Lisa ignored all of it.

She kept her face calm, although her cheeks blushed anyway as she laid her hand on his forearm.

"You know, I really don't appreciate being used like this," Thayer muttered to me.

"Yeah, I'm sure no one has ever said that to you before either." I smiled at Thayer's drop in expression when he caught on to the irony.

Lisa giggled and tried not to look at Thayer, who scowled at me.

"Okay, Lisa." I focused. "Pay attention to his skin. Feel the warmth just underneath it. Can you feel it?"

"I think so." Lisa stared at her hand like it was going to move without her permission.

"Close your eyes, and just feel," I suggested.

She flicked her eyes up to Thayer before deciding it would be safe enough to close them.

"Now, try to get his energy to pass through him. Pull it closer to you," I said.

Lisa's face changed. Her eyes squeezed shut, forming wrinkles on her forehead. She scrunched her nose and held her breath. I waited. Thayer waited.

Nothing happened.

"It didn't work," Lisa opened her eyes and sighed.

Thayer didn't drop his arm. Instead he reached further and touched the side of her arm. He stroked his hand up her arm until she looked at him. He gave her a faint smile, the kind he would give to me when there wasn't anything he could do to fix it other than to let me know that I wasn't alone.

Those were the best kind of smiles, but Lisa still looked over at me with sad eyes.

"Option two." I shrugged a shoulder and turned my body to face the tourists walking a few steps away from us.

Lisa shook her head as her eyes widened at the steady flow of people. Her stare darted from person to person, looking at their faces.

"I don't...I don't think I can do this," Lisa protested and took a nervous step back as she waved her hands at her sides.

"Just focus. I promise everything will be fine," I said and reached for her and pulled her toward me and the people.

"I can't. No. What if I hurt someone?" Lisa whispered and heaved in short breaths.

"So what? They're just humans," Thayer muttered under his breath. "It's not like we haven't done that before."

Lisa's eyes widened even further. They looked like they were ready to pop out of her head. Thayer looked up casually into her scared expression. My stomach knotted as Lisa's eyes narrowed at Thayer, but then she turned her gaze to me.

"Has he killed people before?" she asked me, as if he wouldn't give her an honest answer.

Thayer quirked an eyebrow at her. He shot a stare at me before he walked toward Lisa.

"I see what's going on. Yes, I've killed. She's killed. It's actually quite a thrill," he started and Lisa moved to step away from him. "You're a Legend now. Just like us. And whether you like it or not, humans are no longer your concern."

He was acting too calm, like he was talking about the sunny weather. She shook her head and leaned toward me to protect her.

"Thayer, now is not the time." I stepped around her and stood between them.

"I think it's the perfect time. She's starving and she can't get out of her own head long enough to take care of her needs." Thayer glared.

"I know, but we can take this slow." I raised a hand to get him to back off.

He didn't stop. He kept walking closer to her, keeping his brown eyes locked on Lisa.

"Look at her, Mara." Thayer pointed.

My eyes followed the direction of his finger. Lisa had her tired hands wrapped around my clothed arm. Her pupils were dilated inside her bloodshot eyes. Her body trembled less because of fear and more because it knew what she needed even if her mind couldn't accept it.

She needed energy soon and I knew it.

"You brought me along because you knew she was going to struggle with the transition from thinking of humans as equals to seeing them as prey," Thayer said and my eyes moved back to look at him.

His gaze softened as he looked over to Lisa. "It's different. I know that. But you are different now. And as much as Mara wants to protect you, she can't."

Her hand shook as it held onto me. I didn't want to admit it but Lisa was desperate.

I moved my hand to push her grip off my arm.

"Let him help you," I whispered.

I stepped out from between them. Lisa stumbled when I moved away from her. Without energy, her body would start shutting down. She had a strong-enough will to keep herself away from the energy. What she needed was someone to convince her to let go.

If I wanted her to think of me as a good person, the way she does now, that person couldn't be me.

Thayer was right about the second reason I needed a Shadow with us.

He stepped closer toward her and put his hands on either side of her face. She relaxed into his touch because she didn't have the strength to keep putting up a fight.

"I can't. I don't wanna hurt these people," Lisa sobbed.

"I know, I know." Thayer pulled her face closer.

His lips planted a kiss on her forehead. Her shoulders relaxed. He looked in her eyes and moved her wildly curly hair out of the way. She stared back at him, worry in her gaze.

He moved to her ear and whispered something too soft for me to hear.

I wanted to know what it was, but all I could do was watch. Thayer waited for her response and Lisa nodded. Her eyes still threatened to let out the tears she was holding back.

Thayer whispered something else in her ear. He kissed the top of her ear and stroked a finger along her cheek.

Lisa's eyes hardened almost instantly.

I stiffened, just imagining the things he could be saying to her. As a human, she was sweet and kind and all I wanted was to protect her from this. As a Legend, I couldn't save her anymore.

Thayer pulled back and looked at Lisa's determined face. I cringed.

"Ready?" Thayer asked in a low voice.

Lisa closed her mouth and straightened her shoulders. She didn't look at him, or me. She just stared ahead.

"Ready," she muttered with a straight face.

Thayer turned her toward the crowd and then pulled his hands away. She walked and I stepped forward to follow her.

"What did you do to her?" I asked as I brushed past Thayer.

He looked down and hid a small smile.

"Pretty much the same thing I did to you to convince you it was okay to hurt Legends," Thayer answered.

I stopped. "Are you crazy? I wanted you to get her to relax, not force her to turn into..."

"What? Not turn her into you?" Thayer asked, raising an eyebrow at me.

"I have to fix this." I turned immediately to go after Lisa.

She was getting closer to the tiled path, where humans passed by in each direction. I couldn't just let her walk into the crowd with no inhibitions.

I couldn't let her be me.

Thayer caught my arm and yanked me back to stand with him. I struggled to pull my arm away, but instead, Thayer held me closer. He leaned down to my ear and I felt his breath race across my skin.

"If she doesn't eat someone soon, she's gonna be in rough shape and she is far too pretty to die a sad, anticlimactic death," Thayer hissed in my ear. "Once you get her back to the mansion, we can talk, but for now, just watch."

I did. I watched Lisa's every move. A step forward, a human was within reach. Another step, Lisa moved her hand toward his open arm.

Thayer tightened his grip on my arm and blood rushed to my face, roaring in my ears. I held my breath and Lisa's hand touched the man's arm.

My eyes focused. A tiny burst of yellow light swirled around Lisa's hand. I stopped moving and Thayer released his grip on my arm.

The energy brightened as she pulled more and more. She didn't pull away. Instead, she closed her eyes and relaxed her shoulders. The man turned around, Lisa still held her hand on him.

Every nerve in my body fired, getting ready for a fight.

Lisa opened her eyes and looked at the man as he turned to meet her gaze. She sighed like she had been holding her breath.

"Can I help you?" the man asked her.

She looked at him with a blank stare as her hand casually fell away from him. The energy stopped. She lifted her hand and looked at it, turning it over like it would look different than it did before.

"No. I'm fine," Lisa muttered, still looking at her hand instead of the man.

The man shrugged and walked away. Lisa glanced back

at me and Thayer, her eyes intrigued. She slowly turned away from us and continued walking, reaching her hand out again to the next person.

I glanced up at Thayer out of the corner of my eye. He beamed. I didn't say anything.

"You're welcome." Thayer nudged my shoulder.

I reluctantly smiled and watched over Lisa. It felt like we were witnessing a kid take their first steps. I hugged my arms, wishing that Kylan could be here to see this.

# CHAPTER
# SIXTEEN

*Kylan*

Five long days in the lab made me loathe Alec even more. Every person in that shining, grotesquely clean place either fawned over him or scattered when he walked into a room. But I just hated him.

"Isaac," Nikki sang when she walked up behind me.

I turned around, keeping my eyes to the thin grout lines as much as I could. The tile was so polished that I could see my reflection. The glasses hid most of my eyes if the unruly hair didn't.

"We're going out. Come with us." She waved me forward with a dark smile.

I shook my head. "I'm okay."

The Legends here went out for energy nearly every day if not every other day. I had enough in my body and so did they. But they always wanted more.

"Come on." Nikki sauntered over to me, her black hair swaying behind her. "You haven't been out with me for a week."

Alec walked into the room, shrugging off the lab coat. He rolled up his sleeves as he looked at me.

"I need to finish this." I gave an excuse, gesturing to the papers in my hand.

Nikki pouted as she ran her hand up my bare arm. I could feel her energy underneath her skin. Wild, untethered, and practically jumping out at me. It made my fingers tingle.

The less time around her, the better.

"You can finish that later," Alec said, looking over to me. "It's not like you need to impress the boss or anything."

He smiled and Nikki giggled. Her high-pitched laugh made even Sage's sound like music. She tugged on my arm.

"See, the boss says you should come, so come," she said in a whiny voice.

She leaned her body against mine, touching as much of me as she could without laying her body flat against me. More warmth, more energy. I gritted my teeth as I looked back at Alec.

He turned to hand his coat to an assistant waiting eagerly to help him. The tablet was tucked safely in the back of his jeans.

"You're taking that with you?" I asked, grateful for the distraction from Nikki's insistent hands roaming my body.

It took everything in me not to stop her. I settled for pushing the glasses up my nose to break the touch between us.

Alec nodded, letting his hand reach back and feel the top of the tablet. "I take it with me everywhere."

"No more changing the subject." Nikki waved a finger at me. "Let's go hunt."

I looked at the tablet, at Alec, and then back at Nikki's big eyes. If Alec was taking the tablet with him, I had no more reason to stay here. Not going would only draw more attention to me.

I still couldn't persuade the pit in my stomach that any of this was a good idea.

I looked back up at both of them. Alec had his eyes trained on me, his gaze filling with questions.

"You've convinced me." I smiled back down at Nikki.

She cheered and grabbed my hand, pulling me out the door. I followed with my eyes trained on Alec.

As soon as we stepped outside, we ran. We hit the nearest town in a matter of minutes. The energy in my body blazed with anticipation. I took a calming breath, hoping to clear my mind.

"Where should we go first?" Nikki asked.

"I heard there's a college throwing a dance not too far away," Alec said, looking at Nikki. "You like dances, don't you?"

"I like humans that think they're invincible." Nikki played with the stud earrings in her ear.

"Then to college it is." Alec nodded and looked at me. "What do you say, Isaac?"

I could imagine the energy teeming in a crowded room. My body ached, I wanted it so badly. I had been avoiding going hunting with anyone and I was starting to feel how long it had been.

"Let's go," I said in a gruff voice and nodded.

We wandered through the town, enough time for Nikki to terrorize any person she saw on the street. Alec skulked in and out of the shops along the main road.

"Looking for something?" I asked.

The more I used my voice, the more Alec stared at me. I had to choose my words carefully and I probably could have kept those to myself.

"Just following up on some rumors I heard," Alec answered, narrowing his eyes at me.

"About?" I asked again, forgetting my voice this time.

"Alec won't say." Nikki grabbed my arm and pulled me

toward the college looming ahead. "He doesn't tell anyone his plan before he wants you to know it. Not even me."

"You can't blame me." Alec smiled at her. "You'd spill anything to the first guy that batted his eyes at you."

"Not true." Nikki shoved at him.

Alec dodged her, stepping easily to the side and catching her arm instead. He yanked her close to his body, his mouth brushing against her cheek. "You know it's true. You love telling secrets when it benefits you."

Nikki bristled against him, trying to keep a straight look on her face. Alec spun her and pinned her back against his chest. His hands slid over her arms and stomach.

I wanted to vomit right there, but forced a flare of jealousy to cloud my eyes. Just in time for Alec to look up at me with a dark smile.

"Tell me, darling," Alec whispered. "When was the last time Isaac made a move on you?"

His eyes stayed on me. That look, that knowing, calculating look was too hard to look away from. He knew something, or he was proving a point. The next few seconds would tell me.

Nikki kept her mouth closed, eyes staring straight at me.

"Tell me," Alec breathed down her neck before he planted a kiss there.

Every muscle in my body locked into place to keep me from turning or shifting, anything to keep Alec's attention off me.

But Nikki didn't break. She held a calm face. "No."

So Alec lifted his hands away and stepped back, leaving her to stand on her own. That was when something snapped in her gaze. The brief loneliness was too much for her.

"Eight days," Nikki breathed.

Alec grinned and pointed his hands at her like he had just proven a point. Nikki spun and walked to the college without the two of us. I followed, not saying anything.

He caught my arm as I passed him. "Don't worry, I'm sure she'll find you interesting again soon enough."

His hand touching me ignited a rage inside of me. I wanted to peel away his fingers and twist his wrist out of place. Instead, I nodded and kept walking, following quickly after her. As much as I hated Nikki touching me, I hated it from Alec more.

My breaths became shallow as I tried not to step out of line or gag.

"Are we doing the college or not?" I asked and Nikki put her hands on her hips in frustration.

"Anxious." Alec eyed me. "Lead the way, Nikki."

She ran ahead and he followed. I finally took a normal breath. Music ahead wafted over before I saw any people or sensed their energy. It was going to be loud and intense.

And that was just the energy inside of the people.

Nikki finally stopped giggling when we walked through the glass doors. The hot air rushed over my face. I could sense everyone inside, their energy, their lives. Nikki raced through the room to her first target. He was tall, strong, and a little too drunk for his own good.

Alec faded away behind the rest of the people, out of sight. I walked slowly through the crowd, pulling their energy into my body a little bit at a time, the way I always did.

It should have been fine, so long as they left me alone. But Nikki had a thing for the body I had matched. I understood why I kept seeing flashes of her over and over again.

The poor idiot had a crush on her and she loved to exploit it and use him. It had become a chore to avoid her.

"What's up with you?" her voice asked from behind me.

I spun and saw her crossing her arms in front of her chest. We had made it to the edge of the dance, near the stage but just out of the view of the main crowd.

"What do you mean?" I asked, leaning casually against the wall behind me.

She put her hands on her hips, drumming her fingers as she eyed me carefully. "You're no fun today."

"Sorry." I shrugged. "I've been feeling off lately."

Nikki didn't buy it. She clicked her tongue as she stared me up and down. I slumped away from the wall and started walking away from prying eyes. She followed.

"Sure that's all?"

"What else would it be?" I turned to face her.

She narrowed her eyes at me. A drunk student stumbled against her shoulder. She stepped aside and let him stagger in front of her. Those brown eyes moved from the man to me and back again.

"Hey, hot stuff," the man slurred. "Nice ink."

The student sloppily dragged a finger across her shoulders that were mostly black with intricate tattooed lines. She lazily turned her head to him, a blank stare on her face.

Her hand flashed forward almost faster than I could see. She grabbed him by the neck, pulling him closer to her face as she scowled. Nikki tossed the man forward, his intoxicated body tumbling at my feet.

"Kill him," Nikki ordered.

"What?" I tried to play it off like a joke.

The man's hands slipped as he tried to get them under him. He shook his head, trying to sober up enough to stand again.

"If you're really fine, then it shouldn't be a problem." She shrugged, reaching her hands up to her hair.

They twisted back and forth, pulling the hair into a braid. All while staring at me too closely.

"I don't need to prove anything," I grumbled in a low tone, praying the man would walk away soon.

He stood slowly, still not aware enough to take a step.

"Not even for me?" Nikki stepped forward.

Her hands moved swiftly down the length of her hair. I gulped and looked back down at the person in front of me.

"Isaac?" Nikki asked again.

I rested my hand on the man's shoulder, just barely touching his neck. He looked at me, dazed and eyes darting everywhere.

*I'm sorry.* I thought to myself—words that I could never say out loud.

I pulled his energy from his body into mine. I lit up, warming with the new power. I tried to take even breaths, but my body disobeyed. I was too excited by the energy to care about the man standing in front of me anymore. More energy poured in, more than I had had in a long while.

I looked up at Nikki. Her hands had stopped moving, the hair untwisted on its own from the braid. A small smile turned up the corner of her mouth.

The man's knees buckled. I grabbed his arm with my other hand. The energy scorched faster. His eyes closed, his breathing sputtered.

I kept my eyes on Nikki, trying my best to ignore the energy. It was like ignoring a bonfire burning at your feet. She relaxed further, stepping closer to me.

The man took his last breath. His final energy sailed into me. I instantly recognized the taste, sweet and thrilling. My body shuddered as the power melded with each of my cells.

Even when the influx faded, the taste lingered in my mouth. It wasn't Legend energy. It wasn't Legend energy.

"Much better." Nikki smiled and held out a hand. "Let's go dance."

I took her hand easily, my body moving in graceful sweeps with the new power. I lowered my chin, peering out onto the floor in front of us.

I didn't see a room full of humans. I saw a room full of possibility.

# CHAPTER
# SEVENTEEN

Once Lisa had all the energy she needed, it took too long to convince her to come back to the mansion.

She wanted to flit in and out of the shops, talking to people and touching them. The only thing that got her attention was Thayer giving it another shot at flirting.

That made her laugh and she finally agreed to follow me out. I hardly even recognized her. Probably because she was skipping most of the way home.

We made it down the hall and to her room without many questions. I tucked the door closed and Thayer gave the two of us a moment alone.

"Okay, let's review." I nodded to Lisa.

"Human energy helps me survive, but if I take too much it's bad?" she confirmed.

She settled on an oversized armchair with gold nail heads on the arms. She flung her legs over the side and let her head fall back. The room Thayer had given her had a large bed, original gold-leafed molding around the window, and far too many mirrors.

It was also uncomfortably close to his, but she didn't seem to care. She didn't seem to be worried about anything when we returned.

"It's not bad, it just makes you want more," I corrected. "It's addictive and it can be hard to slow down, even if it means you might hurt someone."

"But Thayer can take as much energy as he wants and you don't care," Lisa muttered.

I stopped my next lecturey sentence. "What?"

She lifted her head. "Why is it that you monitor all of us, yet he can do whatever he wants?"

I raised my eyebrows at her. She ran her fingers along her plush armchair, satisfied.

"I'm not..." I started.

"Not turning a blind eye to everything Thayer does, that the Shadows do?" she asked, leaning forward in her chair now.

She looked different, less feeling and more empowered. I looked at a stranger sitting in front of me. I thought back to Thayer whispering in her ear.

This was his manipulation. It had to be.

"I'm gonna kill Thayer," I muttered under my breath.

The door swung open to the room and Thayer stepped through, his phone near his ear. He smiled his usual wide grin as he glided over to Lisa's chair. She smiled and leaned the other way so he could sit on the arm.

"I heard my name. Burning ears. And Sage just called." Thayer clicked a button on his phone. "Kylan's been in there for almost a week, and still no tablet. He's getting closer though."

"How is he?" I asked, my gaze softening.

Thayer sat on the arm next to Lisa and pretended to be distracted. I snapped my fingers at him. "Uh, he still looks like the other guy, Isaac is his name. He's cozying up to Alec and he talks to Sage every day."

"That's not what I asked." I narrowed my eyes.

"Mara," Thayer sighed and I already knew the tone of voice. "He's in the middle of the Shadows, hiding directly next to Alec. How do you think he's faring?"

"I knew this would happen." I shook my head and stood. "We have to go get him."

"No." Thayer stood with me and put a hand out to stop my movement.

"Notice how I wasn't asking for permission there?" I raised an eyebrow at him and shoved him to the side.

"You can't yank him out in the middle of the plan." Thayer stepped in front of me. "What are you gonna do? Just knock on the door and say, 'Excuse me, I think I left my boyfriend here. Do you mind if I take him back now?' We need to wait."

"You can wait. I'm going," I said.

"I think you should listen to him," Lisa said, still sitting casually on the chair.

I turned my gaze down to her. She smiled at me without a hint of fear for Kylan in her eyes. She looked more like a Shadow than the human she used to be.

"I think you should *stop* listening to him," I said through gritted teeth.

"Why?" she asked. "So you can be in control of me again? Don't like transferring the babysitting duty to someone else?"

"Where is this coming from? I'm not in control of you," I scoffed.

"Really? You decided my fate when you didn't tell me who you were. You let me walk into that lab thinking I was helping my friend. And you've been obsessed with what I do since we got here." Lisa glowered as she rose from the chair.

I tilted my chin at Thayer. He had his hand over his mouth like he was trying to stop a smile.

"You're dead," I said, glaring.

"I'm sorry." Thayer let out a laugh. "I can fix it, I swear."

"Good," I said.

"No, don't." She took Thayer's arm and pled. "I don't want to go back to being scared of everything. I want to stay this way."

I waited, hoping to see a change in her eyes. Nothing came. I turned my head to Thayer and watched his mouth thin into a line. His face changed from a smile to wide, amazed eyes.

"Well?" I raised a hand to motion Thayer forward.

"If that's what you want," Thayer sighed.

Lisa beamed and shot out of the chair, throwing her arms around his neck. He hesitated before wrapping an arm around her.

"Thank you, thank you." She smiled and glanced at me.

Thayer caught the stare and released her. "Get out of here before I change my mind."

Her shoulders dropped in relief as she pulled away from Thayer and went toward the door, brushing past me without another glance before the door closed.

"You wanna tell me what just happened?" I quirked an eyebrow at him.

"Here's the thing," Thayer started. "When I altered her emotions back in the city, I didn't change what she was already thinking. I took away her fear. I released her incessant worry. The personality you see now is who she is without fear. As if she was a Legend all along instead of a simpering human."

"So?" I asked, flicking my eyes back to Lisa.

"So, I made a promise to you a while ago that I wouldn't change your emotions to affect your decisions. Not even if

Alec asked me to." Thayer raised an eyebrow, walking toward me slowly. "I'm keeping that promise now with her. I won't change her emotions unless she wants it."

"Are you serious?" I asked.

"I'll fix it when she asks me to." He shrugged and moved to lean against the back wall.

My hands fell open at my sides. I stepped toward him, trying to contain the anger seething in my body.

"You need to put her back to normal now." I stared at him.

"This is her decision." Thayer stared at me.

"No, it's not." I shook my head. "She doesn't know what she wants. She's too inexperienced with this life to understand what she's asking for. I know better—"

"Don't finish that sentence," Thayer interrupted, glaring at me.

"Why not? Because you know I'm right? Someone else needs to make this choice for her, someone with a clearer head," I explained, walking toward him.

Thayer flinched as I got closer. He stood up away from the wall so he towered over me.

"And that person is you?" Thayer gritted his teeth.

"Yes," I huffed. "I'm apparently the only person in this room who knows what's best for her."

He shook his head and walked around me. "This is unbelievable."

I turned and waited for him to explain himself. He crossed his arms in front of his chest and stared at the ground while he thought.

"What?" I asked.

Thayer looked up at me with a calm face as he tapped his fingers against his muscular arm. A smile flashed across his mouth before he leaned in closer to me.

"I never thought I would say this, not after everything you've been through, but you sound like Alec." Thayer narrowed his eyes at me.

"I do not." I shoved him away from me.

"Sure about that?" Thayer caught himself on the back wall before turning to me again.

The words echoed in my mind.

*I know what's best for her.*

*She doesn't know what she wants.*

Those same words had come from Alec before I left the mansion the first time. The reasons he believed he needed to change my mind.

"The difference is, I'm not doing this for me! I'm thinking about her and what she needs. I'm thinking about you." I shoved a finger at him. "You should be on my side. She'll hate you once she realizes everything you took from her."

"That's exactly the reason Alec had for me changing your emotions!" Thayer shouted, raising his arms. "And you know what? For decades, that crap made sense. I believed him. But I'm not gonna let you trick me into meddling in someone else's life, not when I just got away from that with him."

"This isn't the same." I clenched my jaw. "You changed her emotions to begin with. She wasn't like this when she came here. You did this to her."

"Because she asked me to," Thayer said. "That's what I was telling her when I didn't want you to hear. I asked her permission to do what I did. She said yes. That was a choice you were never given, and I'm sorry for that. But I won't do the same thing to her."

"Why not?" I stopped for a second. Thayer held his breath. "Why does she all of a sudden mean so much to you? You don't even know this girl."

"You're right. I don't know her. But neither do you

anymore. She's never been a Legend before and you have to accept the fact that she may want this life. She may like being a Shadow," Thayer said.

I leaned away from him, taking in his expression. I wanted to see that he would falter, that he might obey me anyway. He stood firm and that only fueled the anger inside me.

"Thayer, just listen to me," I pled.

"No, Mara. In this mansion, I'm the King and what I say, goes. I'm not changing Lisa until she asks me to." Thayer stared at me with the most intense gaze that his brown eyes were capable of.

I thought about what he said, what I had said. He was right. Everything I wanted was exactly what Alec had wanted with me. I shuddered when I realized how alike the two of us really were. I stared at the empty room and felt like I was the only person in the world.

My hands balled into fists. I knew Kylan needed me, but I couldn't leave, not with Lisa hanging on the edge of becoming Thayer's newest Shadow. I hoped that Kylan could hang on for a little while longer.

Just long enough for me to get my friend back.

# CHAPTER
# EIGHTEEN

*Kylan*

The jittery discomfort hadn't faded. I figured after being at the lab for almost two weeks that it wouldn't feel this way anymore.

I walked down the hall, carrying papers that needed to be translated to digital format. I handed them off to the lab assistant. My forearms brushed against her as I transferred the stack to her.

My skin crawled with goosebumps. Her arms were warm, energetic, and I had to clench my jaw to keep any sound from coming out.

I stepped away from her, trying to hide the fact that I was balling my hands into fists and releasing them again. I looked at her, but she didn't suspect anything, just turned to walk the rest of the way down the hall.

At night, I caught myself remembering killing those humans. The feeling of their final energy spun around and around in my head and sleep became my only escape.

But it didn't make me want more from them. It made me want Legend energy. And there were so many Legends here within my reach.

"Have you seen Alec?" I asked.

I didn't want to deal with pleasantries and beating around the bush. Every second I was here, I was slowly losing my control. I stood a safe distance away from the lab assistant and she didn't stop walking to answer me.

"I think Nikki said he was going to take a shower." The assistant shrugged and kept walking.

*Shower.* I smiled.

There was only one place I could think of that Alec probably wouldn't take an electronic device. He had held it so closely to him and had yet to hand it off to anyone I had seen. Not even Nikki.

I turned around, headed toward the basement with all the rooms. The sound of water running led me down the hall, almost all the way to the end.

I pushed the door open to his bedroom. He hadn't even closed it all the way. The lack of privacy in this place made it pretty difficult to slip out enough times to talk to Sage. I couldn't wait to leave.

But not once had Alec left the tablet alone. No one had mentioned 17B or seemed to know what it was at all when I looked in their minds. If it was a carefully hidden secret, they were succeeding.

Alec's room was pristine. Every piece of furniture was dark wood that looked too formal for the white walls and shiny floors.

I still stood in the doorway, my eyes searching for anything that looked out of place. Seconds ticked by, and all I could hear was the sound of the water running and the blood rushing in my veins.

On the dresser, next to the bathroom door, sat a sleek tablet. The exact one that Alec had always carried around with him.

*Two weeks*, I thought. *That was all it took for you to slip up.*

I stepped into the room, focusing on that dresser. It was finally going to be over.

"What are you doing?" Nikki asked from behind me.

I almost jumped out of my own skin when I spun around. Her tiny frame leaned against the door. She crossed her arms and stared at me.

"Isaac?" Nikki raised an eyebrow. "What are you doing in Alec's room?"

I thought about the tablet on the dresser. I stared at Nikki in front of me. I couldn't hear anyone else in the hallway, which meant she was alone.

Against anyone else, she would have been scary enough to intimidate away. But I was an Extractor up against a Shadow with no power and the one thing I've been looking for was just on the other side of the room.

I stepped toward her.

*The tablet.* I tried to force myself to focus.

"Sorry, I thought this was your room," I smiled.

My mind spun. Nikki's eyes were bright with so much energy. To drain her enough to knock her out would mean an immense amount of power coming into my body.

Deadly, cunning power. My body screamed for me to grab her and take it all.

"Really?" Nikki smiled and relaxed further against the door.

I didn't care what she said. Human energy paled in comparison to what stood in front of me. I wanted it and I had a perfect reason to take it. But if I touched her flaring energy, I might not be able to stop.

*Tablet.* I tried again. That's what I was here for.

I reached my hand out to her and she actually stepped

toward me. My fingers tingled as she moved closer. I could almost feel her body heat. I could almost taste her energy.

The water stopped running at the sound of a squeaking faucet being turned off. My hand stilled in the air. I glanced behind us.

Alec stepped through the door, a towel wrapped around his waist. He looked at both of us and quickly glanced down to the tablet before setting his stare on me.

"Can I help you?" Alec asked.

"Isaac was looking for me and accidentally found you instead. What are the odds?" Nikki said in a low, sultry voice.

I looked at her from the corner of my eye. Her eyes looked dazed enough to tell me she had fallen for my lie. Alec was the only one I was really worried about.

"Sorry, we'll just head out now," I muttered and fixed my eyes on the floor.

"Hey, Isaac," Alec called.

I turned and saw him picking up the tablet from the dresser. He held it in his hands and looked down at it too long. His eyes snapped back up to me and he settled his shoulders.

"Don't let me catch you in here again," Alec said and waved his hand.

A rush of air slammed the door to his room shut in our faces. I staggered back at the sudden movement and Nikki just leaned against the now-closed door while she stared at me.

"So, what did you need me for?" Nikki asked in a low voice.

She dragged a finger up my chest, continuing past the collar of my shirt. My stomach turned. At least now I was so distracted by my distaste for her that I wasn't thinking about her energy anymore.

"Um." I glanced at the floor, nudging my glasses up. "I don't...don't remember."

"Aw, you're so cute. Come on, you can tell me." Nikki stepped even closer to me.

Her body pressed up against mine and a gag pulled at my throat. I looked at Alec's door, the wall, the ceiling, anything but her.

"Hunting," I blurted and stepped away. "I wanted to go hunting with you."

More energy was the last thing I needed, but the only valid excuse I could think of before Nikki threw herself at me completely. I took a breath now that I had enough room to move without touching her.

"Too bad." Nikki looked me up and down.

She closed the distance between us and moved her mouth to my ear. Her breath felt like acid on my skin. I froze, not wanting to blow my cover, but also hoping she would back off on her own.

"That's not what I was hoping you wanted," Nikki whispered.

I cringed and wanted to die right where I stood.

Nikki peeled herself away from me and sauntered toward the stairs. I paused to take a few free breaths, preparing myself for what was coming up.

With her swaying black hair and upper body mostly covered in black markings, she looked like walking death.

"You coming?" Nikki waved me forward without turning to look at me.

I didn't want to move. I wanted to burst into Alec's room, snatch the tablet, and run as fast as I could back to Kate. Against only Nikki, I could have taken her down, but against them both, it was too dangerous.

I stared ahead at my only other option. Following the walking death out the front door.

"Yeah, I'm right behind you," I muttered and took a reluctant step forward.

# CHAPTER
# NINETEEN

I only saw one way to solve this problem. If Lisa wanted to feel what it was like to be a Shadow, then I was going to push it as far as it could go. She should see everything she'd be stepping into.

First up was getting Thayer off my back.

"I've been thinking about what you said," I tapped his shoulder and whispered. "About me sounding like Alec. I wanted to say I'm sorry. I shouldn't put you through all of that again."

Thayer furrowed his brow as he turned to face me. He crossed his arms in front of his chest before looking me up and down.

"That's it?" Thayer asked. "Five minutes of contemplation and you're all fine?"

"What can I say?" I shrugged. "I've always been a faster learner than Alec."

Thayer laughed and I knew I was winning already. I leaned in closer to him, catching his attention even more.

"So where's your newest protégé?" I looked around the room.

"I wouldn't call her a protégé quite yet." Thayer smiled as he turned. I rolled my eyes at how easily distracted he could be. "But she's in the courtyard. She's working with Fiona to break through another Level. Intriguing girl like that is definitely more than a Level One."

"Careful now." I nudged him. "Sounds like you have a crush."

"Ah, I don't do crushes. You know me." Thayer smiled and guided me to where Lisa was.

"Yes, I do," I muttered.

I smiled, but my stomach turned. The Lisa that he saw now was not who she was, but that was exactly the type of person that would make Thayer's next girl on his hit list. The Lisa she was would fall hard for someone like Thayer. He wouldn't know how to do anything but watch her crash and burn.

He was a good person at heart, but the rest of him was rough.

My thoughts were interrupted by the sound of cheers coming ahead. Thayer turned around and walked backward to look at me.

"Sounds like someone just became a Level Two." Thayer fluttered his eyebrows like it was just another day in the mansion for him.

I moved around him to see Lisa standing in the crowd of people. She held a dagger in her hands and smiled down at it. The tip of the dagger dissolved into black dust, falling all around her.

A shiver prickled down my spine as I stared at her holding a Shadow's dagger.

"Reading and destroying." Fiona nodded. "A deadly combination."

Lisa's eyes flinched at her words. For a brief second, I

thought I almost saw guilt pull at her eyebrows and slow her breath. But Thayer came and put his arm around her and all of that emotion faded.

"Excellent work." Thayer smiled down at her.

She blushed and lowered her chin. Even without the fear of being human, she was still Lisa. I had to hold onto that hope for what I was about to do.

"He's right." I clapped my hands and walked forward. "You found another Level and that's not something that happens every day. I think we should celebrate."

"Really?" Thayer asked, scanning my face.

A quick smile and he relaxed back into holding Lisa closer to him.

"Of course. If Lisa wants to see what the Shadows are all about, then we should show her." I looked at her now. "Who's up for a party?"

The Shadows around me cheered, clapping their hands and raising their arms. I glanced around at everyone. A party to the Shadows meant death to the humans, but to them, it was fun. When my eyes fell back on Lisa, she stared at me.

"Well, I'm always ready to party." Thayer smiled and turned to the Shadows around him.

The women fawned over him and the men studied him with awe. I was the only one who had a fake smile plastered to my face as Thayer accepted their praise. Lisa walked up to me.

"Thanks for understanding," she said. "I know it's not what you wanted, but I'm happy. More than I've been since… you know, the whole Chase disaster. Anyway, I appreciate you respecting my decision."

I forced every muscle in my body to comply so I could put my arms around her. I hugged her close to me and finally let the worry fall on my face.

"What are friends for?" I whispered into her curly hair.

She pulled away from me and bounced her way back to Thayer. I clenched my fists at my sides and caught Fiona's attention.

"Hey, have you seen Cassie and Derek?" I asked.

"The Rogues?" Fiona asked. "I think they're huddled together on the balcony somewhere. Turns out, Shadows aren't really their thing."

"Shocker," I muttered.

I raced up and saw Cassie sitting on a bench, pointing at something in the sky. Derek knelt at her feet, smiling as he followed her hand.

"There you guys are." I smiled and walked over to them.

They looked up at me and Cassie scooted over on the bench to make room for me. All the worry finally flooded through my eyes as I glanced over the balcony at Thayer and Lisa standing too close to each other. Derek stood and waited for bad news to drop.

"What's going on? Is it Kylan?" Cassie asked, letting her hands fall in her lap that was mostly covered by an oversized sweater.

"No, he's okay for the time being. Apparently, being at the lab is starting to get to him, but he's strong." I tried to smile.

"I knew it. I have a bad feeling about this." Derek looked down at Cassie.

"How much longer is he gonna stay?" Cassie cringed.

"Sage says he's close. He should know Alec's schedule by now and there's gotta be a time when he leaves the tablet alone at some point," I said and their shoulders relaxed slightly.

"So then, what's wrong?" Derek asked.

"Take a look." I moved my eyes to the scene below.

"Yeah, we heard. Lisa broke through another Level," Derek edged.

"Well, I guess everyone gets to be a Two or higher, don't they?" Cassie grumbled.

My gaze snapped back to her for a second. She glared at the ground. I looked up at Derek and his eyes went back and forth between the two of us as his mouth hung open, just waiting for words.

"Oh um...Just don't mind her. She's a little emotional today." Derek tapped his toe against Cassie's shoe.

"Yeah, sorry," Cassie blurted. "Just ignore me."

"Anyway, what's up with Lisa?" Derek turned his attention back to the courtyard.

"Thayer helped her feel a little less worried about hunting and she took it a bit further than he expected. But he won't change her emotions again unless she asks him to," I explained.

"What? He messed with her head? That's not fair," Derek said.

"Well, no. But I get where he's coming from. This needs to be her choice. So, I'm planning on...helping her in the right direction." I gestured my hands in the air to explain my plan better.

"So, what does that mean?" Cassie asked.

"That means that tonight there's gonna be a party. Shadow style. And I think you two should steer clear of the courtyard." I looked at Cassie.

She stared back at me thoughtfully before she turned to the courtyard. She stood from the bench and walked to the edge so she could get a better view.

"Are you sure you don't need our help?" Derek asked, sitting on the bench next to me.

"I appreciate that, but no." I shook my head. "I need to

show her what it's like to be a Shadow and I already know exactly what to do."

"Okay, we can lay low for the next little bit. Right, babe?" Derek asked her.

Cassie turned, crossing her arms a little lower than looked normal. She looked at the floor, her eyes flicking back and forth between the stones.

"Cass?" Derek edged again.

"I wanna watch," Cassie finally said with a steady gaze.

"No, no," I glanced at Derek. "This isn't something you want to see."

"Yeah, honey." Derek knelt in front of her, putting his hand on her shoulder. "I don't think this is the safest option for you."

"It's not like I want to stand in the middle; I just want to see." Cassie looked up at him like she was asking permission.

He didn't object.

"Cassie," I started.

"No." She raised a hand. "I've spent my whole life hating the Shadows. I can't really explain it, but I want to know if I am still right to despise them. I wanna see it for myself."

I looked at Derek and he stared down at her a little while longer. When he looked up at me, he stood with her and set his shoulders.

"We'll stay up here," Derek said. "Will that be out of the way enough?"

"Yeah." I nodded.

I looked at Cassie's small frame. She slumped over and held her hands in front of her stomach. She used to be all smiles and sass, but ever since Rachel died and I came back, she was a little different. More emotional maybe, but more somber, like Rachel used to be.

Derek stood next to her like it was the two of them versus

the world. I wanted to protect them. But for tonight, I needed to act like a Shadow or at least look like one. Something inside split in my stomach when I thought of how their opinion of me would change.

Cassie wanted to find something to hate. And tonight would do just that.

"I won't stop you from watching, but let me just warn you..." I stared at both of them.

They looked back at me with serious expressions. Their shoulders held far more weight than they should have. But there was nothing I could do to fix that now.

"You aren't going to like what you see," I finished.

Cassie nodded. "I know."

# CHAPTER
# TWENTY

*Kylan*

Nikki burst into the spacious inventory room followed by two Legend lab assistants.

"Ugh, I'm telling you, I don't know," Nikki said.

I turned my back to them and rolled my eyes so they couldn't see. I took a breath and put on a neutral face again before turning back around. I reached into the box and the glass vials clinked in my hands when as I pulled them from the box to stock them on the shelves.

Nikki sat on the table as close to Alec as she could get while he studied his precious tablet.

"Alec doesn't talk about why he chose the dagger mark. Even to me." Nikki glared at the women below her.

Alec glanced up from the tablet to look at Nikki, then me. He paused for a second, a flicker of thought in his eyes. I continued stacking the vials, hoping he would look away.

My blood pounded in my ears.

"So there is no way he's gonna tell—" Nikki started in as condescending a way as she could.

"Actually," Alec interrupted and turned his attention to

the others in the room. "Maybe now would be a good time to talk about it."

My gaze shot up to Alec. He suddenly wanted to reveal information? Something wasn't right. I stayed exactly where I was to decide what I should do next. Alec tucked the tablet he was holding into that unreachable, interior back pocket of his lab coat.

"Excuse me?" Nikki pulled her hair behind her ear as she stared at Alec.

"Darling," Alec purred to Nikki and put a finger under her chin. "You don't want to hear the story? I promise it'll be a good one."

Nikki didn't say anything. She held her lips in a tight line until Alec held out a hand to her. She cracked a smile as she took his hand and hopped down from the table.

"The day I found Nikki," Alec said, still watching her. "I knew that I wanted her."

Nikki smiled even wider as Alec stepped closer to her, moving around behind her. I tried not to gag. She was the most obnoxious person I had ever met and Alec was so full of himself. Any relationship between the two of them would be oozing with ego.

"She could destroy anything. She could create a mark for me. A way to identify my Shadows from the rest of the Legends," Alec continued.

He lifted his hand to Nikki's hair and pulled it toward him and over her shoulder. She turned her face toward his touch.

"Now, all I needed was to give her the image. The one thing that shaped me more than anything else," Alec explained and grabbed her arm, pulling her into him. "This dagger."

He held up her forearm that had a black dagger pointing toward her hand. His arm underneath hers had the exact same one.

"You see, growing up, Father taught me to follow my sadistic instincts. Most of the time, I listened. I liked being bad," Alec said and stepped in front of Nikki again.

The women in the room had their eyes locked on her and Alec. Nikki had her gaze pinned to Alec. The only sound I could hear when he paused the story was my own breath.

"But every once in a while, I did something kind. A small reminder of the good that was still in me. When Father saw that, he wasn't happy," Alec said.

He turned around and faced the two women in the room. He created a dagger in his hand, the same as the one on his arm. The dark blade shone in the harsh lights of the room.

"So, he would take this dagger and show me what it felt like to be good." Alec pointed the dagger at one of the women.

He rested the tip of the blade on her sternum and stepped toward her.

"Every day, the same dagger. Every day, a new part of my body was gashed or stabbed," Alec shoved the dagger into her skin, far enough to draw blood.

Everyone on the room sucked in a breath. I could picture the image of Father standing over a younger Alec. Throwing the dagger toward him. Slashing the dagger across his chest. Shoving the blade through his arm, his hand, his shoulder. Anything he could reach.

Alec would scream, but he would learn. Father was incredibly effective at getting a point across.

"I adapted. That little voice inside of me that told me to be good? It died. Even after he was gone, it never came back." Alec pulled the blade away from the woman and she stepped back, watching her wound heal.

He turned back to Nikki and glanced at me before looking down at her.

"Being good is overrated anyway," Nikki said in a low voice.

"Yes, it is." Alec smiled at her. "But, there was one thing that was the only exception to Father's rule. One thing I was allowed to love, allowed to care about."

I pulled my eyebrows together. If father had wanted Alec to be pure evil, there shouldn't have been an outlet for him, not unless it served a purpose.

The answer crashed into my mind. My heart dropped in my chest. I stared at my brother in front of me as he stared down at a woman that wasn't anywhere close to the one he wanted. The one he was allowed to have.

"Her," I breathed before stopping the audible word from flying out of my mouth.

Alec's eyes snapped up to me. Nikki turned around to look at me with a confused gaze. Alec only smiled.

"Mara," Alec agreed.

My breath stopped in my chest. I glanced at the door. Both of them were in the way. I knew not to look around for a window. We were in one of the inner rooms. I was stuck.

I waited for Alec to make a move. His eyes moved around my face, not trying to put anything together, just watching me. He moved his gaze away as easily as he had looked at me. But the inner struggle was lost on Nikki. The only thing she focused on was Mara's name.

"That's why you want her so much. She's the only way you can feel what it's like to be good? I thought you didn't want that anymore?" Nikki asked with a raised eyebrow.

It made sense. Alec was tortured into becoming the monster that he was now. The exact monster I would have become had I stayed.

"I don't," Alec answered her, pushing her hair behind her inked shoulder. "I did at first. But Father realized that's what was happening. He still wanted me to stick with Mara no matter what happened. But, I didn't love her yet. We were just kids."

Alec leaned in close to her face and changed direction at the last second. He moved his mouth to her ear.

"He had to make sure I never would. And there was actually still one person in my life that I did care about, that I loved more than anything," Alec whispered in her ear, loud enough for the rest of us to hear.

"If it wasn't her, then who?" Nikki asked just as Alec pulled away.

I could hear the hope in her voice, and it even made my stomach turn. Alec didn't glance down at her again. He turned around to the other women in the room, leaving Nikki by herself and breathless.

"One night, Father and I sneaked away from the rest of the Shadows. We traveled all the way to that person's house," Alec explained slowly.

The women in the room had their eyes glued on Alec. Nikki sighed and walked over to me instead of standing there and appearing to be waiting for him to give her attention again. She stood next to me and crossed her arms in front of her chest.

I looked down at the mark on her arm before she pressed it against her body. I knew I should have been more worried than I was. But I had to hear the rest of the story.

"I remember walking through the front door. It was a quaint little house on a quiet street. I went up the stairs and into the back bedroom. I opened the door and saw my target lying asleep in the bed," Alec said and turned slowly to face Nikki and me.

"A dagger would be too obvious. I shot a bullet into her chest." Alec stared at me. "The last of my kindness toward anything else died that night. The night I watched my mother choke on her own blood."

My mouth fell open. Alec's story was too similar to what

happened. I remembered the night I found her dead in her bedroom. Anger flooded through my body. My breath came in short spurts.

He was telling the truth. He was the one that killed her.

"She stared up at me. She still knew I was her son, though we hadn't seen each other in decades. She asked me why. I realized that I didn't have an answer for her. Not one that would make sense. She bled to death right in front of my eyes." Alec stared at me, waiting.

"How could you?" I asked, without a worry of what anyone would think. "How could you kill your own mother?"

"When she closed her eyes, all that happiness was gone. The only things I wanted to possess were power, pain, and Mara. I was exactly what my father wanted me to be," Alec smiled at me.

"You're a monster." I gritted my teeth.

"And yet, I'm not as bad as Charles," Alec stepped closer to me. "Am I, Kylan?"

I used the rage-fueled energy in my body to change my appearance back to who I normally was. The energy seeped out of my body, I barely noticed until I tried to take a faltering step forward.

I ripped the annoying glasses from my face and pulled the lab coat off of my shoulders. Nikki stepped away from me with a small smile.

She knew too. It didn't matter, though. The only thing that I could focus on was Alec.

"No, you're not," I answered. "You're worse."

I stepped toward him again, wanting to rip his smile off of his face. I wanted to plunge his precious dagger in his chest. Then he could feel what it was like to choke on his own blood.

Before I could launch myself toward him, I couldn't see

Nikki anymore. I knew where she was when I felt a sharp tip of a blade press into my back. The women in the room gasped.

"One more step, and I will ram this through your gorgeous body," Nikki called from behind me.

"It looks like that little identity change cost you a bit more energy than you planned, huh?" Alec lifted an eyebrow.

I knew if I moved, Nikki would stab me. She was obsessed with Alec, and if I threatened him, she wouldn't hesitate to kill me. I wouldn't have enough energy to heal from the wound.

I clenched my fists before I looked back at Alec.

"So, that's it then? You're just going to let your little minion kill me? I thought you would've wanted that privilege yourself," I asked, hoping his ego would make a stupid decision.

"Oh, I do." Alec smiled even wider. "But I want one thing a little more."

Alec lifted the dagger he still held in his hand toward my chest. The tip of the blade almost touched my skin. He was just far enough out of reach. So was Nikki. They had planned it perfectly.

"You know, I wasn't sure that it was you for a moment. But then, you didn't want to hunt for energy like Isaac did. You didn't flirt with Nikki endlessly the way he used to. And you asked far more questions than that idiot would have. It didn't take very long to put it together after that," Alec said.

"What did you expect me to do? Sit back and watch you tear her life apart?" I asked.

"I didn't think she would send in her second string to get what she wanted," Alec snarled at me.

I glared back at him, fighting the urge to move forward. Alec reached into his lab coat and pulled out the tablet that held all the answers. He lifted it up for me to see. He turned it in his hands so the lights flashed off of it and into my eyes.

I looked down and gritted my teeth.

"What are you gonna do?" I asked, looking back up at him in defeat.

Alec had everything. Every card I could have played was gone. I had been here for almost two weeks and I didn't know anything more than when I started. I needed him.

And he knew it.

"If she wants this"—Alec kept his eyes on me—"tell her to come get it herself."

# CHAPTER
# TWENTY-ONE

The music blasted as loud as the speakers could manage and it still wasn't loud enough to drown out the dread in my gut.

Tonight was all about excitement and freedom of the Shadows. So tonight, everything was black and red. I added the final details to the courtyard decorations when Fiona walked in. She was followed by a string of unsuspecting humans.

I tried not to look at their eyes. None of them would be walking out of here alive, but they didn't know that. Every smile on their faces brought a pang of pain in my chest.

I glanced up at Derek and Cassie, waiting just out of the way on the balcony. Even from down here, I could see Cassie's eyes welling up as she looked at the line of people who had just been walked in.

Lisa bounced up next to me and grabbed my arm.

"Wow, this looks amazing," she gushed. "You should have planned the company parties for Mr. Lyle instead of me. Man, that would have saved me so much stress."

"But the gala you planned was fun." I jumped at the chance to talk about her human life. "That was where Kylan and I had our first dance. You and Chase had your first date. It was a memorable night."

"Yeah…" Lisa paused, thinking about it.

I waited for emotion to cross her eyes, for a flicker of worry at how different this event would be. Nothing came before she was interrupted.

"Memorable, huh?" Thayer walked up to her and put his arm around her. "Well, then, tonight ought to blow that memory out of the water."

He pulled Lisa closer to him as she giggled. Any thoughts she had left as her eyes looked up at him. He released her and she bolted over to Fiona and started talking too fast for me to follow. Thayer stepped in my sight line.

"I know what you're doing." Thayer leaned down to me as he turned to look at Lisa with me.

"Do you now?" I asked, crossing my arms as I watched her laughing next to the Shadows.

"You're trying to get Lisa to feel a connection to humans anyway," Thayer said, barely moving his mouth.

Lisa glanced up at him and waved. He smiled and nodded back to her.

"Are you sure?" I asked, turning to him now and staring blankly.

"What else would you be trying to do?" Thayer shrugged and leaned forward. "I figured I would just offer the chance to give up now. The only person to break through my emotional manipulation was a Level Five. And last I checked, little miss beautiful over there is only a Two."

Thayer smiled when he looked at Lisa and then the smile melted when he turned to me. He wasn't angry. He was actually happy that he was winning. This was his first taste of real power, and I understood why he wanted to hold on to it. But in that particular case, the "it" was one of my best friends and I was going to fight for her even if it meant going against Thayer.

"Thanks for the offer." I extended a hand out to him.

To him, this was another game. He was playing to win and I was playing to save Lisa. He smirked at my hand before he shook it.

The music changed to a steady, slow beat and Thayer still held onto my hand.

"Could I have the first dance?" Thayer smiled.

I nodded and Thayer pulled me out onto the floor. We spun around in circles in silence. Both of us were beaming and enjoying the temporary fun.

While I didn't want to support what the Shadows did, I still felt the allure of being in the glamorous mansion where all your darkest desires could thrive.

"We miss you here, you know." Thayer pulled me close enough so I could hear him over the music.

He held onto my hand like he didn't want to let go. A lump formed in my throat as I looked around at the Shadows. A few humans had already hit the ground and Fiona dragged the first one into the corner of the room.

"I don't miss being here," I muttered. "This isn't who I am anymore."

I pulled away to look at him and tried to ignore the obvious death going on around me. Thayer stared at me with a somber expression pulling the corners of his mouth down.

"I know." He nodded.

No matter what his words said, I know he didn't agree. It didn't matter what I said. So when I kept talking, it was only for me. Thayer just let me talk.

"We just live in two different worlds now." I shrugged.

Thayer smiled and pulled me closer to him. "For what it's worth, you'll always have a place on this side of the line."

I wrapped both arms around him and hugged him as tight as I could. We both stopped swaying and just held on to each other.

When I pulled away from him, I looked down at the mark on my arm. Thayer raised his arm and held it next to mine.

We each had a black dagger marked forever on our bodies.

I looked up at him and a rush of emotion twisted through me. I was a Shadow on the outside, and I always would be. But standing in the mansion, next to Thayer, with this mark burned on my arm, I never felt more like a Rogue.

"If you ever want to join the good side, I want to be the first to know." I smiled up at him.

He nodded and took a step away from me. His mouth stayed closed, his jaw muscle twitching from the effort.

"Deal," he finally said.

Lisa ran up behind him, her eyes bright with new energy. Seeing her high was like all her neurotic stresses and worries flipped on their head and doused themselves in steroids. She was a totally different person already. I gulped.

"Do I get a dance now?" Lisa asked, extending her hand out to Thayer.

I just stared at her. She was bold and flirty, beyond anything that I thought she could be. All of her previous personality was tied to her human life. Without that emotion, she was a flatter version of herself and it made me cringe.

"Absolutely." Thayer winked and snatched her hand.

He spun her around and pulled her into him. She crashed into his chest and giggled. The music sped up and the two of them danced circles around each other, ignoring everyone else.

I felt a pull toward her, to protect her, but I remained standing where I was.

I glanced up at Cassie and Derek. She hugged her arms around herself as she stared down. Derek rubbed her shoulders, trying to keep his eyes anywhere else but on us.

I wanted to run up to them and convince them to leave but Cassie was too stubborn to listen to anyone right now. I couldn't blame her. She had the chance to watch her own nightmares play out in real life. Watching someone die, she wanted to look away but couldn't.

I turned back in time to see Thayer spin Lisa around to face a human girl. He whispered something in her ear and she laughed as she shied away from him.

Lisa danced her way toward the human girl and ran her hand up the human's arm.

The energy brightened Lisa's hand, and the human's steps slowed. Lisa pulled her hand away and the human slogged off to the corner, into another Shadow's arms.

Lisa sauntered back to the crowd without another thought. The human was safe and Lisa was moving back to Thayer, back to the Shadows, back to everything I knew she would hate later.

"I can't watch this anymore," I muttered to myself and darted to the nearest human, a short, impossibly young man with dark hair.

For a breath of a second, I was sorry for his fate.

I grabbed the human's wrist and he didn't fight me as I pulled his energy from his body. He smiled at first, and then his smile drooped. He stumbled into me and I caught him with my free hand.

My eyes snapped over to Lisa, who was only a few steps away. I dragged the human along with me, closer to her. She was still smiling, dancing, and letting her curls bounce all around.

But Lisa sensed the energy and she turned.

I looked at how happy she was and tried to mirror her smile on my own face. I shoved the human toward her. He didn't have much energy left when he staggered toward her. She caught him with both hands on his arms.

Her eyes trained on the human. He looked down to her and her smile softened as she stared. Judging by the fact that neither of them looked away, she was reading his mind.

All the blood in my veins froze as I watched. I hoped she would see how exhausted he was, or how he must be scared to be here and not know why he's so tired. I wanted her to see anything that would give her a reason to want to understand humans again.

Her face remained the same.

Instead of looking around or pausing, she brushed her hand along his arm. She pulled his energy from his body and his knees buckled out from under him.

My mouth fell open as I watched. Lisa just grinned as she took more of his energy. The human's head hung down and his scrawny legs gave out completely.

Lisa didn't slow his fall to the floor covered in glitter. He hit with an uncomfortable thud.

I waited. Lisa stared down at him, unmoving.

I still waited.

I held my breath as I watched her brown eyes glaze over with apathy.

The music changed to a slower pace and Thayer came out of the bustling, black-clothed crowd to find Lisa again. The quieter song matched the soft look on Lisa's face.

"I don't feel anything," Lisa whispered.

I would've missed what she said if I hadn't been watching so closely. I wanted to rush to her and tell her that all she had to do was ask to get it fixed.

But Thayer was right about one thing, I couldn't make this choice for her.

All that would bring is resentment toward me the way I resent Alec. She meant too much to me to do that. So, instead, I waited. I stood far enough away to remain out of her sightline, but close enough to see it all.

Lisa stared down at the human as Thayer walked up behind her.

"Hey, are you ready for another—what's wrong?" He stopped when he saw her face.

She shook her head and kept looking at the human. Her eyes remained wide and emotionless.

"Oh, here, let me take care of that." Thayer waved Fiona forward. "Would you mind?"

Fiona nodded and grabbed the human's wrist. She pulled him away and Lisa finally broke her stare. She looked up at Thayer with that same vacant expression.

"Take it back," Lisa said.

"What?" Thayer tried to laugh it off but his face dropped the longer he looked at her.

"Why...what changed? You were having a great time a minute ago." Thayer glanced around the room and locked eyes with me.

I shook my head at him. He opened and shut his mouth without words coming out before he turned back to Lisa. What could he say to me? I hadn't done anything.

"I want you to take it back," Lisa said again.

"Okay, I will. Just come back to the party," he begged and grabbed her hands to pull her with him.

She ripped her hands out of his grip. Hope bubbled up inside of me as I saw Lisa stand her ground and shake her head.

"I just killed a person," Lisa said, "and I don't feel a thing. Nothing. I don't want it to be that way."

"Why?" Thayer asked, probably honestly wondering. "Isn't it easier that way? To not feel anything and just…live."

"It's not who I am." Lisa's voice remained even and steady. "Please, please just undo whatever you did."

"Okay," Thayer whispered.

He pulled her to the side of the courtyard, under the glittering streamers and away from any prying eyes. They hid under the balcony and Thayer pulled her to face him.

I thought he would try something else, force her to stay this way. But I trusted Thayer's word to know he would let her go. He cupped her face in his hands.

"It was fun while it lasted," he said.

Lisa smiled and put a hand on his wrist. I walked closer to them to get a better view of her face. I was only a few steps away, but neither of them saw me.

I didn't think it would hurt as much as it did to watch the change. But when I saw the first twist of pain on her face, I wanted to melt into the floor.

Her eyebrows pulled together, and her hands shook by her sides. The sobs sputtered out of her mouth as she kept looking at Thayer. He finally released her face and she collapsed, landing on her hands and knees as she struggled to pull in a breath.

Thayer slowly turned to look at me.

His face looked like Lisa's used to, vacant, calm, and slightly bored. Only for him, it was a mask. I saw the way the agony tinged his gaze. He walked away without looking down at Lisa again.

Lisa curled into a ball on the floor. I ran forward and knelt on the ground beside her.

She leaned into me and just shook her head while she cried. I rubbed my hand up and down her back as the other hand pushed the hair away from her face.

"What...what happened to m-me?" Lisa's voice shuddered. "Everything hurts. I don't...I don't know what to do. It just...I want all of this to stop."

I lifted her shoulders and forced her to look at me. Tears streaked down her face. Stray strands of hair stuck to her wet cheeks.

"Your mind is just adjusting to your original emotion. Thayer replaced it with something else and now you are feeling everything," I explained.

She stared at me with eyes searching for any source of relief.

"Just take a deep breath." I showed her what to do. She followed. "And feel just one emotion to start. Then another, and then before you know it, you'll be able to deal with it all."

"I killed someone," she muttered.

I nodded.

"I *killed* someone," she said again, like she didn't believe the words.

"I'm sorry," I said.

"I should have listened to you," Lisa cried again. "I was such an idiot. It was easier the other way, but I shouldn't...I just..."

"Hey, hey." I shook her shoulders. "Blaming yourself won't do you any good now. Just accept what you need to feel."

"I'm so sorry," Lisa said and fell into my arms.

I held her as her tears dripped into my lap. Out of the corner of my eye, I saw Cassie and Derek edging their way closer and closer.

Derek nodded and held on to Cassie's hand like he was afraid to drop it. Cassie clenched her jaw until she looked at Lisa. Her eyes softened as she moved forward and knelt on the ground with us.

"Lisa?" Cassie said.

Lisa lifted her head up enough to see Cassie. I kept my arms around Lisa until she sat back on her own.

"I've seen people die. People that didn't deserve it, and it really hurt to watch," Cassie started.

"Maybe you shouldn't—" Derek interrupted.

I shook my head at him and he backed off again. I felt Lisa's body relax a little.

"But that wasn't the worst part. The part that hurt the most was that they didn't care, the Shadows. They actually enjoyed it," Cassie reminisced.

I thought of the memory she showed me. Her parents had been murdered by Shadows. Alec's father had led the group that took their lives. Cassie saw it all and escaped just in time to save her and her sister.

I looked down at my arm again, at the mark that would always stain my past.

"But you're different. You made a mistake, a big one," Cassie scoffed. "But all of us have done things we aren't proud of."

"We're all here for you." I rubbed her cold arm.

We sat on the ground, all holding each other. Cassie and I tried to shelter Lisa from the Shadows all around her.

Thayer walked up and shattered the illusion of temporary safety. I looked up to tell him to leave, but the words stopped when I saw the worry clouding his eyes as he lowered his phone from his ear.

"Guys," Thayer started.

"What do you want, Shadow?" Cassie snarled up at him.

She had an enraged expression all ready to go, but even she stopped when she looked up at him.

"It's Kylan," Thayer said, his voice changing, and I felt every piece of me crumble apart.

Cassie stood instantly and Derek moved closer to hear every word. I helped Lisa to a standing position and kept my eyes glued on Thayer. Someone stopped the music and the silence was pounding in its place.

"Alec caught him. And he wants to see Mara," Thayer finished.

My blood felt like slow lava in my veins. I dropped my hands to my sides, forgetting everyone else around me.

"Can we get him out?" I asked, already knowing the answer.

Thayer shook his head. "Sage said Alec wants you to help him become a Five. If you do, then he'll give you what you want."

Now I shook my head. "There has to be a way to keep Alec from getting that power. Once he does, no human is going to be safe. That's the only thing holding him back. Ask Sage if we can—"

I was already moving toward the door. We needed a plan, but we had the whole trip there to figure something out.

Thayer grabbed my arm. "He's not just offering to give Kylan back. He promised to help fix you. You won't have to steal energy without thinking."

"What?" I stopped. "He wouldn't do that. What did he say exactly?"

"I don't know. I'm hearing it secondhand from Sage anyway. If he really is promising this, then you'll have to be there in person to hear it." Thayer dropped his hand from my arm.

"How do you know this isn't a trick?" Cassie asked.

"It definitely is," I said. "But what other choice do we have?"

Thayer sighed. "This is Alec. You don't have another choice. He'll kill Kylan if you don't show."

"Then let's get going." I started walking again and no one stopped me this time.

The others still wanted to argue. Discuss all the options.

Their voices sounded like they were a million miles away. I couldn't even hear the sound of my own footsteps. I took in a breath and all I wanted was to see that Kylan was okay.

I staggered to the front door. The others clamored after me, but I ignored all of them.

*Kylan was taken.* That was all I could think.

The one icy thought that sharpened my mind to focus on anything was this.

*I can save him.* I said it over and over.

All the way out the door. All the way across the states that stood between me and my goal.

# CHAPTER
# TWENTY-TWO

The iron doors opened. My breath stopped.

The light fell through the doorway, revealing a glisteningly clean lab in front of us. Shining floors and the smell of nothing in the air. I stepped through the threshold and moved my gaze to a figure walking toward us.

I'd know those cold, indigo eyes anywhere.

"Mara," Alec hummed. "It's good to see you're back to your old self, baby."

I looked straight ahead and took in a steady breath. I balled my fists so hard I could feel my nails stabbing into my palms. My heart pounded in my chest.

The doors closed and Alec stood in front of me in fluorescent-lit clarity. My eyes adjusted back to the harsh lights shining off every white surface.

But I found what I wanted. Kylan was standing next to Alec, dagger pointed at his side and metal cuffs on one of his wrists. Nikki stood just behind him.

Alec smiled directly at me, ignoring everyone else in the relatively crowded space.

Before saying another word, Alec nodded to Nikki. She walked around with a handful of glowing cuffs. She put one on each person's wrist except mine.

Thayer grinned when she placed his. Derek and Cassie grumbled. Lisa didn't make a sound. Kylan stared ahead at Alec, despite Nikki trying to catch his eye.

No one fought her, though, not even Cassie.

When she stood by Alec again, she took what must have been the remote to the cuffs and shoved it down her shirt, daring anyone to try and reach it. Thayer stifled a laugh.

"As promised." Alec shoved Kylan forward.

Kylan walked toward me and I threw my arms around him instantly. I buried my face in his shirt and took a deep breath in of his clean scent. He smelled so familiar, calming.

When I finally peeled myself away, I turned to face Alec. He stepped forward like the next hug was for him.

"Don't take another step." I raised my free hand in the air.

Alec froze, except for a crooked smile pulling at his lips. I lowered my hand slowly but never took my eyes away from him.

"Before we go any further, I need to clarify the terms." I raised an eyebrow at him.

"Are you really in the position to be negotiating anything?" Alec smiled and relaxed.

"First, as soon as we figure out how to create a Level Five, you will help fix whatever it is you did to me," I ordered.

"Of course," Alec nodded. "Once I am a Five and I have everything I want, I will give you every piece of information I ever gathered on you and your...condition."

I thought about his exact words, looking for the trick. But I wasn't focusing for this long before I noticed the lack of other people in the room. I listened and it was utterly quiet. It was too empty.

Alec and Nikki stood together, the only other people in sight.

This wasn't normal. Kylan and Sage said there were other Legends here—humans, too. The lab should be far from empty.

"Wait, where is everyone?" I asked Alec.

"He dismissed the entire staff when he figured me out. Everyone left a few days ago," Kylan answered instead.

"Safety reasons. Don't need you turning anyone else against me." Alec smiled.

His smile made my skin feel like it was being pricked by a thousand needles. I hated it when he knew he was in control. A chill swept over me.

I kept myself from shivering, long enough to focus on what I wanted.

I narrowed my eyes. "My next demand is about everyone that just walked in here with me. If you hurt anyone in this room—"

"Then, you're dead," Kylan finished my sentence.

Alec pursed his lips as his eyes glanced around at the people here, probably considering how he could get out of that part of the deal.

Kylan. Cassie. Derek. Lisa. Sage. Thayer. Me.

It was a long list, and I knew how much I was asking. It also wasn't something I was willing to give up.

Alec looked back at me and tapped his fingers against his leg as he thought.

"Meaning, even if I hurt their feelings? That seems a bit drastic," Alec drawled.

He was looking for a loophole. I ran the scenario through my head and I couldn't see how that would help him.

"I guess asking you to be nice would be too steep of a request," I said.

"You do know me so well." Alec smiled. "But I'm afraid that rule has to be a two-way street. If they threaten me, I will defend myself."

"They wouldn't do that." I shook my head.

"Okay then, on the slight chance that one of these entirely perfect people decides to go behind your back and attack me or Nikki, I can break rule number two. Deal?" Alec asked.

I waited, hoping I would see what his end game was. Nothing came to mind. I couldn't trust Alec, but once again, I didn't exactly have a choice.

"Deal." I nodded.

I let go of Kylan's hand and stepped forward. Alec took a step toward me too, smiling at my outstretched hand.

It wasn't a welcome. It was a threat. My skin was dangerous now, thanks to him. His cold, blue eyes looked back up at me as he raised his own hand.

Alec never backed down from a threat.

"One more thing." I pulled my hand back. "Can you promise you'll answer all of my questions truthfully? The whole truth. Including what you just said."

"You know how this works." Alec's smile glistened in the harsh lights. "Ask the right question, and I will."

I stared at him, ignoring the pyrotechnics going off in my body. Every nerve told me this was a trap. He was danger. Nothing about this situation was safe. Even though I knew better, I lifted my hand again for Alec to shake.

"Stop," Kylan interrupted.

Alec's eyes turned icy as they moved to look at his brother. Kylan stepped forward to stand beside me. The warmth of his body allowed me to relax slightly. With him standing so close, there was nothing I couldn't handle.

"Kylan, if you're unhappy with your end of the bargain of keeping Mara, I'm more than happy to renegotiate," Alec sneered.

"I have a demand as well." Kylan looked straight ahead at his brother.

Alec stepped away from me and crossed his hands in front of him. He raised both eyebrows lazily as he waited for Kylan to talk. Kylan's warm hand touched the small of my back, and my muscles released the tension.

"She gets one free hit without you blocking her," Kylan said.

My eyes widened as I turned to glance back at Kylan. When I turned back to look at Alec, he just smiled at me.

"You want to hit on me?" Alec grinned easily. "Baby, you don't have to ask to do that."

"You know that's not what I meant." Kylan lunged forward.

I shoved against him and stopped him from moving closer to Alec.

I nodded to let Kylan know that I was fine on my own. He backed off. I faced Alec. The way his eyes burned at me made my skin crackle with rage.

"Be a little more specific next time," Alec warned.

I wanted to smack the expression right off of his face and I was instantly grateful that now was my opportunity. Kylan knew what I wanted before I even did.

I grabbed the bottoms of my sleeves and rolled them up over my elbows. I took my time rolling up the right sleeve, making sure Alec saw the mark on my arm.

"One punch. After everything you did to me. I think that's fair." I moved my head from side to side to stretch the muscles.

The more I prepared, the more Alec tensed up. He

swallowed as he watched me. His eyes changed. They weren't calculating, they were soft, almost guilty.

"Alec..." Nikki edged.

He held up his hand to stop her from talking. She stepped back again and locked her eyes on me instead.

"Whatever it takes," Alec said slowly.

He stared forward at me and straightened his shoulders. He moved his hands to either side of his body and held them still. His breath came in quick spurts until I raised my hand. My fingers curled into a fist and his breath stopped.

My hand coiled back, adrenaline flooding through my body.

I thought back to my time here. I pictured his face standing on the opposite side of those glowing bars. I imagined his sick smile as I lay on the cold, metal table. I saw his eyes the moment I turned around and saw a gun in his hands when he stood next to Rachel's dead body.

I hated everything he had done. It was an effort to keep from exploding at the sight of him. My fist tightened.

Alec closed his eyes. I paused. Every muscle in his face relaxed. He wasn't going to fight me. This would be so easy.

But I thought of Rachel and I lowered my aching hand.

"I can't," I whispered.

Alec's eyes snapped open.

"What?" Kylan's voice asked behind me.

"You can't?" Alec asked.

"No." I shook my head and turned to the rest of them. "This hit doesn't belong to me."

Alec stared quietly at me.

I listened for him to move forward anyway. He stood perfectly still. I looked at the group of people in the room. Kylan stood next to Thayer and Sage. Derek stood in front of Cassie, her eyes on the floor.

"Despite everything you've done to me, there is one person in this room you've hurt more," I explained. "Cassie."

Her eyes flew up to meet mine. Her mouth dropped open as she stared back at me. I smiled and nodded to let her know that no one was going to hurt her, especially Alec.

Derek smiled as Cassie walked toward me slowly.

I turned back to Alec and waited for her to join me. He didn't glance at the others. He didn't care about them. When I was in the room, all he could see was me.

"Your father killed her parents," I started. "And you killed her only remaining sibling. If anyone deserves a moment of revenge, it's her."

Alec finally glanced down at Cassie. She stood firm in front of him. His eyes roamed over her face while he made the connection.

"Rachel," he mumbled.

"Yes, Rachel," Cassie growled at him.

I took a step back and pulled Cassie in front of me. I looked up at Alec. His eyes followed me instead of looking down at Cassie.

"Same rules apply. Don't block the hit," I said and took another step away from her.

Cassie's red hair spilled down her back as she tugged at the bottom of her bulky jacket. Alec's eyes reluctantly moved back to the Rogue. He didn't flinch or move, just waited.

"Knock him dead, honey," Derek called from the back of the room.

Cassie's shoulders rose and fell as she took a breath in. I assumed she would wait and relish in the moment.

I was wrong.

Cassie's fist knocked into Alec's jawbone and his head snapped to the side. His body twisted as his knees hit the floor.

Nikki rushed forward and caught his shoulders before he completely fell.

Cassie spun around and cradled her punching hand close to her stomach. She looked up at Derek and smiled.

He stretched out his arms and she walked into his enveloping hug. Her head tucked just under his chin. Derek looked up at me with a soft smile.

*Thank you*, he mouthed. I nodded.

I turned back to Alec, who rubbed his cheek and stood. He looked over to me and took a step forward. Nikki stilled, not walking forward with him. Alec stepped close to me and the lights reflected off the red mark on his face.

I brushed my right hand along his jawbone and his energy seeped into my body.

"That looks like it hurt," I said in an empty voice.

Alec stared at me, not pulling away from my hand. "I've had worse."

His eyes filled with sadness. I knew what he meant.

Worse would have been me choosing to leave. Worse was also the day his father died. Worse was every moment he had to spend knowing that I loved Kylan, his brother, instead of Alec.

Yes, Alec has had worse.

That didn't mean he didn't deserve most of it.

Without warning, my left hand curled into a fist and punched him in the stomach. The air forced out of his body. He doubled over around my hand.

"I lied." I looked at Nikki now.

She didn't move. Her wide eyes trained on Alec crippled over in pain. She held her breath as she waited for Alec to stand.

He slowly lifted himself back up again as he caught his breath in sharp gasps. I watched his eyes narrow at me and a grin spread on his face.

"Didn't see that coming," Alec coughed. "Good job, baby."

I scowled and pulled my right hand back this time. I let it fly forward, aiming for Alec's face. His hand shot up and caught my fist in the air. He held it in place, right in front of his mouth.

"I agreed to one," Alec threatened. "Anything past that, and I'll take you down."

I almost couldn't hear his voice over the rush of his energy flooding into my hand. It spiraled all the way up my arm and filled my head.

I didn't move, I just froze. My mind reeled at the rush of energy in my body.

Alec watched my eyes. A smile appeared in the corner of his mouth. He knew I was taking his energy. He wanted anything that connected me to him even more.

I yanked my hand away and Alec dropped his.

"Let's get started." I straightened my shirt and glanced between Alec and Nikki.

Alec stepped forward, too close to me. I stared back at him, not willing to back down. Even if I was in his territory now.

He handed me a pair of cloth gloves made out of a spandex material. I couldn't touch anyone, and Alec was only rubbing it in. I took the gloves from him and frowned.

That was when I heard Alec say the words that I never expected to hear.

"I'll follow you." He grinned.

# CHAPTER
# TWENTY-THREE

It took Alec at least two hours to explain most of the tests he had done and the information he already had about a Level Five.

I did my best not to cry when he explained everything. He was watching for my reaction and I couldn't handle seeing him smile at my pain. Not again. Not like how he used to when I was here as a prisoner.

After a few rounds of baseline tests, Alec finally let me go. These experiments weren't as bad as I remembered. If anything was too painful, they gave me something to numb the pain. And Kylan sat with me during it all, even if he was jittery and couldn't touch me.

"I think that's the last one we need for now," Alec said, resting the syringe on the tray that Nikki was holding.

"Good," I said, rubbing my arm at the injection site.

Kylan forced a smile, wringing his hands.

"This will take an hour or two to process. After that we can start the next round, which will be way more exciting." Alec stood, entering information on his tablet before tucking it in his coat.

Kylan remained seated, staring at the ground. Something wasn't right with him and I wasn't going to find it out with Alec standing so close.

I stood. "That'll have to wait until morning. I'm pretty tired."

These tests were draining. I needed a break, from Alec, from this room, from all the needle stabs.

"Oh, here," Alec said, reaching a bare hand out to me.

I hesitated before I leaned away from him.

"No. I want to sleep," I said.

Alec just laughed. "Sleep? Are you joking?"

"It's not so hard to fathom. You've slept before." I rolled my eyes, moving closer to Kylan.

Alec nodded with a growing smile. "The last time I slept was with you at the mansion."

Kylan broke out of his trance long enough to stand with me and level a serious gaze on Alec. I touched his shoulder to guide both of us out the door.

"Nightmares don't bother you then?" Alec asked before I could leave.

"Haven't had any since the day I left." I shook my head, trying to keep my tone level and light.

Alec nodded his head, purposely keeping his mouth closed.

"Good luck with that," Nikki said.

Alec turned like he wanted to scold her, but didn't say anything. I left, pulling Kylan out the door with me.

As soon as the door closed, I leaned in closer to Kylan, checking over my shoulder.

"Are you doing okay?" I whispered.

"Fine," Kylan answered curtly.

I stopped us from walking, tugging on Kylan's arm. He looked down at my gloved hand as if he didn't want to meet my eyes.

"Hey." I touched his cheek. "Talk to me."

Kylan finally looked up at me and the expression on his face fell. The dark look in his eyes sent pain in strings between us.

"I'm glad you're here," Kylan said.

That wasn't everything he wanted to say. I knew there was more. Before I could ask, he pulled me into a hug. I tried to keep my skin away from him, and my hair worked as a good enough barrier.

When he took a shaky breath, I wanted to destroy whatever pain he was feeling.

I turned my head into him. "I'll always be here for—"

The skin on my cheek had touched his neck. I felt the warmth a little too late. Kylan hissed and jerked away from me.

Feeling his body leave mine felt like a stab in the heart.

"I'm sorry," I started.

"Don't," Kylan said, closing his eyes and trying to hide the pain. "I just… I think I'm a little drained."

"Well, let's get some rest then." I started walking toward the stairs.

"I'll be right behind you." He didn't move.

I stopped. "Kylan, there's something else going on. If you don't tell me, I can't help you."

I wanted to reach out to him, but I didn't want to make him feel more uncomfortable. Instead, Kylan put his hands on my shoulders and his face softened.

"I'm fine," he sighed.

I opened my mouth to argue. But Kylan just leaned forward and kissed me. I yanked my head back, trying to minimize the amount of energy I took.

"Kate," Lisa called from behind me.

When I glanced over my shoulder, Kylan stepped away.

"I'll meet you downstairs," Kylan said, not looking back.

I wanted to follow Kylan, but Lisa had already bounded up to me and latched on to my arm.

The words flew out of Lisa's mouth almost faster than I could listen. "Okay, I know I've been here before but I really don't remember anything and this place is giving me the creeps. Have you ever walked through an empty hospital? That's exactly what this feels like. I mean, I don't even know—"

"Lisa." I put my hands on her shoulders. "Take a breath."

She did. I did as well. The air didn't settle the pit in my stomach with what was going on with Kylan, but it did take the edge off.

"This is gonna sound like a stupid question, but is there somewhere I can sleep? Like, are there bedrooms that aren't... experiment rooms?" Lisa looked around warily.

I laughed and linked my arm with hers. "Yes. I was actually just going down there."

"Good." Lisa heaved a sigh and walked with me.

We went down the stairs to where the other people stayed. Alec had showed it to me when I had first arrived. He wanted me to see what everyone else was getting before he locked me in the cage.

That was the first step in breaking me down. I had to feel like I was less than nothing. It had worked.

Feeling the tests today, how easy they were, it only made me hate Alec more for everything he had done to me. All the pain had been unnecessary. It was only so Alec could break me and shape me into what he wanted.

The first two rooms were labeled in elegant calligraphy etched into metal. Alec and Nikki's rooms. I tried to glance inside Alec's room, but the glass was obscured.

"Here we are," I said. "Pick a room."

Lisa's eyes caught on Nikki's nameplate before moving to the next empty room. She opened the door and her eyebrows shot up.

"Yes?" I heard Thayer's voice.

Lisa jumped back and I didn't hold back a laugh.

"I'm sorry." Lisa's hands flew to her face. "I didn't... didn't know this room was taken."

Thayer ate up the bashful look on her face and Lisa's cheeks were only getting redder by the second.

"Come on." I nudged Lisa's shoulder to face her to the room across the hall.

She followed, keeping her eyes on the floor. The next door she opened much slower. Once she was sure it was empty, she bolted inside and shut the door.

I laughed and turned around to Thayer. He was leaning against the doorway, shirtless and displaying his long, slender body. His arms were crossed in front of his broad, bare chest. His eyes roamed Lisa's door.

"Across the hall." Thayer finally looked at me. "Are you trying to tempt me?"

I rolled my eyes and knocked on Lisa's door lightly. "Hey, if you need anything I'll be in the room down the hall."

"Thank you," Lisa's voice answered.

I locked eyes with Thayer again and whispered, "And I have excellent hearing."

I pointed my fingers at my eyes and then at him. He just smiled at my gesture before he stepped back into his room.

Even the brief moment of distraction didn't take my mind off Kylan. I needed to know why he was acting off. I'm sure the lab couldn't have been an easy experience. But the only other person that would know was out of sight.

"Hey," I said and Thayer paused. "Have you seen Sage?"

"Why?" Thayer put his hand on the door again.

"I want to talk to her about Kylan. I think something's off and I thought maybe she'd know something," I answered, crossing my arms in front of me.

He didn't answer or move at all.

Suspicious, I narrowed my gaze. Thayer heaved a sigh and shoved the door open. I looked behind him to see Sage walk around the corner from the attached bathroom—dressed, thankfully.

I raised my eyebrows. "Oh."

I started to back up.

"It's fine." Thayer waved me inside, taking a glance at the room across the hall. "Mood's kinda spoiled already."

I walked in, trying to ignore the awkward feeling pressing on me. Sage pulled her white hair back into a ponytail as she sat on Thayer's bed.

"You're worried about what happened while Kylan was here," she said easily.

Her red eyes looked up at me, not needing an answer. I sat on the bed next to her. Thayer pulled on a shirt and grabbed a chair from the corner, straddling it backward.

"I just know what it can be like when you're around Alec too long. I think there might be something he's not telling me. But I don't want to keep pressing unless there is something to ask about." I wrung my hands in my lap, pulling at the tips of the gloves.

"Well, he didn't talk to me much even when he checked in," Sage said, glancing at Thayer.

She was hesitating. Thayer looked back at her and nodded. There was more.

"Sage, please." I reached forward and rested a hand on her leg.

Her red gaze twisted in discomfort. "There was one time when I ran into him in the city. He was out hunting with

Nikki. I didn't see Alec anywhere, but he may have been there too."

"They took him hunting?" I asked.

"They had to. How was he supposed to get back into the lab without Isaac's actual eyes? If he didn't leave with someone, his cover would be shot," Thayer interrupted.

Sage flicked her stare over to him. He lowered his head and raised his hands in surrender.

"Anyway, there was this woman in the park. It was really late, so it was kinda hard to see. Nikki was watching him and Kylan went up to her." Sage stopped, watching me pull my hand back. "The woman didn't leave the park alive."

I paused to process the information. Kylan killed someone. It made sense logically and I really had no room to blame him, but it still felt like a betrayal that he at least wouldn't tell me.

"He had to, right? Nikki would have known if he refused," I tried.

Sage let out a breath. Thayer moved to sit on the bed with me but I stood up before he reached me.

"That wasn't the only body that night. I followed them for a little while," Sage started again.

"You've got to be mistaken. Nikki must have killed the other ones." I wanted to jump down her throat and stop the words from coming out of her mouth.

"Mara," Thayer started.

"No, Kylan would have told me." I narrowed my eyes at her.

Sage stood. "I'm not a liar and I'm not stupid. While I don't think what Kylan did was wrong, I know he does. It's eating him alive."

"You knew?" I pointed to Thayer.

Thayer leaned back farther on the bed. "Sage told me

everything over the phone. I didn't realize how bad it was until I got here and saw him. He's in rough shape."

"You don't think I know that?" I scoffed. "Why wouldn't he talk to me? I mean, I know why he wouldn't want to tell me, but he has to know that I love him no matter what. This doesn't make sense. I just wanted—"

Thayer stood from the bed and wrapped his arms around me as I rambled on. We stood there until I could take a deep breath. Sage even hung her head as she left the room.

When it was just the two of us, it felt real. All of this was real.

"I hate this. I hate Alec," I muttered.

"Talk to Kylan," Thayer said. "He's the one who needs you right now. I'm sure Alec is already enjoying this. No need to hand him any further ammo."

"Kylan left. He said he needed a break for a minute." I pulled away from him.

"Then go get some sleep." Thayer pressed a gentle kiss to my forehead. "He'll come to you when he's ready."

I was grateful for the energy. It made the storm of anger rest for a moment. I put my face in my hands, feeling the exhaustion again.

"Sorry for interrupting your night," I said as I walked toward the door.

"Nah." Thayer shrugged. "What are friends for?"

He followed me to the door. When he opened it, I walked into Lisa holding up a piece of paper.

"Oh, sorry," she backed up.

I glanced at the ripped page of a notebook in her hand. It said Thayer's name on it. A matching one was already on her door that listed her name.

"Couldn't get enough of me, huh?" Thayer asked, leaning against the doorway again.

"Thayer," I warned under my breath.

Lisa gulped, pulling a shaky hand through her curls. "I just thought maybe we should label the rooms. You know, that way there isn't any, um, confusion later."

"Great idea," I said. "Isn't it, Thayer?"

"Anything sounds like a great idea when she says it," Thayer answered, smiling down at Lisa.

I shoved him and he laughed. Lisa handed him the paper awkwardly. He took the opportunity to touch her hand when he grabbed the page. His eyes never left hers as he attached it to his door.

Lisa's mouth hung open a little. I couldn't tell if he was manipulating her or not.

"Well, I'm going to my room," I said, and Lisa snapped out of it.

"Good, good. That's good," Lisa nodded nervously. "I'll come put a name on your door. That way Kylan can find you later."

She shuffled down the cold hallway and I followed her to a darkened room. I turned back to see Thayer staring at her.

"Thank you," I said and he looked down to me.

He winked and I waved. He shut the door and I wandered to a room near the end of the hall.

I heard Derek's voice talking to Cassie from the last room. Of course they had chosen the one farthest away from everyone else.

Lisa scribbled on a paper and taped it to their door before turning to the door I chose. I smiled at her, but I couldn't think of anything besides Kylan.

She hurried back to her room and I looked at her rushed handwriting.

*Kate and Kylan.*

I went in and fell on one of the twin beds in the room.

I didn't bother turning over, just rested on my stomach, counting the seconds until Kylan came back.

My eyes closed without permission as my breath became steady.

# CHAPTER
# TWENTY-FOUR

*Kylan*

I avoided Alec and Nikki, still awake and working, when I came back inside. The cuff on my wrist glowed and lit my path down the deserted halls.

I snuck down the stairs near the bedrooms, listening for any creaks. My body buzzed with energy, making each step feel like a crash. I hated this raw feeling after taking energy, but I also loved having it in my body.

When I rounded the corner, I hoped that everyone would be asleep. That hope vanished when I saw Thayer in the hallway.

"Oh, hey," he whispered, stepping away from one of the doors.

"Is everyone asleep?" I whispered back.

"You mean, is Mara asleep already? Yeah, she's in the back." Thayer pointed down the hall.

I walked up to him, noticing the door behind him with his name on it. The one he had stepped away from had Lisa's name on it.

"Labels were her idea." Thayer nodded to Lisa's door.

"Okay."

I didn't stay to talk and I didn't want to guess why he wanted to talk to Lisa. I had too much energy and guilt battling in my head to care. I walked past him.

"Hey." Thayer grabbed my arm.

I could feel his energy against my skin. It was so much better than the energy I had just taken. I already could tell. Filled with emotion, exciting and new.

I looked down at his hand, and wondered how much I could take without him noticing.

"Mara's been worried about you. We can all tell something's off," Thayer said.

"I'm fine," I scoffed and yanked my arm away from him.

"Sage saw you in the park," Thayer said quietly.

I thought I misheard him. I really wanted to have misheard what he said. I had only been to a park once since I had been here. That was on the hunting trip with Nikki.

I spun on my heel to face him.

"What are you talking about?" I scanned his eyes to see how much information he knew.

"She knows," Thayer said.

"Sage?"

Thayer shook his head. I knew who he meant. Kate knew. Anger flooded through my body, ending in my fists.

I moved to slam a fist against the wall of Lisa's bedroom, but Thayer caught my arm and flung it back too easily. Energy difference or not, he was too strong.

The lights flared on his cuffs and Thayer gritted his teeth.

"You just couldn't wait to tell her, could you? Are you really that desperate to make sure you can have her all to yourself?" The words flew out of my mouth as I rushed toward him.

Thayer grabbed my shirt and tossed me against the wall

by his door. It was almost too quiet to even wake anyone but strong enough to hold me still.

He looked at my eyes, not saying anything as he squinted in the dim light radiating from his metal cuff.

"The calm, composed Kylan I've come to accept wouldn't be punching walls and slinging insults. You're high right now, aren't you?" Thayer asked and dropped his hands from me.

He stepped away and looked at me with understanding eyes. I hated that he knew what I was feeling. I hated how much he could see.

"I'm sorry." I put my hand to my forehead. "I just got a bit carried away."

"I'm not the one who needs an explanation," Thayer said, walking toward his door.

"What's going on out here?" Derek hissed in a whisper. "Cassie and I are trying to sleep."

"Nothing," I said and walked straight to the room with my and Kate's name on it.

I kept my eyes on the floor and away from Derek. I heard Thayer close his door. At least he wouldn't be spilling to anyone else tonight. I turned toward my room and forgot how to move again. I just leaned on it with my shoulder.

Derek's hand hit my shoulder.

I kept facing the door, pressing my forehead into the metal now. He squeezed my shoulder and I bit my lip to keep myself quiet.

"You're slipping," he whispered.

I didn't say anything. He didn't say anything else. I pushed my fist into the door, hearing the metal groan under the force. He kept his hand on me and I remembered what body heat could feel like when it wasn't flowing into me. I remembered it could be different. Tender, comforting.

I finally turned my head enough to make eye contact. He looked exhausted. I'm sure I looked anything but tired.

But he just stared at me, with the quiet kindness that only the rarest version of Derek showed.

I hoped if I opened my mouth that words would come out and make it all better. But they never came. Derek pulled on my shoulder until he had his arms around me.

My first thought was that his energy seemed faded, wispy. But it still sung, purring under his skin. I clamped my teeth together.

"I'm not letting you go," Derek said. "Cassie and I. We're here. We're holding on."

I nodded into his shoulder. Cassie opened the door behind him, with bags under her eyes and a confused smile. She wiped the sleepiness from her eyes and the cuff on her wrist brightened her face. Cassie looked so much like Rachel when she wasn't wearing makeup.

"We love you," she whispered.

I nodded again.

And I remembered Rachel lying there. I remembered my family hobbling out of this lab the first time. We were back here and everyone was holding it together, sloppily, but they were in one piece. Even Kate after everything she'd been through.

Out of all of us, I was the one who was slipping. I was the one with the least likely chance to walk out of here.

Which is where I deserved to be. Alone, on the floor and in pain. I'd left too many other people to die at my hands.

I pulled away from Derek. He didn't stop me when I turned and ducked in the room with my name on it. With our names on it.

When it clicked closed, I fell against it.

My family stood right outside, probably wanting to know

what was wrong with me. Thayer already knew. Sage knew too. I gripped my hair in my hands.

Too many people were finding out. Too many people would be hurting if they knew. I wanted to hide under the floor so no one else could see me. I hated the energy flowing through my body even though I was the one that wanted it.

It was a painful reminder now.

"Kylan?" Kate's voice called in the dark.

I didn't answer. I waited, hoping I would somehow fade away. I heard the blankets on the bed stirring and I sank against the door.

My head rested in my hands. I couldn't bear for her to see me like this. But she was also the only person that could make that ringing noise in my head go away.

Her warm hands found me.

"Are you okay?" she asked so sweetly. I wanted to break at the sound of her tender voice.

She sat next to me, putting her gloved hand at the back of my neck and the other on my chest. In between her hands, I felt the smallest crack of relief.

I took in a breath, already feeling the empty void setting in that usually followed an energy binge.

"No. I'm not."

She pulled me closer to her. My head rested against her chest. She didn't ask for any details, didn't press to know the number of people's energy I now held in my body.

With the pressure of her body against me, her Legend energy burned underneath her skin. The warmth was intoxicating, even if I was already staggeringly satiated.

"I'm sorry," I whispered more to myself than her. I shook my head and leaned away.

Her hands held firm. Her gloved fingers pulled my chin around to face her in the dark. I didn't need to see her eyes to guess they were angry or disappointed. Either one would kill me.

But instead I heard her whisper, "You don't have to be okay."

The energy surged in answer to her. I crumbled against the door, letting my full weight rest. She moved her head closer, and I hoped she couldn't see the tears spilling from my eyes.

She whispered close to my ear, "You just have to breathe. You have to focus. And you have to try to be better. And the next time you feel like this, you breathe, focus, and try. Do that over and over again, until you don't need to think about it anymore."

Her breath tickled my neck but her words pierced inside of me, awoke the good part of me that was buried under so much raging energy and twisting cravings. I felt at home in my own body for those few moments.

"Tonight, just breathe."

With the love of my life holding me up, my determination finally rumbled to the surface. I took a breath and it felt like it fit in all the right places now.

There were no more words between us. No questions, no judgment, just the groundbreaking support that I needed to tether me back to reality.

I was Kylan again. And for a few breaths, that was all she expected me to be. All I could expect me to be. So I didn't push her away or bring her any closer.

She hovered near me, and I let her erase the pain for as long as she was willing.

# CHAPTER
# TWENTY-FIVE

I stirred to consciousness, feeling the bed under my shoulder and expecting to hear Kylan's deep breathing next to me.

"Wake up! Kate!" Kylan's strained voice shouted.

My eyes flew open, already feeling the heat on my hands. I was holding Kylan's wrist in my grasp. The gloves were gone and his energy burned against my skin.

I dropped his hands and shot out of the bed. My legs tripped over the other bed and my back slammed into the far wall.

"What happened?" I asked.

Kylan doubled over, swinging his legs to the floor. His breathing was ragged as he adjusted.

I stared at him, wanting to make it better. Touching him would only make it worse.

"You were talking in your sleep. You kept saying you wanted me over and over. Then you took off your gloves and…you wouldn't let go," Kylan explained.

I looked at the spandex gloves on the floor.

"I'm so sorry," I breathed.

The new energy in my body made me feel like I was floating despite the obvious guilt I should be feeling. My body was replenished and then some. Kylan had told me he had taken too much energy last night, but I hadn't really asked him to elaborate.

Judging by the amount I was feeling and that Kylan was still breathing, he must have been out all night to slowly get that much.

"It's not your fault. Alec said this place was going to affect you." Kylan sat up straight, groaning with the movement. "Guess he was right."

I stared at him wide-eyed. Kylan tried to fake a smile and that only made my head spin more.

I snatched the gloves from the floor and dashed out of the room before he said anything else. I marched up the stairs, ready to get rid of this energy as fast as possible.

Nikki was just leaving a testing room when I made it to the next floor.

"There you are," Nikki said. "Alec was just saying—"

I brushed past her. "I'm here now. Let's get started."

Alec tapped on the tablet in his hands. His eyes darted back and forth. When he looked up, he locked eyes with me.

He must have noticed the wild look in my eyes as I tossed the gloves on the table and walked toward him.

Alec only smiled. "Rough night?"

"None of your business," I snapped at him.

I wanted to pace back and forth because I was so riled up. Really, I wanted to run but I had to force myself to stay still.

"Have you told her about the first test?" Nikki said, closing the door behind her.

I thought about all that time in the lab with him torturing me. Just the sight of his eyes was enough to make my blood boil.

"We've got the biological inventory we needed. Now we have to test your reactions," Nikki explained.

My fists clenched at my sides and I took my breath in short huffs but my eyes never broke away from Alec.

"Translation. I need you to get angry," Alec whispered.

My eyes narrowed on him. "I'm already there."

"Great. Show me." Alec gestured to the machine against the wall.

I stood in the empty space between hanging wires and a monitor hung on the wall near my left shoulder.

Alec surveyed me moving willing toward the machine and smiled. There wasn't a glare cutting enough or a snarl menacing enough to explain how much anger I felt toward him. So much of my pain, discomfort, and sadness was a direct result from him.

He and Nikki placed adhesive monitors on the backs of my hands, my temples, and my chest. The cords hardly bound me, but they made me feel tied down to something.

I took a deep breath. Alec reached his hand forward and adjusted the monitor on my head without breaking eye contact.

Before he moved his hand away, his finger brushed my skin. His energy jolted into my body. My muscles stiffened as my cells eagerly welcomed the crazed energy.

I yanked my face away. The tablet beeped in his hands. Alec looked down at the screen again and smiled.

"That's better," he observed. "Right now, nearly every mental pathway is closed."

"Told you," I confirmed and tried to remain still in the midst of all the wires attached to my skin.

"I said nearly." Alec pulled his eyebrows together, still looking at the screen. "When the mind is experiencing too much anger or pain, it shuts down to focus on fight or flight. Since every Legend or human undergoing the transition serum feels that, we need to replicate it in a perfect test subject. You."

"So, what do I need to do?" I asked.

"You need to get overwhelmed. All-out rage. Anything that would trigger a response strong enough to close down your mind," Alec said.

I just had to look at him. That wicked smile. That perfect lab coat. The way he held himself when he stood too close to me. My ears felt hot and my fists balled at my sides.

"I am," I argued.

"The monitor disagrees. It's either this or we can induce a pain simulation that will force your mind into it anyway." Alec didn't even try to hide the smile playing on his mouth. "Your choice."

"Wouldn't you just love that?" I snarled and shook my head. "I can do this."

"What are you thinking about?" Alec asked.

*You.* Annoying, incessant, and couldn't leave me to think for even a few seconds.

"How much I hate you," I answered.

"Aw, and you don't hate me enough. How sweet," Alec teased.

I kicked a leg forward and it connected with his shin. He grunted and stepped away. I stared at him and tried to get as angry as I could. "What else do you want me to do?"

"Well, you better think of something, because if you don't want me to torture you—" Alec stopped.

He glanced down at the tablet and smiled again before he looked up at me.

"What?" I groaned, not wanting to know the answer.

Alec just stared at me. He turned his head toward Nikki, but kept his eyes on me. I glanced at her, already not liking the idea if it involved her.

"Hey Nikki, come here," Alec said, still watching me.

Nikki hopped off the table and sighed as she sauntered over to us. Alec held out his hand to her as she stepped up to him. He put his hand on the small of her back and looked down at the tablet again.

"Hold this," Alec said as he handed the tablet to her.

"Sure," Nikki replied warily as she gave Alec a look.

I sucked in a breath. He actually handed it off.

I looked back to Alec, expecting him to realize his mistake. Silence infiltrated the room other than errant beeps or whirring sounds from the machines surrounding me. But I should have known, Alec had thought this through.

Alec stared at me again and the mischievous smile of his meant I wouldn't like what I saw next.

Without warning, he tangled his hand in the back of her loose hair and pulled her face toward him. Their lips met and every muscle in my body seized.

He pulled her into him and I stopped breathing. She moved with him so easily. He kissed her harder, faster, and my heart launched like a rocket. My mind completely shut down. I felt it.

Not a single, coherent thought formed, just sheer anger and shock racing through my body.

The tablet in Nikki's hands beeped faster than it had before. Alec broke the kiss and looked down at the screen, still holding her in his hands.

"Now we're getting somewhere." He smiled and grabbed the tablet again.

Nikki stepped away easily, like nothing had happened. Although the look she gave told me she knew exactly what she had done.

The beeps on the machine were coming so close together, I almost couldn't tell them apart.

"Thank you, Nikki," Alec smacked his lips and looked at her.

"Anytime," she said in a dark voice.

She brushed her hair over her shoulder and glanced at me before she walked back to her seat on the table, practically skipping.

"Say it." Alec turned back to me and sighed, waiting for a lecture.

"I don't have anything to say." I shook my head, reaching for the sensors on the backs of my hands.

Back at the mansion, she was the one person he swore he had never touched. The only one I was ever worried about. I knew she had always wanted him, but I never imagined...

"You sure? You've got that look on your face like you just can't wait to say something." Alec smiled.

I just shook my head, not falling for his trap.

Alec glanced down at the tablet, paying attention to the beeps and levels displayed in the screen. The anger built inside of me, almost beyond control.

"Well, then, maybe you should know something else." Alec looked back up at me, moving his face closer.

His breath danced across my face. Nikki smiled in the corner of my gaze. I clenched my fists even tighter.

"That's not the first time I've kissed her," Alec's excited blue eyes stared into mine.

I shouldn't have been jealous. Guilt crept up my back. I should have been happy that Nikki finally had someone show her a speck of affection, but I wasn't.

Any control I had, I lost it.

My stomach twisted in on itself. My chest heaved in hot, angry breaths to fuel the energy building inside of me.

The beeping from the tablet stopped being intermittent, and gave off one steady sound. Alec smiled down at the screen, ignoring me again.

"Got it." Alec touched the screen with his finger before he looked back up at me.

His eyes stared through his eyelashes, his chin still lowered to his chest. An infuriating smirk pulled at the corner of his mouth.

"Nice to know you still care," Alec taunted.

"I don't," I threw back.

Alec shook the tablet in his hands as proof.

"Science doesn't lie." Alec smiled even wider.

My hand shot forward to rip that piece of metal from his grip. The sensors attached to the back of my hand ripped off. Alec yanked the tablet away from me just in time.

"Ah, ah, we're not done yet," he chided as he tucked the tablet in what seemed like a back pocket of his lab coat.

"What else do you need?" I asked.

"Well, that was the first part, where we needed you to get angry, and may I just say, bravo. You nailed it," Alec reminded me.

"And?" I waited.

"That was just a test to see how in control of your emotions you were and to get a baseline." Alec smiled. "We actually need the exact opposite of that."

"Of course you do." I clenched my teeth, mad at myself for falling for it.

"But hey, you did a spectacular job of getting mad at me, baby, so I'm sure you can handle the next part," Alec teased.

"I hate you." I glared back at him.

"I believe you," Alec answered back, reaching to put the sensors back on my hands.

"Don't touch me," I shoved his hands away and replaced the sensors myself.

"Breathe, Mara," Nikki condescendingly coached. "We

need you to let all the barriers down in your mind. You can't do that with steam pouring out of your ears."

My anger flared again as I looked up at her smug, happy face. She wiped a finger across her lip to remind me of the intense kiss that just happened in front of me.

"That might be easier if you two weren't in the room." I moved my gaze back to Alec.

He just chuckled as he pulled the tablet out from his coat again.

"Oh, come on, baby. If we left, your imagination would fill in the blanks with an image far worse than anything you just saw," Alec chided.

He tapped in the next combination of keys. Nikki laughed in a low-pitched, dark tone that made my skin crawl almost more than Alec's laugh.

"Stop talking." I shook my head.

I took slow, steady breaths. I closed my eyes and tried to focus on anything that wasn't Alec and Nikki, or Alec's mouth on Nikki's.

I thought about the reason I was here.

Kylan.

I wanted to be with him. I wanted to be able to touch him again, to hold him in my arms. The sharpness of the anger dulled as images of kind, green eyes came flashing across my mind.

I loved him. He was the source of safety that I needed. With him, I felt like my life wasn't so broken. All the missing pieces of me didn't matter as much when I was with Kylan.

My breathing slowed naturally. I counted the seconds between each one.

"That's good. You're getting close," Alec's voice called through my thoughts.

"Close to what?" Kylan's voice asked.

I hadn't even heard the door. I opened my eyes and saw him in the back of the room, walking toward Alec.

Thayer whispered something in his ear and Kylan shrugged off the hand pressing on his shoulder. I didn't really care what he'd said. Having anyone in this room with me besides Alec and Nikki was a relief.

"Good," I sighed.

"Ah, there you are. Get enough energy to make it through to the end of the day?" Alec teased.

"I'm fine," Kylan answered.

Alec turned around to look at him, sizing him up and down. I noticed the ease of his movement, the lightness in his eyes. He had more energy than he needed. He wasn't quite high yet, but he was so close.

"You look better than fine to me. Now that Mara's here, I thought you would've gone back on your diet by now." Alec turned back to look at me.

"What is he talking about?" I asked Kylan.

"Nothing. While I was here at the lab, I had to convince them I was Isaac. I got used to taking more and more energy every time we went out because Nikki wouldn't ever leave my side." Kylan nodded toward her.

"Guilty." Nikki waved. "Can you blame me though? With that gorgeous body and incredible power, I didn't want to let him out of my sight. But, I mean you know what I'm talking about, right?"

Thayer slid a somehow hateful yet intrigued gaze over to her.

"Adjusting has been harder than I remember." Kylan rolled his shoulders and shoved his hands in his pockets.

"None of this is helping," Alec announced with an annoyed voice.

"What are you trying to do?" Kylan asked.

"The main problem with the serum is that the pain of transition makes the mind shut down before it can penetrate every area. For Lydia, somehow it worked just fine. They either used a gentler way of administering it, or a different serum entirely. Regardless, we need to find out how," Alec answered.

"In other words, maybe you can work your magic and calm her mind enough to get everything to open up?" Nikki suggested, walking back over to Alec.

Kylan took a step away from her and looked up at me.

"Just talk to me," I begged. "Anything to block out their voices."

"Okay," Kylan tentatively said. "I talked to Cassie and Derek this morning. The two of them had been mostly keeping to themselves—you know how they are. Cassie has been more irritable than normal, and Derek is even more protective of all of us now that we're in the lab. But they just left for a break and I think it'll be good for them."

I focused on his voice and paid attention to each breath in and each breath out. I closed my eyes again and felt my body relax, despite the wires tangled around me.

"But honestly, being here, it's not as bad as I thought it was going to be. I mean, don't get me wrong. It's weird seeing Alec every day and Nikki freaks me out," Kylan continued.

I smiled. That sounded like the man that I loved. Honest as can be.

I thought about how nice it was to have him with me this time. The lab wasn't as bad as before. At night, I had a safe, warm bed with Kylan by my side. It was better.

"But, it's all going to be worth it," Kylan said. "When it's all over, you and I can get out of here. As far away from here as you want to be. We'll be free to just be together. The two of us."

I followed the thoughts with him. I could see it. The two of us in a little house somewhere. Honest. Happy. Safe. Everything that I wanted from him.

"Well, with Derek and Cassie, of course. They'd kill me if I left them behind," Kylan laughed.

Thayer cleared his throat. I smiled.

"That's great, Mara. You're almost there." Alec's voice interrupted my thoughts again.

It was a reminder though—a real one. Our life was never going to be as simple as a little house and a little family. Not with Alec alive or the humans forced into submission because of him.

I yearned for a simpler time. A time before I met Alec, when it was just me and my mother. The two of us, together against the world. Even that picture wasn't perfect. As long as the humans hated us, and she was a Level Five. We would always be hunted.

Even my imagination had flaws.

"And, we just lost it," Alec groaned. "Looks like even you can't will your mind to comply."

Emptiness creeped inside of my body, traveling through all of my veins. It was the only thing that was perfectly real. At least for now.

I opened my eyes to see Alec's frustrated gaze looking back at me.

"Interesting. She doesn't love you as much as she hates Alec," Nikki chimed in. She turned to Kylan. "Don't take it personally, gorgeous. You tried."

Thayer jumped in and grabbed Nikki. "I heard there's a beauty pageant in town this week. How about we go snag ourselves a queen or two?"

"Just as long as we don't have to bring your human friend," Nikki drawled, and I could already hear Thayer's argument for Lisa as they left the room.

"What was she talking about?" Kylan asked.

Alec looked up at me. "Mara can explain it to you."

Kylan looked over at me. I shook my head to tell him not now. I peeled the sensors off my body. I could tell him later. I could explain that as much as I loved him, I didn't know if it was everything I would ever want.

I looked at Alec. He was the person standing in between me and utter happiness. I expected him to smirk or rub it in my face. Instead, he just gave me a sad nod. I stared, unsure of how to react.

Kylan helped remove the sensors, careful not to touch any of my skin.

My eyes followed Alec as he left the room with Nikki tailing closely behind him. I hated him more than anyone on the planet. I wanted to be free of him, and yet, I couldn't imagine a life where Alec didn't exist either.

# CHAPTER
# TWENTY-SIX

I rushed to the metal table, looking at the paper charts Alec had left behind of my brain patterns and what pain caused which areas to react.

"I need to figure out what went wrong." I ripped off the last sensor and it left a sting in its place.

Rifling through these papers brought a chill over my skin. I realized how immaculately he had documented my pain when I was trapped here.

"You need to take a break." Kylan shook his head.

I leaned closer to the chart, taking note of the biggest part of my brain that reacted to the agony. I wondered what trial he had done to get that reaction.

"A break?" I scoffed. "I can't just take a break. Every second that your family is in here is another chance for Alec to hurt them. And I can't be here much longer before I lose my mind again. Everything here reminds me…the cage, the tests…I can't. I can't stop until I get what Alec wants."

I waited for Kylan's response. The clever comeback that would put me in my place or the sweet sentiment that would soften my harsh words. I searched the pages for what other functions that biggest part of my brain controlled.

*Maybe I could work it backward?* I wondered as I flipped through the papers.

The sound of a body hitting the tile halted my movement. I spun and looked at Kylan laid out on the floor. He stared up at the ceiling as peaceful, easy breaths made his chest rise and fall.

"What are you doing?" I asked, setting the papers down.

"Taking a break," Kylan smiled and patted the floor next to him. "Wanna join me?"

I laughed. His beautiful smile didn't falter as he looked up at me expectantly. The papers didn't seem so important anymore.

"I should be working." I pulled my hand away from the charts.

"And you shouldn't be lying next to me, staring at the ceiling, doing nothing. Come on." Kylan lowered his voice and his smile changed. "It can be our secret."

"You're impossible." I rolled my eyes and laid myself on the floor next to Kylan's warm body.

"It's a good thing you like me so much." Kylan smiled and looked back up at the ceiling, in between the fluorescent lights that hung above us.

I moved my hand closer to his before I realized I didn't have my gloves on and pulled back. Kylan didn't look down, but I knew he saw it based on the grimace that pulled at his lips.

"Sorry," I muttered.

"Can I tell you something?" Kylan asked, a little too abruptly.

I looked over at him, waiting for him to answer his own question. He stared at the ceiling instead of me.

"Being here," Kylan started, a blank look on his face. "It's starting to get to me. Being around Alec again, and all of the energy, the Legends, everything. I catch myself itching for more all the time."

"What would happen if you gave in?" I asked.

"It would be fine at first. I'd be high, and maybe a little too happy." Kylan laughed like he remembered the feeling.

"But it won't stay that way?" I clarified.

Kylan's smile fell. His mouth closed and thinned into a line. He shook his head back and forth, making his longer hair shuffle with the movement.

"I'll start rationalizing. I start hiding how much I'm consuming from other people. When it gets that far, human energy isn't good enough anymore," Kylan said. "I become something worse than the Shadow that Alec is now."

"Hey." I waited for him to look at me. "You aren't Alec. No matter what happens, you'll always have that desire to be good and that's what I care about."

Kylan looked at each of my eyes. His breathing had stopped as he waited for me to turn on him, to look at him with the same disdain that I look at Alec with. I kept a soft smile on my face until Kylan finally believed me.

"Thank you," Kylan whispered, his voice breaking.

I nodded and smiled wider.

Kylan turned on his side to face me. His index finger dragged along my long-sleeved shirt. The fabric didn't stop me from feeling his body heat.

"Can I tell you something else?" Kylan raised his eyebrows at me.

I paused too long before answering. His face was closer to mine than it had been in a while. His hand had reached my shoulder and turned around to go back down my arm. My entire body ached as I waited to see what his hand would do next.

"Y-yes," I stammered, focusing my eyes again.

Kylan chuckled as his eyes roamed before settling on mine. He tilted his head to the side and my stomach knotted.

"It feels weird calling you Kate," Kylan said, a serious look in his eyes. "You're not the same person that I met. You've changed so much in the time that I've known you."

The entire room shifted out of my view. I saw Kylan's somber expression and nothing else. My breaths became shallower as I waited to hear anything else other than what I thought was coming.

I turned my gaze away and stared at the bright lights above me. I wanted to be anywhere but right here.

"I'm sorry," I muttered.

Kylan kept his hand on me, but it had stopped moving. It rested on my upper arm, keeping me painfully aware that he was still almost touching me.

"Me too," Kylan sighed. "I had a pretty big crush on Kate."

The words sliced through the air and straight into my body. Lines of stinging pain ran everywhere as I kept my eyes away from Kylan.

But what else could I answer? "I can't bring her back." I winced.

I finally dared to look over at him. A tear spilled from my eye and ran along my cheekbone back to my ear. Kylan looked at me and took a breath.

He moved his hand to my hair, it was the familiar dark curls that he was used to. He twisted the brown hair around his fingers.

"I know," Kylan muttered. "It isn't who you are anymore. It's who you pretended to be."

"No, it wasn't—" I started.

"Just like I pretended not to be an Extractor. Or even how I pretended to be human when I first met you," Kylan rushed.

The rest of my words stopped in my throat. I stared at him, unable to care about anything else at the moment.

"You may not be Kate anymore," Kylan smiled. "But the longer I know you, the more I catch myself falling for Mara."

"What?" I asked, a smile distorting the sound of the word.

Kylan paused and took a deep breath. He stared at me like I was the only thing holding him on the ground.

"I'm Kylan Stone, son of the man who created the Shadows and a powerful Extractor with little self-control. But I love you," he whispered.

He smiled down at me and I could hear the icy protection around my heart cracking. I turned to sit up on my side so our faces were at the same height.

I looked at his eyes and watched as my reflection changed. Within his light green irises, my hair shortened and brightened to the shiny blond I had always known. My face changed from round and innocent to sharply featured and dangerous.

I smiled when I looked at myself now in his shining eyes.

"I'm Mara Hayes, daughter of the Level Five and former Shadow. I've killed people, I love stealing energy way more than I should, and I've been trained to never trust anyone." I shook my head. "But despite all of that, I find myself in love with you."

I had never felt so honest and open. I wasn't Kate anymore. My time in the lab under Alec's control had taught me that. I was Mara. I always had been.

But now, Kylan knew everything. He saw all of me. When

I looked like Mara, the person he should despise. The Shadow, the murderer, the liar, the manipulator.

When he looked at all of me, he smiled.

"It's nice to meet you, Mara."

Kylan lifted a hand to my face. I forgot about everything, about all the rules, and so did he.

His hand moved through my hair to the back of my neck, pulling me forward. His lips touched mine and energy burst between us. His mouth moved like he was racing against time itself to kiss me.

I reached for him, pushing him onto his back. My hands stayed on his shoulders as I kissed him. A tingle ran all the way from my mouth to the tips of my toes.

When I drew in a breath, a shudder moved through me. I wanted more of him, with every touch of his lips and flame of his energy.

I tangled my fingers through his hair that had grown out. We pulled each other closer. He held me tight enough to him that I could barely breathe, but I didn't care.

"Mara," Kylan muttered against my mouth.

My heart soared. I hadn't even known I had been waiting for him to say my real name, but when he did I forgot all about Kate Martin. A hazy cloud formed in my mind; nothing mattered except Kylan lying beneath me.

His hands fell away from my body, leaving me enough room to finally take a full breath.

"Mara," he said again.

This time I heard the pain in his voice. I jerked my head back to see his cringing eyes. His energy.

I yanked my hands away from him and stood faster than I could blink. He lay on the floor, catching his breath and staring at the ceiling again. His eyes fluttered open and closed as he rolled onto his side. The cuff on his wrist lit dimly with his movement.

"I'm so sorry." I shook my head and pulled my hands to my mouth.

"Ugh." Kylan shook his head. "That really hurts."

"I shouldn't have touched you for that long. I forgot... I'm...I'm," I stammered, backing away toward the door of the room.

"Don't." Kylan smiled weakly. "Don't blame yourself."

I spun and left the room, not able to stand another second seeing Kylan in pain. I caught Lisa in the hallway and told her to go get Kylan. That was all I could do to take care of him.

Once I saw her enter the room, I ran. I sprinted through the hallways, trying to get as far from him as I could. No tears came anymore. I wasn't sad or longing for him.

I was angry. The rage ripped through my core as I focused on the one person that had put me in this position.

I narrowed my eyes and kept running.

# CHAPTER
# TWENTY-SEVEN

My hand shoved against the steel door. The lights were on, and that was the only thing I noticed before I rushed in the room. My hands flew to my hair. I wanted to rip something apart.

I lunged forward to the table in front of me and flipped it over. The miscellaneous papers, syringes, and everything else scattered to the floor.

"Someone's in a mood," Alec's nonchalant voice said.

I whipped my head over to him. He leaned forward to look into a microscope, the light shining against his perfect blue eyes. I clenched my fists even harder when he flicked his eyes up to me.

"Sorry, didn't realize you were busy," I snarled.

"Don't apologize for something you can't control," Alec answered without looking up.

He grabbed another slide and loaded it into the microscope.

"Yeah. None of this is my fault, right? I'm not the one that created this trap in the first place." I seethed with anger and walked toward him.

"Right," Alec answered, only glancing at me.

I grabbed the nearest stool and tossed it across the room and into the wall. Alec didn't even flinch at the sound.

"I'm not the one that made it impossible for me to touch the people I care about without hurting them," I growled.

My hands reached for the next table in the room. I flipped it over with one hand. I ripped off one of the metal legs and shot it into the glass cabinet behind the table. The shards flew in every direction around where the metal bar lodged into the back of the cabinet.

"I'm not the one that is so obsessed with power that he can't even let the girl he loves be happy!" I shouted.

Alec still didn't look up at me. My pain wasn't enough for him. The energy scorched through my body, begging me to show him the pain I felt. Without thinking, a familiar, cold dagger formed in my hand.

I gripped the handle of the blade and threw it straight for Alec's head. He dodged the blade at the last second, and turned to look at it stuck in the wall just behind his skull.

He grabbed the blade from the wall and pulled it out, turning it over in his hands. I saw a flash of fear in his eyes before he looked up at me.

"I see Kylan told you my story about this dagger," Alec tapped the top of the blade against his fingers.

His eyes looked at me with the look of a little boy who just got caught in a lie. The sharp sadness filled his expression. He walked around the table and toward me slowly, like he was afraid to get too close to the person that threw a dagger at him.

"He didn't need to," I answered, narrowing my eyes. "I lived it with you. I watched your wounds heal every day."

"And you chose to use it against me." Something dark and raw rested in his gaze. "That's something I would have done."

"I don't want to be like you." I shook my head.

Alec looked me up and down, watching my breaths. His gaze softened even more as he stared up at me with those big blue eyes.

"Baby, you already are." He smiled.

Something about that smile ignite a flaring rage inside of my chest. My entire body launched forward without me thinking. Alec stepped aside just before I could grab his shirt.

"You're wrong," I huffed as I whipped around to face him again.

"Are you sure about that?" Alec smiled, waiting for me to come at him again.

"No," I grumbled.

I should have stopped myself and taken the high road. I should have bottled my anger and left the room. Instead, I just froze in place, deciding if I wanted to give in to the sweet revenge banging inside my mind.

"Come on, baby. Do your worst," Alec whispered.

My fumbling control of my anger snapped. My eyes narrowed on my target and my body carried me forward. I raised my hands to wrap around his throat.

"Stop calling me that!" I screamed.

Alec's gaze ignited at the sound of my rage. His hands opened, ready to catch me. I darted forward, forgetting the dagger in his grip. Alec ducked underneath my arms and spun around behind me.

One of his arms wrapped around my waist, yanking me back toward his body. The other hand lifted the dagger blade to my throat.

"There's the Mara I remember," Alec whispered into my ear.

His hot breath sent shivers down my neck. My hands flew

up to his arm, pulling back his sleeve and clasping my hands around his open skin.

"The Mara you remember couldn't do this." I smirked as the blade shifted against my neck.

His energy sparked against my hands and raced through my body.

"That's why I love you. You're always surprising me." Alec pulled the blade away from my neck and spun me around to face him.

"Be honest," I said, swallowing around the lingering pain on my neck. "When all of this is over, when you have your Level Five power and the humans are all cowering at your feet. What do you want then?"

Alec paused, waiting for me to explain my thought further.

"Don't ask me something you don't want the answer to." Alec shook his head.

"I want the answer." I narrowed my eyes.

"Fine." Alec smirked. "After I have everything, I guess I could either go for an ice cream sundae or drain a high school cheerleader. Both of those sound delicious."

He stepped forward, running the dagger up my body until it reached my neck again. I didn't move as the blade moved from my shirt to my skin. I only balled my fists at my side as I looked at his smile.

"That's not what I meant, and you know it," I glared.

"Then, ask me your real question. The one you're too scared to ask," Alec encouraged.

He turned the dagger on its side and laid it against my collarbone. The cool metal pressed against my skin and I felt it with every breath.

"Once you have the power, will you let me go?" I asked, trying to steady my heaving breaths.

The energy in my body screamed for me to move, to run, to rip the dagger from his hands. My mind told me to get as far away from this room as possible. But my feet stayed frozen in place.

"There it is." Alec smiled. "Before I answer that, I need to know something."

"That's not fair. I asked my question first," I scoffed, grabbing the dagger.

Alec shrugged, still holding on. "Didn't know you played by the rules."

I wrapped my fingers around the blade and twisted it out of his grip. I turned the tip of the blade to point directly at his heart. The one place I could stab that might actually kill him. He stood perfectly still.

"For once in your life, just be honest! There's no other way for you to get around this. Just answer. The. Question." I glared into his everlastingly glib gaze.

Alec leaned forward, forcing the dagger to pierce through his shirt and his skin. He stared at me, his eyes wincing from the pain.

"You want to know if you'll ever be free of me. If after I have all the power I want, if I'll stop chasing you?" he whispered.

"Yes." I nodded.

His hands wrapped around mine. Instead of pushing the dagger away from him, he pulled it deeper into his chest. The blood trickled down his dark shirt.

"Do you want me to stop?" Alec asked.

The dagger was moving too close to his heart. It could have punctured a lung by now. I could end Alec's life.

I looked up into his pained gaze and knew exactly what he was doing. I saw the worry, the amount of trust he had in me.

"The day I let you go is the day I no longer have a purpose for living. So, the answer depends on you," Alec gasped in pain and he turned the dagger, opening the wound further.

"W-what are you saying?" I asked, not wanting to hear the answer.

"If you want me gone, kill me. It's my life, or yours," Alec said through clenched teeth.

I thought of all the pain he caused me, all the torture endured at his hands. I wanted him gone.

*Didn't I?*

The longer I held the blade in my hands and the more blood poured out of him, the more I wasn't sure. I looked at the man standing in front of me. I was the one source of goodness in his life. He was the allure of darkness in mine.

I saw his desperate gaze and I knew my choice.

I released my grip from the dagger, and Alec's hands let mine slide away from the handle. He pulled the dagger out of his chest, the yellow energy rushing to close the wound and heal him.

I didn't move away from him. I only dropped my hand by my side, stained with dribbles of Alec's blood. I looked down at the ground, feeling the shame of my decision already.

Alec lifted his hand under my chin, pulling my face upward. My eyes reluctantly met his. He moved his hand from my face to reach down for mine. He lifted it gently and placed the dagger in my open palm. His hand moved back to my face, spreading the warm blood on my cheek.

Alec was the most broken person I had ever known. He was the Legend who had been ripped apart the most. Other than one.

Me.

Alec looked into my eyes and used one hand to tuck a hair behind my ear and the other to tighten my grip on the dagger.

"When you're ready to end my life. I will let you go," Alec whispered.

A tear stung the corner of my eye. As twisted and malicious as he was, I couldn't kill him. I hated him. I wanted him dead. I just wasn't strong enough to do it myself.

"Why?" I asked. "Why can't you just leave? Just bow out gracefully. Why is that so hard?"

"For the same reason you won't shove that dagger in my chest." Alec leaned forward and kissed my forehead.

A soft sob shuddered through my chest. I clutched the dagger in my hand, desperately wishing I had the courage to put an end to all of this. As Alec's lips connected to my skin, his energy flew into my body again. It was softer this time, kinder. Everything I wished Alec could have been.

"The choice is yours, Mara." Alec rested his forehead against mine.

The dagger shook in my grip. I wanted to kill him. I just couldn't, not when I understood him more than anyone else around me.

"Now, if you'll excuse me." Alec touched the still-bleeding wound. "I'm suddenly in need of energy."

He turned and left the room, trying not to limp around the pain. I watched him take every step. Alec turned and looked at me, waiting. He always did know me so well.

"I need you to promise. If I'm willing to kill you, then you'll leave forever," I said, loud enough that he could hear me at the door.

Alec's smile still didn't look weak despite the blood dripping down his hand and his slightly hunched-over body.

"I promise," Alec nodded.

He closed the door behind him, and left me alone with the worst thoughts possible. Alec left the decision to me. I was the only one keeping all of us in this never-ending cycle of torture. I let myself fall to the floor, landing on my knees. I should kill him. I should want to.

But I remembered the little boy that walked into my room while my mother was being killed on the other side of the wall.

*I curled up in the corner by the bedside dresser, hoping no one would see me. I heard footsteps, too soft to scare me. My sobs were the only sound in the room. I looked up and my quivering mouth stilled for a breath.*

*A little boy came around the corner. He didn't look much older than me. His dark blue eyes reminded me of a darker version of my own.*

*"Father," he called. "I found her."*

*I looked around, but I couldn't see past the boy. I should have been scared, but the little boy smiled. He walked slowly to me. He sat. I didn't budge. The boy reached his hand out and looked up at me with trusting, hopeful, intrigued eyes.*

*I took it. Our tiny hands held each other as the rest of our worlds spiraled out of our control. A woman's scream came from the other room. I already knew who it was. Hot tears filled my eyes as I wanted to sink back farther into my corner.*

*The boy held onto my hand relentlessly. I looked over to him as he stared at the floor in front of him. Those dark eyes turned sad. Just before he looked up to me, a tear dropped from his eye onto the old wooden floor.*

*I held him and he held me. Both of us awaited what came around the corner next.*

For that one moment and centuries after, Alec was everything I needed. He didn't want this life at the start. Neither did I.

The difference now was that I didn't want it anymore and

he did. But as much as I wanted to blame him, I couldn't. My heart crashed in my chest.

I hated him. But I also loved him. I wondered what he could possibly do to push me to kill him, if he hadn't done it already.

I took comfort in one final thought.

Alec always kept his promises.

# CHAPTER
# TWENTY-EIGHT

*Kylan*

I needed energy and I needed Lisa to not be around when I took it. I couldn't take her looks of disappointment. That look from anyone would kill me.

"Trust me, I can make it the rest of the way," I repeated.

"Really? Show me," Lisa challenged.

I staggered for a moment but used every muscle in my legs to catch myself in time to stand up. I still wasn't standing straight, but close enough.

"See. Fine." I smiled.

"I don't see what the big deal is. Thayer wouldn't let me go out with him and you're trying to shove me away too." Lisa crossed her arms in front of her.

She was a little different after spending some time at the mansion. Not coarse, but definitely more assertive.

I knew why I was pushing her away. But all I could hear was the roaring in my ears and my body screaming for me to get energy. It had taken every ounce of self-control to not grab for her energy when she helped me up.

I shook my head and turned toward the door.

"I need to do this on my own," I said.

It was barely a good-enough excuse, but at least Lisa took it. She spun around and left the room without another word. I finished walking toward the front door.

Each move sent pain shivers through my body. I reached for the door but stopped when Alec came around the corner, clutching his stomach.

The hunched-over position looked a lot like mine, but Alec had bloodstains on his hand and shirt.

"What happened to you?" I asked, still feeling a little dizzy from the lack of energy.

Alec looked down at his stomach and smiled.

"I won an argument." He shrugged, and then tightened his grip on his stomach.

"With who?" I stiffened.

I looked around in a futile hope that I could see Derek and Cassie walking around. If Alec went after someone, I knew it would be them first.

"Relax, your precious *siblings* are safe." Alec smiled.

"How did you—" I started.

"Even after a couple centuries, it's still so easy to read your face. Though it doesn't look like you have much energy to keep me out of your head anyway." Alec looked me up and down.

"You're one to talk." I nodded to him, still not wanting to walk so Alec could see all the pain I was in.

"Mara do that to you?" Alec asked, his eyes looking at me too long.

"Shut up." I managed to take a few steps without looking too pathetic.

He laughed and walked up behind me. I flinched when he put an arm around my shoulder.

"Let's go get you some more energy then." Alec smiled.

"With you? No," I edged.

Alec took his arm off my shoulder and reached for the door. He bit his lip to stop whatever sounds the pain wanted him to make.

"We both need it. What's the worst that could happen?" Alec asked, propping the door open with his foot.

"You could rub off on me," I scoffed.

I was about to tell him to leave. But I saw the agony on his face and blood on his hand.

And at least I knew he would be the last person to judge me for the energy I wanted.

"You should be so lucky." Alec laughed and followed me out the door.

The run to the town was long and painful for both of us. Alec's wound had reopened by the time we got there, but that quickly changed once the first human girl saw him and ran up to see if everything was okay.

He thanked her by leaving her dead body in the nearest alley.

But that wasn't what bothered me. When Alec walked back up to me, moving easily and finally having lifted his other hand from his abdomen, he looked different.

He seemed more normal and less villain-like than I had ever seen him.

I shook my head and tried to focus on all of the terrible things Alec had done. But all of that faded away when I thought about how easily he had killed someone. It was simple, thoughtless for him.

He stood taller, his injury healed and a new smile on his face.

"Now, let's get you fixed up, huh?" Alec slapped my shoulder, sending pain through my back.

"I'm not killing anyone," I said through gritted teeth.

"You don't have to." Alec shrugged, already setting his sights on the next human girl.

The girl had dark hair tied back into a ponytail. She had her eyes set on her phone until she rounded the corner and looked up at the two of us.

"I'll finish this one off when you're done," Alec whispered to me.

The girl saw Alec's blood. That and his looks must have been a magnet for any concerned stranger. I didn't hate him for how easy it was. He had nothing to lose by luring one person in further. The lack of guilt made him free.

"Can you help me?" Alec asked the girl, moving his bloodied hand back to his stomach and doubling over.

"What happened?" The girl's hands fluttered over Alec. "Are you okay? You need a hospital."

"Actually," Alec winced, looking up at her. "Would you mind helping my brother?"

The girl looked over at me. At the most, I looked tired to her, but Alec's wound made it look like he was dying.

"He doesn't need help. You do." The girl shook her head and put her hands on Alec's shoulders.

Alec stood up perfectly straight, dropping his hand. The girl gasped and took a step back.

"You have no idea how right you are. But for now, my brother's a little hungry." Alec grabbed her arms and spun her around to face me.

"Whoa, w-what are you doing?" The girl shoved back into Alec to get away from me.

Me. I was the person she wanted to get away from.

Her energy spiked in her body. Every nerve was on high alert. My body shrank into nothing in the presence of such warm, vibrant energy.

"Alec, this isn't how I do things," I said and my mouth went dry.

"Maybe not." He grinned and walked the girl closer to me.

Her energy taunted me. "But your body needs it. Everything Mara stripped from you can be put back. All it takes is one little touch."

"No, no, no. Stop. Don't touch me," the human pled, flailing her arms as much as she could under Alec's grip.

"Hey." Alec smashed his mouth to her ear and the girl froze. "My brother's gonna take your energy. It won't hurt a bit. But if you keep moving, I'll crack a few of your bones before he gets the chance."

The girl stilled into a statue. The only movement was her trembling lip and shuddering breaths.

"Go on, Kylan." Alec nodded before he shoved the girl forward. "Take it."

Her body tumbled into mine. I grabbed her arms to stop her from falling, and her energy raced into my body without even thinking. I needed it, and that desire took over before I could stop it.

Once her energy flowed through me, I didn't want to pull away. My fingers spread across the skin on her arms. I tried to ignore Alec smiling in the background.

The girl fell harder into me, her knees no longer holding her up. That was enough to snap me back to reality and I stopped pulling her energy.

The pain had been dulled enough for me to stand up straight. I held the girl a little more carefully, reminding myself that she was a person and I was killing her.

"You don't want the rest?" Alec asked, crossing his arms in front of his bloody shirt.

"I'm fine." I clenched my jaw and held the girl awkwardly in my arms. Her heart was still beating. Her energy still flowed. And I still wanted it.

"Well, if you won't kill her, I will." Alec stepped forward and grabbed for the girl.

"No." I pulled the girl away from him.

She was more like an object in my arms than a person. I looked down at the back of her head, her face pointed toward the ground.

"Come on, you killed people not too long ago. Can't you still feel what that last energy is like?" Alec asked.

"I did that because you forced me to. If I hadn't it would've blown my cover." I narrowed my eyes at him.

"I already knew." Alec shrugged.

"You knew? And you still made me do it anyway?" I asked.

My hands gripped the girl even harder. Her soft arms formed around each of my fingers and all I could think about was her energy thrumming through her body.

I shook my head and focused on Alec.

"I just wanted to see how far you'd go to keep it up. Gotta say, I was impressed at your commitment," he said.

Alec smiled and stepped closer to me and the girl. He ran a finger through her hair. When I didn't move, he reached down and took her from my arms. He lifted her head up so she was facing me.

"But I didn't force you. Just like I'm not forcing you now," Alec said easily.

"You never told Mara that I killed while I was here." I stared at him, trying not to look at the human. "Why not?"

"Wrong question." Alec shook his head. "You want to know if I'll tell her after this little outing."

I waited. Alec stared ahead at me as he touched the girl's neck with his hand. Her energy swirled around the tips of his fingers.

"What you should be worried about is this human. I'll kill her in a few seconds if I keep my hand right here." Alec lowered the rest of his palm, touching more of her skin.

"Let her go," I started, but even I didn't know how to end that sentence.

"If you want her, then stop me." Alec smiled, moving his hand along her neck.

All the thoughts cleared out of my head. I was left with nothing. Nothing but the sound of my heartbeat racing, and her heartbeat fading.

I reached forward and Alec lifted his hand from her neck. I didn't stall to test him further. The girl was going to die no matter what. Her final energy sparked into the palms of my hands.

My entire body buzzed with utter relief.

"Welcome back, brother." Alec smiled.

The girl slipped and fell to my feet. I looked ahead at Alec, hating the smug look on his face. But the energy didn't make me want to kill another human. It just made me want to kill a Legend.

The energy I wanted the most was the one I swore to myself I would never take. But every time Mara touched me, I thought about it. Kissing her made me think about it more.

I shook my shoulders and tried to focus on something else, other energy maybe. But I couldn't shake the feeling of wanting Legend energy.

And the only one I could see was Alec.

# CHAPTER
# TWENTY-NINE

It was almost an hour before anyone found me in the lab room. That gave me enough time to get Alec's blood off my hands and face.

But no matter what I tried to change or clean or destroy, I couldn't shake the sound of his heart nearly stopping and me dropping that dagger.

"There you are," Lisa sighed as she opened the door.

I hadn't moved from my kneeling position on the floor. I had hoped some desire to do anything would come, but it never did.

I reluctantly looked up at Lisa. She held the door open for Cassie, who came rushing behind her.

"Kylan said you...Anyway, he made it out okay, but I wanted to come find you." Lisa came and knelt down beside me.

"Are you okay?" Cassie asked, her voice softer than it normally sounded.

"Yeah, I'm fine." I shifted, preparing my lie. "I'm just struggling to adjust back to being here."

"I'm sorry." Lisa rubbed her hand on my arm.

"Yeah, me too. I mean, if that's what was actually wrong with you," Cassie added, still standing.

"What?" Lisa asked up to her.

Sometimes I really hated Cassie.

"No, no, she's right." I hung my head. "I just...I thought things would be different by now. I thought Kylan and I would be perfectly happy and that I could chalk this entire lab up to a bad dream. But it's all still here, all still the same."

"Now, you're talking." Cassie knelt on the floor next to me, taking each movement slower than usual.

"Sometimes change isn't all it's cracked up to be either." Lisa shrugged.

I turned to look at her. She glanced around the room to avoid my gaze. I reached a hand toward her and she looked down just in time to take it.

"I guess I shouldn't be complaining." I smiled at her.

"That's not what I meant."

"Hey, you've both gone through a lot over the last little while. But the important thing is that you don't have to go through it alone." Cassie put a hand on each one of us.

"You know what we need?" I smiled. "We need something exciting to look forward to. Something that has nothing to do with what happens here."

"I like that idea." Lisa smiled. "What about someone's birthday? Maybe we could—"

"Uh, birthdays? No, that's not—Oh, I've got it!" Cassie patted my leg. "New Dec."

It was perfect. The party, the music, the food, the dancing. I could see all of it now, even if it was under the Shadows' roof. It was an event every Legend could appreciate.

"What's that?" Lisa asked.

One more thing to explain about our people, now Lisa's

people too. "Since Legends age slower than humans, a new year isn't as important to us."

"So instead, we celebrate the turn of a decade," Cassie finished excitedly.

"New Dec, I get it." Lisa smiled. "But that already happened?"

"Pssh." Cassie waved a hand at her. "Close enough. And we never really celebrated anyway. We'll just pick a day and party at midnight then."

"I like the way you think." I smiled at her.

"Okay, I'll start working on the details and what time we want to celebrate. Lisa, could you maybe—um...I think I hear Derek yelling," Cassie paused, listening.

"Is he okay?" I asked, glancing at the door.

"Ah." Cassie dismissed my concern. "He's probably just complaining about how there aren't enough windows or his sheets aren't a high-enough thread count. He's a little high maintenance sometimes."

"That's ironic, coming from you," I blurted.

Cassie swatted a hand at me, but I leaned into Lisa just in time. We both laughed as Cassie left the room, slamming the door behind her for emphasis.

"Should we go see what the commotion is about?" I looked at Lisa and nodded toward the door.

"Actually, I wanted to talk to you about something." Lisa wrung her hands and I noticed the cuff on her wrist. Guilt tugged in my chest.

"What is it?" I asked.

"I know I shouldn't be so worried about this, but..." she started.

"But what? You can tell me anything now," I smiled at her.

"I haven't heard from Chase. I've left messages. I just kinda thought he would have said something by now." Lisa stared at the floor.

"I'm sorry." I put an arm around her.

"Am I an idiot for thinking that we can somehow still..." Lisa asked, too scared to finish the sentence.

"Love makes people do crazy things." I shook my head. "It kept me from telling Kylan I was a Shadow. It still makes it impossible for me to really hate Alec. Sometimes, it's not fair what you get stuck with."

Even I was shocked at how much I had just said. With Lisa being a Legend, it was so much easier with her. She put both of her arms around me, holding onto me like I was the only thing keeping her upright.

"Yeah, maybe you're right." Lisa nodded. "But still, my other option is a Shadow and I don't think—"

"Thayer?" I said slowly.

"What? No." Lisa's mouth fell open. "He's...I mean he's like really good-looking and he's actually pretty nice. But I was joking. He's a Shadow."

I shrugged. "So am I."

"No, I mean, yes. But that's different." Lisa pointed at me, her finger shaking slightly.

"I know." I looked down at her wavering hand, a little confused at why this was starting such a reaction.

"I just...I have an idea of the kind of stuff he's done, that he still does. How can I be okay with any of that?" Lisa asked.

The fact she was asking that question meant she wanted to be okay with it. I wasn't sure I was ready for Lisa to be subjected to Thayer in all his glory. I know he wouldn't hurt her intentionally, but they were different.

One wrong move and he could break her, even with how strong she had become.

But I also thought of Thayer, if he actually fell for someone after all his centuries of living. And if that someone rejected him because of who he had become as a Shadow. I shuddered.

Neither sounded like a good option.

"Ugh." Lisa let her head fall in her hands. "I wish nothing had ever changed."

"I wish everything could change." I laughed a painful, sad giggle that Lisa reciprocated.

We held each other, sitting on the cold floor. At least for those few seconds, I was content. The world had stopped spinning long enough for me to catch my breath.

"Hey, this life isn't all bad." I pulled away from her. "You'll see how much fun we can have at New Dec. Cassie will make sure of that."

"It's not gonna be like the Shadow party, is it?" Lisa shied away.

"No." I shook my head vigorously and she relaxed. "It won't be anything like that. This will be a Rogue party."

"Rogues?" Lisa asked. "There's so many things I don't know."

"Well, you're new. A Rogue is just something that Thayer always called Legends who aren't Shadows like him. It kinda caught on."

"Why are you still so close to him?" Lisa asked. "He's... I don't know...not good?"

I laughed as I thought about everything that Thayer was.

"I know you didn't have the best introduction to him." I looked at her. "His morals may be way off base, but he is the most loyal and self-sacrificing person I've met."

"He's always gonna want to be a Shadow, won't he?"

I thought about her question. She may be right—Thayer may never change. But he had gone from blindly following Alec to becoming a king of devoted followers. He had grown a lot over the last little while.

But he was still a Shadow King nonetheless.

"I wouldn't put anything past him at this point." I shook my head. "I know Thayer likes his life the way it is. But, as you know, people can change."

"Yeah." She smiled. "I guess you're right."

I wanted to ask her why she wanted to know so much about Thayer. I started to wonder if the doe eyes had not just been all on his part. Before I got the chance, I heard a voice shout from where Cassie had left.

It wasn't a shout anymore. It was a scream.

Any thoughts of Lisa or Thayer or anything else vanished because I recognized the voice. I ran toward Kylan as fast as I could.

# CHAPTER
# THIRTY

*Kylan*

I had just sauntered into the room, rolling my shoulders as the energy still mixed with my blood. Alec followed behind me slowly. But I wasn't expecting Derek anxiously pacing before he laid eyes on me, his breath already coming in short huffs.

"It's been hours," Derek accused.

"Aw, Kylan didn't say he had a curfew," Alec mocked Derek as he rested his arm on my shoulder.

"You need to back off." Derek narrowed his eyes at Alec, fidgeting with his metal cuff.

"Why? Jealous of how much time I've been spending with my brother?" Alec asked.

"Alec, don't—" I started.

"Ah come on, your *friend* can't have a little fun." Alec poked a finger into Derek's shoulder.

"Friend?" Derek raised an eyebrow as his mouth tightened into a line.

"Hey, hey, come on, let's go—" I stepped between Alec and Derek.

"Yeah, friend. You know, a person that gets dragged along and isn't related by blood," Alec insisted.

"I've been more of a brother to him in the last century than you've ever been," Derek snarled.

"And yet," Alec smiled, "I'm the one he wants to spend all this time with."

"Stop this." I turned and held both of my hands against Alec.

He just smiled past me. "I'm not the one that started it."

I turned and looked at Derek, who was already fuming out of his ears. He shook his head at me with a look that told me he wanted to pummel someone.

"Derek, you know the rules. If we don't go after him, he won't come after us," I explained slowly.

But he ignored me and shook his head. "You're not seeing this, are you?"

"Please, be a little more specific," Alec drawled.

"Ever since you came in here, you started acting differently. Cassie and I can tell. Even Lisa can see it." Derek leaned closer to my face. "Don't you think it's possible that he's not targeting her. That he's actually aiming to manipulate you?"

"Don't be ridiculous. I'm still the same person you've always known me to be." I shook my head at him.

"Staying out later and later. Avoiding me and Cassie." Derek grabbed my face and forced me to look at him. He could see the raw energy in my eyes. "Coming back higher every time."

"Get off me." I shoved him away. "I can handle this."

"What? You think it's a coincidence what's happening to you? He's playing you." Derek shoved a finger in my chest.

I leaned into him. "I don't care what Alec is trying to do. Mara made a specific deal that we can't touch him."

I didn't know why I was defending Alec. Part of me worried he might give details of our hunt to Derek, but even Alec wouldn't waste precious information like that on someone he didn't perceive as a threat.

Derek backed away as he stared, dark and disappointed. I turned to face Alec, who had a smug grin that made me want to smack him. Derek remained at my side, even if he was struggling to look at me.

"Didn't mean to cause strife in the *family*." Alec smiled.

The anger stirred in my body. I wanted to scream at him to back off. Derek was too important to me to let Alec disparage him. My hands clenched uselessly at my sides.

"I promised her," I breathed.

It was a lame excuse, and Derek knew it. I turned to walk out of the room, to find Mara. When I noticed that Derek wasn't following me, I turned back around a little too late.

"Well, she's not my girlfriend," Derek seethed just before he threw a punch across Alec's smiling face.

My breath seized in my chest as Alec's body twisted to the side. Instead of a sound of pain coming from Alec, he laughed like a person who just got what he wanted.

"You know, I had my money on the little redhead breaking the rule first." Alec rubbed his jaw. "After all, how many forced flashback nightmares can someone take before they snap. Turns out, a lot."

Derek froze. "You did what—?"

"Alec don't." I stepped forward, hands raised. "You promised Mara you wouldn't hurt us. What will she think?"

I hated using her against him, only because I knew it worked so well in the past. Whatever she'd want, he'd give. But this time, he was already too excited. His eyes never moved from Derek. They only narrowed in on his target.

"You really saying you don't want to hurt me for what happened in the city a little while ago? Or for your little wife tossing and turning all night?" Alec looked between us.

I didn't move and thankfully, neither did Derek.

"Although, it doesn't really matter." Alec brushed a finger on the fading red mark across his cheek. "I promised not to hurt anyone unless they came after me. Something you should know about me, brother," Alec cooed. "I always keep my promises."

With that, the cuff on Derek's wrist went dark.

It blocked him from using his power. But it also kept Alec out. Nikki walked in the room, holding the small remote in her hand, and my stomach dropped.

Derek's hands flew to his head as he screamed. The wailing cry echoed down the sleek halls.

Nikki smiled at Alec as he stared down at Derek, amused.

"No!" I shouted, rushing to Alec.

My cuff went dark next.

Alec's eyes didn't even look up to me before he shot out a hand. A rush of air shoved hard against my chest. Derek's cry cut off as soon as I slammed into the nearest wall.

My vision shifted painfully as the oxygen filled my lungs again. Derek stood with his cuff now alight again, moving toward Alec. When Alec's eyes moved to Derek, my stomach dropped.

Alec smiled as he shoved Derek into another wall. Two daggers appeared in his hands before my feet touched the ground again.

I had heard whispers about Alec's power but I had yet to see it in full force with my own eyes.

It was strength that seemed as easy as breathing for him. Trained and perfect, deadly. His practice, the obscene amount of energy in his body, all of it made him untouchable.

The daggers flew straight into Derek's wrists, pinning his arms against the wall. His scream rang into my ears, loud enough to drown out my own pain. Blood streamed from his wrists, pooling on the floor.

"Alec stop!" I screamed, peeling myself away from the wall and moving my aching body toward them.

The energy raced to heal my impact wounds. I had less energy to fight Alec with now. But one look at Derek's pain and I didn't care if I was left with nothing. I had to save my brother.

"Sorry your brother has such a temper." Alec laughed at me, glancing over to Derek.

One flick of his finger and Nikki turned our cuffs back on, bright and terrible.

"You don't have to hurt him anymore." I begged, crouching and debating how soon to move forward. "You proved your point. He'll leave you alone."

I wanted to hurt Alec. But if I lunged for him, that would only direct his fire toward me and leave Derek bleeding out on the wall.

Nikki was still casually standing in the back of the room, her careful eyes on Alec too. I couldn't get to the Shadow if I tried. So I moved toward Derek.

Every motion against the cuffs on mine and Derek's wrists was only taking more energy out of us. Coupled with having to heal new injuries, we were draining fast.

"I never said I would exact the same pain on them. Only that once someone hurt me, all bets were off. And I don't like leaving unfinished business with enemies." Alec lowered his gaze on me, watching my hands reach out to block his view.

"He's not an enemy, he's family," I begged.

"He's not my family." Alec narrowed his gaze on me like I should choose a different side, his side.

"You're right," Cassie called from behind Alec. "He's *my* family. And no one touches my family."

Alec spun slowly to look at her instead. Derek lifted his heavy head to look at her. His eyes widened as much as he could before they drooped again.

"C-Cassie, get out of here," Derek stuttered.

His hands twisted, trying to move. That only shifted the knives in his forearms. The motion was followed by a cry through his gritted teeth.

I took the distraction and used it to rip the daggers out of Derek's arms. His limp body fell forward just in time for me to catch him and lower him to the floor. Blood was coming out of him too quickly.

Dark liquid smeared underneath his arms on the floor. He twisted around to be able to see Cassie.

"Careful," I muttered to Derek even as he still tried to move closer to Cassie.

"Get off me," Derek growled. "Help Cassie. You have to get her away."

"Cassie can take care of herself." I ripped the hem of my shirt to tie around his arm. "Isn't that what you've always told us?"

"No, not this time." Derek shook his head, his hands pushing me away. "She needs help."

I ignored him. He wasn't making sense, probably due to the blood loss. I secured a bandage around his other arm. I looked up to see Cassie and Alec circling each other.

She was the first one to swipe at Alec, which he dodged just in time.

"I let you hit me once." Alec glared. "I'm not letting that happen again."

Alec went low, swinging a leg out, buckling Cassie's knees. He stood just in time to shove her shoulders back, slamming her body to the tile, which cracked on impact. Her red hair splayed on the floor in every direction.

I wanted to jump out to her, but my hands were tied up keeping pressure on Derek's wounds while they closed. Alec didn't waste any time before creating another dagger in his hand.

Cassie lifted a hand to her head as her eyes blinked away the pain. Not my sister. *Not my sister.*

"Alec, you got even with Derek. Now, leave her out of this," I begged.

He didn't even look at me. He knelt, straddling her body between his legs as he moved the dagger toward her.

"Recovering hurts when you don't have enough energy, huh?" Alec cocked his head when he looked at Cassie.

"Don't hurt her!" Derek cried, trying to drag his body forward.

I shoved him down, pressing my hands against his wrists. He clenched his teeth and thrashed against me in spurts. The blood seeping slowed.

"Someone's been gaining weight." Alec craned his head lower to look at Cassie like she was an experiment. Her stomach did look larger, especially laid on her back. But she had been wearing oversized clothes and hiding from us for most of the time here so I hadn't noticed until now.

Was she...?

Derek thrashed in my arms and I held him like he was the only thing keeping me back too. *Not my sister.*

Her arms were pinned to her sides by Alec's legs, but that didn't stop her from squirming underneath him and snarling through her teeth.

"What's going on?" Mara's voice interrupted.

I snapped my head up to look at her. She stood in the doorway, hands ready at her side to act as soon as she decided what to do. Lisa's eyes went wide and she darted the opposite way, gone.

"Do you want to tell her, Kylan? Or should I?" Alec asked as he lowered the dagger toward Cassie's stomach.

"Derek attacked him," I muttered, trying to hold Derek back by his sopping wet bandages.

Mara raised her eyebrows, instantly crouching to the floor. She saw what I saw about Cassie. Something I guessed Alec would ignore. Mara's gaze focused on Alec and the dagger he pointed at my sister.

"Alec." Her sharp voice got him to at least lift his head.

"I'm doing exactly as you said." Alec smiled up at her. "You should have chosen your words more carefully."

"No, they wouldn't have..." Mara breathed and flicked her gaze to me and Derek.

"Rules are rules. This little girl deserves what's coming to her." Alec smiled.

Mara took a staggering step back. Was she leaving? I needed her. I couldn't save Cassie and Derek at the same time. Alec pressed the knife into Cassie's stomach, sending the first trickle of blood through her shirt. Cassie grunted through her clenched teeth.

I couldn't look away. I had walked in on one of my sisters already dead before. I wasn't about to let it happen again.

"Stop it! Stop!" I shouted, at the same time Derek screamed, "She's pregnant."

The room fell silent. Alec froze, still holding the dagger uncomfortably close.

Alec only smiled. The confirmation he needed.

He glared down at Cassie. She tried to avoid his gaze, but was too scared to watch Derek bleed in front of her either.

"Why didn't you tell us?" I asked. "Why did you come here?"

"We couldn't let you come all on your own. You're our brother." Derek's face twisted in pain as he collapsed farther onto the floor.

"Why did you say that out loud?" Mara asked.

"What?" I asked. "Why not? I mean, Alec wouldn't..."

"You don't know him very well," Nikki snarled.

Cassie groaned again as Alec dragged the dagger from her stomach to her heart. My breath left my chest at the sound of her pain. It sounded different, sharper than before.

"Stop him," I breathed. Not my sister. Not again.

Mara looked at me, her eyes heavy. I knew I wouldn't like what she needed to do. But Cassie's life was more important than my pride.

I nodded to her.

She smiled, sadness penetrating through her gaze. She walked toward Alec, taking slow, long steps. Each one felt like she was pounding my chest.

"Alec," she called and her voice had changed.

It was cool, calm, and inviting. I hated the way it slithered through the air. It sounded too close to the way she called my name when we were alone.

"Don't listen to—" Nikki interrupted.

"Take the remote. Follow the curly-haired friend. She's probably going to Thayer," Alec said. Nikki didn't move. Alec snapped his teeth. "Go."

The Shadow turned, tossing her loose hair over her shoulder and stepping over Cassie's legs. Mara didn't look up at her as she passed. She was locked in a stare over Alec as he contemplated just how much my sister's life could hurt us.

With the sound of Nikki's clicking heels leaving, the room fell silent.

"Alec," she sang. Shivers rocked down my arms.

My blood brother's head lifted slowly, still pressing the dagger into Cassie's rib cage.

"You don't want to do this." Mara knelt next to him, close enough to touch.

I could hear the smile in Alec's voice as he responded. "You know me better than that."

"I do know you." She smiled at him, her gloved hand reaching toward him as she slid closer. "I know you care about getting even, about maintaining your reputation as a ruthless tyrant."

The words sounded like a compliment instead of an insult the way she said them. Anger burned in my eyes, but I couldn't look away.

"You're right," Alec said and shoved the dagger forward, drawing blood from Cassie as she groaned underneath him.

"But you're not going to kill her," she hurried.

"Wanna bet, baby?" Alec chuckled.

"Yeah, I do," she smiled easily. "I'll bet you anything."

Anything. Why would she promise that? Alec could call in that bet and make her do what he wanted. A man that always kept his promises wouldn't let this go. But her gaze was confident and totally focused on him.

So I didn't stop her. Didn't ask her to change. I just relied on her to save my sister.

"Deal," Alec scoffed and scraped the dagger down Cassie's chest, sending more blood down her shirt that was being torn in half.

My hands twitched. I had to do something. Mara moved her gaze to me for the briefest moment. A flash of sympathy crossed her face before she turned back to Alec.

*She knows what she's doing.* I had to tell myself.

"Drop the dagger," she asked, moving her hand to Alec's face.

Her finger stroked along his jawbone before her hands shifted back into his hair.

"Tell me why." Alec leaned into her palm.

The dagger remained on Cassie, the pressure lifting just enough to stop new blood from coming out. Her shuddering sobs still brought her stomach to touch the tips of the dagger when she took a deep breath.

I looked in her wide, brown eyes. She bit her lip as she stared at me, tears streaming down her pale cheeks.

*You're okay. Just hold still, all right?* I tried to create a thought in her mind.

The energy dissipated, brightening the armed cuff on my wrist. I held back a grimace as my body adjusted to losing the energy.

But maybe Cassie guessed what I was trying to do because she nodded. She was so impossibly brave, but that was Cassie.

"You love power, and Legends, and that sinister future you have in mind for everyone," Mara said.

Alec's eyes locked on hers now, hanging on her every word. His chest stopped moving; he couldn't even take in a breath while he stared.

I hated it. How much he was wrapped up in her.

"This child isn't an innocent baby that you should leave alive. In fact you should kill both of them just to add to your reputation. Who would dare go against Alec Stone then?" She twisted her gloved hand in his hair.

"What?" Derek muttered from the floor, finding the strength to launch himself forward.

I clamped a hand down on his shoulder to get him to shut up. My eyes strained as I stared at her. All hope relied on her knowing what she was doing. I had to trust it.

I couldn't lose another sister. I couldn't watch Derek lose

his wife. I think he knew if we attacked, Cassie would die faster than we could get there. He shook against my hand and I knew he hated this too.

All we could do was watch.

"But this is also a Legend child. Perfect and pure, with a completely malleable future," she continued, not moving her eyes away from Alec.

He lifted the dagger a little farther.

"Just imagine the potential," she whispered, as she leaned her face closer to his. "It's exciting, isn't it?"

She was offering something to manipulate. Offering up my unborn niece or nephew. Even if I knew it was a lie, that didn't stop me loathing that it was working. Alec would happily take that kid.

If Cassie and Derek lived through the next few minutes, I was going to kill Alec myself.

"Now," she moved even closer, only a breath away. "Drop the dagger, Alec Stone."

She said his name and everything in my mind shattered. My shoulders slumped as my mouth fell open. Her face changed, lighting up with excitement and mischief.

This woman looked more like the Mara everyone addressed her as than she looked like my Kate.

Alec's hand opened, and the dagger fell on Cassie's body, hitting sideways and bouncing onto the cold floor. She immediately looked at Derek, hopeful and still too scared to move.

"Thank you," Mara said, lifting her hand away from Alec's hair.

Alec turned to look down at Cassie, his eyes blank. Cassie didn't wait anymore, not for those eyes to change to cruel again. She squirmed out from under him, wincing from her cuts.

We both opened our arms as she staggered into them. Her body fell against Derek's, her blood joining his on the floor.

"Let's get you two out of here," I said, not able to take my eyes off Mara. "You need energy now."

We stood slowly. Both leaned against me as we turned to the door. I looked back to see Alec and Mara standing a little too close.

"You." Alec glared down at her.

"Yes?"

She was grinning as she moved around him, toward me and my siblings. I wanted to reach a hand out to her as relief washed through me.

"I don't think so." Alec's hand caught her arm. "You and I need to have a little talk."

Her eyes glanced back at those hateful eyes before she turned to me. A sad smile passed her mouth.

"Go." She nodded.

Leaving was the last thing I wanted to do. The air was thick with a brooding connection between the two of them. A result of her saving Cassie's life. I didn't want to blame her, but it didn't make the jealousy in my stomach bite any less.

"I'll be right back, I swear," I said as a promise to her, but more of a threat to him.

Alec yanked her down the hallway in almost a dead sprint before she could say anything else. I clutched my two bleeding siblings. I needed to get them to human energy soon.

For now, that was all I could think about.

# CHAPTER
# THIRTY-ONE

Alec pulled me down the hallways, around two corners, and far away from any prying ears. I stumbled along behind him, trying to keep up.

*I did it.* I smiled.

I had actually convinced Alec to do something he didn't want to do. No one was around to see my joy, but it still felt good.

Alec opened a metal door to a small storage closet and tossed me in before him. I raised my hands to catch myself on the back shelves as Alec slammed the door behind the two of us.

"What was that?" he demanded through clenched teeth.

I grinned. "I don't know what you mean."

Alec balled his fists as he turned away from me. He took a breath big enough to move his shoulders before he turned around.

"Don't play games."

Those stony eyes settled on me and I wanted to break in half with the building victory.

"Isn't that my line?" I asked, still smiling at him. "You're just mad because I bested you. For once."

"I'm mad because you claim you want nothing to do with me and then you go and do something like that," Alec gestured to where we had been.

"But you deserved it," I complained.

Alec stared at me, speechless. Another accomplishment. I leaned back against the shelves behind me, waiting for his next response. Seconds passed and we just stared at each other.

I became intensely aware of how small this room really was. Alec's presence took up all the space, all the air. If I moved at all, I'd only feel more of him.

"Can I ask you something?" he asked.

A tingling, freezing sensation stole across my skin. I needed to get out of here, away from Alec. But I didn't even dare to breathe.

"Did you enjoy it?" he finished.

The air pressure lifted off me. "What? Playing you?"

Alec nodded slowly, carefully, as his navy eyes narrowed.

I didn't dare say my answer out loud. But I couldn't ignore the fluttery, triumphant feeling in my stomach. If that had come from manipulating Alec, I waited for the guilt of doing something wrong.

But that didn't come.

He deserved it. He could handle it. He wouldn't mind me twisting him like he did to me for so many years. We could take it from each other because it's all we had ever done. A constant game of cat and mouse.

"It was easy, wasn't it?" Alec breathed, daring to step closer to me. My feet were pinned to the floor. "Easy to get in my head, make me see something different. So easy to watch me do what you wanted."

"I didn't enter your mind," I said.

Alec clicked his tongue, still keeping those dark eyes on mine. "Not literally."

A fierce heartbeat pounded in my chest. I knew what he meant and he could see that in my expression. I was only denying the obvious answer that both of us waited to hear aloud.

"After all the years of you doing it to me, of course it was easy," I said with heartbreaking smoothness.

"Ah, and you see it now." Alec stepped even closer, his chest nearly close enough to touch my body. "The temptation to manipulate even a person you care about? You could have exactly what you want, even save a life."

I pulled myself away from him. "You never used that ability to save a life. You used it to kill and lie and—"

"We're not talking about me," he interrupted.

I was the one who took a step forward now. Alec didn't bother to hide his smile. My eyes glared up at his and just as I was about to open my mouth, something else caught my attention.

Behind him, my gaze landed on a small stack of vials at rest on a shelf. The small, glass bottles weren't what really pulled at me. It was the label written on them.

*Antidote 17B.*

17B.

I knew that number.

It was the one I had repeated in my head over and over again since that lab assistant had blurted it out in front of me. The answer to the *insurance* problem Alec had created.

"What," I breathed the word, pushing Alec to the side.

He didn't fight me. I didn't notice. My hand shot forward and latched onto the cold, beautiful vial.

I spun it in my hand, holding the key to my happiness.

Searching and screaming and nightmares faded away. It was here in my hand. In this room. The room that Alec had led me to.

My eyes shot up to his.

"Mara," he warned gently, his eyes wide as he looked at the bottle.

It was real. It had to be. He wouldn't be worried if it wasn't. This was the antidote to my energy-siphoning problem.

I scanned the shelf and snatched the nearest needle. Trembling, I shoved the point of the needle through the metal-laced lid. My hand slid easily as the contents emptied into the syringe. It was light in my hand, too light to be the salvation I wanted.

But it was real. It was in my hand.

"Mara." Alec seized my hand with the needle.

"What?"

Alec simply shook his head, a breath escaping his lips. "Don't."

My mouth parted, but my hand remained tight on the very breakable glass syringe in my grip. Alec held my wrist, still on the glove and away from my skin.

"Don't?" I snorted. "Don't? Everyone I care about is in danger from *you*. You were just leaning over Kylan's sister with a dagger. Why, *why* would I stop?"

Alec visibly gulped as the color drained from his face. "If you're healed, you won't have a reason to stay."

"That's the point," I snapped and yanked my hand free.

Alec didn't reach for my arms again. Instead, he rested a hand on my shoulder and let one finger drag down to my waist. His head leaned in to mine, not touching, but close enough for me to see the sweat on his forehead.

A breath of a whisper that danced along my cheek.

"Don't."

I pulled up the sleeve on my arm but I didn't force his hands away. Even when his fingers fell down my shoulder, dragging along my arm.

Not when his other hand traced a line to the bottom of my spine. A touch I hadn't let him do for a long time.

"Please," Alec said, a little stronger now.

A shuddering breath as I lowered the needle to my arm. I wasn't sure if it came from him or me. But he leaned imperceptibly closer, his voice nearly too low for me to hear.

"Don't leave me."

With those words, I paused. I halted my breath, my movement, everything. I could've lived for centuries in that one breath of a pause. Alec froze too, both of us still as death.

I wanted to muster something to say to him. But nothing fit. Nothing could end the years of love and anger and pain and lust and betrayal between us. So I stabbed the needle in my arm.

Alec's hands fell limp as the plunger pushed the serum into my arm.

Antidote 17B.

The solution to everything. The last reason I ever needed to see Alec again.

It was all over now.

The serum was cold in my arm, but I couldn't feel anything else. Nothing different flooded my system. I even wondered if it would knock me out. But that same stillness that existed between us before, remained.

The silence was charged with a fiery hope and a sharp sadness. The sadness I didn't understand. The separation didn't actually exist yet—Alec was still hovering over me with a perfect quietness.

The needle fell from my hand, breaking the peace. I didn't want to remove my gloves, didn't want to really move. I let my head lean closer to Alec, my cheek brushing against his forehead.

Energy flared between the two of us.

I forced myself to stop, forced my body to reject the energy coming from him. I pushed it away with all the mental force I possessed.

But the energy continued anyway.

My head snapped away from him, eyes wide. Alec kept his head lowered, so I couldn't make out his expression. I ripped off my left glove and rested my hand on his neck.

More energy roared into my body.

I didn't know what to ask, or what to say. It didn't work.

Maybe it needed more time? Maybe I needed a stronger dose? I reached back and grabbed one of the identical vials. Instead of picking up the needle, I yanked off the lid.

Cool, clear liquid poured in the palm of my hand. I took in the scent of nothing. When I touched it with my finger and raised it to my mouth, I tasted the reason it didn't work.

"This is water," I said, crushing the bottle in my bare hand. "It's Nikki's stupid flavored water that she loves."

Glass stabbed into my skin, drawing blood. The energy from Alec raced to heal the cuts as I allowed the glass to fall to the floor.

When I spun to look at Alec, I already knew the face that would be waiting for me. He grinned, a calm, wicked smile that touched his cold, dark eyes.

"You changed it," I accused, stepping toward him to lock my hands around his neck.

He slid to the side, out of my warpath. "My changing skills are lackluster compared to yours."

"That doesn't mean you couldn't do it," I snarled.

He was lying. Not really lying, only deceiving by dodging the truth. He was *always* doing that.

"You're right," Alec sighed happily. "But I didn't change this. Every one of those is filled with water and they always have been."

"To throw me off from the real antidote?" I asked, waiting to see a flicker of expression in his eyes.

Nothing came. "I haven't created the real antidote. It doesn't physically exist."

I stepped away from him, remembering the small room again. I shook my head, hating the pooling dread in my stomach. Alec stepped forward, a light hand ready to brush my cheek.

"Why bring me in here? Why would you lead me right to the—" I stopped, connecting what happened.

Alec attacked Cassie. I played Alec. He took me in this room. This room in particular. He wanted me to see this and know that he was my only option out of here.

He planned every step.

"Cassie was bait," I whispered.

"For you. Don't worry, I'm not angry that you turned out just like me." Alec finally smiled.

My stomach dropped. Alec had done the same thing to me over and over again. This was the first time he fell for me. And it was too easy.

"You played along," I snarled.

"In truth, you did convince me. I wanted to do what you said. It just so happened to already fall under my greater interests," Alec said in a condescending tone. "You didn't actually think you beat me."

I moved away from the shelves at my back, throwing my arms down at my sides in defeat.

"Why do it then? Why not just kill Cassie if you didn't fall for it?" I asked, moving closer to him.

Even in the dim light. I wanted to see every expression on his face to know if he was lying or not.

"I had three reasons." Alec raised three fingers in my face. "One, I wanted to see if you'd manipulate me the way that I do to you. I'm quite pleased to know I was right."

That was true. His eyes were steady and the rhythm of his breathing hadn't changed.

"Two?" I asked.

"Kylan was watching." Alec smiled down at me as he lowered a finger.

True again. There was so much I wanted to say about that. But I couldn't let myself feel all the jealousy and rage that Kylan was probably thinking about. I had to focus on this moment.

"And the last one?" I asked, shocked he was even answering my questions.

"Bringing you here, seeing your reaction to the antidote, and watching your decision. I wanted to find out what exactly you'd do. And I saw it," Alec said and I thought he'd go on a monologue about how he was hurt I wouldn't choose him. But he didn't. "That one second of hesitation. That is the Mara I will keep fighting for. The one that paused just a second before running away. You had every reason to leave then and now, but you stalled both times."

I shook my head, stepping away from him and into the shelf behind me. Alec took up my entire vision. That smile, that laugh, that knowing gaze sucked all the air out of my lungs.

The moment seemed as long as the breath before I shoved the plunger down. As long as possible for forever to fit into a single second.

"You're wrong," I finally said.

Alec smiled wider. "Careful, Mara. You just hesitated again."

# CHAPTER
# THIRTY-TWO

I snapped. I shoved him until his back crashed into the opposite shelves. My fingers dug into his shirt, his skin that I wanted to tear away from his body.

"Was that fast enough for you?" I wanted to scream the words.

The rage flooded down my arms, even when Alec let out a strained laugh. "I always know how to get a reaction out of you."

My hands dropped and Alec's feet touched the floor again.

"Stop meddling in my life," I threatened. "I'm here in your precious lab right next to you all the time. I'm stuck, just like you want me to be. Leave my family alone."

"Family?" Alec glanced at the door. "You don't know those people. You didn't even guess that Cassie was pregnant. What family misses that?"

"We've been a little busy fighting with you." I shook my head, closing the space between us so he could read the threatening glare in my eyes. "Unless you need me for a test, do not talk to me. Don't look at me. Don't touch me. Leave me alone."

"You're just upset you didn't see my plan first." Alec brushed a finger along my chin. "Maybe there was another reason. You look so cute when you're angry."

His energy flashed into my skin before I pulled my face away. A shudder crawled down my spine.

"I hate you," I said.

But I didn't leave. I was defeated and angry and should've stormed out of the room. But no one was waiting for me out there. Kylan had left to take care of his family. A family that didn't even share secrets with me.

I understood why they kept it to themselves. The lab, Alec, everything was unsafe. What family misses that?

It haunted me how much he was right. So I stopped my hand reaching for the door. I paused before I left the room with the person who knew me the best.

I took a breath, trying to prepare for the colder world out there.

"Stop," Alec said and I looked over my shoulder. "Stop doing that."

The pain was honest in his voice. That honesty that made me want to hear the rest. It was the same voice when he asked me not to leave. No swagger or bravado masking the tone.

It was just him with a simple request.

"Stop pretending to leave and then…hesitating. It's killing me." His eyes shifted to that of a little boy looking at his little girl. "Every time you stop, I see my Mara. I have to fight for her, even if it hurts. I have to. So if you're going to hate me, then do it."

I looked back at the floor, but let my body turn to face him. "You don't need to doubt that I hate you. I do. I almost want to strangle you every moment I see you."

"Almost," he repeated.

I closed my eyes. "But you have to stop looking for something that isn't there. I don't love you that way anymore. I never will."

"And yet here we are, all alone, and all you want is a reason to get a little closer," Alec smiled, catching my eyes again.

"You're wrong." I stared back at him.

The little boy was gone again, replaced by the villain he grew up to be. "Then why can't you take your mind off me?"

Alec's crooked smile widened before I could look away again. In those few seconds and with a whiff of his energy fluttering inside of me, it was too easy for him.

"Don't—" was all I could get out.

"Don't," I said.

We stood in a small storage room. Alec's face lingered a little too close to mine. I tried to look around, but all I could see was Alec's eyes.

The cold blue captured my attention, wrapping my mind in an icy embrace.

He moved closer to me. I wanted him to. The ways his eyes looked at me, I never wanted to turn away.

Too real. Everything felt impossibly real. As much as I yanked on my mind, I couldn't get it back.

It felt like pulling on a rope that kept dissolving in my hands. My mind swirled, unhinged and scrambling to latch onto anything solid. So Alec came in and filled that space again.

Alec cupped my face in his hands. He leaned forward and kissed me. My entire body melted in his touch.

He pulled back, not quite enough to look at me before he came in again. His mouth touched mine, igniting a flame of energy and desire all at the same time.

I could feel him. I could feel how much he wanted this, how being so close to me was driving him insane. It drove me insane too. His energy, his mouth, his haunting eyes. My vision blurred beyond belief when he pulled away again.

"Stop kissing me," I muttered against his mouth.

My breath was hot inside my throat. Alec's lips pulled into an arrogant smile against mine. Energy flowed from his hands. Excitement, rage, unrestrained need swirled inside me all at the same time.

"Aren't you going to say please?" Alec chuckled as he kissed me again.

My hands moved from being limp at my sides to grabbing his back, clutching at the fabric, for anything to keep me from drowning in him. Alec took that as a hint and pulled his shirt off before I could suck in a breath.

It was. It definitely was a hint. I needed more of his skin.

While we were parted, he stopped before he moved to kiss me again. I took in the sight of his muscled body straining not to tear me apart. He stared at me as he brought my other glove to his mouth.

Crushingly gentle. He bit the tip of the finger and pulled the glove with his teeth. Both of my hands were bare and free.

"Touch me," Alec whispered.

Begged. He needed my touch as much as I needed his.

I ran my hands down his bare, muscled chest. Energy burned under my fingertips. It felt like silk running against my bones.

His hand grabbed the back of my head, pulling me into him. I kissed him back. My lips moved against my will, at least what my mind thought was my will.

I couldn't tell anymore. His mouth was warm and hungry against mine.

"Please," I muttered as I moved my lips to his jaw.

It was a different word now. Not to get him to stop anymore.

Alec's laugh rocked in his chest as I kissed down his neck. More energy flooded through me. He tasted like murder and danger. His hands moved against me like a dance. I wanted it all. I wanted every part of him.

I moved my face back up to his. Pain pulled in my expression as I looked at him.

Heat spread on the right side of my neck, but Alec's hand wasn't anywhere near there. They were lower, so much lower as they wrapped around my waist.

But my neck warmed even more. It was too hot, too much. It pulled me back and I clung to that heat. I winced as I looked at Alec's intense gaze.

"Stop," I breathed.

"Stop," my voice rang differently.

I looked around at the room again. This was real, right? I looked back to Alec, feeling his hand pressed against the right side of my neck.

I reached up and shoved his hand away. His energy immediately stopped and my body cried.

"Your energy." I shook my head, still spinning. "The mind games. You have to stop."

"Why, because it's working?" Alec moved his hands to hold my waist.

My fingers tingled at the thought of him lifting my shirt, his hands touching bare skin. More of his energy would become mine.

"Because it's wrong," I snarled at him.

He blinked and stepped back, his hands pulling away.

Don't go, my body begged.

"How much I want you? Or how much you want me back?" Alec raised an eyebrow, daring to lean in again.

I put a hand on his chest to stop him from getting any closer. My body was screaming, crying to get closer. My mind was the only thing holding me still.

"Don't," I ordered. "I'm with Kylan. I love him. This thing between you and me has to stop."

"Then why do you still want it?" Alec begged now.

"I'm trying not to!" I screamed.

The honesty was too much, way more than he deserved. I should have played it off, but my mind was collapsing in on itself. I could barely think enough to keep him away from me and I wasn't entirely sure if that was his influence on my mind or not.

I was more worried that he had nothing to do with that outburst.

"Do you know how impossibly hard it is to see you with my brother?" Alec asked. "The only thing that makes it worse is knowing you still care about me too."

"I never meant to fall for your brother." I shook my head at him, sympathizing with his pain automatically.

"Oh, please. You're telling me you really had no idea that the two of us were related when you found him? You were chasing the locket. You think it's just a coincidence that you fell for the person who had it," Alec huffed, crossing his arms over his chest.

"I didn't know he had it...I didn't—" I shouted just to interrupt his stream of sentences.

"Fine, maybe you didn't." Alec lifted a hand to my face but lowered it again. "But then you came back to me. You fell for me again. I saw it. If you say you're done with me, then why can't you just do the honorable thing and stop loving me?"

Alec looked down at the floor and he never looked so sheepish and small.

A trick. It had to be a trick.

But he was so small and broken and careening in his own mind. I knew what that felt like, all too well.

"I want to." I leaned back on the shelves again. "You're despicable and psychotic. You hurt the people I care about. You tortured me, manipulated me—"

"And yet that's not good enough for you to kill me. All you can do is leave, and I'm sitting here hoping I can somehow get you back." Alec raised his arms like he didn't know where to put them anymore. "Why?"

"I don't know."

"That's not an answer. Why?" Alec moved closer to my face.

"Because you won't let me."

"Ha." Alec grinned before his eyes turned dark again. "I wish I had that much control over your decisions. Try again."

I shoved him away. "I don't know, Alec."

"Yes, you do," he came right back. "Think, Mara."

"Because you're home to me!"

His mouth fell open and the pain created lines around his eyes. I just stared at him for a moment. I saw all the same years of complications that I felt in mine. We weren't just similar. He and I were mirror images of each other.

"No matter what you do, no matter where I go. When I think back on my life, you are all I can see for centuries," I said.

"I get it." Alec backed off. I caught his arm.

"You don't. You're a terrible person. You're the nightmare that just won't go away." I looked at the floor. "But you're also a huge part of my life, whether I hate you or not."

"I hate you too," Alec muttered.

My mouth opened to protest. But when I looked at his pained eyes, all the words turned to dust.

"I hate you for being with my brother. I hate you for leaving, even after I think you'll stay. I hate that no matter how many times you fall out of love with me, you can fall back in again. When I brought you to the lab, all of that was real for me," Alec whispered. "I wanted you back so badly."

"Don't lie." I shook my head, closing my eyes and hoping he would stop talking.

"It's not a lie. I really thought you'd want to stay with me again. I was even willing to…" Alec shrugged. "But the second Kylan showed up, I knew what your decision would be. I could see it in your eyes."

He paused, trying to find the words. "I never hated you so much. That day. I hated you."

When he said it, hate sounded more like love. Even when I had chosen Kylan over him, he hated—loved—me.

I knew it would only break his heart more to hear it again, if there was even a heart left to break. But I said, "I love him."

"You love me." Alec grabbed my arms, in utter free fall as he latched onto the one thing that held him still. Me. "What makes him so special?"

I reached down and pulled the sleeve of my right arm up, revealing the dagger. I took Alec's right arm and brought it next to mine. Our marks were identical.

"You and I are the same in so many ways," I started. "We've both done horrible things. But when we're together, I want to keep doing horrible things. We…we make each other worse."

"And he makes you better?" Alec asked.

"Yeah, he does." I smiled up at him.

"What if one day, you don't want to be better?" Alec leaned in and whispered in my ear.

"Don't hold your breath," I laughed. "There's this spark in me that makes me want something more, something good. As long as that's there, I don't think anything will change."

I moved my eyes to the floor. I heard Alec's breathing change as I explained. I should have looked up at him again, but I didn't want to see any more pain.

"I noticed that spark in the mansion, before you ever left the first time. I saw what it was doing to you. I just had no idea how to get rid of it," Alec whispered.

"But you tried to get rid of it. That's the reason you and I won't work." I shook my head. "I need someone that fuels me. I want the kind of love where I can feel supported and warm and that kind of love…"

I stopped and thought about my next words.

That kind of love is powerful. I wondered.

My mind raced. Alec couldn't find a way to calm the mind enough to overcome the pain of transition. The reason no one could be a Level Five.

That kind of love.

I smiled, standing up a little straighter. Alec stared at me as his eyebrows pulled together. I looked back at him, already enjoying how he would react to this.

"The locket," I breathed.

"What?"

"The locket. Give me the locket." I stared directly at him.

"No," he whispered, trying to hold on to anything tied to me. But this wasn't about that anymore.

"You bet me anything." I stared him down with a steely, unwavering gaze.

"For a bet I let you win? I don't think so."

I stepped closer. He still leaned against the shelves so I

had to look down. His blue eyes looked even darker from up here somehow.

"Give me the locket." I raised a hand out to him. "And I can make you a Level Five."

# CHAPTER
# THIRTY-THREE

I rushed down the hallway, headed toward the testing room with the machine that monitored my mental pathways. The one where Alec had strapped me to it and sent me into a rage.

The one where I would soon be able to fix the one problem standing in between me and...

"Kylan," I breathed when I spotted him.

He was strong, but exhausted from helping his siblings. He looked at me with grim eyes. Lisa held each of his family with her hands and guided them toward the stairs.

"Are they okay?" I slowed my walk.

"They're recovering, but they'll be fine. Lisa was a big help when she found us. Derek lost a lot of blood and Cassie's wounds are taking a little longer to heal than normal. Apparently that's a Legend pregnancy thing." Kylan glanced at the floor with a strained gaze. "I can't believe they didn't tell me."

"Can you blame them? With everything going on, when would have been the best time to drop that bomb?" I touched a gloved hand to his shoulder.

Kylan looked up and past me. I heard Alec's footsteps stop in the corner of the room.

"Did you two have a nice chat?" Kylan grumbled.

"*Very* nice," Alec answered first.

Anger pinched Kylan's eyes and I didn't blame him. Alec could twist anything that just happened. But I caught Kylan's gaze instead, forcing him to focus.

"Don't listen to him." I waved a hand at Alec. "I think I figured out a way to stop someone's mind from closing off during transition."

Kylan's eyes shot down to mine instead.

"What? That means—" he started.

"That means we're one step closer to getting me back to normal and leaving this place. Me and you and anyone else that wants to come with us." I smiled.

Even as I said the words, I was painfully aware of Alec watching silently.

"I'll follow you." Kylan smiled.

The three of us rushed back to the lab room. We picked up Sage and Lisa along the way.

I walked straight to the machine. I pulled my long-sleeved shirt off, revealing the tank top underneath. I kept the gloves on. I turned back to Kylan, shirt in hand.

His eyes stared at me as his expression changed. Those eyes seemed to ask, *are you trying to torture me?*

The metal cuffs would have blocked any actual thought from him, even with all of Alec's energy now racing through my body. But I didn't need to be a Legend to read Kylan's dilated eyes.

I smiled and tossed my shirt at his gawking face.

I moved to the machine, attaching the sensors to the backs of my hands. Alec reached for the other sensors, brushing my skin again.

"I've got it," I snapped at him.

He yanked his hands back, taking a retreating step. I attached the sensors to my chest before reaching to the ones for my temples. Once everything was in place, I nodded to Alec.

"Give me the locket." I reached a hand out to him.

"What if I don't know where it is?" He shrugged.

"That's a lie."

"I don't have it on me," he tried again.

"Another lie." I glared at him.

"How do I know you won't just take off?"

Finally, an honest question from him. The one he was really worried about. He liked to hide the truth as much as the rest of us.

"You don't." I smiled. "How badly do you want to find out if I'm right?"

He glared at me before he reached in the front pocket of his jeans and pulled out the locket.

"You actually kept it on you?" Kylan asked.

"The best hiding place is the most obvious." He turned to face Kylan. "Plus, the only person brave enough to go searching around in my pockets is Mara. And I doubted she would. Sadly, I'm disappointed—"

"Enough, Alec," I said.

He walked over to me and raised the locket to my neck. I tried to lift a hand to take it from him, but the sensor pulled against me.

"You're a bit tied up," Alec smiled. "Let me handle it."

He reached around my neck and clasped the locket, taking every opportunity to brush his fingers against my skin. I shivered at the sensation of new Legend energy.

"Power me up." I glared. "You're only helping."

"I know how personal taking energy can be. Trust me, I'm only doing myself a favor." Alec winked.

He finished the clasp on the locket and I pulled my head away. The wire attached to the sensor stretched, but not enough to remove it. Alec chuckled as he backed away.

"So, how'll the locket help?" Kylan asked.

"I have a hunch." I shrugged. "I want to see if I'm right."

"For all their sakes, you better be," Alec challenged. And he was the calculating leader again.

I leaned back against the wall, resting as many muscles as I could. The familiar warmth of the locket radiated into my chest. Tears immediately stung my eyes as I closed them. It felt so right to have the locket back, like everything in the world fit into place.

"All right, let's get this going." Alec tapped on the screen.

The sensors buzzed to life. I concentrated on my breathing.

*You are loved.* The locket reminded me.

I took in a breath. The weight resting on my chest, shifting with each breath, reminded me of how close the memory of my mother really was. I wasn't alone.

Another breath. No matter what Alec threw at me, no matter what obstacles Kylan and I had to overcome, I could handle it.

"It's working," Alec's voice breathed.

"There's nothing that woman can't do," Kylan's voice lowered and I could almost hear the smile.

A flutter of hope and happiness entered my body. Strong enough that I wondered if Thayer was around.

But it was just me, the locket, and the mother it reminded me of. I took one more breath and felt every nerve in my body sing. For the first time in months, I was at utter peace.

"Whoa," Alec muttered.

I didn't hear any beeping coming from the tablet. I didn't hear anything. I opened my eyes to see Alec and Kylan gaping down at the bright screen.

"What?" I asked, feeling the calm penetrate even my voice.

Alec looked up at me, his eyes moving straight to the golden locket on my chest.

"It worked," he breathed.

I just smiled and moved my eyes to Kylan and he smiled back at me. This was all I needed. The locket, him, and an open future.

"You need to try," I said, looking at Alec.

He didn't say anything as he quickly ripped the sensors off me and took the locket all at once. His fingers clutched around the delicate metal as he stepped into the machine.

I walked back to Kylan as Alec hooked everything up. I took my shirt back and pulled it over my head, noticing Kylan's frown.

As much as I wanted to leave it off, it was safer for everyone if I kept as much of my skin covered as possible. I yanked my gloves out of my back pocket and pulled them on as Alec hooked up the last sensor.

I stepped forward, holding out my gloved hand.

"I can hold that for you," I said sweetly, pointing to the tablet in his hand.

"Don't push my trust," Alec threatened and rested the tablet on a shelf beside the machine, turning it so it was still within his view.

"Paranoid much?" I said.

Alec just stared at the tablet, tapping the buttons required to run the program. He looked back up at me with a smile before he closed his eyes.

"Okay, clear everything from your mind," I started.

"Shouldn't be too hard," Kylan muttered.

I laughed. Alec opened one eye and squinted at Kylan before focusing again.

"Remember what the locket says," I continued, not wanting to say those words aloud to him. It just felt too strange. "Focus on that feeling. Let it fill you up and relax you."

The tablet beeped slower and slower. The gold chain hung from Alec's fist. It looked wrong in his hands, but I shoved that thought down.

We all waited in silence. The beeping got slow enough to get my hopes up, but never stopped the way it did with me.

After a few frustrating seconds, the beeping increased again when Alec opened his eyes.

"Well, in a surprising turn of events, Alec is incapable of feeling," Kylan said.

"You're not exactly helping. Would you mind giving us a moment alone?" Alec asked.

"Should I leave my girlfriend here while you try to get in touch with your emotional side? Yeah, no thanks," Kylan threw back at him.

"Kylan's not the issue." I looked at the locket again. "That is. Maybe you'll finally believe me that it can't help you."

"It has to." Alec narrowed his eyes. "It's the only thing that helped you."

"Because it's meant for me," I wanted to scream at him, but settled for gritting my teeth.

"It's a piece of jewelry, it can't really mean that much." Alec shook his heading, pulling at the sensors.

"Of course you don't get it," I scoffed. "How could you? You've never felt…"

I stopped. Silence swallowed up my words as everyone in the room probably just stared at me. I looked Alec up and down. I shook my head when I came up with an idea.

"What is it?" Kylan asked and put a hand on my lower back.

"Alec needs to feel what that locket allows me to feel," I whispered to him, looking up at his curious eyes.

Kylan's eyes looked back and forth between mine. A twinge of pain made its way across his face and my heart thumped in my chest.

*I'm sorry*, I wanted to say.

I turned back to Alec slowly, my eyes dragging along to avoid looking at him. Instead of asking Kylan to leave, I said nothing. He could make his own choices and honestly, I would feel better if he stayed anyway.

I finally met Alec's gaze.

His intense stare looked like it could be carved out of porcelain. I took in a breath, feeling the oxygen awaken the rest of my senses. I gave one brief shake of my hands before walking forward.

Every step was painful, so I rushed forward. I threw my arms around his neck and was too aware of every part of my body that pressed against his.

"What..." Alec started but his hands immediately wrapped around my back. I knew they would.

"Let me talk," I ordered.

Alec's muscles tensed at the sound of my voice. I tried to keep it low enough that Kylan couldn't hear, or anyone else but Alec and me. It created a small sense of privacy in this vulnerable moment.

"Despite everything you've done, you...you amaze me," I said.

As much as I wanted it to be a lie, it was real. My breath came in spurts that barely kept my vision straight.

"You've built an empire that falls at your feet. People hate you or fear you, but all of them respect you," I continued.

Alec's hands twitched behind me. A soft laugh moved his chest against mine. I glanced down to the tablet and watched the flashing representation of the beeping noise slow.

"Even I respect you," I muttered in a lower decibel than before.

I pulled him tighter against me. Alec leaned his head forward and rested it against my shoulder. My shirt and hair blocked his skin from touching mine. I was grateful for that because otherwise I wouldn't be able to say the next thing.

"And you're right, no matter what you do"—I tried not to clench my teeth—"I'll always care for you."

I didn't want to say love. The word would have choked in my throat. The tablet showed the beeps slowing even further. Alec's breaths became deeper and sluggish.

"You know what I think?" I asked.

"What?" Alec asked, the beeping sound rising for a moment.

I ran my gloved fingers through his hair and turned my mouth to face his ear. My lips touched his skin and his energy trickled through my mouth.

"Your father was proud to have a son like you," I said.

Alec let out a long breath and his arms relaxed around me. All sound ceased from the tablet. I moved my eyes to see what the screen showed. Every part of the brain image lit up in a soft green color. The line at the bottom was steady and unmoving.

It worked, and I should have thrown myself away from Alec immediately.

But I felt the way his hands started to shake, the way his breath pulled in his chest. For one second, I just wanted to hold the little boy I grew up with. The one that held my hand in that little old house.

It was silent between us as we held each other. So quiet it could've been just the two of us in the room.

"I can't believe it worked," Sage muttered.

My body tightened against Alec, now aware of all the people around. I still couldn't bring myself to let go of this soft, feeling Alec. Even with their voices, the tablet didn't beep again. Open, relaxed, and vulnerable.

"So? Mara's hugs are the magical key?" Lisa asked.

"Well, that's not sustainable all the way through a transition," Sage explained.

Their voices trailed off as Sage explained what exactly a person undergoes to become a Legend. Lisa agreed along with her, finally understanding something based on her own experience.

The sounds shattered the tender illusion I had been in. I pulled away from Alec and tried to just look at the floor.

Alec stopped me from moving too far away. His hands held me tightly, digging in with his fingers. I dragged my eyes up to look at him. He stared, his mouth not moving.

A tiny, frail connection slithered its way into my mind. I didn't stop it. Alec, like me, wasn't wearing a cuff.

*I don't care if you meant it or not.* The words played in my mind and the light in Alec's eyes shifted, softened. *Thank you.*

I nodded to him, not wanting to answer. I did mean it. Every word was true, even if I didn't want them to be. It was enough that Alec got to hear them at least once.

His hands finally fell when I pulled away from him. I walked back to Kylan and already braced myself for the look of pain on his face. He just looked at the floor and then over to the other women in the room.

Avoiding me. That was worse.

I wanted to change any emotion he was feeling. I wanted

to take it away. But no matter what I did, it wouldn't change the fact that Alec and I had a connection. We always would.

That would always hurt Kylan. And me.

# CHAPTER
# THIRTY-FOUR

I turned to Alec, barely containing my anticipation. We had an answer—well, half of an answer. We just needed to make it work in a real trial. Something sustainable.

"Could Thayer do it?" Lisa asked, looking up from her notebook for a moment.

"He might be able to mimic the emotion, but holding on for long enough to pass all the way through the transition...I don't know." Alec shook his head.

"But it's worth a shot, right?" I looked around the room like I already expected him to be here. "Anyway, where is Thayer?"

I glanced automatically at Lisa and Sage. If anyone knew where he was, it was likely to be one of them.

Sage just shrugged and looked at Lisa. Lisa bit the end of her pen and shook her head. "Haven't seen him."

"Hmm," Alec chuckled from behind me.

I spun and looked at him, waiting for him to explain the smug smile that was painted on his face as he removed the sensors.

"Do you know where he is?" I asked finally.

"No, but I have a guess." Alec shrugged. "Anyone checked Nikki's room?"

The sound of a pen clattering to the floor interrupted the awkward silence. I cringed, already knowing where that sound came from. Alec looked back at Lisa, and then to me, always smiling.

"You've got to be kidding me." I raced for the door and shoved it out of my way.

I couldn't hear anything over the sound of my footsteps as I moved through the hall, down the stairs and into the basement where all the rooms were. I hoped I wouldn't hear anything else when I walked up to Nikki's door.

I was met with a high-pitched giggle just before my hand landed on the knob.

Already cringing, I opened the door to find Nikki sitting on a dresser and Thayer pulling her closer to him. He wasn't wearing a shirt and she wasn't far behind.

A string of insults and jabs came flooding into my mind and I had to bite my lip to keep them from coming out. Instead, all that followed was an unintelligible grumble.

"Can we help you?" Thayer asked, focusing on kissing Nikki's neck and playing with her loose tresses of hair.

"I—uh, you're needed upstairs," I said, gripping the handle like I wanted to shatter it in my hand.

"I'm sure whatever it is, it can wait." Thayer smiled, glancing at me as he pushed Nikki's hair behind her ear.

His lower lip grazed over the various piercings and diamond studs until they reached the hollow below her earlobe. Nikki shivered and Thayer smiled.

"Yeah," Nikki finally chimed in. "Can't you give us five minutes?"

Thayer stilled and pulled away from her to look her in the eyes.

"Five minutes?" Thayer scoffed. He lifted her from the dresser and wrapped her legs around him as he moved both of them to the bed. "This is going to take much longer than five minutes."

Nikki shrieked in a giggle and Thayer let her drop to the bed. He glanced at me again before putting the cuff near Nikki and lowering himself down to her. "I could go a lot longer if you took this cuff off."

She shook her head and Thayer narrowed his eyes. He attacked her with kisses while she laughed.

"Thayer, this is important—" I started.

They both ignored me. My anger fumed in my body and the metal door handle started to warp in my palm.

"Alec needs you," I said.

That finally got his attention. Thayer sat up and looked at me, trying to see if I was lying. I stared back, and his shoulders slumped.

"Fine," Thayer griped and stood.

He walked straight past me, leaving his shirt behind on the dresser. I grabbed it before glancing at Nikki's pout and slamming the door. Thayer was already halfway down the hallway when I looked up.

I jogged up to him. "Nikki? Seriously?"

"You got a problem with it?" Thayer asked, not looking back at me and still not caring that he didn't have a shirt.

"Um, only the fact that she's terrible, she tortured me, and come on, she's—"

He spun and glared down at me.

"You of all people don't get to judge me for who I choose to be with," Thayer snapped. "Just because you changed and want to be all goodie goodie now doesn't mean I have to."

"What? Where is this coming from?" I raised my hands.

"Nothing." Thayer shook his head. "It's nothing."

"Well, while you're thinking about it, wanna put your shirt back on?" I held up his shirt to him and he sighed.

"What, you don't like me shirtless anymore?" Thayer grinned.

And he was back again. He stood taller as he pulled the shirt over his head, covering up those impeccable muscles. His familiar smile changed the tension in the air.

"Oh, some things never change." I smiled up at him. "You want to talk to me?"

"There's nothing to talk about." Thayer dropped his smile and shrugged. "I'm just me. Being with whoever I want and not tying myself to anything."

"I get that. But, Nikki?" I raised an eyebrow.

Thayer leaned against the wall and slid to the floor, leaning his back against it. I remembered the people upstairs and everything that hung on Thayer's talent.

But right now, he needed someone to hear him, not use him. I could give him this.

"I just don't see the appeal." I sat on the floor next him, our knees touching.

"Everyone's a little different, different appeal. With you, it was all hot and forbidden because if Alec ever found out, who knows what he would've done." Thayer nudged me with an elbow.

I played along. "Yeah, what were we thinking?"

"That's the point." Thayer nodded, happy to continue talking. "We weren't. Being with Nikki is just...I mean, wow."

"Okay," I raised a hand at him. "I don't need all the details."

Thayer laughed. "No, not in the way you think. It's just... it's like an out-of-body experience being with someone who is so self-absorbed. For that time, you don't even matter, only she does. It's kind of a...relief?"

We both laughed and Thayer leaned his head back against the wall. I looked thoughtfully at his face, scanning for any clue to his emotion. He always wore his heart on his sleeve, and if you looked long enough, he'd tell you everything.

"What are you getting relief from?" I asked.

Thayer's brown eyes snapped over to me. He pulled his head away from the wall and turned his chin down.

"Her," Thayer whispered.

I waited. He didn't need me to talk. If I sat in the silence, he might just tell me what he's dying to get out.

"Why'd you bring her?" Thayer groaned and I knew who he was talking about. "I was fine with everything. The Shadows, my life, everything was what I wanted. And then she was there and she seemed like she wanted that too. But then she just…broke it all."

I nodded. "I understand the allure of wanting something you shouldn't have. But Lisa has been through so much. She's fragile and I think you're making a good choice to stay away from her."

"Fragile?" Thayer asked, looking confused and almost indignant. "What part of her is fragile? She got her life ripped away from her and decided to stick by her friend anyway. She walked into the Shadows' mansion because she trusted you. That woman stood up to *me*. Even being here, she's the one who still has the same brightness that she came in with. The rest of you are starting to look like death warmed over. She's the strongest person I think I've ever seen."

My mouth fell open. Thayer looked at my expression and immediately winced. I smiled and before I made a sound, Thayer put a hand up and shook his head. "Don't, don't say it."

I ignored him. "You like her!"

"No, that's not—" he protested.

"Yes, you do. You think she walks on clouds, you're confused around her, and you've been going out of your way to ignore her since we got here. You so like her." I laughed, nodding.

"It doesn't matter!" Thayer shouted. He glanced around and then lowered his voice. "I'm a Shadow. I've always been a Shadow and it's everything I've ever wanted. She is nothing like that. I can't be a Shadow and want her too. It doesn't work."

He put his head in his hands and pulled at his thick brown hair. I laid my hand on his shoulder.

"It's okay to change what you want," I whispered. "I know this better than anyone."

"I don't think I can be *good* enough for her." Thayer shook his head, still holding onto his hair. "I kill people. And I like it. I can't change everything about my life. It's not...If I wait long enough, I'll get over it."

"I still care about you, even if I no longer agree with all of your choices. You mean the world to me. Who's to say that won't be the same for her?" I said.

At that, Thayer lifted his head and looked at me with a grim expression.

"Thank you," he said with a pained face.

I nodded and patted his shoulder with my hand. I thought about the two of them together and everything Thayer said made sense. But I knew how deeply he cared for people and that was exactly something Lisa needed right now.

"But I've already made up my mind." Thayer gestured to himself sitting on the floor. "This is all I'm ever going to be."

"Good," I said and he looked surprised. "How many people have you killed today?"

I stared at him with a calm face, preparing myself for his answer.

"Two," Thayer sighed. "Oh, wait. No, three. I almost forgot about that other girl."

"Wow, okay." I nodded, about to stand.

"Look, I promise I didn't drain anyone in front of her. Not after I saw her reaction in the mansion," Thayer sighed, staring at the floor.

"You took Lisa hunting with you?" I asked, sensing that steely protectiveness snapping back into place.

"Nikki and I wanted to go alone but she wanted to come!" Thayer threw his hands in the air. "I tried to talk her out of it, but she asked so nicely...ugh. But I stopped when I noticed her watching me."

"You actually stopped?" I waited, watching Thayer's face. He kept holding his breath like he wasn't done talking.

"I waited for her to walk around the corner and finished the human anyway." Thayer shook his head. "I don't even know why I'm telling you this. I just...I feel like there's this weight on my chest whenever I think about her seeing me..."

I knew what the weight was. I knew how heavy guilt could feel when someone you care about watches you do something repulsive. Even if I understood what he was going through, that was something Thayer needed to figure out on his own.

"Hey." I grabbed his shoulder and shook it until he looked at me. "I'm not saying I'm good with you killing people. Seriously, I think you should rethink some priorities, but for the moment, I need Thayer, the King of the Shadows."

I smiled and stood, extending a hand down to him.

"Because you are what we need. Thayer—exactly as you are right now," I said.

Thayer took my hand and smiled. We turned to walk down the hall and Thayer put his arm around me. His body heat made the dank basement seem a little less tragic.

"Thank you," Thayer muttered.

"For what?" I smiled.

He grinned, grateful that I wasn't bringing it up again. We walked arm in arm down the hallway.

"So, what do you need me to do?" Thayer asked in a more serious tone.

"Okay, just go with me here." I put my hands up, ready to explain the story. "I think I figured out how this is gonna work."

# CHAPTER
# THIRTY-FIVE

"All right, everyone can calm down. I'm here," Thayer announced as he walked into the room and raised his arms like he was seeking applause.

I followed behind him and smiled at how many people either laughed or rolled their eyes at his comment. It brought an odd amount of joy to see other people accept Thayer's personality the way I did.

"Look who was exactly where we expected him to be," Alec said.

I looked at Lisa, who tapped the pen on the top of the notepad as she stared at Thayer's feet.

"What?" Thayer asked.

"Nothing," I interrupted before Alec could finish. He smiled and turned back to his tablet.

"So, you know what you're supposed to do?" Sage stepped forward.

"Mara told me everything," Thayer said, rubbing his hands together and turning to Alec with a hand held up. "May I just say it was shocking to hear that you actually do have a heart?"

Alec smirked and removed the cuff, dropping it on the other table. Thayer rubbed where it had probably been chafing.

But that didn't stop Thayer from lighting up in a smile. "Does this mean you're finally gonna let me inside your mind?"

"Not if my life depended on it." Alec shook his head.

"What? How do you expect us to test it out?" I asked.

The answer came strutting in the door, still pulling down her shirt even though she'd had plenty of time to put it back on.

"Sorry it took me so long." Nikki smoothed her hair and pretended to be out of breath. "What are we up to?"

Thayer kept his eyes on either the floor or Alec. He seemed to purposely keep his feet turned away from Lisa at all costs.

"Alec wants to see if I can hold an emotion long enough for someone to transition. But he doesn't want to volunteer himself," Thayer crossed his arms in front of his chest.

"Can you really blame me? I've seen firsthand what you're capable of," Alec argued.

"I think that was a compliment?" Thayer smiled.

"Well, you can do me," Nikki said in a flirtatious voice.

Thayer cringed before he turned to look at her. When he finally faced her, his face was smooth again. It remained smooth when he glanced up at Lisa and back down again.

"There you go. You've got a volunteer," Alec said. "We'll have to give you this serum to induce pain. Don't worry it won't change anything."

"And since this kitty already lost her claws it's not like you have much to lose," Thayer muttered.

"Excuse me?" Nikki narrowed her eyes at Thayer.

"This is good. It's probably easier going up against a Zero than anyone else," Thayer grinned.

Nikki scoffed and tossed her hair behind her back. Thayer moved to the table, standing at the head and patting the surface for Nikki.

She took her time walking over and lying down. Her hands fluttered to make sure her hair was just right before she finally stilled and looked at Thayer upside down.

"All right, it's ready." Alec raised the syringe.

"Give me a second." Thayer put his hands on Nikki's head.

"Be gentle, okay?" Nikki asked as she craned her neck to look up at him.

"Don't fight me then," Thayer said back to her with a smile.

She let out a breath and let her shoulders relax into the table.

His fingers just reached her temples and he leaned closer to her. He stared into her eyes as she stared back. The connection was obvious when Nikki's sarcastic eyebrow lowered and her lips parted.

"Ready," Thayer mumbled as he closed his eyes and scrunched his eyebrows to focus.

Alec didn't wait another moment before sticking the syringe in Nikki's neck. Her face remained still, not even flinching her eyes at the injection.

Alec pushed down the plunger and the clear liquid emptied underneath Nikki's skin. He pulled away and reached for his tablet without taking his eyes off of her.

"The serum is pretty immediate," Alec explained. "She should be feeling the pain now."

All of us stared at Nikki. Her eyes didn't blink as she looked at the ceiling; her chest rose and fell evenly.

Alec tapped on the tablet screen, taking notes and watching Nikki. Lisa scribbled in her notepad in the corner.

Sage and the rest of them stood near the door, all of them holding their breath as we waited.

The minutes seemed to tick by painfully slow. I was grateful there wasn't a visible clock in the room.

"That's ten minutes," Alec announced.

Thayer didn't move. Nikki still stared blankly at the ceiling. I had never seen her so calm before.

"How long does a transition last?" I whispered to Alec.

"Everyone's a little different," Alec shrugged. "I've never seen someone take under an hour to wake up again."

"An hour? He can't hold it for an hour," I hissed back to him.

"Depends on how much energy he's using. Thayer's the best at this. If anyone can do it, then it'd be him," Alec said, still not looking at me.

I turned back to Nikki and Thayer.

She lay perfectly still on the table. Thayer still had his eyes closed and his hands on her. His fingers twitched from holding his muscles so tightly. I listened for Thayer's next breath.

The sound wasn't right when he took in the air. He was getting weak already. He wouldn't make it to the end of the hour at this rate.

I stepped forward and wanted to put my hand on Thayer, but that would only make things worse. I stopped.

Lisa saw me and moved toward him instead. She rested a hand on his back, Thayer didn't move at her touch.

"Just hold on," Lisa whispered.

Thayer's fingers relaxed, almost falling away from Nikki's face. His eyebrows smoothed for a moment but he kept his eyes closed.

"Incredible," Sage breathed as she watched with her bright red eyes. In however many centuries she had been alive, I wondered if she had seen anyone hold on that long.

"Fifteen minutes," Alec breathed.

I glanced at Kylan. He had his arms crossed in front of him as he watched. Doubt cast a hint of gray in his usually warm eyes.

My mind begged for Thayer to hold on. If he could make it long enough to last through a transition, Alec would put the experiment to the test. As soon as he got what he wanted, I'd be free. My fingers tingled at the thought of touching Kylan freely.

Everything else could fade away and it would just be the two of us, holding each other, feeling everything.

But there was no antidote yet. Alec hadn't made one and we might still be a long way from the happy possibility of touching anyone.

Kylan turned to look at me. No doubt he could see the hope written all over my face. An understanding smile pulled one corner of his mouth up. I sighed as I wished and wished that this would all be over soon.

Kylan just nodded back to me.

That one little motion was everything I needed. My body released the stress that had been festering inside. His soft green eyes made the rest of the world make sense.

A groan came from Thayer. I snapped my head back to look at him. He shook his knees and forced them to hold himself up again.

"You're doing it," Lisa whispered again and I could have sworn I heard another moan from him. His head moved from side to side like he was following the connection he was about to lose.

"Twenty minutes," Alec said.

*Twenty minutes.* We weren't even close and Thayer was already losing it.

"Let's get a human in here," I suggested, quietly to Alec.

He only shook his head. "Energy would be too distracting. He'd lose the connection."

"He's not going to make it," I muttered.

I turned and looked at Alec's face. His mouth was closed and his eyes couldn't look more apathetic if he tried.

"No," Alec said easily. He already knew this would fail, but he wanted Thayer to try it anyway.

I waited and counted each breath in and out of Thayer's chest. They spread further apart as he sucked in harder and slowly let the air out again.

I shrank when I didn't hear the next breath come in on time.

Thayer's knees buckled underneath him. His hands pulled away from Nikki as he fell to the floor. He caught himself on his elbows just in time to stop his face from smacking on the tile.

Nikki lurched, crying in pain. She clamped either side of her head. Her back arched off the table as she twisted on her side.

"Twenty six minutes," Alec muttered over the sound of Nikki's cries and Thayer's heaving breaths. "Not good enough."

"Are you serious?" I asked, pointing to Thayer curled up on the floor. "I've never seen anyone use energy straight for that long."

"And yet." Alec tapped the screen on his tablet. "Still not good enough."

Nikki's crying had dulled to an incessant whimper as she squeezed her eyes shut and pulled her knees up to her chest.

I moved to Thayer, who was trying and failing to sit up on his knees. Lisa had one arm locked around his shoulders and her fingers barely reached the other side of him.

"Do you think you can move enough to get outside?" I asked.

Thayer lifted his head enough to look at me. The pain that wrinkled around his eyes gave me the answer.

"I'm sure you can manage to stumble downstairs," Alec errantly commented as if we should know what he meant.

"What?" I asked the question that everyone waited for.

"Let's just say we didn't dismiss all the staff." Alec glanced up from his tablet to lock eyes with me.

"What's downstairs?" Lisa asked. "The rooms?"

Flashes of me previously wondering this same question when I came back to the mansion the first time. Kylan was waiting for me downstairs and Alec had done everything in his power to keep me away just long enough to make sure he couldn't trigger anything.

"No, below them. Nikki?" Alec asked, a little too loud.

"What?" Nikki snapped, still holding her head with one hand and wincing as she tried to sit up.

"Drag Thayer downstairs with you," Alec ordered.

"Ugh, fine," Nikki grumbled and ventured a step off the table.

Her foot landed shaky at first, but solidified once her other foot hit the floor too. She immediately grabbed Thayer and pulled on his arm.

"What's down there?" Lisa said, the fear cracking in her voice.

"Come on, sweetheart," Alec drawled. "Put two and two together. They need human energy and I just told them to go down the stairs…"

"Oh," Lisa said, taking it way easier than I expected. "So, they've just been working down there this whole time?"

Nikki laughed and yanked Thayer up as hard as she could.

He stumbled into her and Lisa stood, still waiting for Alec's answer.

"Just wow." Alec widened his eyes and laughed. "It's like talking to a wall."

Thayer loosed as fierce a growl as he could manage. Even I took a step back at the sound. Alec froze.

"They don't work down there. They are *kept* down there. And we're gonna go pay a couple of them a little visit," Nikki sneered at Lisa as she ran her hand against Thayer's arm slowly.

Lisa yanked her hands away from Thayer and held them close to her chest. Her lips tightened as she glanced between the two Shadows.

"Hurry back," Alec called while staring down at the screen.

Nikki guided the two of them out of the room. Before they left, Thayer looked up at Lisa in a long glance. A pit formed in my stomach. She staggered back to her notebook and sat on the stool in the corner where she was before.

Thayer moved his gaze over to me.

He wasn't angry. He was barely even sad. He just stared into my eyes as if to tell me that this was how things were supposed to be. Lisa hating what he does. And him being his normal, Shadow self.

I shook my head at him before Thayer dropped his chin and let Nikki drag him out of the doorway.

"What a waste," Alec sighed.

"Waste? You sent him to do something you knew he couldn't do." I narrowed my eyes at him.

"Sometimes people have a way of surprising me. Just look at you." Alec finally looked up and smiled at me.

"So, is that it? We've hit a dead end," Kylan said.

"Seems so." Alec shrugged.

"No, there's got to be another way to get that emotion in the body." I ran a hand through the ends of my hair mindlessly.

"Unless you're volunteering to try your hand at emotional manipulation, I don't see how that's going to work," Alec answered.

"A chemical," Lisa muttered from the corner.

The three of us turned to see her hunched over her notebook, staring down, and tapping the pen on the top of the pages.

"What chemical?" Alec asked, giving Lisa one chance to impress him.

"Well…well, I'm not sure…let me just—" Lisa flipped to the next page.

"This is why I don't take advice from humans," Alec sighed, pressing his fingers to the bridge of his nose.

Sage stepped closer to Lisa, looking down at the notebook with her. Lisa buried her nose in the book as her eyes raced back and forth across the words.

"She's a Legend now, remember?" I asked.

"Sorry." Alec raised a hand. "Former human."

"Stop that," I said. Alec just raised an eyebrow at me. "Just stop attacking her. She's been through enough at your hand."

"Oh." Alec tsked. "Such fragile feelings. Too bad your deal didn't cover emotional harm. I'd say that's my specialty, wouldn't you?"

"Oxytocin," Lisa blurted, looking up from her paper.

"Come again?" Alec said, probably already getting his next insult ready for her.

"Oxytocin. It's the chemical that can calm the brain. The same response as when you give someone a hug. I think that's the emotion that Mara just gave to you." Lisa pointed at Alec.

Alec's mouth hung open, the words dying in his mouth. I smiled at her. Lisa pushed her hair back behind her ear so she could stare at Alec.

"Where did you learn that?" Kylan asked.

"One of the general education classes at night school." Lisa stood from the chair, tucking her notebook under her arm.

"Hear that?" I smacked Alec. "Human school just bested your centuries of knowledge."

"Lucky guess." Alec narrowed his eyes.

"And there's no way your cold heart would have ever thought of it." I pointed a finger at him. "Which means you—being you—are actually the thing that is holding you back."

"The irony." Kylan grinned at me.

I turned to him and snickered like a child. We both just smiled at each other, enjoying the one moment of victory over Alec.

"Don't get too excited. We don't even know if it's going to work," Alec scoffed and looked back down to the screen.

"So, what do we need to do?" Sage asked.

"We need to create the chemical and test it again," Alec said.

"But it could work?" I asked, trying to hide a smile.

"To be determined." Alec clenched his teeth.

"And that's as close to a compliment as you're probably going to get." I smiled at Lisa now.

She straightened her shoulders as she looked Alec in the eye. Bravery emanated off her body, and it drove Alec crazy because he was the one who had created it.

Kylan chuckled behind me and it sounded like the pure music of relief.

# CHAPTER
# THIRTY-SIX

Alec couldn't believe that it worked, even if he didn't say it. After we finally tailored the dosage for his body to get the same result as before, he still didn't say anything to Lisa.

Thayer and Nikki walked back in like nothing had happened. Nikki sauntered to the table and sat down.

"How are you feeling?" I asked as I put a hand on Thayer's shoulder.

"Better." Thayer grinned but pain still hid in his eyes.

He kept his face turned away from Lisa, who was whispering with Sage in the corner. I didn't want to think of the dead people downstairs in their wake, not just the ones from Nikki's hand.

Judging by the smooth way Thayer moved now, he had at least drained one. Kylan came back in with Derek following him.

"Kylan said you guys are close?" Derek asked.

"Yeah. We're ready for trial," I answered with a smile.

"Where's Cassie?" Lisa asked.

"She's resting in our room. I told her I'd come get her if this amounted to anything," Derek said.

"Well, now all we need is a volunteer," Alec said, prepping the clear chemical for someone to take.

"No, no. Uh-uh. Nope." Nikki shot off the table and stood behind Alec without anyone even looking at her yet.

"All right, anyone else?" Alec was unfazed as he held the bottle up to the light.

I expected silence to follow, for everyone to take a step away from being the next guinea pig.

"I'll do it," a soft voice rang.

I whipped my head around, instantly grateful that it wasn't Lisa who had said it. Sage moved quietly to the table and lay down as we watched her.

"You sure?" Thayer asked.

Sage just reached for the sensors that Alec had placed near the table. She stuck one on each temple before she rested her head back.

"Someone has to. The sooner we get it over with the sooner we can all get out of here. Even if it strips my powers, at least we won't have to hear Nikki complaining as much," Sage sighed as she settled her shoulders into the table.

The tattooed Shadow snapped her teeth at Sage as she walked instinctively over to Alec.

"Nikki, take this." Alec handed the syringe to her, explaining the process as he pointed from Sage to the tablet.

"You don't have to do this," I said.

Sage moved her red eyes over to me.

"What's the worst that could happen?" She smiled.

I stepped back into Kylan's open arms and nodded to her. Nikki sidled up to the table with the bottle and syringe. She stabbed the needle in the top of the bottle, pulling up the liquid. Alec readied another syringe that must have held the serum to change her.

"Good luck in there, princess." Thayer stepped in and

held her hand gently. "I'll be right here when you wake up."

Sage nodded and then turned her head to the side as Nikki lowered the first needle. A prick of pain flickered in Sage's red eyes as it stabbed in. After a second, Sage wrinkled her nose and shifted her fingers, even in Thayer's hand.

Alec lowered the next needle and I stopped my breath as he stabbed it into the back of her neck.

None of us said anything as her eyes fluttered closed.

None of us said anything when her breaths slowed.

None of us knew what to say when the monitor beeped erratically and her body started convulsing on the table.

Alec jumped forward, studying the screen. Nikki set the bottle and needle on the table next to Sage's seizing body and stepped away.

Lisa and Thayer worked like an automatic team to hold her flailing limbs.

"Nikki, what did you do?" I lunged at her.

"Nothing! I just gave her the dose!" Nikki jumped back even farther.

"But you adjusted it for her, right?" Lisa asked.

"Well... no," Nikki answered.

"No? What do you mean no? Her body is way smaller than Alec's. You didn't think that would be important?" I said.

"Not to mention she's still sensitive to everything around her, even the sun," Thayer said.

"Alec didn't tell me to!" Nikki pointed a finger.

Alec kept eerily silent.

He was actually at a loss for words, just in the moment when I wanted him to explain how exactly he could decide to move forward with a trial and not have thought through every possibility.

"You're so eager to get what you want, you couldn't have thought about how she would react compared to you?" Kylan said.

Kylan reached for Alec with a hand tensed in the shape of a claw. Alec ducked in time to miss Kylan grabbing his shoulder. Before Alec could retaliate, a loud ominous sound silenced us all.

The beeping from the machine to indicate Sage's heart rate had changed to one solid sound. Her body went still on the table, falling awkwardly back into place.

"She's dead," Thayer breathed.

We all froze, except for Alec. He moved slowly around the table, as if he wanted to get a better look.

"The combination must have been too much for her to handle," Lisa said, a tear spilling from her right eye.

She wiped it away before it reached her chin. By the time Thayer turned to look at Lisa, the tear was gone. Lisa tucked the notebook in the back of her waistband. She pulled her shirt over the edges of the book.

I spun and reached for Kylan, his arms already open.

So much of this experience was different from before. When I was here, there was no end to the torture and nowhere to turn for relief. At least this time the aching pain had an outlet. I buried my face in Kylan's shirt and the sting subsided enough for me to take a deep breath.

"Alec! What are you doing?" Thayer's voice shouted.

I ripped myself away from Kylan and turned. Alec had Lisa's arm and pinned her back to him. A dagger shined in the light as it pressed to Lisa's throat.

"Get on the other table," Alec ordered Thayer.

"Are you crazy? Sage just died in your experiment. I'm not—" A trickle of blood fell down Lisa's neck when Alec pressed harder.

"Would you rather the former human take your place?" Alec wiggled his fingers on the hilt like it was easy for him to hold her there.

Lisa's eyes locked on Thayer. She bit her lip to stifle a cry. Moving her throat would only hurt her worse.

"Sage didn't even want to stay here. I talked her into it and she listened to me. She's gone! And it's my fault. You're not even going to give any of us a second to process this?" Thayer looked between Sage and Lisa.

Alec glowered. "It's sad to see such a waste of talent."

"Waste of talent? If that's all she meant to you then that's fine. But she was my friend. I cared about her. After all the decades I spent serving you, can't you give me this?" Thayer's hand landed on Sage's leg.

"Alec, you know this isn't fair." I raised my hands, walking slowly toward him.

"I'm not falling for that again." Alec smiled at me. "If someone doesn't get on the table for the next trial, I will slit her throat. Now, Thayer is almost the same body type as me. I mean, Kylan and Derek would work just fine, but I doubt Derek wants to risk leaving his pregnant wife all alone. And I'm sure you'd rather volunteer Thayer's life than Kylan's. Am I wrong?"

"I don't want to volunteer anyone," I said, shaking my head.

"This is insane," Kylan growled at his brother, just as powerless as I was.

"I'm sorry, I'm sorry. It should have worked," Lisa finally sobbed.

Alec tightened his grip, pulling her closer to his body. When Lisa tried to lean away, another drop of blood streaked down her neck. He leaned into her wild curls, getting as close to her ear as he could.

"One more word out of you and I might just cut you anyway," Alec snarled.

"Alec, we're only asking for some time," Thayer begged.

Alec turned his gaze to Thayer. Those blue eyes didn't hold a shred of empathy in them. He didn't even glance at Sage before answering.

"You're already responsible for one Legend death today. Do you wanna add one more to the list?" Alec asked.

Lisa froze in his grip. Instead of shaky hands, they remained loose at her sides. Lisa looked over to me with pleading eyes.

"Stop!" I said. "Alec, please…"

"No!" Alec shouted back at me. "I've waited centuries for this to work and I'm not waiting another second."

"Please," I whispered.

"Maybe this will be it, huh? The final, unforgiveable act," Alec whispered back to me.

I was the only who knew what he meant. I hadn't even told Kylan about his ultimatum yet. I shifted my feet as I wondered if seeing Lisa die at his hands would make me ready to end Alec's life.

It might.

But the thought that scared me more was that it might not.

"I'll do it," Thayer said, already walking to the second table.

Lisa's eyes went wide in horror. She opened her mouth like she wanted to scream, but no sound came out. My heart wrenched in my chest as Thayer grazed the metal table with his strong hand.

He was one of my best friends. When he looked at me, I saw how much he was doing this for Lisa, but also how much he was doing this for me. It was him or Kylan. And Thayer was always so giving.

One thought chilled my entire body. *This might be the last thing he can give me.*

That thought stuck to my skin as Thayer lay down on the other table only a few feet away from Sage's body. The chills shuddered down my arms as I watched the sensors get attached to Thayer's olive skin.

"I'm so sorry." I stepped forward and put a gloved hand on his shoulder.

The hot tears built up in my eyes as I looked at Thayer's brilliant smile. His bright brown gaze looked back at me and I felt centuries fly between us.

"I just wanted what you had," he whispered to me.

The thought wasn't tainted with anger. In fact, I almost saw a tear shimmering in Thayer's clear brown eyes. I didn't have anything to say back to him, anything to give. I let my hand fall from Thayer's shoulder.

I balled my fists at my sides as Nikki administered the doses and Thayer's beautiful eyes closed.

# CHAPTER
# THIRTY-SEVEN

Minutes ticked by. Achingly slow. Then nearly an hour was gone.

Thayer's heartrate had fluctuated here and there, but nothing compared to the way Sage's had skyrocketed. Derek had moved Sage's body to another room, where she would wait until we could have a proper burial for her.

Alec sat on a stool as close to Thayer as he could get while keeping one hand on his tablet and the other wrapped around Lisa's wrist. Lisa didn't struggle; she just stood silently next to Alec.

The only two sounds in the room were Nikki picking her nails in the corner and the steady beeps from the machine.

My eyes shifted to Kylan, who was still standing next to me. I didn't need to say anything aloud for him to hear my impatience. The tension pounded in the room so hard I struggled to breathe.

Derek came back in the room with a somber look on his face.

"Any change?" Derek asked.

Kylan shook his head and I stared back at Thayer.

"This is the longest I've ever seen him stay quiet." I forced a smile.

To my surprise, Alec was the first to laugh. Nikki followed along with a giggle. For one brief second, the tension wavered and I took a normal breath.

The beeps on the machine increased in frequency, cutting off the laughter. The beeps came faster and faster, while Thayer's body remained still.

"Not again," Alec murmured.

I couldn't lose him. Not Thayer. But I was already wondering who Alec would sacrifice next. Who else's life he could threaten to get the next person on the table.

My fists turned into claws, raking down Kylan's shirt as the beeping sped.

Thayer's eyes flew open.

Alec jumped back, yanking Lisa by her arm. Thayer sat up in one fast motion, the sensors ripped off his skin and flung back to the table as the beeping halted.

"It's real." Thayer touched his body with his own hands like he still needed confirmation.

"Thayer," I breathed, smiling.

He lifted his head and looked at me with a look of innocent awe. My friend, my loyal friend back from the impossible. He jumped off the table, still running his hands on his chest and arms.

"I made it," he laughed. "I made it. I can't believe it."

"Next question is, did it work?" Alec asked.

Thayer's hands dropped, deadly fast as he turned his head to look at Alec. His eyes settled on Alec's hand around Lisa's wrist.

"Thought you'd never ask," Thayer said.

He launched himself forward, not leaving Alec enough

time to reach for his dagger or create a new one. Thayer grabbed Alec by the shoulders and shoved him against the back wall. Thayer's hand clasped around Alec's throat.

Yellow light flushed from Alec into Thayer's hand.

He was a Five. An actual Five. A sense of solidarity formed between Thayer and me now that I wasn't the only one.

If anyone deserved to share this power, it was him.

The reminder of Sage was still too vivid in my mind. That could have been Thayer. But instead he was smiling and sucking energy.

"Yeah, it worked," Thayer whispered in a threatening tone.

Alec grabbed Thayer's hand and tossed it away. Thayer stumbled back and looked down at his palm with a smile. He rolled his shoulders, adjusting to the new power.

"That feels incredible," Thayer said and pointed at me. "You. Thought I was jealous before, but now I definitely hate you a little bit. You had this the whole time?"

"Welcome to the Five club." I smiled and shrugged.

Alec glared at him. Thayer dropped his hand and turned on his heel to face Lisa.

He opened his mouth to say something, but closed it before any words came out. Instead, he walked forward and took her face in his hands.

He pulled her forward and kissed her.

Energy left from Lisa into Thayer as they kissed. He didn't stop holding her until she put a hand on his chest and pushed him away gently.

He immediately pulled away and pulled his hands back to himself.

"I'm sorry." Thayer shook his head as he touched his mouth. "I'm sorry, I didn't mean to… I just wanted…"

Lisa glanced at me. I raised an eyebrow at her and she smiled when she turned back to Thayer. She reached her hands up and laid them on Thayer's chest.

Without any words, she stretched up on her toes and kissed Thayer again. He melted against her as she put her arms around him.

I lifted my head to Kylan and he just gaped at the two of them.

"Man, I did not see that coming," Kylan said.

"Same, bro." Derek shook his head.

Alec pulled away from the wall and Nikki moved to stand next to him. Both of them looked equally disgusted, as if Thayer was kissing an actual human, caring for a human.

"As much as I hate to break this up," Nikki said, "I think I'm next in line."

"For the serum? Or for Thayer?" Alec smiled at her.

Lisa pulled away when she heard that. Thayer rolled his eyes over at Alec and locked a death stare on him. Nikki ignored the comment anyway, but that didn't stop Lisa from blushing a bright red and staring at the floor.

"You promised to fix me. I'm calling in that promise." Nikki walked to the table and lay down as she talked.

"I guess it's only fair. Anyway, one more trial couldn't hurt." Alec shrugged and started readying the next serums.

It only took a few minutes to set the dosage for Nikki. Both needles went in and Nikki's face finally relaxed again. In the meantime, Lisa and Thayer scuttled out of the room. Derek left too, I assumed, to go talk to Cassie.

That just left me, Kylan, and Alec in a silent room.

"When are you going to fulfill your promise to me?" I asked, pointing at the tablet.

"What? Giving you the information on what I did to you?" Alec clarified.

"Yes, what else would she mean?" Kylan rolled his eyes.

"Well, to be perfectly *clear*, you haven't fulfilled your end yet." Alec smiled. "I'm not a Five, am I?"

"Close enough." I begged with my hands.

"Close enough has never worked with me." Alec shook his head and moved to the door.

He was leaving, to go where I had no idea.

"You're not going to stay and watch? I thought you cared about her." I pointed to Nikki.

Alec looked down at her. I expected him to say something, a quick comeback at least. Instead, he just stared lazily at her motionless body. He pushed the door open and walked out without saying anything.

"Cold," Kylan scoffed.

"That's Alec for you," I sighed.

"Good news though." Kylan stepped in my view, bringing a welcome distraction. "It's working. As soon as she wakes up, Alec will get what he wants and we can leave this whole place behind."

"You have no idea how hard I'm holding on to that idea." I closed my eyes and let out a breath.

Kylan smiled, taking my gloved hands in his. He squeezed fingers in his palms and looked up at me.

"I do," Kylan said with a shaky voice while he looked down. "I want to believe that in a little while, everything will be okay. But, I don't know that. Neither of us does."

"Thanks for the pep talk," I muttered.

"I'm sorry." Kylan shook his head like he was trying to focus. "I'm just...I'm not saying any of this right."

"Hey, what's going on?" I asked, studying his face even more than before.

His eyebrows switched between pulling together and

perfectly relaxed. His feet moved awkwardly underneath him. Both unsteady hands held onto mine like they were a lifeline.

He took a deep breath and looked back up. All the stress on his face melted away into a warm smile.

"Follow me." Kylan pulled my hand and raced out the door.

"We can't just leave her. What if something happens?" I protested, but followed him anyway.

"She seems pretty tough. I doubt she'd let herself die." Kylan chuckled.

"Good point," I said. "Where are we going?"

"It's a surprise," Kylan called back to me.

"Downstairs? Why are we—" I tried.

"Asking again isn't going to make me tell you," Kylan said.

I smiled and looked ahead for where we could be going. We slowed as we reached Kylan's room. He opened the door, pulled me inside, and shut the door immediately.

When I looked inside, I lost my breath. Trees stood in the two far corners. Their roots sat on top of the hard floor. The leaves hung so low, they almost brushed the top of my head. In between the two trees was a little stone bench.

The bench was the same one in the park by where Kylan and I used to work. A smile pulled across my lips.

A small, white card rested on the center of the seat. *Reserved.*

I turned around, feeling all of my emotions catch in my throat. My heart was no longer beating in individual beats, but was flying out of my chest.

"What is this?" I asked, covering my mouth with my hand.

"I wanted to do this at home, but the longer we stayed,

the more it seemed like that might not happen," Kylan said.

"This must have taken so long to create. Is that what you've been doing with the energy?" I gazed around the room at the intricate details of the trees and the carved bench.

But mostly I kept looking back at his still-glowing cuff. Making any of this impossible.

"Believe it or not, Nikki has a romantic side. She turned the cuff down only long enough for me to do this in stages—heavily monitored, of course," Kylan explained.

She just wanted Alec to herself, and if throwing me at Kylan was the best way to do that, then that's what she'd do. But I didn't say that.

The last while it seemed like Kylan had been dodging me. I assumed from the sleepwalking scares. Maybe this was why. Kylan nodded. He led me to the bench, swiped the card, and we both sat.

"I don't know what the future holds. I hope I'll be able to touch you. I hope my siblings and I will make it out of here mostly intact. I would give anything to know the future right now. But above all of that, I know I want to be with you," Kylan said.

"I want to be with you—" I started to smile.

"Nope." Kylan shook his head sharply. "Please, let me finish."

I nodded and closed my lips while I waited.

"I know this isn't the time or the place, but I'm tired of waiting for things to be perfect. I'm starting to think that with you around, life will always be an adventure," Kylan laughed.

"Wait—" I finally realized what he meant.

"Nope," Kylan said again, "This place could burn down around us, and I'd be fine with it, as long as I'm with you. I haven't felt this way about anyone in my entire life. I love you, as Mara and as Kate. I love all of you," he said.

My heart pattered unevenly in my chest. I tried to keep my mouth closed, but I couldn't stop my lips from opening when Kylan slid off the bench and down on one knee.

I couldn't stop the sound coming from my mouth when he pulled a ring from his pocket and held it up. I couldn't stop my smile when he said those words.

"Mara Hayes, will you marry me?" Kylan smiled, breathless.

All the words I wanted to say before flew out the door. I looked down at him, at my precious Kylan Stone, and I smiled so hard I laughed.

The room didn't matter. The beeping machines were irrelevant. I could be standing anywhere in the world, and I wouldn't care. He was here, in front of me, and I knew everything else would fall into place eventually.

He was here. And he wanted me.

I laid my hand on top of his as I gazed into his green eyes.

"Just try and stop me," I said.

# CHAPTER
# THIRTY-EIGHT

Just as I was contemplating kissing Kylan, the door flew open.

"All right, I'm ready," Alec said, glancing up at the trees. "Interesting."

"For what?" I said, still a bit dazed.

Kylan had his arms around me, and I must have had a mark on my face from pressing my cheek into his shirt for so long. If I couldn't touch his skin, I wanted as much of him around me as possible.

Alec didn't seem to care that he interrupted the moment. In fact, he smiled a little too much for my comfort.

"The trial," Alec said, leading the way down the hall.

"You're going under now? Nikki hasn't even woken up yet," I said, glancing back at Kylan.

"Yeah, don't you need her to...I don't know, guard you?" Kylan asked.

Alec snatched my left hand, lifting it up to look at the ring. His energy swirled around my hand, glinting in the diamonds.

"Engagement ring? Cute." Alec smiled at Kylan.

I ripped my hand away from him and pulled it to my chest. Kylan looked unfazed by Alec's comment. So he took it one step further.

"I'm sure a big, white wedding is just what Mara's been dreaming about her whole life. Isn't that right?" This time Alec looked at my right arm, at where the dagger would be.

I pulled that arm behind my back. I knew what Alec meant. Shadows didn't marry the way humans did. Based on the engagement, the wedding Kylan had in mind was very human.

Alec knew that I had been dreaming of a Shadow's bonding ceremony, and up until all of this started, I had been dreaming of it with him.

"I'm aware Nikki won't wake for a while." Alec shrugged. "If you tamper with me when I'm sleeping then you'll never find out how to fix Mara. Judging by that shiny new ring on her finger, you're really committed to that whole thing working out. Right, brother?"

"Fine." I followed, not wanting to talk Alec out of this any further.

"By the way"—Alec turned to Kylan—"I don't blame you for not wanting to upstage me. You were never good at that anyway."

Kylan made a fist but kept it to himself. I didn't know if Kylan knew what Alec was talking about. I didn't even know how to explain that I wanted to marry him, even if it meant giving up the tradition I grew up with.

Even when I said it to myself, it sounded sad.

We followed him up the stairs, down the halls, and into the room where Nikki's still frame was lying on a table. The monitors still beeped regularly and her chest rose and fell easily.

I stepped forward. "Hand me the needles and I'll do it myself."

Kylan didn't miss a beat. He walked forward and helped load the liquids in the needles. Alec double-checked the dosage before lying back on the table.

"I mean, I don't think you've thought this through but whatever," Kylan shook his head. "Just know, the second you close your eyes we'll be looking for the tablet."

Alec turned his cold eyes to Kylan.

"Happy hunting, brother." He smiled.

I moved the needle down to the base of Alec's neck. He stared at me the entire time I moved. The first needle, the second needle. His eyes never left mine until they started to close.

"See you on the other side," Alec muttered before his eyes shut completely.

I hope not. I smiled.

"Let's go," Kylan said and grabbed my hand.

He pulled me out the door as we both rushed back down the stairs to Derek's room. I dropped his hand and went to where Thayer had been staying. We glanced at each other and smiled.

Today was the day we figured it all out.

Without bothering to knock, Kylan shoved the door open.

"Where's Derek?" Kylan asked.

"I don't know. I think he went out," Cassie said.

Their voices grew muffled as I moved farther down the hall. I reached the room I needed and stopped listening to Cassie and Kylan.

I knocked on the door, trying not to hear what was happening on the other side. Thayer whipped open the door and his crazed brown eyes landed on me.

"Seriously, Mara?" he hissed. "Look, I appreciate your friendship but I'm sure whatever you need it can wait a little bit—"

"Alec took the serum. He's asleep upstairs," I interrupted anyway.

Thayer bent his knees and rolled his eyes to the ceiling.

"Great, I'm still not seeing what the—" he begged.

"Nikki's asleep too." I raised a hand to stop him.

"What?" Thayer paused, and relaxed his grip on the door. "They both took it at the same time? How dumb can they be?"

"I don't care. All I know is that we have less than an hour to find that tablet and get out of here before Alec wakes." I stepped away from the door.

"Give me two seconds and we'll meet you in Alec's room." Thayer nodded, closing the door.

"We?" I smiled, trying to lean around him to see.

"Come on." Thayer beamed and pulled the door tighter against him. "I'm not that complicated."

Thayer closed the door and I turned to see Kylan walking down the hallway alone.

"You didn't find Derek?" I asked.

"Cassie said he probably went out for energy. He should be back soon." Kylan touched my left arm, moving his hand down toward mine.

The tips of his finger reached my wrist and stopped at the end of my sleeve. He smiled at the flashing ring.

"Is Cassie still not feeling well?" I asked.

Kylan's shoulders dropped.

"No. She's just shaking off the last of the pain. I think she's had enough of the Shadows to last her a lifetime. I can't blame her," Kylan said.

"Thayer and Lisa are going to meet us in Alec's room. I know that's where he's keeping that tablet." I started walking to the door.

"In such an obvious place?" Kylan asked.

"Alec loves his mind games. That's exactly where he'd put it." I glared at the floor, talking to it as if it were Alec himself.

When I opened the door to the room, I could almost taste the victory. The room smelled exactly like the mansion, a mixture of dust and stone. I shook my head, not knowing how Alec managed to do that.

Dark wood furniture had pewter knobs on the faces of so many drawers. It had to be in here.

I stepped forward and went straight for the bed. My hands felt up the sheets as Thayer and Lisa walked in the room, both of them looking a little more disheveled than when they had left the testing room.

"Nice of you to join us," Kylan chuckled.

Lisa blushed and came to the other side of the bed, glancing up at me. I paused my search for a moment to look at her. She just waited.

I nodded to her and she smiled.

Thayer took it all in stride. "So, I take it none of you would be interested in this?"

I spun, hoping it was the tablet in his hands. What he held up was small, metal, and the second-best thing to a tablet.

The remote to the cuffs.

"Where did you get it?" Kylan asked and I winced.

"Do you really want the answer to that question?" Thayer leveled a stare on him. Kylan shook his head, which made Lisa and I both let out a breath of relief.

Thayer clicked the button and the cuffs went dark. Without a moment's hesitation, he looked at his own cuff and destroyed it. The flakes of black fell to the floor. I did the same to mine and Kylan's.

Thayer glanced at Lisa's before she turned and insisted on trying it herself. It took longer than the two of us, but it worked. She grinned as her hand brushed off the black, smudging it on her skin. Thayer smiled and winked at her.

We both resumed feeling the bed sheet until I reached the pillow. I ripped it away from the bedpost, revealing a sleek, black tablet.

I reached for it, my fingers touching the cold surface as I lifted it from the soft bed.

"Found it," Thayer's voice called.

I spun, holding my own tablet. Thayer held an identical one in his hand, hovering it over an open drawer.

"What?" I asked, looking between the two of them.

"Guys," Kylan said and we all looked. "Found another one."

"What is this?" Thayer asked.

I threw my tablet on the bed and raced to the nightstand. In the first drawer, another tablet waited in plain sight, perfectly centered among the clothes. I tossed it on the bed as well. The next drawer held the same thing.

Everyone followed, revealing more and more tablets.

"Alec did this on purpose," Thayer snarled.

"It's a game. That's why he didn't care about him being asleep, the chances of us finding the actual tablet were so low." I shook my head.

I watched more tablets fall onto the bed. There must have been at least thirty shining black rectangles covering the sheet.

"They all have passcodes," Lisa said, clicking onto the screen of the tablet.

"Okay, let's start there," I said, pushing the tablets out of my way enough to sit on the other side of the bed.

"I mean, I don't wanna be the downer here, but there are literally a million possible things it could be." Thayer crossed his arms.

"Try Alec's birth year," Kylan suggested. "1752."

Lisa typed in the numbers. The keypad jolted as the words incorrect passcode flashed at the top.

"Maybe try the year his father died? 1903," Thayer sighed, kicking his feet against each other.

"You remember that year? You weren't even with us when we attacked the lab," I said.

"That's exactly why I remember it. That's the last time I ever sat out of a fight, wasn't it?" Thayer replied, looking over to Lisa. "Everyone learned I was too valuable to leave behind."

She didn't blink at his accomplishment or puffed-out chest. Lisa just shook her head. "That's wrong too."

"1813. The year I joined the Shadows." I toyed with the fabric of the top sheet.

"We're in," Lisa smiled.

"Way to go, beautiful." Thayer smiled and sauntered over to Lisa.

I glanced at Kylan. He tried to hide the annoyance on his face but that only made me laugh under my breath.

"There's nothing on here," Lisa said.

"What?" Kylan shot his gaze to Lisa.

She turned it around for the rest of us could see. There wasn't a single app. Nothing. The screen was just blue and blank besides the time in the top corner.

"So, that one's a decoy." I picked up another tablet and typed in the same year.

Incorrect passcode flashed again.

"They all have a different code," I grumbled in defeat. "We'll never find the right one for all of them if this even is all of them. There could be rooms filled with tablets."

"Just when I think he can't be any more cruel or clever. He always proves me wrong." Thayer shook his head.

"Well." Kylan rolled up his long-sleeved shirt. "Let's get started. If we have to crack every passcode, then we have an hour—less than an hour—to do it. Thayer and Lisa, track down any other tablets you can find and bring them here. Mara and I will work on the passcodes."

"Good idea." Thayer reached for Lisa's hand. "I think we, uh, should start looking in my room."

I stopped my fingers from moving on the keypad and threw a glance at Thayer. He finally looked over to meet my eyes.

"What? He could have stashed some in there, you never know. And we just got these cuffs off..." Thayer purred.

I jerked my chin at him to leave. "Make sure Cassie's cuff is off too."

"Come on." Lisa pulled him toward the door. "We only have an hour."

"Fine." He dragged his feet as he followed her. "But after that..."

Thayer leaned into her ear and whispered the rest of the sentence. I didn't know what he said. I could see Lisa smile at the floor as they left the room.

"You honestly think it's worth trying?" I asked as Kylan moved to sit next to me.

"I have no intention of sticking around long enough to see my brother get everything he wants. Do you?" he asked back to me.

"Not on my life." I nodded.

"Good." Kylan smiled at me.

We spent the next while typing in numbers, thinking of every important year or random combination. We had made it through nine of the tablets before Lisa brought in another box of them. Thayer came in a few minutes later. "Cassie's is off. If Derek is anywhere near here, his could have turned off too."

But I didn't care about what he was saying. I just stared at the new set of tablets in his hands. More. How could there be more?

The mounting stack of tablets seemed like a threat. I could almost hear Alec laughing at us.

"This is impossible! We've only unlocked nine and there's no way we'll get through all of these before they wake up." I let a tablet fall from my hands to the floor.

It landed so the blank screen faced up, reminding me that I spent the last few minutes attempting to open nothing.

"One of these has to be the right one," Kylan said.

But instead of reaching for the next one, we all stopped. The time was ticking by, but it hardly mattered. Not with the challenge we were up against.

"Did anyone search Alec's body?" Thayer asked.

"Uh, no…we just came down here," I answered.

"You don't think…" Kylan breathed

Thayer smiled at the tablets and shook his head. He ran a hand across his light facial hair.

"He had it on him the whole time," I said.

I left the room of fake screens and raced up the stairs. I rushed down the hall and to the testing room. When I slammed the door into the wall, Nikki stirred.

We didn't have much time. My eyes narrowed on Alec and I walked silently to his side.

I reached for Alec's chest, feeling my hands down his shirt. I tried not to focus on his chiseled muscles that his thin

T-shirt hardly concealed. My fingers prodded around his waist and to his lower back.

They stopped when they felt a hard surface, too hard to be Alec's skin.

I almost didn't want it to be true. I lifted the back of his shirt enough for me to touch the metallic tablet warmed to his body temperature. I pushed him to the side enough to pull it from under his belt.

When I lifted it up, a chill swept over me.

"You found it," Kylan breathed from the doorway.

"The passcode, I need the passcode," I said, clicking the screen to life.

A light shined in my eyes, brighter than the rest of the screens. This tablet had faint scratches in the corners from being carried around so much. It was the one that belonged to Alec. The real one.

Alec's hand snapped up to wrap around my left wrist.

"Time's up," Alec said as his grip tightened.

# CHAPTER
# THIRTY-NINE

My energy raced from my body and into Alec. He was a Five now. My body automatically pulled energy too. Our power melded together between our skins.

I yanked my hand away from him but he held tightly. Alec grabbed the tablet with his other hand and tucked it under his leg.

"Mara," he breathed.

His eyes went wide. I knew he felt just how personal and intimate my energy was to him. My skin crawled like he had somehow taken a secret from me and I couldn't cover myself up fast enough.

Kylan jumped in and twisted Alec's wrist away from my arm. I stood, eager to get away. Energy poured from Alec into Kylan.

"You may be a Five, but I've been an Extractor a lot longer than you have. If you touch her against her wishes, I will drain you," Kylan threatened.

Nikki woke and set her eyes on Kylan immediately. She launched from the table with her hands ready to shove Kylan to the floor.

They tumbled away from us as she growled, "No one hurts Alec without answering to me."

"Aw, look who's back. Missing something?" Thayer announced as he walked into the room.

He held up the remote and Nikki instantly reached for her chest. Nikki and Alec both noted our bare wrists, but they didn't say anything. We wouldn't take them down, not as Fives, and not without Alec's information.

Even with the tablet, it would only be a start.

They knew that. It's the only thing that kept them safe as the Rogues outnumbered the two of them.

Nikki stood and moved to Alec, who was just standing on his own now, marveling at his own hands. They talked to each other, smiling, triumphant. Alec whispered something to her and Nikki left the room.

I helped Kylan stand and wrapped my arms around him.

"Okay, Alec, you have what you want. You're a Five. Time to keep your promise," I said.

"You're not even going to give me a moment to revel in my victory?" Alec smiled as he grabbed the tablet from the table.

"That wasn't part of the deal." I glared at him.

"Fair enough," Alec said, tucking the tablet back under his belt. "You know, I'm almost a bit disappointed that you didn't figure it out earlier. I thought you'd be smart enough to guess where it was."

"I don't think like you anymore," I said.

"Shame. Could've saved you a lot of trouble," Alec said.

"Enough chitchat," Thayer said. "I'm tired of being holed up here with everyone. No offense, but I'd like to have at least a few moments of breathing room every once in a while. Give her the information."

With just Alec in the room, I thought about taking him down. About forcing him to give us the information. But if I thought I held up well under torture, Alec would wipe the floor with me.

It would take years to break him. Even I couldn't imagine years of not touching Kylan, or anyone. I couldn't bear it for another second as it was. I understood his impatience when you get so close to what you want.

It's utterly unbearable.

And Alec knew all of that. It's why he didn't waver at Thayer's vague threat. He only smiled and said, "Oh, someone's excited to take down his next conquest."

Lisa flinched, but still held her hand in Thayer's.

"Shut your mouth. You forget who else just became a Five because you were too scared to try it out yourself." Thayer narrowed his eyes. An empty threat. We all knew it.

"Finally standing up to me," Alec smiled. "The new power suits you well."

But the Shadow King kept a cold gaze. "Keep your compliments. I don't need them anymore."

I stepped forward. "You owe me a debt."

"About that," Alec dragged. "There's something you should know."

"Here comes the other shoe," Kylan said.

Alec paused, looking only at my eyes. The smile playing on his lips sent an aching pang of regret down my back. Kylan moved his hand forward and grabbed my right hand. The ache subsided, briefly covered by warmth.

"I know I've been less than honest before," Alec said. "But I'm about to tell the truth."

"What, Alec?" I said through gritted teeth.

"I have no idea how to fix what I've done to you," Alec said easily.

I clenched my teeth. He said the antidote didn't exist. I thought it just meant he hadn't created it. But he hadn't even tried to create it. He'd just injected me with a drug he had no idea how to reverse.

That ache in my back raged to a burning hatred. He had tricked us into staying here under the guise that he was the only one who knew how to fix me.

I didn't need to ask for clarification, Alec saw the fury in my eyes.

"I know what I had to do to get you this way, but I didn't lie when I said the antidote didn't physically exist. It just doesn't exist at all," Alec explained.

The only reason I had kept him alive, the only reason any of us stayed clear of him was because of that antidote. *Antidote 17B*, the fake. But surely there was a real one. He had to know how to undo it.

But if he didn't…no one did.

Instead, we wasted over a month here, suffering through all of his mental manipulation every day. This time it wasn't just me he had hurt. It was all of us. My hands turned into claws as I moved to clasp them around Alec's throat.

Before I could reach him, a scream echoed down the hall.

"Cassie." Kylan went pale before he bolted out the door.

Before I followed, I turned my icy gaze back to Alec. "What did you do?"

"I'm standing in front of you. How could I possibly be doing anything?" Alec tilted his head to the side, looking scarily like Kylan.

My stomach heaved at the thought. I couldn't look at him. I left after Kylan. I caught up to him easily as I had more energy in my body.

Cassie's screams continued, long and painful.

"It's gotta be Nikki," I said to Kylan as we rounded the corner of the hallway.

"If she's killing her..." Kylan shook his head, unable to finish the sentence.

"No, Nikki wouldn't drag it out this long. She knows we'd be coming to see..." My breath stopped in my chest. "No."

"What?" Kylan asked as he launched down the stairs.

"She's not killing her. She marking her," I warned, rushing faster toward Cassie and Derek's door.

Kylan burst inside first. His large body moved out of my view to reveal Nikki standing over Cassie, who knelt on the floor. Nikki had Cassie's right arm in her hand, and only released it when she saw the two of us.

Cassie cried and screamed, the sounds mingling together as she curled into a ball around her pregnant stomach. She clutched her right arm like it was on fire.

I remembered the agony all too clearly.

A black dagger stood where her white skin used to be on the inside of her arm. Pink tinged around the edges where her body was still recovering from the pain.

"Cassie," Kylan breathed.

"Why would you do this?" I wanted to scream, but my voice shook with just those words. "You know how much she hates the Shadows. How could you?"

Nikki just smiled at me and backed away. I wanted to tear her throat out, but my movement was stopped by a sad voice.

"Cass," Derek said from behind the two of us.

He knelt and slid to her side, wrapping his strong arms around her. His eyes locked on the dagger and his face crumbled.

Cassie was wearing a tank top, which was a huge change

from her usual sweaters that had hid her body. Judging by her stomach, she was quite far along. Far more than any of us had realized.

"Where were you?" Cassie sobbed as she leaned into him, maneuvering around her large belly. Her freshly marked arm dangled in front of them.

"I…I'm sorry…I didn't know they would do this to you." Derek pulled her closer, like that would take away the pain.

"What do you mean?" Kylan asked.

"Congratulations, Derek," Alec called as he waltzed in the room toward Nikki. "Your debt has been paid."

"Debt?" I asked.

Thayer and Lisa followed Alec in. Lisa gasped when she saw Cassie's arms. She turned to Thayer.

"Yes, Derek insisted on being a Level Five. I went to go inject him while you put Nikki out," Alec explained easily.

"A Level Five? Why?" Kylan asked.

"I did it for you, Cassie. I wanted to make sure I could always protect you. That no one could attack you the way Alec did earlier. I had to, for you and the baby," Derek explained.

Cassie's cries rocked through her frail body. "But you left me. I didn't need you as a Five. I just needed you."

"I'm sorry, I'm so sorry. I only promised that Alec could hurt me like he wanted to before Kylan stopped him." Derek turned to Alec now. "You were supposed to take it out on me. That was the deal."

"I did take it out on you," Alec said. "By hurting the thing you love most. I knew marking Cassie would do far more damage than anything I could inflict on you physically."

"I'm sorry," Derek said into Cassie's ear again. This time he stroked her arm where the new mark probably still burned.

"Don't take it personally. People who don't have

experience making deals with me always end up with something other than what they thought." Alec smiled at me. "Then again, even people who know, somehow fall for the same thing."

"Alec, I—" I started to threaten.

"You'll what? Kill me? Or can you still forgive me after damning your future sister-in-law to the stigma of the Shadows? Every Rogue or decently educated human will be afraid of her now. All because of one deadly mark." Alec moved forward.

I froze. His eyes stopped me.

I wanted to hurt him, maybe even kill him. But when I looked at his blue eyes, he almost looked scared. He wanted to push me too far, he wanted to know that I couldn't love him anymore.

But I couldn't give him that.

I stepped back into Kylan's arm, looking at Cassie again.

"Incredible," Alec breathed. "Even this."

"Well, she doesn't have to kill you. I will," Kylan snarled.

Before any of us could move, a loud crash sounded and the wall on my right broke apart, sending concrete pieces flying into the room.

Kylan shielded me with his own body. Concrete cracked against his back.

Alec yanked the tablet from his belt, clicking on the screen as the dust settled.

"Humans," he spat.

"What?" Kylan asked.

"Humans have surrounded the lab. With a lot of firepower." Alec turned the screen toward us.

The video feed showed the view from the cameras outside the lab. Human soldiers dressed in heavy armor waited around tanks and missiles.

Another blast sounded and another wall came tumbling in the room. This time the shards flew to Thayer and Lisa. A piece of metal rebar lodged in Thayer's shoulder. Blood spewed from the wound as he crashed to his knees.

Kylan looked up at his sadistic brother, dust covering both of them. "Alec, what did you do?"

"This wasn't me." Alec shook his head like he was trying to get a ringing out of his ears.

I took in the concrete falling loose from the ceiling and fluorescent lights flickering. The blasts weren't coming in quick succession. They could have blown it all up at once if they really wanted to get rid of us.

They were stalling for something. I just didn't know what.

"We've got to get out of here. The humans, the weapons. We won't escape alive." I grabbed Kylan's arm.

"Maybe *you* won't," Alec muttered as he glanced at Nikki.

I glared at him. I hated it when Alec was vague and judging by the returned smile, he knew it.

"Allow me to clarify. There is a tunnel that leads out of the lab and comes out far away from where these tanks are standing," Alec said.

"That's perfect. Let's go," Kylan said.

Alec lifted a finger. "Ah, ah, ah, brother. Let me finish. Nikki and I will be using the tunnel."

"You wouldn't leave us here to die." Kylan swallowed.

"Wow." Nikki laughed. "It's like you haven't even met your brother."

Thayer coughed as he tried to stand. Lisa held on his arm as tight as she could to help him up. His blood trickled down the both of them. Derek was still huddled around Cassie on the ground.

"I would change my mind for one thing," Alec said.

My eyes shot up to him. The glimmer in his eyes made my stomach turn over. A bitter hatred settled on my shoulders.

"Me," I finished for him.

"You see? We do still think alike," Alec smiled.

Kylan stepped in front of me. "She'll never go with you."

Another blast shattered the broken wall around us. Metal scraped across Alec's foot. He winced, but the wound healed before much blood even hit the ground.

Derek wasn't so fortunate.

The metal piece ricocheted into him and gashed down his arm. He clapped a hand over the wound and blood seeped in between his fingers.

"You think because you put a ring on her finger that she's yours forever? Mara is the only one who can decide her future," Alec said, shaking his injured foot.

Thayer popped his head up, forgetting his own pain. "You guys got engaged?"

Lisa gasped and looked between me and Kylan with a sweet smile. This wasn't how I wanted to break the news.

"Nothing gets by you, does it?" Nikki said. Thayer made a face at her.

"Choose, Mara," Alec threatened. "Me or them."

He thought this was a hard choice. He must have expected me to debate for a while, for me to feel shame about what I wanted. But that wasn't the case anymore. I didn't hesitate.

"Them."

"Hmm. Allow me to sweeten the deal," Alec said and raised the tablet in the air.

Kylan shook his head. "She gave you the answer. She doesn't want you anymore."

Alec ignored him, focusing his cold eyes on me.

"Come with me or I'll destroy your only chance at figuring out how to fix you."

I stared at the tablet in his grip. Nothing I could do would let me reach the tablet before Alec or Nikki destroyed it. I flexed my fingers, trying to think of another option.

"You wouldn't dare," I gasped. "You promised to give me that information. You've never broken a promise before."

Alec lowered his chin in an easy, condescending motion.

"Only after I had everything I wanted. Remember me saying that?" I gulped and he raised his chin. "So, tell me, Mara. If I don't have you, do I have *everything* I want?"

A stabbing pain shot through my chest. I stared at him with my mouth open, unable to form words yet.

He knew. He knew this whole time he wouldn't have to fix me because he didn't actually know what to do. Even if I forced him to figure it out, he still wouldn't have to. In our deal, he didn't risk anything.

Unless he had me. Those were my exact words.

I should have known. I should have worded it differently. Actually, I should have never come back here. Regret washed through me as another blast rattled the room, but didn't strike directly.

Alec just watched me, no doubt loving all the emotions in my eyes. I shook from anger as I closed my mouth and stared back at him. He just smiled.

"Time is running out. Two of your friends are already bleeding on the ground and the humans are getting closer. I can keep you safe, make you happy. Eventually, you'll forget all about them. I can promise you that." He wanted to move closer to me, I could see it in his eyes.

But he stayed where he stood. I wasn't alone. Even if he could convince me not to move, he couldn't control the entire room. Especially not his brother—who was shaking nearly as much as I was.

"There is nothing you could give me to make me abandon everyone I love." I shook my head.

"You love me too!" Alec shouted. "Just give it a chance."

His tone changed with the last sentence. He looked at me like I was the only person in the room. Despite the chaos surrounding us, the only thing that mattered was me.

His intense devotion was intoxicating and repulsive all at once. My toes still curled at the sound of his voice when he used that tone.

I stared at him and the world silenced. It was just the two of us. I wished that things had been different, that I had never met Alec. That Kylan was the first and only person to sweep me off my feet. That I still had my mother.

There was so much that I wanted. So much that had always been out of reach ever since the day Charles brought me into the Shadows.

But it was no good to dwell on impossible wishes.

"I want Kylan," I said in a final tone.

Alec's face hardened. All the tenderness of the little boy I knew was gone again. He reached his free hand out to Nikki, where she pulled out a familiar, blue journal and placed it in his hand. His cold eyes settled on me.

I sucked in a breath as he placed my mother's journal and the tablet in the same hand. He just upped the offer. I didn't have time to wonder how she had gotten it or if it was even the real one. My mouth fell open.

"Are you sure?" Alec asked.

I hesitated. Longer than I wanted to. I resisted the urge to touch the locket still safely around my neck.

"Sure? Am I sure?" I mocked. "Yes, I want Kylan."

"So, I'm guessing you don't know then, do you?" Alec asked, tapping his finger on the two invaluable items in his hand.

"Know what?" I asked, taking the bait too easily and already regretting it.

"Alec, don't," Kylan interjected too quickly.

I glanced at Kylan. His hands were out, fingers splayed like he wanted to surrender. I squinted and moved my gaze back to Alec.

"Don't what?" Derek asked, looking Kylan up and down.

I sensed he already had a guess at what Alec was going to say. Something told me that I didn't want to know.

"Please," Kylan whispered.

The soft sound was out of place with the loud crashes and the sound of fire starting to crackle around us.

Alec just looked at Kylan and smiled.

# CHAPTER
# FORTY

*Kylan*

Terror clawed at my spine. I could see the words on Alec's lips. I wanted to launch forward and stop this moment from happening.

I stopped when I saw Mara. She looked at me with wide eyes, hopeful that anything Alec could say wouldn't change her mind. At least, that's what I wanted to see in her gaze.

"You don't know how many people he killed," Alec said slowly.

Mara relaxed. "I heard about disguising himself as Isaac. He shouldn't be on the hook for whatever situation you forced him into."

"Killed?" Cassie asked with a quiet voice.

I closed my eyes as the guilt consumed me where I stood. The world blacked out and I still didn't feel hidden enough.

"I'm not talking about the handful of bodies he left behind when he was masquerading as Isaac." Alec wagged a finger. "I mean the ones he drained after the rest of you arrived."

I opened my eyes again, immediately looking at Mara. Her face fell as her eyes slowly shifted to me.

"Kylan?" she said with a shaky voice.

The dust from the explosions clung to parts of her face and clothes. Her hands laid lifeless at her sides as she stared at me. The blasts had continued, but far enough that all they did was rattle the lights.

The humans must have been trying to break the outer concrete and clearly didn't know where anyone was in the building.

We had a little time, but not nearly enough for me to fix the way Mara looked at me. I cringed and couldn't find the words to answer her.

"That's not the best part. I mean, what's so intriguing about eleven dead bodies over the last few days?" Alec prattled on.

*Eleven.* The word shattered into the room.

Cassie gasped. Lisa stepped away from me and into Thayer. He was the only one with a sympathetic gaze.

Mara stared.

My entire body ached and I hated every twinge of energy I still had in me.

"The best part is how much he enjoyed it. You should have seen the smile on his face. Poor guy probably hasn't taken a life in decades," Alec continued.

"Is it true?" Mara asked me.

I looked at the ground instead. The change in her breath told me she knew the answer. Derek stood slowly, wincing as he moved to me.

"You're not even gonna try and lie about it? Come on. She loves you so much she might even believe you," Alec taunted.

Derek's hand landed on my shoulder. It felt like it weighed a million pounds. I wanted to dissolve under his touch.

"I don't want to lie to you." I glanced at Derek and then up at Mara again.

Derek closed his eyes, but still held his hand on me. She twisted the glittering ring around her finger, not looking at me anymore.

"How..." Mara started, turning to face Alec and then stopped.

"I'm sorry," I blurted. "I just, uh...I'm..."

Mara clenched her jaw, still facing Alec. My words turned to vapor in my mouth.

She walked toward Alec and my legs turned to liquid. Derek's hand wasn't holding me down anymore, it was holding me up. Each step she took seemed to send another crack through my body. My insides felt exactly like the building shattering all around us.

"What are you doing?" Alec smiled and studied her.

"You know what I'm doing," Mara replied easily.

"Alec," Nikki started a warning.

Alec raised a finger and Nikki closed her mouth. Her eyes still burned as they stared at Mara.

"What do you want?" Alec tried a different question, his eyes wandering down her body.

I shifted forward and Derek's hand gripped tighter on my shoulder. I glanced back at him, but he just stared at Mara's feet. He couldn't watch, but he couldn't let me chase someone who no longer wanted me.

I wanted to slap him and thank him all at once.

"Read my mind," Mara cooed. "You'll see what I want."

She took her gloves from her hands and let them drop to the floor. Her bare hands and bare arms reached for Alec.

I tried not to show my worry. But Derek's fingers had turned white at the tips from holding me back so hard.

Images flashed in my mind and I froze.

*Mara smiled. Her fingers ran across a man's bare arm. Energy didn't flow. It was just a touch.*

*Her hands moved up to a shoulder, a neck. Her light touch slithered down a bare chest. Another hand joined in as she pulled the person closer to her body.*

I stopped breathing. My mouth fell open. The thoughts weren't mine. She was creating them in my head. No doubt at the same time Alec was reading them.

The man's face was hidden in the images. I couldn't tell who it was. I wanted so badly for it to be me. But I also braced myself for seeing Alec's eyes staring back at me.

I wouldn't blame her. How could I?

Curiosity eventually forced me to look up. Alec's face looked exactly like mine, awe-struck and hopeful. I gritted my teeth to keep me from moving.

Mara's hand touched Alec's shoulder, right where his lab coat started. Her other hand went around the back of his neck. Energy brightened between the two of them and I wanted to vomit.

"You can see it, can't you?" Mara said.

"I think you'll have to be a little more specific," Alec said, glancing around to me.

Mara laughed in a low tone. "Allow me to elaborate."

*Her hand touched the back of a neck. The other rested on a shoulder, sliding down the arm. She leaned forward, closer to the man's face.*

*Mara's lips brushed against his. The face still unseen. Her sliding hand moved closer to his wrist.*

*She caught her breath. The image widened somehow and the man became obvious.*

*It was me. My arms held her. My lips kissed her back forcefully.*

"I want Kylan," Mara growled.

I blinked and nearly missed what happened. Mara reached for the tablet. Nikki jumped forward and snatched it from Alec's hand before he had a chance to pull back out of her mind.

"Nikki," Mara spat her name like it was poison.

She leaned past Alec, craning to get her hand closer to the tablet Nikki had yanked away. Alec snaked a hand around her waist and pulled her away.

"Much better attempt, baby," Alec said, yanking her ear close to his mouth. "You got me that time."

Mara snarled, a little too close to his face. "How could you think that I'd judge him for making the same mistakes I did when I was a Shadow?"

My shoulders lifted. I stared ahead at her, mouth gaping open. Derek's hand relaxed and he fell back next to Cassie. Either he knew I didn't need him anymore or the blood loss was finally getting to him.

"He murdered people. He liked it. Wasn't that the exact reason you said you didn't want to be with me? Wouldn't that make us the same?" Alec narrowed his eyes.

"The same?" Mara laughed. "You two are nothing alike. I don't know how to make this any clearer. I. Want. Him."

"Then you can have him," Nikki said.

She held the tablet up. Cracks shattered across the screen in her tight grip.

"No!" Mara reached for it again, squirming to get away from Alec.

He grabbed both of her arms and tossed her across the room. Her feet stumbled on the broken rubble and she fell. I caught her in my arms just before her body hit the floor.

My energy peeled away from my skin and into hers. My automatic reaction was to let go, but I held on until she got her feet underneath her.

She yanked her hands off me as soon as she could balance.

"Why?" I asked, rubbing the pain in my arms from losing energy.

Mara smiled up at me. "You still cared about me when you found out I was a Shadow. You came back anyway after I caused Rachel's death. You've always stood by me. Why would I leave you the first time I see you fall?"

Words left my mind. Breath vanished from my lungs. I watched her honest, blue eyes and it felt like all my broken pieces were mending.

"I love you, Mara Hayes," I whispered.

Before she could talk, Alec interrupted. "You've made your choice."

Alec took the tablet and journal from Nikki's waiting hand. He knelt down to get eye-level with Mara. He didn't break eye contact as the two items melted into black dust that fluttered to the ground.

"No!" I screamed and jumped forward.

Mara put a hand in the middle of my chest and shoved me back.

"He has nothing to lose anymore. You go after him now and he'll kill you," she said.

"Oh please, give it a try. You're the one thing standing between me and what I want." Alec smiled.

"Come, defeat the monster." Nikki wiggled her fingers, her rings clinking together.

Alec stood and walked toward the open holes in the walls. Nikki moved with him, almost mirroring his steps exactly.

Dust, concrete, and metal pieces surrounded all of us. There was no way we could get Derek and Thayer up in time to follow them together.

"Alec, you can't just leave us here," Mara called after him.

"You always underestimate what I'm willing to do," Alec glanced back at her and stopped.

"Risking my life? You've never been willing to do that." She shook her head. "What's changed?"

"Nothing. I'm still betting you'll somehow find a way out here." Alec winked. "Impress me, baby."

He vanished behind the next wall, Nikki following him. I turned to Thayer to see the wound already closing with energy. His constant high from being a Shadow helped him. I knew what he'd have to do to get that much energy.

Still, my mouth watered as I looked at his energy healing his body.

"He's gonna be all right," Mara said to Lisa. "The wound is almost closed."

"It's because of all the energy, right?" Lisa said with pain in her voice. "Could he have that much without...um... without..."

She was smart enough to put together how Thayer could have that much energy in his body. I could see in her eyes she already knew it.

Thayer avoided her eyes, instead focusing on his arm.

"Listen to me." Mara grabbed Lisa's shoulder. "Thayer is a Shadow, and you knew that. If you can't accept it then you better walk away now because even he doesn't deserve to be toyed with."

Derek groaned, collapsing further against the floor. Cassie caught his head before it hit the hard tile. His gash was still bleeding, unlike Thayer.

"Mara," I called.

She spun and looked at Derek and the blood pooling beneath him.

"He's losing too much blood, and Cassie's running low on energy too," I said as I wiped blood off Cassie's arms and shoulders.

She had scrapes and cuts all along her right arm. With all that blood and a dagger mark, she looked way too much like the Shadows she hated. A mix of anger and agony warped her freckled face and I couldn't fix it.

*Derek's an Extractor now.* I widened my eyes, finally grateful for Derek's choice to leave Cassie and become a Five.

"Take my arm," I said without hesitation.

"Kylan, no. You don't have enough." Mara grabbed his arm with her gloved hands to hold it away.

"None of us do. He's my brother. I'm not leaving him here to burn," I said.

I touched Derek's good arm, energy immediately leaving my body. The familiar pain clouded my thoughts and I had to focus on my breaths to stop myself from taking his energy back. I slumped over without noticing as Derek's cut began to scab enough to stop the bleeding.

"That's enough," Derek said and yanked his arm away.

"We've got to get out of here before this whole place collapses," Mara said, already looking down the halls.

My vision shifted back and forth as my body argued with my conscience. I wanted energy and everyone had it. My fingers twitched and I clenched my muscles to keep myself still.

"So, we've got to find a secret tunnel with no guide and probably half the lab broken in pieces?" Thayer asked. "You do like trying the impossible."

"Isn't that part of the fun?" I forced a smile.

Mara glanced back at me and smiled. She lowered a hand to me and helped me stand. Black spots formed on the edges of my vision. I shook my head.

We moved through the hallways as fast as everyone could manage. More blasts came, more blood was spilled. Even I was having trouble keeping my feet moving.

Mara looked back at me. Her blue eyes scanned my body and I hated how she saw my weakness. But I couldn't change what I had done.

It also hurt knowing how much she understood my position. I admired her bravery even more. So when I looked at her eyes now, she became my entire world.

"Do you trust me?"

I smiled down at her and wanted so badly to take her away from all this, to have her all to myself. I wanted to see our future in her eyes.

Even though all the odds were stacked against us making it out of here alive, the bravest woman I knew was willing to try it. That was good enough.

"Just try and stop me," I repeated her words.

# CHAPTER
# FORTY-ONE

We had stumbled down the halls, getting as close to the edges of the building as we dared. The blasts kept coming and more of the passages were consumed in flames. We were running out of options.

"The basement," Lisa whispered.

"The tunnel. It's probably in the basement. Lisa you're a genius!" I grabbed her by both arms and searched for the safest way down there.

"Thayer, you've been down there. Did you notice anything that might lead out?" Kylan asked as he bound Derek's wound with a strip of his sleeve.

"I, uh, I didn't notice anything...else."

He must have been too busy taking energy. Lisa looked up at him with a brief look of sympathy. Kylan helped Cassie and Derek stand.

"I'm sure we'll figure it out." I pushed Thayer toward the biggest opening in the wall. "Lead the way."

Thayer dashed down the hall, a little too fast for the rest of us. Lisa ran after him, somehow managing to keep on his heels.

I wrapped my arm around Cassie's lower back to shield her scraped arm from the flying dust and exposed concrete. Derek slung his arm across Kylan's shoulder and they both hobbled behind us.

We rounded the corner slowly and another blast crashed far away into the building. I expected more concrete to chip off, or the floor to crack. Instead, a crackling, whooshing sound followed us down the hall.

Heat singed through the air before I even saw the flames.

"The stairs. Get down the stairs." I nudged Cassie forward and hurried the other two in front of me.

The flames licked up the walls and hovered over the tile in the far corner. I stepped down the hidden stairs and shut the door as hard as I could. The metal already felt warm. My heart pounded in my chest.

The stairs were wooden. We didn't have much time to find another way out.

"The exit better be down here," I said as I stepped down the last steps and into the dimly lit basement. "Because the other way is no longer an option."

The ceiling felt so low I wanted to stoop. The air was disturbingly cold. The metal doors had small windows about eye-level. It reminded me of the dungeons at the mansion.

I noticed in the corners the spackle streaks and the metal that had been scratched around where the screws held the walls and doors together. This place was new to the lab. An addition that Alec probably suggested.

"There are so many rooms. Do they all have people in them?" Lisa said.

"Man, I hope so. I could use a little energy right about now." Derek coughed into his arm and winced.

"You're gonna have to wait a little bit longer," Thayer said, shutting a door to a cell.

"Why?" Lisa asked.

Thayer stared at her. "You don't wanna know."

She didn't hesitate before she walked forward and peered inside the tiny glass window. She gasped and I could only guess what she saw.

Thayer lowered his chin.

Lisa rushed to the next window and raised a hand to her mouth. She moved to look across the hall but Thayer caught her arm and stopped her.

"They're all the same," Thayer said.

"You don't know that." Lisa quivered as her eyes darted at all the doors, then her gaze landed on me.

Thayer pulled her around to face him. "I know Alec. If he came down here, then he wouldn't have left anything for us."

"Anything? Any energy? That's all these people are worth to you?" Lisa shrugged him off.

"Why would I think anything else?" Thayer asked.

"This is a good sign," I interrupted.

"Good?" Lisa heaved in breaths faster than her body would be able to process.

"They're dead. That means Alec came down here and we're on the right track," I explained and started down the hall to look for any sign of an outlet.

Without my saying anything, everyone who could stand on their own fanned out. Derek and Cassie leaned against each other.

Even Lisa—still sobbing—felt around the walls.

Alec would hide the exit somewhere I wouldn't think to look. In the most obvious place.

I watched the people around me, shuffling in and out of the cells. Probably stepping around dead bodies. That would be an obvious place. But they weren't finding anything.

*Where is the one place I wouldn't look?* I asked myself, hoping to spark some sort of epiphany. I turned in a circle.

I decided to start at the entrance. I moved down to the landing where the stair stopped before the dungeons began. I faced the cells again, my back to the stairs. When I looked up, I was hoping to see what Alec would.

All I saw were dead ends and frantic people. This should be hopeless. But it was only over if I gave up.

"I'm not letting you win this one," I muttered, glancing at the flames reaching under the door at the top of the stairs.

"There's nothing down here," Thayer called, walking toward me from the very back of the hallway. "It's a trick."

The thought settled that I might have been the one to lead everyone to this fiery death. Guilt boiled in my stomach. I shook my head and let my hands pull through my hair.

There had to be something. Some place that only Alec would notice. I stepped off the landing and heard a faint squeak.

*The entrance.* The one place I wouldn't think to look.

I dropped to my knees and scrambled to feel the corners of the landing. Hidden on the edge of the last stair were hinges.

"Here!" I shouted and dug my fingers in the opposite side of the landing.

I didn't even see the seam I was grabbing for. I definitely couldn't wedge my fingers in there. I changed my hand position and tried again. I still couldn't feel anything. But there were hinges. It had to open. It *should* open.

I drew my hand back and slammed my fist through the center. The thin wood shattered and a cool draft of air met my face.

The lid was in splinters, but I hauled it up to crash against the stairs. The wood on the top steps was already igniting.

A ladder beneath extended farther than I could see. I flew down the rungs, taking them two or three at a time.

Cassie came down next and I helped her on the last few until she could balance on the ground.

"Thank you," Cassie muttered.

"Of course." I nodded and looked up the ladder.

"Not for that," she said, taking my arm. "For Kylan. I think you're really good for him."

Her brother had just admitted to killing people. To being way more like the brother she loathed. But she still cared about him. Her gratitude was for me not leaving him. For loving him as much as they did.

But staying together in the impossibly hard times is what made a family. And I wasn't about to give this one up without a fight.

"We're good for each other." I smiled and watched Lisa climb down next.

Kylan followed. Derek's hand thunked against every other rung from not using his bad arm. Thayer slid down the side without touching a single rung.

When his feet hit the ground, he grunted and I recognized how exhausted he was.

We all were. Derek hobbled forward into Cassie, even though she wasn't walking straight either. The others moved forward, but Thayer stayed still. He stared at the ladder.

"Thayer?" I asked, reaching out to touch him.

He pulled his shoulder away from me. My hand wouldn't have touched his skin, but apparently the threat was enough. I curled my fingers into a fist.

"Sage." The name caught in Thayer's voice. His breath hitched like he was trying to avoid the emotion.

"Consider this her cremation," I said.

It was the honorable way to die as a Shadow. Not by old

age, or at the hand of someone else, but when you decided to finish your life. Thayer touched the ladder with his hand, bowing his head in a silent moment. I tried to ignore the sounds of fire breaking the room above us.

"Rest in peace, princess," Thayer whispered.

"Rest in peace," I agreed, touching the ladder as well.

"Let's go," Thayer said, his eyes turning cold and void of all the emotion I had just seen.

We joined the others, catching up to their slow, limping speed. Even Kylan's steps faltered.

Lisa crossed her arms in front of her. She was the most energized out of all of us. And the one person none of the Extractors could bear to take from.

Kylan walked as close as he could to me without touching. "How did the humans find us? This lab's been here for decades and it's gone undisturbed until now."

I hated the distance. Intensity burned the air between the two of us. I wanted the heat of his body just a little closer. But I didn't have gloves, sleeves, or the energy to create either.

Most of my attention was focused on not touching him, so I almost missed his question.

"The lab," I blurted and shook my head. "Yeah. I don't know how they found it. I can't imagine that Alec would tip them off."

"He said he didn't. Have you ever known him to outright lie?" Thayer chimed in.

"No, I guess not." I pursed my lips.

"What about the other girl? Nikki?" Lisa asked.

"Maybe." Thayer considered, tilting his head from side to side. "She's held a big grudge against Mara for sapping away all of Alec's attention and for dropping us like a rock when she found out about Alec's manipulation of everything."

I nodded. "She wants me dead. This would give her a plausible way to do it without Alec knowing."

"Nah." Thayer waved a hand. "If it's her, he'd figure it out though. She wouldn't risk it, at least not when she's so close to having him all to herself."

"Maybe the humans just got smarter and figured it out," Lisa suggested easily and shrugged.

Thayer laughed, unrestrained and mocking. "That's about as likely as us walking out to a purple sky."

Lisa glared up at him and walked faster, leaving him behind. Thayer groaned and moved quickly to catch up.

I smiled. She was actually standing up to him. She didn't need to and the old Lisa would have just agreed. She was usually a peacemaker, quiet and calm.

"Oh, my," I muttered, starting to rush my own steps farther into the cool, underground tunnel and away from the emanating heat.

"What?" Kylan asked, too low for them to hear.

"She's in love with him too," I whispered back to him.

I remembered Thayer leaning his head back against the hallway, so frustrated that his own feelings had betrayed him. That he had fallen for her. The only thing holding him back was that she'd never care for him and he'd never change.

But she already cared.

"Love him?" Kylan muttered and frowned.

Lisa turned on her heel and walked farther down the tunnel. I glanced over at Thayer, who had a mix of rage and wonder on his face. He shook his head and walked ahead of us, and a gnawing feeling crept in my stomach.

We hobbled down the dark tunnel, far away from the threatening flames. Half the group needed to lean on each other to move at all. The only light came from holes that had been blasted by the missiles outside.

"I see the end," Derek announced, ahead of us.

My eyes shot up and I saw it too. Daylight. More than could come in from holes in the ceiling, it flooded the tunnel ground.

"I can't believe it worked," I breathed.

Relief washed in me with each word. The pain in my body seemed less, easier to move. Hope took over whatever energy I lacked, as it did for most of us.

"You really should stop doubting yourself. I don't," Kylan smiled, even in the dark.

"That's it," Cassie said. "The outside."

"We're almost there." I turned to Lisa and Thayer.

Both moved slower than the rest of us, probably not from a lack of energy. We moved toward the daylight until it engulfed us and our feet landed on wet soil.

# FORTY-TWO

We were out. I took in the surroundings and I didn't recognize any of the trees. We must have been over a mile away from the lab.

I breathed in the fresh air, lifting my head to the sky. The overcast clouds were so thick and dark. It was a swirl of violet and gray above me, but I was hardly worried about the rain.

We were out, and far enough away from any sign of trouble. My arm relaxed around Kylan.

"Over here!" A shout sounded to the left of us.

I snapped my head to see three armed soldiers advancing toward us. They were clad head to toe in black armor. Two more soldiers headed back toward where the rest of the reinforcements must be.

"Alec showed them the tunnel," I said.

"He wouldn't," Kylan argued. "They're humans. Why would he trust them?"

"He doesn't have to trust them." I shook my head. "He just has to use them to slow us down."

Thayer stepped forward, still favoring his injured arm. He joined me as we focused on the guns rising toward us.

"Shadows versus humans. Nothing we haven't handled before," Thayer said as the first bullet whizzed past me and missed.

"Go left, I'll go right," I ordered with a grin.

He didn't hesitate. We ran at the three of them. I knocked the first one's legs out from under him. He landed on his back, knocking the wind out of him long enough for Thayer to break his legs.

The human screamed and blacked out in pain before Thayer stole his energy. He moved to the second human and grabbed him by the arm.

I ripped the gun from the last man and slammed the butt of the gun into the man's helmet. A loud crack sounded as his head snapped to the side and his body fell limp. Too limp. The force hadn't just knocked him unconscious.

His remaining energy would be untouchable now that he was dead. I hated that that was my first thought. But I could either save us or the humans.

My family came first.

I turned to the last standing human attacking Thayer. He ducked under the gun as the human fired. His hands grabbed the gun and yanked it from the human's grip, using the arm Thayer still held to throw him onto the wet ground.

"Don't kill him." Lisa balled her hands near her mouth as her eyes went wide.

"He would've killed me if he had the chance," Thayer said back to her as he aimed the gun at the human who had been sprawled out in front of the Shadow King.

"You don't have to stoop to his level," Lisa said.

"His level?" Thayer scoffed, not looking up from his target. "I think you mean my level."

The human propped himself up on his hands. His head visibly moved from Thayer to Lisa.

"No, that's not what I—" Lisa walked toward him, a small hand reaching out.

Thayer stepped away from her like touching her would burn him. But Lisa stepped in front of the gun and Thayer immediately lowered it. I thought she would say something to defend the human, something Thayer could argue.

Instead, she reached back and yanked the helmet off the man's head.

Light blond hair tumbled out, reflecting the overcast sunlight almost as much as his fair skin. Lisa caught a glimpse of him and went still.

"Chase," I breathed.

We forgot about the gun Thayer was holding. Lisa's mouth fell open, matching the rest of our faces.

"What are you doing here?" Kylan asked.

I looked him up and down. "You were the one that led them here. Weren't you?"

Chase glanced at me before looking back at Lisa. Her mouth gaped as the helmet fell from her hand, making a slick sound as it stuck in the mud.

"You?" She just stared. We all did.

"Yes," he grunted. "After that video went viral, I used an app to find your phone and it led me here. I knew you'd be with *them*."

Thayer threw the gun away and raked a hand through his hair. Lisa just blinked and struggled to find words.

"A human figured it out." Thayer rolled his eyes up to the sky.

Gray clouds, almost lavender, hung over all of us. Thayer grumbled something to himself.

"You hate me that much? You want me dead?" Lisa finally choked.

"Who is this?" Thayer asked Lisa, but she didn't answer.

He glanced around for anyone else to fill him in. When his eyes landed on me, I didn't know what to say. Where to start.

"The guy stupid enough to fall in love with her," Chase spat.

Thayer tsked and kept a hungry gaze on me. "I'm guessing he's an ex now?"

"When Alec turned her into a Legend…" I trailed off.

"You left her?" Thayer gaped at the human now. "This woman, who is worth more than a thousand humans—no doubt the best thing that happened to your miserable life—you left her because she was a Legend?"

"Yes," Lisa's answer pierced through the air.

Just like that she was timid, quiet, and powerless again. I stepped forward and raised a hand, but stopped myself. I couldn't force her to be strong. She needed to do it herself.

"Tell me this." Thayer focused on Chase. "If I handed you that gun, would you point it at her? If you got the chance, would you kill Lisa?"

"Yes."

"Chase," Lisa gasped.

"I'd save humanity from all of you if I could," Chase answered in the coldest voice I had ever heard from him.

My heart seized at the sound of surprise in Lisa's voice. No matter how many times we explained, she didn't understand why humans hated us so much. She saw both sides, and it was a lot easier to sympathize with us than she wanted to admit.

She was more Legend than human now.

"Give me a reason not to," Chase challenged. "Since you became… this thing, have you killed anyone?"

Lisa hung her head instead of answering him.

It was an unfair question. Chase's mouth tightened into an even thinner line. Her hands should have been shaking at her sides, but they hung still.

Thayer stood and walked over to her. He put a gentle hand on her lower back. I thought she'd fall into him, or at least lean on him. But she just stood still and raised her gaze back to Chase.

Chase shook his head. "I won't love a killer."

I recognized the slump in Thayer's shoulders. He was the one who had toyed with Lisa's emotions, taken away what made her human. Even if she had asked him to. The murder was more his fault than hers.

But Thayer could take that guilt, he wouldn't mind. The shoulder slump was for her, because she didn't deserve to feel this way.

"She's the furthest thing from a killer." Thayer scratched his chin. "Unfortunately for you, I'm not."

"Thayer, don't!" Lisa shouted.

Thayer didn't listen. He lunged forward anyway, locking a hand on Chase's wrist.

Chase snatched a handgun from his hip and aimed it directly at Lisa. Thayer noticed and yanked Lisa down with him. The bullet fired into the person standing directly behind them.

Cassie grunted and doubled over. Blood spotted in the center of her chest.

Everyone froze. The only sound was Cassie's ragged breathing and Chase's body hitting the ground.

"Cassie," Derek cried. "No."

The blood rushed out too quickly from her body. Her brown eyes searched for something to stop the pain.

"Energy. She needs energy." Kylan rushed to Cassie as she fell to the ground.

Derek looked at Chase's still form. Cassie sucked in a breath, it sounded like she was choking on liquid rather than air.

"The city is miles away and the only other humans have guns waiting for us on the other side of the hill," Derek said.

His hands fluttered over Cassie's wound. The blood spread up to the collar of her shirt and down over her large belly.

"Get her to the city," I said.

As soon as I said the words, I could feel the deafening silence from everyone around me. Derek glanced at me briefly with heavy eyes. Kylan held his breath.

Derek touched his weak arm. "I can't carry her."

Kylan immediately pulled Cassie into his arms. He groaned with the movement and I knew how low he was.

Derek took off running as fast as he could. Kylan glanced back at me. I waved him forward and he followed after Derek.

"You shouldn't have done that. I asked you not to kill him," Lisa cried as she fell to her knees.

"He would've killed you," Thayer muttered back. "He just killed Cassie and you're worried about his life."

"She's not dead yet," I said.

"Mara," Thayer groaned. "You saw the blood. They won't make it within city limits before she dies. If they get there fast enough they might be able to save the baby."

"If you didn't kill Chase, then they could have taken his energy to save her," Lisa said.

"I was trying to stop him from shooting anyone else." Thayer leaned down and glared at her.

Lisa only ignored him. Her shoulders quaked with either anger or sadness, I couldn't tell. She pointed a shaky hand to Chase.

"He's dead. Should…should we bury him?" Lisa asked in a low voice to avoid the tears from breaking her words.

"The humans will find him soon." I tried to hide the pain in my eyes.

Lisa sniffled and stepped even closer to Chase. "We're not just going to leave his body here. I can't do that."

"Why do you care about his life?" Thayer cocked his head.

Lisa stiffened and wiped the tears from under her eyes. She stood tall and didn't flinch even when Thayer got way too close to her.

Her gaze locked on him, unflinching. Thayer studied her face.

"Because he was a person. It doesn't matter if he hated me. His life wasn't yours to take!" Lisa shouted at him.

"I'm not going to apologize for saving you," Thayer hissed. "I would rather watch a hundred awful humans bite it than see you get hurt."

"Why do you assume every person is beneath you?" Lisa shoved a hand against Thayer.

He stumbled back and crossed his arms over his chest before he stepped back to her. She didn't budge, but we all slowed our walk.

"Not every person. Just humans." Thayer gave her a long glance and a half-smile.

"*I* was human. Do you think I'm beneath you?" Lisa asked.

Thayer bit his lip, obviously trying to not turn her last sentence into an innuendo. I was shocked that he tried at all.

"*You* are a Legend now. Above and beyond where any human could be mentally or physically," Thayer said and leaned in to her personal space.

Lisa grabbed Thayer's shoulder and threw him on his back. My mouth fell open. Thayer stared up at her in equal shock.

"I might be a little stronger and a lot braver than I was before. But nothing about me has changed from who I used to be." Lisa shoved a finger in his face. "You just can't admit that you actually like a former human."

He launched to his feet and didn't bother to brush off the dirt. Lisa opened her mouth to say something, but Thayer moved too quickly.

He kissed her more forcefully than should be allowed in public. But Thayer was never one for rules. Lisa went still. I couldn't even tell if she was kissing him back.

But we didn't have time to see how this would turn out between the two of them. Shouts echoed from over the hill.

Thayer broke the kiss and snapped his eyes over to me. I smiled at him but nodded in the direction of the approaching voices.

"Your humans are coming," Thayer muttered, stepping away. "They'll take care of him now."

"We need to get out of here," I said.

Lisa nodded, perfectly silent. She and I sprinted in the opposite direction of the voices. Thayer followed behind the two of us, watching over his shoulder.

He turned and caught eyes with me. I smiled at him, understanding his risk of wanting Lisa even if they were too different. That was me and Kylan.

Thayer actually blushed and ran faster so he wouldn't have to look at me.

Judging by the sounds behind us, the humans weren't following anymore. But danger still lay ahead of us. Cassie needed an energy source in the middle of a barren forest.

I called Kylan, hoping by some miracle that everything would be fine.

The phone rang and rang until his voicemail message played. I shoved the phone in my pocket and ran faster, feeling the screaming burn in my muscles.

Kylan didn't deserve to lose another sister. Derek definitely didn't deserve to lose his Cassie.

I was almost glad Thayer had killed Chase. He had taken a shot at my family. If Thayer hadn't, I would have.

# CHAPTER
# FORTY-THREE

It took too long to find the other three. Lisa narrowed down their location when we got closer to the city.

We walked up to what looked like a house on the outside, but inside it was lined with bookshelves, books, and paper scattered everywhere. I stepped in to find Kylan shouting and Derek shoving his back as far into the bookshelf as he could.

"Derek! Get over here!" Kylan screamed.

He leaned over Cassie, his hands already stained with blood. Derek put his hands in his hair and shook his head.

"I can't. I can't." Derek's tears flooded down his face.

"What do you need?" My knees hit the floor next to Cassie and waited with hands ready.

"The bullet missed her heart. But the baby is still pulling her energy too fast. We have to get the baby out," Kylan said.

"She's still alive? Thayer, go get her energy," I ordered, and I heard the doorbell ring when he left.

Kylan locked eyes with me. He already had a knife in his hand. Kylan sucked in a breath and I nodded. He lowered the blade to the bottom of Cassie's stomach.

"Where's the owner of the house?" Lisa bent down and asked Derek.

Derek shook his head. They must have already looked. Lisa rushed around the bookshelves and up the stairs.

Kylan's hands were shaking too much to hold the blade correctly. He blinked, holding his breath as he tried to start the incision again.

I finally heard the unsteady breaths of someone else in the room. It wasn't Lisa. Another pair of footsteps followed her.

"You're okay. You're okay. We're just trying to save our friend," Lisa whispered. "See? She needs your help."

The gray-haired woman stared at Lisa with wide eyes. She was so old and frail already. Her energy might not be enough to save Cassie even if she did take it all.

Lisa brought her to Cassie and knelt the two of them down next to Kylan. The woman allowed her hand to be guided to Cassie's arm. Energy lit up between the two of them.

"Do you know what you're doing?" I muttered to Kylan.

"Nope," he said curtly.

His hands stopped and his eyes widened. I took the blade from him and switched places with him to move closer. Cassie stared at the ceiling, tears in her eyes. I sliced through Cassie's skin and tissue, deeper than I wanted to imagine was possible.

My time learning to be a doctor in one of my past lives hadn't quite covered this. But I was the closest thing we had to a viable medical professional.

Kylan wiped the blood away with his hands before he reached inside. I watched Cassie's face. It was a mix of emptiness and pain.

"I feel the baby," Kylan whispered.

"Derek," I called, reaching back for him with bloody hands.

The tears had stopped and Derek stared up at Cassie's face. The blood, Kylan's hands, nothing pulled at his attention as much as Cassie's blank stare.

"Derek, you don't want to miss this." Kylan breathed a laugh.

He moved his hands out slowly, like he was afraid to break anything. His arm muscles flexed from focusing so hard.

Cassie stirred, pulling her arm away from the woman. Lisa pulled the human's hand back and caught her as the old woman collapsed. The human's eyes stayed open, just barely.

We all saw it. If Cassie took any more energy, the woman would have died. I knew she understood that. I admired that she wouldn't take a life, even if it was to save her own.

She didn't deserve the brand of a killer on her arm. That dark, ominous dagger she now bore. Cassie was a hero in a way that I could never hope to attain.

"I can't," Derek choked.

I turned to Derek and grabbed his hand. "This is your kid. Whether Cassie makes it or not this baby is gonna need their dad."

Kylan continued to pull his hands out. A tiny foot came into view, followed by impossibly small legs and frail body.

"It's a girl," Kylan announced as the head appeared, resting in his hand.

The baby struggled for a few seconds. After a few taps on the back, she cried. Cassie's hand twitched at the sound, but no other movement came from her. Blood began to clot on her chest, but she was already bathed in it. She had lost too much.

Lisa helped Kylan cut the cord. Derek still sat in the corner with eyes on his wife, swimming in her own blood.

"She's beautiful," Lisa whispered to the baby.

The human linked arm-in-arm with her seemed a little less scared once she could see the child. She even reached toward the baby, touching her tiny hand. A yellow thread of light pulled from the human, helping speed the baby's adjustment to living away from her mom.

A tear slipped down Cassie's face. Her breaths came in sputtering gasps. Any energy she wasted on talking or moving would only bring her one step closer to death.

Derek took off his shirt and handed it to me, still not wanting to touch her. I took it and wiped the baby's face before moving down her little arms. My muscles stiffened when I reached the inside of her right arm.

"No," I breathed.

Kylan turned to stone beside me. "That's not... That can't be..."

I held out her little arm, and Lisa's face drained of color. Kylan glanced down at Derek, who finally craned his head toward the kid.

A heavy weight settled in my chest when Derek crawled forward, his eyes locked on the baby's arm. I wrapped his shirt around her and held her out for Derek.

He touched the soft, dark fabric of the shirt and halted. His eyes filled with pain as he glanced at Cassie. Derek held out his hands and I rested the child in them. She was so little in his large grip.

"We have a daughter, Cass." Derek pulled her into his chest. He didn't mention the arm, just swallowed that information.

The baby girl cried, reaching her hands out into the air. Derek kissed her right palm. Cassie let her head roll to the side so she could see her daughter. It should have been unconditional joy when she looked.

But a dark dread filled her stare as she saw a black

dagger mark on her daughter's arm, just like the one Cassie had.

"The dagger..." Cassie choked on the words.

"Don't talk." Kylan's hands immediately flew to her, trying to stop the blood from her stomach and her chest. The words only brought a new gush of red spilling to the floor.

"I'm so sorry," I said, biting back my own tears.

Derek shook his head and looked at Cassie. "This is my fault. He marked you because of me. I just...I never thought he'd mark her too."

The baby's arm was tucked inside the makeshift blanket. Derek reached in and brushed his finger over where the small black dagger would be. I knew how much he thought this was his fault. But it wasn't. This was Alec, through and through.

Just when I thought the painful reminders were over.

I offered to take the baby and Derek reluctantly allowed her into my arms. He fell on his elbows next to Cassie's face.

"It doesn't matter if she has a mark. She's alive. You're alive. That's all I care about," Derek said, stifling back a sob.

Cassie smiled up at him. Her face looked like she was at utter peace despite the pain she must be feeling.

Stuttering and grimacing, Cassie got out, "I...love you."

"Shh," Derek whispered. "Save your strength. We're gonna get you fixed up."

Cassie just shook her head and looked over at her daughter. Another tear fell from her eye, leaving a shiny trail down her cheek. She sucked in a breath and winced from the pain.

More blood trickled through Kylan's fingers pressed against her wounds. I tucked my chin in to the baby in my arms, not wanting to watch the light fade from Cassie's eyes.

"Take more energy. You'll be fine," Derek begged.

Lisa's eyes filled with tears as she guided the woman closer to Cassie. I watched as Lisa shook with a sob as she held the woman's hand against Cassie's shoulder, even when the woman struggled against the new Legend's strength. I could barely see through the blurriness from my tears.

Kylan leaned forward, looking at the little baby. "Just focus on your daughter," he whispered.

A sob rocked Cassie's chest as the woman's eyes fell closed and went limp in Lisa's arms. She was bleeding and too close to dying, but she pulled her shoulder out of reach.

Lisa pulled the woman back, laying her down to rest.

Derek shook his head as his wife's eyes still fluttered. "Don't stop, please. Please, Cass."

"Not a...I'm not a Shadow," she said, and it sounded like her mouth was filling with liquid. She tried to swallow, but coughed out a splatter of red.

Lisa was sobbing. The woman was unconscious. Kylan was fighting his own tears. I just focused on the large, hulking mass of Derek hunched over his little wife covered in blood.

"Please don't leave me," he begged.

But Kylan reached forward and put a hand on his brother's shoulder.

"We'll tell her all about her brave mother," Kylan said and the pain lifted from Cassie's face. "How she risked her life for her family. How she would have given anything to see her daughter grow up."

Her brown eyes brightened momentarily when she glanced back at her baby.

"We love you, Cass," Derek said. "I love you."

Cassie smiled up at Derek. His huge hand brushed a tear from her cheek, smearing the wetness and red downward. She laid her face against his palm and closed her eyes.

Her chest lifted, ever so slightly, and everyone in the room held their breath.

# CHAPTER
# FORTY-FOUR

The room smelled of salty tears and careless dust. The silence seemed to shake the floor we knelt on as we stared at Cassie's lowering chest.

It didn't rise again after a second. After two seconds. Three seconds.

None of us moved. None of us dared to breathe without her.

The shrill bell rang against the door as it opened. All of us jumped, except Derek. I spun and saw Thayer holding the door as three people rushed inside.

"Good gracious," the teenage boy gasped.

"We're here now and we're here to help ya," the blonde said.

A man followed behind the two of them. All three of them raced to Cassie and knelt down immediately.

I couldn't see Cassie's breath rising in her chest anymore. The humans laid their hands on any open skin they could. They didn't even glance at the Shadow mark on her arm or the blood, too eager to help.

Their hands rested on her skin. Perfectly still and useless.

I sucked in a breath and pulled the baby closer to my chest. Derek clawed his hand into Cassie's red hair, letting it twist in between his fingers as he made a fist. A sob shook his entire body as he rested his head against hers.

Out of the corner of my eye, I saw yellow lights spark in three places. My eyes locked on one of the human hands.

Energy flowed from them into Cassie's body. The light moved to her wounds, swirling and floating into her. The blood stopped and the wounds pulled shut. For one breathless moment, I thought she might actually survive this.

Cassie opened her eyes and took her first full breath in a long time.

"Cass!" Derek cried and yanked her even closer to him.

He wrapped his arms all the way around her. Cassie even lifted her own hands to touch him. The humans shifted so they could keep contact with her. All of them still had smiles on their faces.

They were too happy to be here.

I looked up to Thayer to ask how he did it. He looked down at me with dim eyes, his shoulders sagged from little energy. He must have spent it convincing them to get here.

"I had to do a lot of things you wouldn't approve of," Thayer said, letting the door close behind him. "Manipulating emotions, ignoring free will. But she's alive."

"You did the right thing," I said, nodding to him.

He looked down at the floor before his eyes wandered over to Lisa. She hadn't wanted to move from the unconscious woman's side. But now, she stared at Thayer and stood.

She stepped around Cassie and Derek. The three humans were looking tired. They watched Thayer like they were waiting for a command. With a single nod from him, they pulled their hands away, sitting back on their heels.

"You're controlling them?" Lisa asked.

"One more thing to hate me for," Thayer said, locking eyes with her like he was awaiting her backlash.

"Thayer," Lisa started but it seemed like even she didn't know how to finish that sentence.

"I did you a disservice when we first met. I showed you my charming side and you fell for it," Thayer stared at Lisa like the rest of us weren't there.

She waited with steady hands at her side as he continued, "I should have never protected you. I should have used you in the game against Mara. You'd think differently of me now."

"I didn't fall for your charm." Lisa shook her head. "You sacrifice everything for people you love. You stayed with the rest of the Shadows; you helped Kate instead of following him. You became a king because everyone around you respected you. I fell for your loyalty."

"Don't say things you don't mean." Thayer pulled away from her, already wincing. "I've had enough people lie to me to get what they want."

This time Lisa stretched on her toes and wrapped her arms around his neck. His hands hesitated instead of hugging her back.

"It made me want that kind of loyalty, that kind of love," Lisa whispered into Thayer's shoulder.

"Please don't," Thayer begged, flexing his hands to stop himself from touching her.

He wasn't worthy of this, her pure love. He honestly believed that. She was so good, and he wasn't sure he wanted to be. It broke my heart that he looked at her and hated himself.

Lisa pulled away, letting her hands rest on either side of Thayer's face. He held himself like one wrong word would shatter him.

"It made me want...to be one of the people you cared about." Lisa shuddered.

Lisa placed a gentle kiss on his lips. She leaned on him like she would fall over otherwise. He pulled her in closer, desperate to accept the deep, unending emotion she offered him.

Thayer smiled against her mouth and whispered, "Congratulations. You just made the list."

In a second, they became a tangle of breathing and hugging and whispering back and forth, melting into each other like the rest of us weren't here.

"Looks like you were right," Kylan whispered, looking at the two of them.

I moved my gaze to Derek and Cassie. Her blood covered almost every part of her shirt, and now Derek's upper body. Cassie's cheeks had tears streaking in pink as they mixed with the blood.

She looked over to the baby in my arms. I immediately held her out and Cassie took in a breath before laying hands on her daughter.

I leaned back against Kylan as I watched her eyes fill with even more tears.

"She's beautiful," Cassie said.

"What's her name?" Kylan asked.

Cassie glanced up at Derek. "Well, we've been arguing. I really like Gretta."

"And I hate it." Derek laughed like the debate hardly mattered now. "It's such an old name for such a young girl."

"She'll be old one day," Cassie countered.

"Centuries from now, yeah. She shouldn't have to wait that long to fit into her name," Derek said. It sounded like a rehashed fight from the recent past.

"What about just Etta?" Lisa suggested from behind us. "It's cute, but not too weird."

Derek pursed his lips and nodded. "Hmm...not bad."

"Hey, baby Etta." Cassie smiled down at her daughter as she tried out the name. "I think I like that one."

"Then welcome to the family, Etta." Kylan reached a finger out and touched the shirt that wrapped around the baby.

Etta clasped her fingers around her uncle's and both parents smiled even wider. Despite the blood, tears, and the strangers in the room, I had never felt so surrounded by comfort in my life.

Kylan placed a kiss on my forehead. The warm bloom of energy on my skin brought a smile to my face. The problems weren't over yet, but we were alive. We had each other. I had a family around me.

# CHAPTER
# FORTY-FIVE

*Kylan*

Lisa had been playing a game with the destroyers and Thayer hovered over her to coach or block her. It took nearly an hour before Derek ventured to join.

But Lisa took him in, the two of them working together, ripping things apart until the courtyard was covered in black dust. Even Thayer stepped back after a while.

"He needs training for sure," Thayer said to me, still watching them. "Lisa's brand new and she's already kicking his trash."

I rolled my eyes at how proud he sounded, but even I couldn't deny that Thayer was right. Derek was rusty, uncoordinated. Being a Level Five would be useless to him if he never learned how to use it.

"I suppose you're volunteering to train them?" Mara said, sliding her arm around my waist.

Thayer smirked. "I'm already thinking of some exercises we could try." His voice was too low and his gaze was too intently focused on Lisa to be talking about both of them.

Mara punched at his arm. Thayer jerked away. "What? Oh, you want me to train both of them?"

"I doubt Derek would let you," I answered, watching him.

His lack of talent and training was so obvious around the Shadows. But that didn't stop him from trying. Cassie had been sitting on the side with Etta, or locked in a room with her, since we got back. She hardly ever let the baby out of her sight.

I didn't blame her. None of us did. After everything that happened, and the new Shadows crooning over their fresh marks, I'd want to hide too.

"Speaking of which," I said, switching the topic just as Lisa obliterated another obstacle. "How about those New Dec plans?"

Mara peeked up at me. "Did Cassie tell you?"

I shrugged. "She may have mentioned it. But then once we got back…I haven't heard her bring it up."

Lisa was already rushing back to Thayer, black dust covering her hands. She was grinning from ear to ear and he swept her up in his arms, spinning her around and around. They both laughed.

"I haven't wanted to push her," Mara whispered, glancing down.

I pulled away from her, forcing her to look at me again. "I think it might be just what she needs. Plus, I think Lisa could cool it a bit on the training anyway."

That brought a smile to her face. I loved those smiles, real and uninhibited. I had only seen a few since we left the lab.

"Yeah, she's starting to make the rest of you look bad," Mara muttered.

"Agreed," Thayer answered in a cool voice as he walked

Lisa over to us. She happily followed, brushing dust off her hands onto her already black pants.

"Kylan and I were just talking about New Dec," Mara started and Lisa's eyes lit up.

"That's right," she gushed. "I totally forgot about that."

"Maybe we should grab Cassie and nail down some details?" Mara suggested, holding out her gloved hand.

Lisa snatched it and the two of them leaned their heads together, already whispering furiously back and forth. They didn't even wave as they rushed off to where Cassie was hiding behind the balcony.

"Mara's always been a sucker for a good party," Thayer said casually, trying to find a way back into the ring with the other destroyers.

He had every Level now and he took it upon himself to become a master at every game. So far, only Mara had bested him at changing. Creating was a breeze and even destroying looked like it was getting easier.

It was something about having all the Levels that made him understand how to use each one. At least that's how he described it. When I asked Mara, she had agreed, finally putting it together herself.

But Mara had had every Level for a long time. Even as a Shadow she had still possessed the ability. Every Shadow seemed to know she was different, special.

They adored Thayer and took every chance to shake his hand or make him laugh, but they looked at Mara with a solemn respect that I couldn't deny. She was a symbol to them.

This was so utterly her world, the mansion and the Shadows. The world she had grown up in. She may be a Rogue now, at least according to Thayer, but this place was her home.

I couldn't stop thinking about what Alec had said about a big, white wedding. Of course it wasn't what she wanted. I knew that. I also knew that I didn't understand this world and what she might be missing out on by being with me.

But I didn't want her to sacrifice anything. She had given too much already.

"I need your help with something," I started, not sure what I was even asking for.

"Sure, anything," Thayer said, not glancing back at me. Derek got thrown on his back and Thayer laughed, almost doubling over.

I reached out and touched Thayer's shoulder, asking for his attention. He turned to me and immediately noticed the look on my face.

"It's about the wedding…"

I wanted to know how to show Mara that a union with me could be the one she dreamed about, but I wasn't sure if it was that different than a human one.

"Look," he sighed. "I can walk you through the wedding night, I'd just rather not…"

My eyes went cold, angry, and he grinned. He didn't make me finish before he put a hand on my shoulder and said, "I was hoping you'd ask."

He gave me a gentle push and led me down to a room far away from the rest of the group. Part of me was already regretting the decision to ask for help.

But this was for Mara. She deserved one thing in her life to be perfect, one special day that couldn't be ruined.

I took in a breath and followed him into a room that had an eerie lack of sound in it. Once we were alone, he started talking again.

"First thing you need to know," Thayer said, "is that a Shadow bonding ceremony is nothing like a human wedding.

Knowing Mara, she'll probably have New Dec up and running as soon as next week and you can't pass up an opportunity to time it with an event like that. So, you're already behind."

I didn't know what to say, what to ask. But it looked like I didn't need to. "How did you know?"

Thayer smiled. "Because as interesting as I'm sure your Rogue life is, I guessed you were smarter than to assume that Mara would be content with giving everything else up."

I wondered if I should be offended. But Thayer didn't say she'd be unhappy with me. That a life with me would be giving anything up. It was just about the wedding. He cared about her too and wanted to see her just as happy.

So I let it slide and focused on that. That both of us wanted to see Mara smiling and laughing on her wedding day.

"So, where do we start?" I asked, already completely out of my comfort zone being in a room alone with Thayer.

"Honestly, we should have started a couple of months ago," Thayer said. "The bonding ceremony involves a... dance...let's call it a dance. But since we only have a matter of days, I'm gonna speed things up a bit."

"What do you mean?" I asked.

He smiled and I was more uncomfortable than I was before. "Meaning, we're starting with this," Thayer said, pulling a dagger out of the air.

"What?" I asked, flinching instead of taking a full step back.

Thayer didn't budge at all. He settled his intense, all-too-knowing gaze on me.

"Now, you only have a few days to learn this," Thayer ordered. "So pay attention."

# FORTY-SIX

The mansion thrummed with excitement that night. It was finally time to celebrate New Dec. Cassie had been bouncing off the walls for most of the day. It was the first time I'd seen her this excited since Etta was born.

Anytime Etta wasn't under Cassie's constant care, she was with Derek. The new baby thrived pretty well with a healthy supply of energy to her body to solve any lingering ailments.

"Come on. Come on!" Cassie begged as she pulled Lisa down the hallway.

"Mara, let's go!" Lisa shouted back to me.

*Mara.* They had all started calling me that after Kylan did. I thought it would feel strange to have my old name back. But I liked it. I wasn't hiding anything from any of them.

They knew I was a Legend, a Shadow, and now a Rogue. Through all of that, I was Mara.

"I'm right behind you," I called.

They were already down the hall and skirting the corner. I smiled and looked at the jagged stone floors. My fingers ran along the textured walls, lifting only when they reached the polished, wooden doorframes.

I took my time walking down the hall. I listened to the rumble of cheers and people rushing in the courtyard.

Without Alec here, this place felt more and more like a home. I recognized every hall, every detail in the moldings. I brought my fingers to my mouth, my other hand brushing at the locket.

"Nostalgic already?" Thayer said from behind me.

I didn't turn. I just smiled against my fingers and shrugged. My hand pulled into a fist, but I still held it close like I didn't want to let go. That wasn't the only thing I didn't want to release.

"I want to remember all of this," I said, feeling my mouth move against my knuckles.

Thayer ran a hand along my shoulders, pulling me gently to face him. Instead of looking up, I reached my arms around him and leaned into his chest. He laughed.

"You and the Shadows, they mean so much to me. I don't know if I ever really thanked you for everything," I muttered into his shirt.

"Don't talk like you're saying good-bye. Tonight is about new beginnings." Thayer smoothed my hair with his hand.

"After tonight, though...I can't ask the others to stay here." I pulled away from him.

Thayer shrugged. "It's been a month since we all made it back here and they haven't asked to leave. I know Cassie's had this whole New Dec thing and she needed a party space, but they don't seem anxious to go."

"They?" I knew who he meant. Lisa didn't seem like she wanted to leave, not since the two of them had spent every free moment with each other and out of sight.

Every time I saw Lisa, I swear she glowed even brighter.

"I don't think you need to worry. She may choose to stay with you even if the rest of us leave." I said, turning away from him.

He caught my shoulder again and took my chin in his hand. I was forced to look up at his brown eyes and show the pain welling up in my own.

"She's not the only one I want to stay," Thayer whispered. "You're my family. You always have been. I would be honored if the Shadow Queen deigned to live among us."

The Shadows did respect me, if nothing else than as an original Level Five. The dagger on my arm was a reminder that I still had a place here but I was far from a leader anymore. I shook my head.

"I think you might be surprised," Thayer smiled.

I narrowed my eyes. "Why?"

He just shrugged and walked past me. "You'll have to see."

"No. No surprises," I groaned.

"This surprise isn't coming from me. I will say this, though. Your fiancé has put a lot of work into tonight and he would be disappointed to see you so sad," Thayer said.

Before I could ask anything else, Thayer took my hand and led me to the courtyard. I walked in and my breath left me.

My gaze settled on the ceiling. Twinkling lights spanned across the open ceiling. Glitter sparkled on the floor and tables. It was a sea of lights and candles, everything gleaming.

It wasn't the courtyard I remembered at all. It was the night sky, like living among the stars themselves. I smiled.

"Happy New Dec," Thayer whispered and pulled my hand up.

I spun underneath his arm and he released my hand. When I stopped, I faced Kylan. Everything he wore was black. The shirt, the jacket over, and the jeans. It was odd seeing him in such a dark color. It made his eyes stand out even more.

He held out a hand. I took it and stepped close to him. His arm moved around my back, settling at the base of my spine.

"You look incredible," I said, glancing at my own black clothes. "We actually look like we might belong together."

Kylan smiled, pulling at his jacket. He was uncomfortable in black, but he was trying for my sake.

He didn't know how much I appreciated it and I wasn't sure how to express it. Everyone around us was in black or at least a very dark color. The room was the only thing that glittered and it was utter brilliance.

Thayer sauntered up to the stage, just in front of his throne that he didn't have the heart to take down. The Shadows stepped out of the way of their beloved leader.

"I'd like to say something before we get started. I know this past year has been a difficult transition. The Shadows have been ruled under Alec. We were ruthless, cruel, and self-serving." Thayer flashed a wicked smile. "To be honest, I don't think much of that is going to change."

The Shadows roared their approval. Kylan's hand flinched against my back. My eyes found Cassie with her arm threaded with Lisa's. Derek walked up behind them with little Etta tucked in his arms.

"But I can say this," Thayer continued. "I sincerely hope that our guests feel welcome here. Especially on this joyous occasion. Celebrating the turn of a decade has normally been a night of gorging on energy, music, dancing, and a slew of other activities best performed at night under the magic of starlight."

Kylan's arm turned to stone behind me. The other Rogues stared with tight lips and wide eyes.

Thayer's eyes found Lisa and he leapt off the stage. He walked to her slowly, calmly. Cassie unlinked their arms and stepped back toward Derek. He extended a hand to her. She took it and he guided her into the center of the courtyard.

A chill spread bumps on my arms. I leaned forward on my feet, ready to spring into action.

Tradition dictated that the Shadow leader took the first human life of the decade. But Lisa wasn't human, nor did I want to believe that Thayer would kill her. The tradition had been started by Charles, passed down to Alec.

He pulled what looked like a long match from his pocket. Without a breath, the match lit and Lisa leaned away. Thayer smiled and handed her the light, leaning in to whisper in her ear.

"What's going on?" Kylan asked.

"This isn't normally how New Dec starts." I squinted, trying to see what he was telling her. "I mean, normally it starts with the leader making the first kill of the night. After that it's..."

I didn't need to finish that sentence.

Both of us fell silent as we watched. Lisa nodded her head, not smiling. A spark of fear flashed in her eyes when she glanced at me.

I stepped forward, leaving Kylan to wonder behind me. I stopped when Thayer lifted his head away from her and smiled.

Lisa bent her knees and jumped, higher than I thought possible, even for a Legend. She lifted the match with her, reaching it above her head.

Instead of gravity pulling her down, she hovered in the air, inching closer and closer to the top of the courtyard, where a ceiling would be if it had one.

Thayer held his hands out and watched Lisa with a

concentrating gaze. He was holding her up. I relaxed, waiting in awe and silence with the rest of the Shadows.

Lisa's match hit some invisible barrier that we couldn't see until it ignited.

The ceiling lit up in strands of fire. When the lines burned out, glowing orbs sustained the flames. It looked like the starry sky above us, just brighter and closer than it should be, like little suns.

Thayer relaxed his hands and Lisa dropped to the floor, slowing just enough for her to get her feet in position. He caught her with a hand on her back. The gray shirt she had worn left most of her back exposed. A very different outfit for a different Lisa.

When she caught her breath, she looked up at him and smiled.

He held her close as he turned to his Shadows. "Let these stars be a reminder that Shadows need light to exist. Personal desires aside, I think we could use a little more light in this mansion."

The crowd agreed in a slow, accepting clap. They were expecting a murder, we all were. But Thayer was a different kind of leader. Not to say that he wouldn't ever kill again. Even I wouldn't ask him to give that up.

But he had changed tonight. It wasn't about death to humans. It was about life to Shadows, to Rogues, to all Legends.

That was enough for now.

I was the first to drop to my knee, and for one breath, I was the only one. Thayer's eyes fell on me with a smile. The other Shadows followed, dropping to their knee as they looked up at their king.

Even Cassie and Derek lowered to the stone floor. Thayer walked to me and lifted me to my feet.

His bright brown eyes smiled. He was no longer a boy to be toyed with or ruled. He had become the man that I was so hoping was in there somewhere.

No longer a follower, but a leader all his own. The Shadow King.

"With that"—he turned to his audience—"let the New Dec celebration begin."

Music flowed into the room. The glittery décor shined in the makeshift starlight. This was different than I had ever seen the mansion.

Still not quite made for a Rogue, but enough to seem like a home to people even without dagger marks on their arms, especially in the world Alec would surely waste no time destroying.

I didn't want to think about the world outside of these walls. Alec would most likely be turning as many Legends as he could. At least until he had enough to take over the remaining humans. How long would it take before he dominated the planet?

But he couldn't do anything tonight, couldn't ruin this glimmer of happiness amidst the sea of darkness I had just swam through.

That we all had come through. Together.

I turned to Kylan, his hand already waiting for me. Instead of having to form gloves on my hands, Kylan already had. The gloves he wore were black leather, matching the rest of him.

"Care to dance?" he asked.

I smiled up at him and took his hand. Yes, nothing could ruin tonight.

# CHAPTER
# FORTY-SEVEN

I followed his lead as we swayed back and forth. Other Shadows joined in around us and I had never felt so surrounded by what I could call a family.

Cassie dragged Derek out to the floor. Thayer tossed Lisa over his shoulder to get her to join us. He set her down and she was laughing too hard to stop him from dancing.

"This is a good night," I laughed, looking around the room.

"It's a perfect night," Kylan said. "How could it not be? I'm here with you."

I leaned up and kissed him, gently and quickly. The energy flared momentarily between, but broke way too early. I wanted to kiss him more, and I craved his energy.

I pressed my lips together, trying to savor the taste. Kylan smiled and pulled me even closer to him. Our clothing and gloves protected us from any unwanted contact.

"So when do you think we can make this official?" Kylan toyed with the ring.

"You want to get married?" I asked, watching him twist

the band.

"I know that Shadows don't believe in marriage the way humans do. I'd be an idiot to think a preacher and a marriage license would be everything you wanted." Kylan laughed.

*I'm sure a big, white wedding is just what Mara's been dreaming about her whole life.* I hated that Alec's threat had even followed us here. It seemed like yesterday we escaped the lab. Kylan must have been thinking about it over and over again.

"You're everything I need. I'll marry you however and whenever you want to get married." I smiled.

He just spun me away and pulled me back in one fluid motion.

"I know. But I also know that you've been dreaming of this day differently for as long as you can remember," Kylan said.

I thought of the Shadows' tradition. It wasn't a formal ceremony with dresses and speeches. It was more intense than that.

Any dream I had of participating in that ceremony left when I fell for Kylan. A loss I'd happily take if it meant I got to be with him.

"That doesn't matter. A lot of things in my life won't be how I thought they would." I reached up and touch his face. "Not all of the changes are bad."

"Do you think you'll miss it? Your old life?" Kylan asked.

"Yeah, I will." I shrugged. "But I'm more excited about what's ahead."

"Here's the thing." Kylan stopped the dance. "I don't want you to give anything up for me. I want you to have everything you've dreamed about."

"Kylan," I started.

He raised a hand and I paused. He looked at Thayer and nodded. The Shadow King didn't hesitate.

Thayer walked around the room, whispering something to the other Shadows. They nodded and smiled, looking at us.

"What's going on?" I asked.

I glanced at Cassie and Lisa holding each other's hands on the side. Derek was swaying back and forth just behind them.

Each of them had put on something black. Derek had a black t-shirt. Lisa had her backless charcoal shirt and black pants and Cassie had a jacket. That was definitely not normal.

The Shadows around them were already in dark clothing, but flashes of shimmering silver popped up around the room. The light glinted off the new silver, sending shimmering reflections everywhere.

During a bonding ceremony, it was customary to wear black and silver to honor the couple.

I looked back at Kylan, who was still standing in front of me. But the other Shadows had moved away from us. That left him in the center of the room.

"I want to marry you. Right here, right now," Kylan said.

"What about the preacher and the marriage license?" I asked, folding my arms across my chest.

Kylan shook his head. "The only thing you'll need is a dagger."

Hope formed a lump in my throat. He couldn't mean that. He couldn't know what that was. He wasn't talking about a wedding, he was referring to a Shadow bonding ceremony.

I jerked my gaze to Thayer. He now wore a silver sash across his black button-up shirt. He walked toward me, slowly creating something shiny in his hands.

When he reached me, the shiny object had formed into a sparkling crown. It was simple and studded with diamonds. One large center diamond hung lower than the rest of the crown. I almost choked on the words I wanted to say to him.

This was my dream, this moment. He knew that.

His brown eyes understood the centuries behind this moment, the importance and gravity of the commitment. And he wanted me to have it, Kylan and Thayer both did. My family did.

No gratitude seemed like it would be enough.

"You'll always be a queen here," Thayer whispered.

I didn't move as he lifted the crown above my head, resting it perfectly on my hair. It fit a little too snug, which made sense for what would come.

Kylan smiled, touching the lapels on his jacket and they turned silver under his hands.

If it weren't for his green eyes and happy smile, I wouldn't recognize him. He looked more like a Shadow than I had ever seen.

This looked more like the moment I had pictured than I had dared hope for.

Thayer's hands crossed and rested on my shoulders, his fingers digging in just above my collarbone. I looked down just as he dragged his fingers over my shoulders and down my back, leaving metallic trails behind on my black shirt.

His hands stopped when they swooped near my lower back and around to the front of my stomach.

A giant, metallic X would be glittering on my back from his touch.

The weight of the crown shifted as I watched. The glittering streaks stood out from the cotton fabric.

My lips parted and I moved my gaze up to Kylan as Thayer moved back into the audience.

"What do you think, Mara?" Kylan reached his left hand out.

I thought there was no way he learned that routine in this amount of time. The dance was dangerous, to say the least.

It wasn't really a dance at all, more like a choreographed fight.

The Shadows around me pulled out daggers, tips pointing directly at us, creating a ring of danger around us.

Unless he knew the steps perfectly, I would hurt him. Or kill him.

"Kylan, you're not a Shadow. You don't have to do this." I shook my head, not wanting to hope.

"Luckily, the King of the Shadows has granted me honorary status just for this," Kylan said easily.

Thayer whistled. The other Shadows laughed.

I stared at Kylan's left hand, still in the air. I reached out to him and we clasped hands, palms together and thumbs laying over each other.

"I don't want to hurt you," I whispered to him.

"Don't pull any punches for me," Kylan said. "We only get to do this once."

I gripped his hand even tighter and smiled. The only time I ever thought I would do this was with Alec. It should have felt weird, seeing Kylan standing in his place.

But it actually never felt more right.

"Are you ready?" I asked.

Kylan only smiled. I moved my fingers against his hand and spread my stance on the floor. When I took in a breath, it felt like time was slowing down around me. I didn't see anything else, only Kylan's green eyes.

Then I punched my right fist as hard as I could toward Kylan's cheek.

Instead of feeling my knuckles collide with his jaw, he dodged it at the last second and grabbed my wrist with his free hand.

He pulled on both my arms and I jumped. My body flew over him and I landed on the other side, crouching on the rough stone. My fingers grazed the floor as I locked my eyes on Kylan, still standing.

I smiled even wider now. The first move was the hardest to catch. He stepped toward me and I swung my leg underneath him. Instead of falling, he spun in the air and caught himself on his hands.

I slid on my knees over to him as he did the same toward me. We stopped just inches away from each other on our knees.

"You've been practicing," I whispered.

"Give me everything you've got," Kylan said, tipping the crown off my head with his finger.

I smiled. It clinked against the floor as we both stood, keeping our eyes trained on each other.

"You asked for it," I challenged.

I shoved him away and launched a kick at his chest. He caught my leg and spun me in the air. I landed with a dagger already created in my hand.

Before I took another breath, I threw the dagger directly at him. He caught it and tossed his own toward me. I snatched it, stopping the blade from piercing my heart.

We moved toward each other and I grabbed his arm, spinning him around me. He stumbled just enough to lose his balance and stagger toward the crowd.

A deadly mistake. I halted.

The Shadows near him kept their daggers out for him to fall on if he came too far. He balanced on his toes just before his stomach would've pierced the blades.

Without missing another step, he came back at me. Punches flew back and forth, the daggers we had held dropped to the ground behind each of us. We grabbed each other's arms, twisted, and landed in perfect sync with each other.

I couldn't stop my smile now. For the final move, I swiped

the dagger off the ground and spun blind to face Kylan. The daggers clashed into each other in a perfect cross, just inches in front of our faces.

The ring of metal on metal sounded in my ears. I was breathing hard as I looked across the blades and into Kylan's gaze.

We finally lowered the daggers to our sides. Kylan was breathing faster than when we started. Between the dagger, the black and silver, and the mansion around us—Kylan seemed to be as much of a Shadow as I was.

But I had become as much of a Rogue as he was. Together was the place where the two warring sides of our personalities met.

The room was enveloped in silence but there should've been cheers. I turned to look at Thayer.

He smiled at me and got on his knee. His hands rested on his leg as he bowed his head. As the leader, that was the greatest sign of respect possible. Overwhelming happiness choked in my throat and ached in my heart.

He wasn't a king in that moment. He was a best friend, making this the best day of my life.

The other Shadows followed suit, each one taking a knee. The movement shifted all the silver and black, throwing light in the already dazzling room.

It was what they would have done if Alec and I were up here. It was what they would do if Thayer ever chose someone to bond with. I tensed all my muscles, taking in the sight around me.

I hadn't given up anything by not choosing Alec. I had only gained.

The entire room rested in a perfect stillness as I turned back to Kylan.

"Mara Hayes," Kylan said, moving the dagger to my chest. "Everything you are, is mine."

He cut the X on my skin, barely drawing blood. It was the ultimate trust to allow someone else to mark me. No fight, no victory would ever matter as much as this one.

The pain couldn't compare to the tears of joy stinging in my eyes.

I raised the dagger to him, shifting his jacket out of the way. "Kylan Stone. Everything you are, is mine."

My hand pulled the blade down in a diagonal line. I held my breath as I dug the other line on him. His blood glistened on his black shirt, reaching the edges of his silver lapels.

We dropped the daggers to the floor at the same time.

The cheers finally came. Everyone jumped to their feet, clapping and shouting. I almost didn't notice.

I just looked at Kylan, my true partner in life. In every way, he was a part of me. So much of who I had become was wrapped up in him. I loved him more than I could imagine was possible.

He looked back at me like I was his whole world. For the rest of my life, it would be the two of us.

Us and everyone else we loved along the way.

"Ten, nine, eight..." Derek called and everyone chanted with him.

I noticed the time on the big, decorative clock hung high above. It was nearly midnight.

My eyes fell back on Kylan and I wanted nothing more than to kiss him, to hold him without anything stopping us.

Kylan pulled the gloves from his hands and slipped a slender wedding band around my finger. It clinked when it hit my engagement ring.

"Five, four..." the crowd shouted.

I created a shimmering, silver ring for him and placed it on his finger, careful not to touch him. A pang of sadness interrupted the moment.

This wasn't exactly how I pictured it. I looked at his skin, wishing for more. My hatred for Alec tinged what should have been a perfect night.

Kylan reached a hand under my chin, not bothering to avoid contact. Energy warmed my skin. I stopped, not wanting to touch him without permission.

I wanted to ask him why or tell him to stop. But I just waited. The look in his eyes glowed and I needed to see what he did next.

"Two..." the crowd said.

"One," Kylan whispered.

He lifted my chin and kissed me. I should've worried about his energy pouring into my body, but I didn't want to. I had just been bonded to him and I couldn't be happier.

I grabbed his shoulders and pulled him closer to me.

He kissed me harder than I expected. His energy didn't fade, his movements didn't slow. If anything, his hands held me tighter. I kept kissing him, enjoying the rush in my body from everything happening all at once.

His tongue brushed against my lips and I thought I was going to pass out. I clutched the collar of his shirt to keep myself from falling completely into him.

I noticed it when he broke to take a breath. I felt it before he came back in and kissed me again.

My energy was leaving my body too. The sensation had almost been totally covered by everything else.

But I still recognized it. He was taking my energy.

Every touch instantly changed. This wasn't just me kissing him or feeling his power. He was feeling mine. Everything inside of us was in each other, swirling back and forth like we were one body.

My breath caught but that didn't stop me from the

kiss, from feeling every inch of his exposed neck and face. His hands tangled in my hair and I never wanted our lips to part.

He pulled his mouth away, still resting on my forehead and holding my hair.

"I love you," Kylan said, breathless.

I lowered back on my heels and the flow stopped. He stepped away, taking his hands with him. He was breathing just as hard as I was. My eyes begged for him to stay.

"I just had to know what that felt like. At least once," Kylan said.

I knew he meant my energy. His muscles tensed in his arms. His fast breaths hitched when his chest was full. He was restraining himself from taking more. I knew that look in his eyes all too well.

"And?" I asked, not moving forward.

Kylan looked up at me and the cool restraint vanished. His eyes begged to be closer to me. His hands twitched to move forward.

"And you feel better than I could have imagined." He rolled his shoulder, trying to look away from me. "Maybe a little too good."

"I understand." I nodded.

Instead of reaching out to comfort him, I smiled. It was the signal he needed. I would not push him. His shoulders relaxed.

He visibly took in a breath before he focused back on me. "Breathe, focus, and try. Right?"

I smiled at the words I whispered to him when he was falling apart at the lab. The words I had learned would get me through almost anything.

"Exactly," I said, stepping forward. "And after that, we have centuries to figure it out."

Kylan put a hand on my back clothed in silver, relaxing his body even more. I gave his arm a squeeze just before his sister came barreling into him.

# CHAPTER
# FORTY-EIGHT

The intense moment broke and Cassie hugged Kylan so hard he had to let go of me.

"We're so happy for you!" She nuzzled her face into Kylan's shirt—the side without the blood from the now-healed X on his chest.

"Happy New Dec, bro." Derek smiled.

Kylan shook his brother's hand, reaching around Cassie to do so. She finally peeled herself off of him and came to me, leaving the men to hug around the baby in Derek's arms.

"Welcome to the family." Cassie grinned up at me. "And Happy New Dec."

"Happy New Dec," I said back to her. "Sister-in-law."

I glanced up at the crowd. The Shadows were standing, still dressed in hints of silver among the black. Most of them had coupled up a partner to kiss at midnight.

Lisa and Thayer stood closest to us, wrapped up in each other so much it was hard to see where one of them started and the other began.

It wasn't nearly the wedding I had pictured. Rogues and a former human in attendance. Most of all, Kylan as the person standing opposite me. Nothing was like the image in my mind.

But it was everything I wanted now.

I looked to Kylan like he was the only thing giving me a reason to keep breathing. His siblings hugged me and smiled. Thayer even came up for a breath long enough to give me a thumb's up before turning back down to Lisa.

*I love you.* Kylan mouthed across his two siblings.

I laughed at how happy I was. This was what I wanted.

"Okay, okay. Time to open presents," Cassie said, hurrying back to a small table with gifts overflowing.

Even I was surprised at how many of the Shadows wanted to pay their respects to me. Maybe Thayer asked them to, but I'd never know.

"Cassie, we can open those later," Kylan said as he moved closer to me. "I want to dance with my bride."

She rolled her eyes and shoved a pink present in my hands. "You can wait a few more minutes. This is for both of you. Although I had Mara in mind when I got it."

"I knew it," Kylan sighed and narrowed his eyes at her. "You like my wife better than me."

"Aw, nothing could change my love for you." Cassie smiled and tapped a finger on the wrapping.

I ripped open the paper. It fell away and I held a picture frame in my hand. The wood was warm to my touch, but that wasn't what sparked happiness in my heart.

The picture inside was of all of them.

Kylan, Derek, Cassie, Lisa, and Thayer. Cassie held a picture of Rachel to make sure she was never forgotten. A family photo.

"Kylan and I agreed that your walls were a little too blank. Now you have a picture to hang on one of them," Cassie explained, excitedly jumping in place.

"It's perfect." I smiled down at her. "Thank you."

I knew the gift idea probably came from Kylan. But Cassie was so happy about it. It came from all of them, from my new family.

"Here's the next one," Derek interrupted my thoughts and handed me another gift. Kylan took the current one from my hands and I didn't see where he put it.

"That's from me," Lisa said.

I noticed she had moved to stand next to Cassie. Thayer was just behind her, unable to take his eyes off her. I smiled back at Lisa, still trying to wrap my head around the two of them.

I reached into the bag and pulled out a notebook with tattered corners. It was easy to recognize and I lost my breath.

"I took notes the entire time we were at the lab," Lisa explained. "I figured something in there would give you ideas on how to fix your problem."

"Who ever said an assistant wasn't valuable?" Kylan smiled.

Cassie tsked. "No one, Kylan. No one has ever said that."

"Thank you, Lisa," I said, holding the book close. It was the only thing left from our horrifying time at the lab. This book and my mother's locket. "I know you understand what this means to me. But thank you."

"You're welcome," she nodded to me.

"This one looks pretty," Cassie said as she looked down at a pristinely wrapped present with white paper and a black ribbon.

"Who's it from?" I asked.

More people shrugged than offered names. Even Thayer shook his head. Kylan lifted the gift to read the tag.

"To the happy couple," Kylan read the first side and turned it over. "Welcome to the final round."

"What?" Derek asked.

I yanked the gift back and untied the ribbon. I pulled the lid off the box. It dropped from my hand and I tore apart the inside paper layer.

My bare fingers wrapped around a cold, hard metal handle. I raised from the box a black dagger. Everyone around me stared, waiting.

Cassie grabbed her right arm as a reflex. The blade looked just like the one on all of our arms.

I stared down at the familiar curves of the dagger. I knew who sent the gift. It was meant to inspire fear. Remind me that even the happiest day of my life wasn't free from his reach.

The palm of my hand warmed, like the dagger was sending heat into me. The warmth changed to a burn within a few seconds. I hissed and dropped the dagger. I turned my palm over and red welts formed on my skin.

The searing pain shot up my arm, although the red stayed firmly in place on my palm. My knees buckled and I caught myself with my free hand, still holding my burning palm so I could see it.

"It's poison." Kylan kicked the dagger away from me as he bent down to hold my shoulders.

"Is it spreading?" Lisa asked, stepping forward.

"No, no." I dug my teeth into my cheek. "My hand. It's just my hand."

I lowered my head and clenched every muscle to distract myself from the pain. I shut my eyes, silencing the world around me. All I could sense was the raging pain in the palm of my hand.

I took in a breath, and the pain seemed to plateau.

"Wait a second," Thayer said and I heard him step close. "It's a mark."

I looked up at my own hand and saw what Thayer meant. Bulging welts had formed and most of them had ruptured, leaving trails of red blood in the shape of an X across my palm.

It wasn't exactly a cut that had made the mark, but it was the dagger that caused it. I knew what that meant.

"This isn't an attack," I snarled. "It's a game."

"Alec," Kylan whispered.

The pain in my hand had dulled enough for me to have clear thoughts again. My breaths didn't seem so labored and my eyes focused on that bloody X on my hand.

I should've been shaking. But my hand held steady in front of me. I stared forward into the crowd.

If Alec was close enough to plant this dagger, he was close enough to hear this.

I knelt on the floor, not bothering to look around. Alec wouldn't be stupid enough to stay in plain sight. Kylan put a hand on my shoulder and the pain almost disappeared completely.

I wasn't alone anymore. I wasn't the scared little girl that Alec found in that tiny old house. I wasn't an orphan anymore either. I had a family all around me.

I curled my injured hand closed as my energy raced to heal it. The motion brought a new sting, but it only sharpened my vision. No matter what he did, Alec couldn't hurt me.

I wouldn't let him.

He was right about this, though. This would be the final round. It would either end in my death or his. Even though I dreaded both, I knew that this had to end.

My stare grazed the crowd of Shadows, into the faces of people I loved. The flickers of silver among the black clothes caught my eyes as they moved.

I looked down at my fist last and smiled.

"Come get me," I challenged.

THE END

# TO THE READER:

Maybe you're sick of the cliffhangers, but at least you made it this far! I honestly hope you're enjoying the journey of Mara and Kylan as much as I am. These characters have a special place in my heart.

Writing this book came at a time when a lot of things in my life seemed fine on the surface, but I was struggling. Writing characters that I could put through pain, made my struggles seem a little easier. Writing the characters handling their problems and finding happiness despite them, was extremely cathartic for me. I can only wish that reading this book can be of a similar help to you, even if it's just to step out of reality and into the Legends & Shadows world for a while.

Thank you for reading. Thank you for caring. You mean a lot to me because you help make these books real.

# ACKNOWLEDGEMENTS

I have a lot of people to thank for bringing this book about. I was stalling on this book for a while and I needed a little push. Believe me, the people in my life delivered with plenty of encouragement.

To Brandon: You're incredible. You're literally the best proofreader I've ever seen. I know you dislike this genre, but you love my books. It means the world to me that your support me and love me. Thank you.

To Suzanne Johnson, my editor: You are such a joy to work with. I really appreciate your insight and fresh eyes. These characters would not be what they are today without your help. Thank you for giving me the encouragement I needed to make these books a reality.

To Sarah Hansen, my cover designer: Please keep blowing me away with your talent. You have a knack for design and I'm glad I found you. Thank you for all of your help.

To Ryann Jones and Trisa Christensen: You guys are excellent beta readers and proof readers and all-around book-discussers. Thank you for letting me lean on you as I create these books. I don't know where I would be without you.

To my family: I love you guys. I am lucky to have grown up in a loving, supportive family. I'm even more lucky that now that we are grown up, you are still just as loving and supportive. Thank you for loving my books and encouraging me.

## A SPECIAL THANKS

To Mrs. Eyring's 7th grade honors class: I'm so glad to be working with you guys this year! I feel honored that you are using my book in your classroom. Thank you for letting me be a part of your journey to love reading and writing. Best of luck on your short stories!

# ABOUT THE AUTHOR

Angie Day found her love of writing while in college where she studied psychology and eventually went on to a master's degree. She noticed the need for romantic and fantastic adult stories that were still wholesome and clean. So, she took matters into her own hands with her debut series. When she's not devouring the next book, she is spending time outdoors with her husband.

To follow along with her journey, find her on social media or check out her website.

www.angiedayauthor.com
@angiedayauthor